THE
EXILED
FLEET

ALSO BY J. S. DEWES

The Last Watch

THE
EXILED
FLEET

J. S. DEWES

TOR

A TOM DOHERTY ASSOCIATES BOOK

NEW YORK

THE EXILED FLEET

Copyright © 2021 by J. S. Dewes

A Tor Book
Published by Tom Doherty Associates
120 Broadway
New York, NY 10271

www.tor-forge.com

Tor® is a registered trademark of Macmillan Publishing Group, LLC.

The Library of Congress Cataloging-in-Publication Data is available
upon request.

ISBN 978-1-250-23636-4 (trade paperback)
ISBN 978-1-250-23635-7 (ebook)

Our books may be purchased in bulk for promotional, educational, or business use.
Please contact your local bookseller or the Macmillan Corporate and Premium
Sales Department at 1-800-221-7945, extension 5442, or by email at
MacmillanSpecialMarkets@macmillan.com.

First Edition: August 2021

Printed in the United States of America

0 9 8 7 6 5 4 3 2 1

For Anders and Justice.
No hard feelings. If they took my cat,
I'd have done the same thing.

THE
EXILED
FLEET

CHAPTER ONE

"Motherfucker. You better work."

Cavalon slammed the access panel shut. Sweat stung his eyes and he wiped away the moisture slicking his overgrown hair to his forehead. Days since he'd started this phase of the project: twenty-three. Times he'd recalculated, reconfigured, or rebuilt this single fucking subsystem: fourteen. Patience: zero.

This had to be it. It had to work this time, or he'd give up and activate it without any stupid "core stabilization," then stand back and watch the damn thing supernova. Who tried to build a star aboard a fucking space-ship anyway? Bloody void.

He tapped the black nexus band on his wrist, and an orange holographic display slid into the air over his forearm. He found the menu labeled with a hashed half circle, a spiked teardrop, and an inverted triangle—a Viator phrase that unnervingly translated to "anti-explosion box." He selected the icon, and it produced an infuriating "sync in progress" meter.

He waited for the bar to fill, scratching at the few centimeters of blond growth along his jawline. He'd given up months ago, and just rode the stubble wave right into a beard, which had arrived peppered with more gray than felt reasonable for twenty-eight. But there was no time for shaving when there was a "perpetual jump drive" to build. Well, *invent*.

Jump drives required solar energy to function, usually amassed by panels on the hull while a vessel went about its business in a solar system. But they weren't in a solar system—they weren't even in a galaxy—which meant there wasn't a single star even remotely close enough. So, naturally, the solution had been to *build* one. In the damn ship.

For the last six months, every ounce of his effort, day or night, sleeping or waking, had been focused on finishing this ridiculous "perpetual jump drive." This singular task, the only thing that could get all four thousand rescued Sentinels to Kharon Gate before they all died of thirst or starvation, or the Divide finally drove them all mad and the *Typhos* became one giant murder party. As usual, no pressure.

With a placid beep, the sync completed. The screen flashed red and his nexus band blurted out a negative tone. He clenched his teeth, suppressing a low growl. Ever the masochist, he tapped the activation again. Again, a docile negative tone, and again, nothing.

He quirked a brow at the display. Strangely, it showed no error code.

Maybe the wireless controls were acting up again. It hadn't been the easiest task of Puck's career to get the Legion software to interact nicely with the Viator-conceived systems. He'd have to check the primary control terminal to be sure.

Cavalon closed the menu, then headed up the slanted passage and out of the reactor's shell into the hangar bay. Comparatively cool air chilled his sweat-slicked cheeks as he stepped onto the metal walkway.

A framework of scaffolding ringed the outside of the twenty-meter-diameter orb, allowing access to the dozens of systems required to make the monstrosity work. The reactor's components weren't nearly as accessible as they'd been in the versions aboard the dark energy generators, mostly due to the exorbitant amount of improvisation he'd had to do. But hey, he wasn't an ancient alien species with millennia of research and apparently endless resources at his disposal. He was simply a guy with a degree in astro-mechanical engineering, which somehow meant this was in his wheel-house. Most days, he just felt like a guy with a few different types of wrenches and way too much responsibility. The whole thing was really absurd.

Cavalon headed around the arc of scaffolding toward the reactor's anterior, which faced out into the large, empty hangar—bay F9, now pragmatically known as "the reactor bay." Though at least eighty meters square, it was modest compared to what a behemoth capital ship like the *Typhos* had to offer, easily the smallest of their dozens of hangars and docking bays, but also the closest in proximity to the ship's jump drive.

He arrived at the primary control terminal, a two-meter-wide counter covered with jury-rigged holographic interfaces and repurposed viewscreens. He swept open the solenoid controls, and a white holographic menu materialized in the air over the terminal counter.

He grumbled under his breath and tapped the activation switch.

Another negative tone, this one louder, denser, and more judgmental than the one from his nexus band. An error screen taunted him next, along with a brand-new message he'd not seen the other fourteen times he'd taken a stab at this: "Subsystem not found."

Void, he'd made it *worse*.

He clenched his fists, knuckles going white as he pressed them into the console top and muttered, "Goddamn piece of flaming void garbage."

"Maybe if you didn't call it mean names?"

Cavalon glanced over his shoulder, down past the walkway railing. On the deck six meters below, Jackin North stood in front of the cluster of workbenches. He stared up at Cavalon expectantly, hands on hips, looking all hygienic and not grease-stained in his unwrinkled, navy-blue Legion uniform. It'd taken Cavalon about two weeks before he'd given up on maintaining a clean uniform, and Jackin about two more before *he'd* given up giving Cavalon shit about wearing nothing but a T-shirt and duty slacks. Jackin knew how to pick his battles.

Cavalon took a strange amount of comfort in Jackin's composed appearance. It acted as evidence that life existed somewhere outside bay F9. And, as was probably the point, served as a reminder of how a soldier *should* look. As their acting commander, Jackin had to set a precedent. Lead by example, or some such nonsense.

Yet even the highest-ranking officer aboard couldn't hide the impact of months of reduced rations: his face narrower, cheekbones sharper, and a sullen, yellow tinge to the whites of his dark brown eyes.

"How's it going?" Jackin asked, tone unnervingly even.

Cavalon cast an unnecessary glance at the nexus band on his wrist. "That time again already, boss?"

The scraping assessment in Jackin's eyes somehow felt equal degrees judgmental and tolerant.

Cavalon sighed. "I know it's on your regimented daily itinerary, Optio, but I'd work a lot better without you breathing down my neck every morning."

"Remember, it's *centurion* now."

"Right. What's with that, anyway? I thought you were going to be CNO?"

"You don't really need a fleet navigations officer when you don't have a fleet."

Cavalon scratched his chin. "True." They were in fact a fleet of one at the moment—all the other ships that'd survived the Divide's collapse had proven themselves just as stranded as the *Argus* had been. No ion drives, no warp drives, no jump drives, and thus no ability to congregate. Which held its own as an exercise in negligence, but after seeing the monumental—and frankly, creative—ways in which the Legion had recklessly abandoned the Sentinels, Cavalon now knew it to be intentional. If you're going to banish all your criminal soldiers to the edge of the universe, no reason to give them an easy way to escape. Or to mutiny, as the case may be.

Cavalon knelt, letting out a groan as his joints protested. He reached under the console and grabbed a battered multimeter, then tossed it under the railing at Jackin.

Jackin flinched as the device hit him square in the chest. It toppled down into his arms and he awkwardly caught it. He leveled a glower of barely contained frustration at Cavalon. "Void, kid—I'm not a time ripple."

"That's what they all say," Cavalon mumbled. "Just checking. I don't have time to have this conversation again. And again. And again."

"Yeah, I get it," Jackin grumbled, dropping the multimeter onto the nearest workbench. "Why don't you just give me the report, then me and all future mes can get on with our days and leave you alone."

Cavalon grimaced as his hands began to cramp. "The report is: How about you worry about getting yourself a fleet, and I'll worry about creating a star generator from scratch."

"Because I won't be able to get inward to even *begin* to muster a fleet without your star generators. Also, everyone will starve."

Cavalon dug a thumb deep into the palm of one cramping hand. "Void, I know, okay? I don't know what you want me to do. I can only work so fast."

The furrow in Jackin's brow softened. "I know, kid. Sorry." His gaze went unfocused as he rubbed a hand through the scarred side of his trimmed black beard. "Just do your best," he encouraged. "We've got the rest in hand, don't worry about that part."

Cavalon nodded, unable to ignore the forced evenness in Jackin's tight expression. He wasn't a very good liar. And Cavalon was well aware of the primary cause of his worry: Rake and Co. were supposed to have returned from rescuing Sentinels and restarting the other dark energy generators weeks ago. Every passing day they didn't return seemed to age Jackin by weeks—stony gray salting his black hair at the temples, his light brown skin too weathered for someone in their early forties.

Jackin drew in a deep breath, vanquishing the worry from his face with an ostensible effort. "I'll leave you to it. Update me when you can. Will I see you at drills tomorrow?"

Cavalon forced a grin. "Yeah. Wouldn't miss it."

Jackin nodded, then made his way back to the massive bay doors and left.

"Animus."

Cavalon startled, the scaffolding at his feet groaning as he twisted to find Mesa lurking behind him. She regarded him evenly, the bags under her overlarge eyes like inky bruises against her warm beige skin.

He licked his dry lips, then reached out and pressed her shoulder gently. "You real?"

Mesa's narrow chin stayed straight as she swayed back from his push, her round eyes sharpening. "Difficult to say, considering one is not generally aware of one's own dissociation from space-time."

He cleared his throat. "Fair."

"Time ripple or not," she said, holding out a tablet toward him, "I have recalculated the magnetic potential using our altered equations."

Cavalon took the tablet, a frown tugging at his lips as he noticed the way it trembled in her grasp. As a Savant, she had lousy endurance even on an easy day, and the last six months had been nothing but hard days.

"How's it look?" Cavalon asked, glancing at the dozen blocks of Viator code on the screen.

"Promising," Mesa replied. "I believe you were correct in your assessment that we miscalculated the phase shift accumulation. We cannot continue to assume our present understanding of gravitational field generation is wholly accurate."

Cavalon blew out a heavy sigh. Present understanding, in this case, meant "mankind's collective comprehension of particle physics." But redefining their fundamental understanding of science happened once a week these days, so he wasn't surprised. Only annoyed.

He gave a cursory look at the new code. This phase shift hack job was a last-ditch effort. If Mesa's new calculations didn't fix it, he'd have to go back to the drawing board on the whole core stabilization subsystem— *again*—and all Jackin's anxious notions over them starving before they could leave the Divide would likely become reality.

"Well, let's hope you were right," Cavalon said, "and it's really only because we fucked up the math. One small problem first, though . . ."

She tilted her head. "Yes?"

He tucked the tablet under his arm, then palmed the holographic screen over the primary control terminal. He spun it to face her, showcasing the error message. "I kinda broke it."

Mesa made a constrained clicking sound with her tongue, shoulders stiffening with forced patience. She swiped to dismiss the message, then backed through the menus to another screen. She sighed. "It is not broken. You merely left the remote edit permissions lock on again."

Cavalon snorted a laugh, running a hand down the side of his face. Of course he did. It was the engineering equivalent of a child safety lock. Obviously he'd not be able to work it properly.

Mesa had insisted on implementing the feature early on, and at the time, Cavalon had thought it wholly unnecessary. But the longer it went on, the more tired he grew, the more mistakes he made, and the happier he was that Mesa had completely ignored his objection.

"We will need to release the local console," Mesa said. "But we can simply enter the new calculations from there."

Cavalon nodded, and Mesa followed as he headed back around the scaffolding to the posterior access tunnel. They ducked inside, but Cavalon stopped short when he saw two figures ten meters down the sloping passage, standing at the control panel. He squinted at the wavering doppelgängers—he and Mesa, of course, but weirdly, they were grinning like idiots.

Real Cavalon slid real Mesa a weak smile. "If those kids are that happy, maybe we're onto something after all."

Seconds later, the doppelgängers' outlines jittered, and they shimmered like a puddle of water disturbed by a tossed pebble before vanishing.

Cavalon started down the pitched floor toward the console. "What if . . ." he proposed, "we fly this whole outfit even *closer* to the Divide so we get even *more* ripples and maybe one of *those* Cavalons and/or Mesas will have a clue how to finish this thing."

"Regardless of how absurdly dangerous that would be," Mesa replied, "as with the other Sentinel ships, we cannot move this vessel in any appreciable manner."

Cavalon sighed. "I miss Rake. She could appreciate a good joke."

"I am sure you do," Mesa said, "but not for that reason."

He scoffed. "What?"

"You say you 'miss' her because she would tolerate your pointless humor—"

"Pointless? Ouch, Mes."

"—but 'missing' a person is merely a symptom of unfulfilled emotional needs."

A *symptom*? That was pretty calculated, even for Mesa. She must be extra over it today.

"In this example," she continued, "more than likely, the sense of security the excubitor provided as a sympathetic commander. By that account, I 'miss' her as well."

Cavalon sighed. He wasn't sure why Mesa kept air-quoting "miss" as if it weren't a real thing.

"Sure," he said, "but, I think you're underestimating how much I need people to like my jokes."

Mesa pursed her lips.

"And FYI," he added as they came to a stop in front of the console, "by your own definition, you *miss* Puck."

"I do not know what you speak of," Mesa said, with the barest sliver of defensiveness in her tone.

"You know—Jackin's cheerful optio, weirdly tall, shaved head." Cavalon mimed typing in the air. "Good with the hackies? The one giving you a doe-eyed stare all the time?"

"I do not *miss* him."

"Do too. He's too busy running the ship to fulfill your unfulfilled—"

"I suggest you not finish that sentence," she warned.

Cavalon grinned. Mesa was such a damn prude. Watching her get all squirmy about her secret boyfriend was one of the very few bright spots left in Cavalon's day.

Mesa impatiently plucked the tablet from Cavalon's grip. "May we return to our work, please?"

"Yeah, yeah. Sorry." Cavalon activated the control screen and unlocked the remote edit permissions.

Mesa started reading off the new code as he input it. "You have taken to the Viator language extremely well," she commented.

"It's been six months." He hit delete a few times to correct a typo. "Bound to pick up a few things."

"Regardless, I am surprised it is even possible without formal instruction. It would be a difficult task, even for a trained linguist."

"Careful, Mes. This is starting to sound like a compliment."

She sighed.

"What can I say, it's critical to our survival. You do what you have to do in times of crisis."

Curiosity pinched her brow. "For most, it is not that simple."

Cavalon gave a wavering shrug. His rapid proficiency in the Viator language surprised even himself. "Not like you're any different," he countered. "You didn't know shit about photovoltaics six months ago. Now you could build a neutrino capacitor in your sleep."

"Mm," Mesa hummed, then let out a soft yawn. "I will be, at this rate."

"Oh relax," he grumbled, entering the final symbols. "There. Done." He skimmed it over to confirm, then saved the new code and closed out the screen.

He opened his nexus, expanding the orange primary control menu. He tapped to activate. This time, the red error screen was instead a bright green. And not an error screen.

"Holy shit," Cavalon breathed. He took a step back, a rash of heat climbing his neck.

Green. Not red. It'd fucking worked.

A click sounded and the panel behind the control terminal buzzed with electricity as the system engaged.

Cavalon turned to Mesa, whose overlarge Savant eyes had grown even larger. Her lips stretched into a broad smile, exposing her straight white teeth. He scooped her into a hug and accidentally lifted her off her feet—despite her petite frame, she weighed even less than he'd expected.

She patted his back lightly and he let go, suddenly aware of the unfortunate amount of perspiration clinging his shirt to his skin.

"Sorry." He frowned. "I'm sweaty."

"Indeed," she replied, elation returning to brighten her features. The Divide might excel at making them anxious, agitated, and depressed, but after six long months, Cavalon knew the opposite could be true as well. Low lows and high highs. It was a truly exhausting way to live.

An airy warmth inflated Cavalon's chest as the remaining steps of the project fit together in his mind's eye. One larger task and a slew of smaller tasks remained, including testing the gas injection system, finalizing the photovoltaics bridge that would feed the jump drive, and conducting a final evaluation of the operational diagnostics before they had to seal the thing up. But they were close. Really, really close.

He and Mesa climbed out of the inner chamber and descended the scaffolding to the workbenches at the front of the machine.

Cavalon hunted down a towel on the cluttered worktop and wiped the sweat from the nape of his neck, then grabbed his water bottle and took a long drink. Despite being room temperature, the epithesium-infused water felt like an icy mountain stream. Meant to hydrate and energize, the supplement hadn't made much of a dent in his fatigue lately, and he found it took more and more to get the same results.

The rush of water flushed him with a cool tingle, and his damp shirt sent waves of goose bumps across his skin. He grimaced as his calves cramped. Bracing against the workbench, he tried to stretch through it, but the movement only sent more aggressive convulsions through his legs.

He glanced up at Mesa. She stood across the workbench, honed gaze sweeping over him like a biotool's diagnostic beam.

To an outside observer, Mesa had two modes, intellectually discerning and critically discerning, and this one certainly fell into the latter category. During their endless hours working together, Cavalon had grown adept at interpreting the nuance behind her glares. This one was: *You look like death, why are you not tending to your most basic human needs?*

He rubbed the heels of his palms into his eyes. "I'm fine, Mes."

She folded her hands on the counter. "Please visit the medbay during your next break."

He scoffed a laugh. "Break? You mean the four hours a day I pass out facedown in the dark?"

"The greatest danger of this project lies in its many unknowns," she said, ignoring his defeatism. "Many of the metamaterials you are working with are highly radiative—"

"I'm aware."

"—not to mention the extended waking hours and reduced rations."

A feverish chill washed over him, and he curtailed a shiver, then took another long drag of his water.

Mesa stepped around the workbench and laid her cool fingers on top of his balmy hand. All hints of judgment had fallen away, her overlarge eyes round. "It is the same reason, when aboard an aircraft, you attend to your own safety needs before assisting others. If you are dead, you can help no one."

Cavalon swallowed. The muscles at the base of his neck cramped. "I'll drop by over lunch."

"Thank you."

"Speaking of breaks," he said, glancing at the time on his nexus, "your shift ended four hours ago."

"I am aware."

"You know, even though we're the same rank, as project lead I have the authority to have you forcibly dismissed . . ."

She blinked once.

"That's right. I've been reading all about the perks of my new rank." Not so *new* anymore, though. He'd been an overworked animus about twelve times longer than he'd been a shitty, barely passable oculus. He'd been grateful for the shift in duties, though saving the excubitor from getting swallowed by the collapsing universe had been kind of an overly dramatic way to earn a promotion.

Mesa sucked in a slow breath. "Very well, *Animus.* I will take my leave." She arched a brow and gave the mess of schematics on the work-top a once-over. "I know we have many ancillary tasks to attend. However, we should review your strategy for the cryostat's final phase so I may draft the implementation agenda."

Cavalon sighed, glancing over his shoulder and up the scaffolding that enveloped the reactor. He'd made the cryostat the final phase for a reason. It was the one system they hadn't been able to recreate, lacking the metamaterial required to make it function. Which meant he had to craft a new version of the system from scratch. And a rather important system at that. Their superconducting magnets wouldn't stay very superconductive at anything toastier than absolute zero.

"I haven't made it that far, I'm afraid," he admitted. He slung the sweat-dampened towel over his shoulder. "I have a couple ideas. Just need to figure out a few things. I'll have something ready before your shift starts tomorrow."

"Very well." She inclined her head, then started for the exit.

"Thanks, Mes," he called after her. "I mean—adequate work today, Animus Darox. It will be noted in your review."

She threw a characteristically dismissive hand wave over her shoulder and left through the bay doors, leaving Cavalon alone in the sweltering hangar.

He took one last chug of epithesium-laced water, then set the bottle aside. He cleared half the worktop of tools and tablets, exposing a section of the holographic glass, then expanded the schematics for the cryostat shell and thermic shield.

He pored over his notes, reviewed the readouts on the diagnostic systems, and skimmed through Mesa's exhaustive redundancy checks. Though the audits could be a time-consuming nuisance, he'd grown to see the value in that step of Mesa's overly thorough process. One anxious, exhausted brain should not be in unconditional control of compressed star fabrication. Especially when that brain had no idea how to finish it.

Cavalon rested his elbows on the counter as he pressed his face into his hands, breathing slowly. He urged his eyes to return to the screens, but he simply couldn't focus. He'd never felt like he had so little control over his own mind as he had in the last couple of weeks. He'd been brooding over this cryostat issue since day one, yet felt no closer to cracking it now than he had then.

A knot constricted his rib cage, trapping the air in his lungs. Sharp bile stung the back of his mouth. He pressed his knuckles into his chest and closed his eyes to let the twisting room right itself.

He'd grown all too familiar with this sensation lately, which mixed all the pleasantries of a panic attack with the thrill of anxiety-induced nausea. Unfortunately, knowing exactly why it was happening didn't do anything to stop it.

It wasn't because he feared Jackin's disapproval, or that of the other twenty-some Sentinel commanders regularly shooting him judgmental glares, or that he felt he had to prove something to the obnoxious gang of Allied Monarchies hate-mongers roaming the halls. It wasn't even the fact that four thousand lives hung in the balance. He just couldn't bear the thought of letting Rake down.

She'd been gone almost six months, and the more outwardly worried Jackin grew, the more genuinely concerning it became.

It'd been a long time since Cavalon had missed someone, and even longer since he truly worried whether someone was alive. It was times like this he wished there were some worthy deities to pray to for her safe return. Or to blame if she never came back.

CHAPTER TWO

Adequin Rake made her way through the dim, empty corridors of the *Synthesis*. Overhead, a bank of green-tinged light strobed, signaling its death throes with soft clicks and a high-pitched whine.

She coughed as she rounded a corner, inhaling through her mouth while covering her nostrils with the back of her hand. Though they'd managed to improve the general odor of the ship through the application of dozens of bottles of industrial-grade cleaning solution, lingering pockets of putrid, earthy Drudger musk still lay in wait to accost her when she least expected it.

She risked breathing through her nose again as she descended a short flight of metal steps and approached the entrance to the cockpit. Inside, the flight console displayed a single holographic menu showing an FTL diagnostics feed alongside a countdown. They'd be decelerating from warp soon.

Emery Flos sat in the copilot's seat on the right, her neon-orange-laced boots draped across the flight dash. The long sleeves of her navy shirt were pushed up past her elbows, revealing the line of punitive, obsidian Sentinel Imprint squares cutting a path through the black-inked tattoos covering her thin arms. Her duty vest's drawn hood shaded her face as she breathed in soft, whistling snores.

Adequin stepped between the two pilots' seats. "Circitor."

Emery startled awake. "Sir!" Her boots slid off the dash, her jaw resuming its gum chomping as instinctively as her eyes blinked and her lungs drew breath. Her white cheeks burned with an infusion of pink as she shot a quick look at the FTL screen. "Fifteen on the clock still, boss." She creaked out a soft yawn, then seemed to awaken all at once as a wide grin spread across her face, eyes alight.

Adequin lifted a brow. "What?"

"Last one!" Emery beamed. "Aren't you excited? We can finally get off this void-forsaken ship." Her eyes fogged over with a distant, dreamy look. "Eat somethin' other than an MRE. Maybe take a shower hotter than room temp."

Adequin blew out a heavy sigh. "You good to take outlet cowl duty again?"

"Yessir," Emery piped. She followed Adequin to the lockers inset beside the crash seats along the back wall. "Want Owen to run diagnostics first? Or we just assumin' it's busted?"

Adequin pulled one of the white pearlescent space suits from the locker and passed it to Emery. "I think it's safe to assume. The last seven have been blown, after all."

"Yeah, fair enough." Emery stepped into the suit, then ran her fingers up the front seam. The nanite-infused fabric stitched together seamlessly as it reshaped to fit her small frame. She took a plasma torch from the locker and twirled it around by the trigger guard.

"Em," Adequin admonished as she dug deeper in the locker.

"Sorry." Emery caught the torch by the grip, then holstered it. "Guess we can't be too mad about the outlet cowls. The fact this ancient tech works at all is a miracle. You really think the Viators made it? Musta been someone that came before them, right? Cathians or somethin'?"

Adequin passed Emery a tether harness and gave a light shrug. "Mesa thinks it was them."

"Yeah, true. Not gonna argue with that lady."

Adequin helped Emery into the harness, loaded her out with more tools than she would ever need, then double-checked the MMU attachment and suit comms.

When the dash let out a soft chime, Emery stashed her helmet and MMU by the door, and they returned to the helm.

Adequin sat in the pilot's seat and checked the FTL screen. Ten minutes until arrival. "All right, Circitor. Call it."

Emery nodded as she slipped into the copilot's chair and opened the comms interface. She drew her shoulders straight, chin high. "Greetings, passengers of the RSF *Synthesis*," she began, her tone crisp, monotone, and overly pleasant.

Adequin leaned into her periphery and mouthed, "RSF?"

Emery muted the connection long enough to whisper, "Renegade Sentinel Fleet," then returned to the announcement. "This is your captain speaking . . ."

Adequin scoffed, shaking her head as she slid back and shouldered into her chair's harness.

"We shall begin our scheduled deceleration shortly," Emery continued in her same affected timbre. "Please make your way to the nearest crash bench, and remain seated with your harness securely fastened as we will be entering the maw of the ancient alien megastructure in T-minus nine minutes and counting."

Adequin pinched the bridge of her nose.

"After disembarking," Emery went on, "proceed carefully along the extremely narrow walkway to the giant bronze sphere and please do not fall off the edge as there is no—"

"Void," Adequin breathed, swiping the dash and stealing comms control from Emery. "Decel in five," she grunted. "Delta Team, disembark from hold airlock in ten. Helm, out."

Emery frowned, slouching back in her seat. "What? You don't like Renegade Sentinel Fleet? I also considered LSV—'Liberated Sentinel Vessel.'"

Emery went on for a long while about the various ship prefixes she'd considered, and Adequin was relieved when the timer finally hit zero and the ship decelerated from warp.

The deck rumbled softly, and the viewscreen flashed white before being replaced with a sea of absolute black. Adequin stared at the empty screen, eyes scanning for any sign of the structure.

Finally, the massive orb appeared for a fraction of a second, silhouetted by a sharp light cutting a static path across the void: the Divide collapsing toward them, evaporating whatever stray stardust lay between it and the generator. A *"direct affront to the laws of thermodynamics,"* a frenzied Mesa had once ranted.

Adequin expanded her preset array of flight screens and Emery activated the searchlight. The narrow beam caught only a fraction of the structure. It reflected off the overlaid slabs of metal, carved with deep trenches of an uninterrupted, geometric design like that covering the four facets of the atlas device.

Adequin eyed the burnished gold pyramid resting on the dash between the two pilots' seats. Over the last five weeks, the Viator device had allowed them to stay a step ahead of the Divide while locating Sentinel vessels, and acted as a key to unlock access to the generators. Now she wondered if they'd ever have a use for it again. Its range didn't seem to extend beyond the Legion-occupied Divide, and if all went as planned, the Sentinels would be leaving the Divide in short order. Cavalon hadn't come up short on a promise to her yet.

Adequin engaged sublights. From beyond the station, more staticky light erupted, and deep in her gut, right at her core, a tiny, almost imperceptible tug willed her outward, toward the Divide.

She drew in a steadying breath. "On approach," she said, then angled them toward the structure.

Adequin stood just inside the entrance to the bronze sphere chamber and watched Delta Team go about their work. She chewed the inside of her lip, tapped her foot in various rhythms, and checked her nexus every twenty seconds for any missed messages or summons. There never were any. After so many restarts, no one needed their hand held anymore.

Across the room, dozens of compressed hydrogen tanks were lined up in front of a floor-to-ceiling observation window. The thick glass show-cased a distorted view of the reactor's dark interior—a circular chamber lined with reflective paneling, ringed with coiled copper.

Pairs of oculi took turns hauling the hydrogen tanks through the only other doorway, which led to the curved corridor containing the main control array and gas injection valves.

Adequin's eyes caught on the activation terminal on the far wall. She pushed out a breath and forced her gaze down to the dark, grated aer-asteel floor. A dull warmth pulsed in her cheeks.

Every single bronze sphere chamber in every single dark energy gen-erator had been eerily identical. Yet even knowing this was a different place, hundreds of light-years and thousands of lost lives from the first, she couldn't help but feel it was the same place Griffith had died. Only five weeks ago . . . or six months, depending on who was counting.

"Sir?" An oculus approached, her light brown skin cast in warm light by the array of orange nexus screens expanded over her forearm.

"Owen." Adequin inclined her head to the young woman. "How's it looking?"

"We're set on the teracene and the rest of the metamaterials," Owen said. "Circitor Flos has repaired the outlet cowl and is on her way back inside."

Owen tapped her nexus, expanding the remote link to the station's primary controls. Weeks ago, the oculus had somehow found a way to connect their nexuses to the stations' main control terminals. Remote access had made the activations much faster—and far less stressful.

"We're just waiting on the hydrogen," Owen continued. "But I ran the secondary diagnostics, and I'm getting an error that doesn't translate."

Owen angled her screens toward Adequin, showing a highlighted line of Viator symbols. One of the few things she was still good for—translation.

"Oxidation warning," Adequin replied. "Atmo can bleed into the chamber sometimes." They'd seen that warning more frequently in the early days, before they'd started preemptively replacing the invariably shitty seals on the injection valves.

"I see, sir," Owen said. "What's the procedure?"

"There should be an operations preset marked electrolysis; run that before you inject."

Owen gave a curt nod, already swiping through the menus. "Understood, sir." She worked steadily for a minute, then hesitated, gaze lifting to look across the room.

Near the observation window, a duplicate of Owen stood arguing with another oculus—also a duplicate from the way its edges jittered before snapping back into place.

Adequin sighed, then called out, "Ritcher!"

The exceedingly patient oculus she'd assigned to time ripple duty appeared from the open doorway to the curved corridor, his eyebrows high. "Sir?"

Adequin jutted a thumb toward the doppelgängers.

Ritcher took off after them. He punched Owen's duplicate in the shoulder, and it barely had time to look annoyed before its edges wavered. It disappeared along with the oculus it'd been speaking to.

Owen chewed her lip, tugging at the braid of wavy dark brown hair hanging down her shoulder. "Thanks, sir," she said softly. "Still not used to those things."

Ritcher returned to the curved corridor just as Emery strode out. Unsealing her helmet with a soft hiss, she shook out her sweaty hair, pink-cheeked and already gnashing at her gum.

"There a complaint box around here?" she grumbled as she marched toward Adequin and Owen. "You'd think they coulda put a *touch* more engineering know-how behind that stupid outlet cowl, considerin', ya know"—she gestured vaguely around her—"what the rest of this shit is capable of. Doesn't seem like it'd be that hard."

Owen's lips pressed into a restrained smirk. "You'd think," she agreed.

Emery's levity faded as she approached Adequin, lowering her voice. "We got quite a light show goin' on out there, boss. We may be closer to the eleventh hour than the atlas made it seem."

Adequin flexed her jaw, eyes flitting up as another duplicate of Owen appeared across the room. Thankfully the real Owen didn't notice, remaining focused as she continued to input settings.

"Understood, Em," Adequin replied with a heavy sigh. "How about you go aim that abundant energy of yours at the hydrogen crew? Get them to double-time it."

"Copy that," Emery piped, the spun around.

Across the room, two oculi picked up one of the heavy, compressed hydrogen tanks and started ambling toward the curved corridor. Sweat slicked their brows, faces long and weary.

"Where's the enthusiasm, guys?" Emery chirped as she sidled up to walk beside them. "It's the last one! No more carrying heavy shit, no more near-death experiences, no more bein' all time-dilated. The *Typhos* is gonna feel like shore leave after weeks of this bullshit. What's our motto, friends?"

"Get it done fast and don't die, sir," one recited.

"Atta boy." Emery gave him a firm pat on the back. She lifted her chin and called out loudly, "But I didn't hear the rest of you!"

The other members of Delta Team, including Owen and the few oculi working inside the curved corridor all shouted, "Get it done fast and don't die, sir!"

Emery wrapped her arms around the middle of the hydrogen tank to take a portion of the weight. "Here we go! Fastest hinge ever!"

One of the oculi raised an eyebrow. "Uh . . . hinge, sir?"

"Hydrogen injection, Oculus!" Emery barked. "But that's six syllables and we only have time for one! We're settin' a record, get a move on!"

The trio disappeared into the curved corridor, Emery still chattering on, and blissful silence filled the main chamber.

"Sir . . ." Owen began warily, peering up through her screens at Adequin. "All due respect, but you may have created a monster."

Adequin let out a long sigh, crossing her arms as she leaned back against the sloped wall. "Yeah."

Twenty minutes later, they had in fact accomplished one of their quickest activations to date. Adequin squinted as her eyes adjusted to the new light, blinding despite the thick, shaded glass of the observation window. The five-meter-wide ball of hydrogen churned within the containment chamber. Magenta flames lapped up around the sides, reflecting brilliantly off the metallic interior.

Sweat trickled down her spine. She absently thumbed the edge of one of the two sets of dog tags around her neck, the metal and glass hot against her callused fingertips. Only one step remained.

Owen approached. "Reactor stability's great," she said, swiping through a few screens. "Energy levels are strong." She looked up, pity rounding her hazel eyes as her tone grew quiet. "So . . . whenever you're ready, sir."

Adequin forced out a reluctant nod, then tucked the dog tags back under her sweat-soaked tank. Willing her legs to obey, she drew herself toward the activation terminal, which contained a half-cylindrical slot recessed into the slanted glass face.

She slid her right sleeve up to her elbow. Starting at the wrist, she loosened the wrap binding her right forearm. She unwound it slowly, exposing the sores, bruises, and blackened veins underneath. Stabs of pain shot across her skin with each tiny movement.

Clenching her teeth against a tremor, she laid her arm into the clamp. The glass surface glowed white and the apparatus spun closed, encircling her forearm in a metal sleeve.

A metallic tinge flooded her mouth. The silver and copper squares of her Imprint tattoos activated, folding and unfolding as they moved down her bruised bicep. They disappeared beneath the cuff as they tore into the raw skin on her forearm, sending a thousand knife-sharp stabs across her nerves.

In an instant, her consciousness fell away, body vanishing as her mind disconnected and coupled with the mainframe.

Safely inside the network, all sensory input disappeared, and a heavy blanket of peace engulfed her. No blistering heat, no overtaxed muscles, no tangy smell of sweat and hot metal. And no eternal, unavoidable hollowness burrowing ever-deeper in her chest.

Though she now perceived time slower, and only a fraction of a second had passed, she could already feel the mainframe growing impatient, curious as to why its new user had yet to make an inquiry. So she refocused on her Imprints—her liaisons to the machine—imagining them to be hundreds of tiny drones awaiting her orders. She made her request, and in an instant, it was done.

In a terrible rush, corporeality descended.

Her Imprints fled the machine, boring into her wrist. Hot tears welled in her eyes as the metallic squares clawed over her raw skin, up her bruised arm, and back to her shoulders.

As the shock of the concentrated burst of pain dwindled, the nape of her neck tingled with a new sensation. One that, despite everything, felt just as existentially daunting as the first time: the genesis of dark energy.

A thick pressure built, the familiar swell of a bone-deep ache as the space between her molecules expanded, stilling her breath. A sonorous whipcrack rang through the chamber—a sound felt as much as heard, leaving a jittering thrum resonating deep in her chest.

After a few moments, the sensations abated. A dense quiet descended, air slid back into her lungs. Her rib cage loosened like a thousand tiny knots unlaced at once, vanquishing, however briefly, the relentless dread that hovered just under the surface.

The generator had restarted. They were done.

Despite Emery's objections, Adequin helped Delta Team haul the empty tanks and remaining supplies back to the hold. When she arrived at the cockpit, Emery had already finished preflights.

"Hey, boss," Emery said, throwing a sorrowful glance over her shoulder. "Feelin' okay?"

"Fine," Adequin said, masking a grimace as residual jolts of pain shot up her right arm. She dropped the atlas pyramid on the dash, then tugged down her sleeve to ensure it covered the edge of the wrap at her wrist.

Emery's tight-lipped look conveyed a degree of skepticism, but she didn't press the matter. "All yours, EX." She stood, stepping aside to relinquish the pilot's seat. "Let's get the hell out of here and never look back."

Adequin shook her head. "You take this one."

Emery's brow shot up, light kindling in her green eyes. "Holy shit. Are you sure?"

"Positive."

Emery's high brows flattened as hesitation dampened her excitement.

Adequin gripped her shoulder. "You've been training for weeks—don't overthink it."

Emery bit her lip. "Yeah, 'cept that's like a tenth of the time they get at the flight academy."

"By Sentinel standards, five weeks is luxurious," Adequin pointed out, slouching into the copilot's seat. "Besides, no one at the academy had me as a teacher."

Emery smirked, but only some of the worry lines disappeared from her forehead.

"You got it," Adequin encouraged. "Just remember rule number five."

Emery bobbed her head once in an exaggerated nod. "Confidence forges competence," she recited. Her eternal enthusiasm finally made ground on her doubt as she started gnashing on her gum again. "Thanks, sir." She jogged back to the door to spit her gum into the incinerator chute, then popped a fresh piece in her mouth as she swaggered back. "Last pack. Good thing we're headed back."

"Yeah," Adequin scoffed, "I bet the *Typhos* has pallets of gum on standby for you."

Emery beamed, her invigoration unable to be squashed by Adequin's cynicism. "Grape, if they know what's good for 'em."

Emery slid into the pilot's seat, shoving her sleeves up past her elbows. She expanded the flight controls, then navigated the *Synthesis* across the inside of the empty seventy-two-kilometer shell.

The constant onerous thrum of the generator ebbed as they drew closer to the center, where a narrow groove ringed the inside of the sphere. Since activation, the dark silver ring had filled with shimmering bolts of brilliant cobalt light, circling on an endless loop as they snapped in and out of existence—some feature of the dark energy generation they didn't understand, and likely never would. While humanity had managed to reverse-engineer some Viator technology in the thousand-odd years since first contact, there was still plenty that eluded them—relay gates, most metamaterials, and anything beyond the very basics of Imprint technology. The machines from which Adequin had received her Titan Imprints, and Cavalon his royal ones, had been spoils of war, and only a handful still existed that could apply real Viator Imprints. The dark energy generators just happened to be the newest, if not most formidable, addition to that list.

A few minutes later, they exited out the massive, triangular hatchway and back into open space. The generator loomed in the rear cameras, its inward face ablaze with light. The hull's matte black slabs of overlaid aerasteel shone with an ethereal, effusive glow that felt substantive, almost magnetizing, as if the light had its own gravity. The reaction was another component of the activated generator that'd garnered a brow-pinched, *"without further study, I cannot say"* response from Mesa, and a cackling shrug from Cavalon.

"Copilot, clear for warp," Emery requested.

Adequin's focus drifted to the navigation screen, and she gave a cursory glance over the trajectory and coordinates. "Cleared."

"Engaging."

Adequin's stomach dropped and the floor thrummed as the drive activated. The image of the generator evaporated into the void.

CHAPTER THREE

✦

Cavalon crossed his arms as he stood back and watched himself punch Puck in the face. He really hoped his form wasn't as bad as his doppelgänger's—flat-footed, stance too narrow, elbow too low. He would have to work on that.

Puck rushed into duplicate Cavalon's guard, a move real Cavalon knew always flustered any Cavalon, future or present. His unfortunate future self hesitated a fraction of a second too long, and the much taller Puck spun and pulled him into a headlock. The duplicate Cavalon's edges jittered and wavered, his white cheeks flushing red as Puck tightened down. With a jagged flicker, the doppelgänger disappeared. Puck continued clamping down on empty air for a few fleeting moments before he vanished as well.

Cavalon lingered near the equipment racks at the training room's entrance, safely away from the onslaught of future aberrations strobing in and out of existence like jittering, corrupted video on fast-forward. With so many last-second decisions flying around, the training area was a breeding ground for time ripples. Though it could be a feature as much as a hindrance. Without even having to get punched a single time, he could see the mechanics behind a win or loss, gain a great perspective of his own terrible fighting habits, or see from afar how anemic, tired, and half-dead he looked.

He absently sipped on his water bottle, then scratched at the line of black Sentinel Imprint squares running up his left forearm, more nervous than he cared to admit about Warner's pending arrival. It was supposed to be Jackin's turn, and the centurion was much more in Cavalon's "weight class." Though Jackin had managed to put on a degree of muscle Cavalon had been struggling to achieve himself. It was as if his body were resisting the very idea of having more strength, just as a general concept. Like it believed if it forced him to stay weak and ineffectual, they'd never put him in the line of fire again.

In a normal situation, that would probably be a reasonable assumption. As an animus, he was a science officer, meant to provide support with scholarly insight, endless research, and fancy tech. But what his traitorous muscles failed to understand was that sooner than later, there wasn't going to be a difference. Every Sentinel would have to fight, egghead and meathead alike. So Cavalon intended to be both.

That morning, he woke to find himself even more eager to hit things than usual. He needed a distraction. He'd been poring over the cryostat issue for a week straight, and still had no new ideas. His current hope was that Warner might punch the solution out of him.

Cavalon wrapped his wrists while he waited, his chilled fingers shaking with light tremors that made it difficult to secure the clasps. He gritted his teeth as a pang of hunger gripped his stomach. They'd scaled back rations again two weeks ago. It was temporary, Jackin had asserted—only until Rake returned. She'd have more food processors and nutrient concentrates and hydroponics equipment and probably a whole damn agriculture ship along with an actual herd of literal cows, and whatever other tragically optimistic thing everyone was so sure she'd arrive with in order to shower them all in endless caloric intake.

Cavalon had trouble believing any of it. Math and logic and the unstoppable passage of time painted a much grimmer picture, one that meant the last of the rescuable Sentinel vessels had been saved long ago, which meant no more cargo holds full of countless wonders. Rake would be lucky to come back with a few dozen people and whatever shitty equipment those people had thrown aboard their shitty shuttles. If any of them even came back at all.

"Heads up, princeps."

He turned in time to catch a pair of padded gloves as Warner chucked them at his chest. Cavalon grimaced a smile, the unexpected impact causing a swell of nausea in his stomach.

Warner grabbed a set of wrist wraps off the rack and unfurled them. "Surprised to get your message," he said in his gravelly timbre. "Didn't think you'd ever *ask* for a beating. Especially not from me."

Cavalon nodded ruefully. It was true. If literally anyone else had responded, he'd have picked them first—anything to avoid subjecting himself to the stocky man's brutally solid blows. But he saw no reason to admit that out loud, so instead, he slid Warner his most confident grin. "Who better to spar with than the chief of security himself?"

Warner's sandy-brown eyes regarded him evenly. "Whatever you say, princeps."

Cavalon tugged on his gloves, then followed Warner to an open mat nearby. They tapped gloves and Warner shuffled back, stretching out his neck and shoulders.

Cavalon inhaled, sequestering a sliver of focus to ensure his royal Imprint tattoos aided his reflexes, but not strength, what little he had of it these days. He had no intention of accidentally breaking the chief of security's nose.

They traded sets of soft warm-up blows, then Warner launched straight into the real sparring with a barely telegraphed right hook. Cavalon brought up his left arm and blocked the swing, core engaged, stance wide, all the things they'd been drilling into him for the last six months. As if he'd ever get into a fistfight with a Drudger—whether the regular or clone variety. Maybe that was his problem with the stupid cryostat thing. He'd been so concerned with assumptions, maybe he wasn't allowing himself to think outside the box. To think bigger.

He gritted his teeth—he'd been through that loop many times before. It didn't matter how big he let himself think; he didn't have unlimited resources. The *Typhos* was a massive ship, but there was basically nothing of use on board. Their only other Divide-worthy vessel, aptly named the *Courier*, had rendezvoused with Rake a few dozen times over the months to shuttle back rescued Sentinels and salvaged materiel. They'd brought back *some* useful things, mostly in the form of raw materials that could be fed to the fabricator, allowing them to form the thousands of components they needed to build the reactor. But Rake's focus had, rightfully, been on filling her hold with people, food, and life systems parts. Not random tech the animuses might one day find useful for "thinking big."

Warner's fist slid straight through Cavalon's line of thought and cracked squarely against the side of his face. The room tilted and his cheek hit the floor before his hands could even consider reacting to brace the fall. Darkness cut in on his field of vision, waning a fraction of a second later.

"Shit," Warner huffed. "Princeps, you okay?"

The room rolled to the side and Cavalon's stomach lurched. He clamped his eyes shut and steadied his breath, inhaling to a slow count of four, exhaling even slower, just like Jackin taught him.

His royal Imprints shuffled aimlessly around his abdomen, as if they wanted to reach in and sieve the grumbles of hunger from his stomach. Useless pieces of garbage. They'd offered no protection when Warner struck, or when he hit the floor, but they were there to grouse about his upset stomach. Despite his efforts at "training them like a muscle" as Rake had advised, they'd only grown more and more fickle and jittery of late, like waning lamplight trying to draw from a dwindling power source.

Cavalon opened his eyes and the room righted itself. Warner's thick hand unfolded and Cavalon accepted it.

Warner hauled him to his feet. "Maybe we should call it," he suggested, his deep voice wary.

"No." Cavalon stepped aside to take a long draw from his epithesium-laced water. "I'm fine, really."

"You do realize you just passed out for like ten seconds?"

Cavalon scoffed. "Did not."

Warner ran a stiff hand over the top of his shorn hair, the same sandy brown as his skin. "I don't really wanna accidentally kill the guy who's supposed to save our lives."

Cavalon dropped the water bottle, stretching out his cramping jaw as he returned to the mat. "You won't. Promise. Right as rain."

Warner's grimace loosened only a fraction, but he pulled his glove back on.

Cavalon gritted his teeth at the sheer amount of concentration it took to lift his hands above hip height. The backs of his arms quivered, weak, as if he'd lifted weights for five hours straight.

With a deep breath, he shook it off, dedicating his Imprints' remaining strength to bolster the worst of his fatigue. He tapped Warner's outstretched gloves.

Warner bounced backward on the balls of his feet, hands drawn up. He hopped around, giving no indication he intended to attack.

Cavalon leveled a flat look at him.

Warner blew out a stiff, relenting breath, then jaunted forward, offering a quick series of feeble jabs to Cavalon's abdomen.

Cavalon let out a low growl, circling to one side. "No. Don't do that."

Warner didn't bother to avoid Cavalon's combination of quick punches as they thudded into his concrete chest. "Do what?" Warner asked.

"You know *what*," Cavalon replied, breaths labored. "You're pulling your punches."

"You don't look good, man. I don't want to hurt—"

"Don't even finish that thought."

Warner's jaw flexed, his clean-shaven face firming to stone. "Fine. Your funeral."

But before Warner could even draw back his fist, a lead weight dropped into Cavalon's stomach, flushing a wave of nauseating heat through his body. The overhead lights bloomed and his knees gave way as a cool rush of blackness descended.

Cavalon woke groggily to residual images of his dreams strobing against the backs of his eyelids. White and gray and black and red, some spotted, some smooth-coated. Their insides made of milk and cheese and steak. Bovine of every variety.

Disappointment descended as his eyes opened *not* on a rolling green field full of food and manure, but instead onto the pristine, antiseptic cleanliness of the *Typhos*'s medbay. Large panels of overhead diodes bathed the place in flat, diffused light.

He lay atop the white sheets of a half-reclined hospital bed, still wearing his rumpled Legion-issue PT uniform. A diagnostic machine whirred quietly on a nearby cart. He craned his neck to glance around the large outpatient ward.

In one direction, a dozen more beds like Cavalon's dotted both sides of the aisle, all unoccupied. The other way led to the main hub of the *Typhos*'s large medical facility, where he caught glimpses of a few white-coats working at various tasks around the central lab station. The intercom system output a constant drone of white noise.

Cavalon's heart sank as his eyes fell across the central hub and onto the lineup of privacy screens cordoning off the opposite corridor. Beyond led to the psych ward, or rather the overflow area the overpopulated psych ward had expanded into—inhabited by unfortunate souls who'd grown more distressed than most by their protracted proximity to the Divide. No Sentinel ship had ever sat as close as the *Typhos* currently did, and as far as Cavalon knew, no one had ever lived this close to it for this long. Some merely needed a break, a chance to reorient before returning to their normal tasks. Others had given up on drinking or eating or sleeping entirely, and were essentially comatose. The latter filled more and more cots each day.

Cavalon let out a creaking yawn as he shifted to sit up. Down the aisle, one of the physicians looked up from the hovering holographic display over his tablet. The man's eyes landed on Cavalon with the same mild interest of realizing your instant coffee had finished reheating.

He wore the standard Legion navy blue under a white lab coat, sleeves pushed up to his elbows. Cavalon guessed him to be in his early fifties, with weathered skin and ashy, textured hair that seemed at once neat and messy—as if it'd been cut for style, but the time to maintain it had become an impractical luxury.

Cavalon thought he recognized him, but couldn't place from where. Not the medbay, he didn't think—not that this was Cavalon's first visit. He'd managed to injure himself in a variety of creative ways over the months.

The familiar-ish man dismissed the screens on his tablet and headed over. He arrived at the bedside and touched his palm-sized tablet to Cavalon's nexus band. "Welcome back," he said, his smooth voice low, thick with a heavy Cautian brogue.

"How long have I—" The dryness in Cavalon's mouth swallowed the rest of his words. He tried to clear his throat, but it only itched worse, throwing him into a coughing fit that sent cramping pains firing through his torso.

"All right, all right, lad," the doctor said, giving Cavalon a firm pat on the back. "Try'ta relax."

Through a haze of cough-induced tears, Cavalon blinked up at the man. *Lad* . . . he knew where he'd seen this guy before—hanging around with Jackin, sometimes at drills, a few times in the mess. He'd even seen him hovering in the doorway of the reactor bay while Jackin performed his daily nagging ritual. Of all the sundry Cautis Prime natives aboard, this guy had the accent to be reckoned with.

The doctor grabbed a glass from a nearby food cart and passed it to him. Cavalon took a drink, and the cramping subsided. The wracking pain ebbed as he drew in a series of long, slow breaths.

"Better?" the doctor asked.

Cavalon nodded. He set the glass down and cleared his throat. "It's Ford, right?"

He inclined his head. "Aye—Circitor Ford Kellar." He stared down at his tablet. "And you look to be Animus Cavalon . . . no surname. What's goin' on there?"

Cavalon let out a crackling sigh. "Let's just say, good riddance."

Ford didn't appear to react. He set the tablet down, then produced a scope from his coat pocket and clicked it on. He fired the beam of light into one of Cavalon's eyes, then the other. "Blink."

Cavalon complied.

Ford turned the light off and pocketed it. He scratched at the salt-and-pepper stubble on his jaw. "What of your symptoms?"

"Symptoms of what?"

"You lost consciousness for a reason."

"I got punched."

Ford shook his head grimly. "The chief swore blind he didn't do it. Said you—and this here's a direct quote—'looked like tepid pigswill' before you even started fightin'."

Cavalon cringed. "He really didn't knock me out?"

"Afraid not."

"Well," Cavalon said, clearing his throat. "I guess it's true I haven't been feeling a hundred percent."

The diagnostic machine nearby bleeped. Ford stepped aside and his eyes grazed the readout. He let out a low, growling whistle.

"What's wrong?" Cavalon asked.

"You been skippin' meals?"

Cavalon laughed.

Ford quirked a thick, ashy eyebrow.

"Sorry," Cavalon said, scratching his brow as he dismissed the pained humor from his expression with an effort. "No, I definitely don't miss meals. I'm constantly starving. I happily eat every bite I'm given."

Ford shook his head. "Well, you've got protein and vitamin deficiencies, though I think our primary offender is hyponatremia."

Cavalon scoffed, convinced he'd misheard the word in the man's muddled accent. "Uh, you think I'm overhydrated?"

"If you wanna call it that, sure. It's low blood sodium."

"Right, but why?"

"Have you taken anything recently?"

"Drugs? No, sir, clean as a whistle." Cavalon saluted, elbow high, fist to chest—a move he still couldn't perform with any degree of grace. "I swear on . . . well, shit. I don't really have anything to swear on these days."

"I don't mean narcotics," Ford explained. "Anything at all. Any kinda medication? Supplements?"

"Oh, uh . . ." Cavalon cleared his throat. "Epithesium, I guess."

Ford picked up his tablet and swept open a new screen. "Dosage?"

"I add a vial to every bottle of water I drink."

Ford's gaze lifted and the tablet lowered. "And how many bottles are you drinkin' a day?"

Cavalon gulped. "Eight or nine. More on training days."

Ford shook his head. "Void, lad. That's *way* too much."

"Water?"

"Void, no. Epithesium. You need'ta cut way back."

Cavalon wrung his hands. Only he'd be capable of making a problem out of something as innocuous as epithesium. "Uh, I don't think that's going to work. I need it—I'm so unfocused without it."

"Then you'll be findin' other ways to focus," Ford said, his rigid tone allowing no excuses. "Limit it to twenty milliliters a day."

Cavalon sighed. "I thought it wasn't habit-forming?"

Ford's brow furrowed. "It's not. Some mutagen defects can cause substances like that to turn addictive, but . . ." Ford's eyes drifted over Cavalon. "Considerin' your lineage, that's not likely the case."

Heat stung Cavalon's cheeks, and as evenly as he could manage, he said, "I don't know what you mean, doc."

Ford's lips pressed thin as he turned to the synthesizer beside the diagnostic machine and began tapping instructions into the control screen.

"If it's not habit-forming," Cavalon began, "why's it matter how much I take?"

Ford pinched the bridge of his nose. "Void, lad. Just 'cause somethin's not habit-forming, doesn't mean you're free to take as much of it as you want," he admonished. "With that much epithesium, you're flushin' all the nutrients from your system before you can absorb them."

Cavalon rubbed the heels of his hands into his eyes and let out a long sigh. "That's probably also why I haven't been able to put on any muscle, huh?"

Ford loaded an empty biotool cartridge into the synthesizer. "Likely, aye. And with rations goin' down tomorrow, that'll be even harder—so cut it out with the epithesium."

"Rations are going down again already?"

"Aye . . ." Ford muttered, the single word nothing but a deep crack in his throat. He kept tapping at the synthesizer and left the rest unsaid: that rations would go down again after that, and not stop going down until something changed. Until they could get this ship inward. Until they could set up supply chains and put down some roots. None of which could happen until Cavalon finished the jump drive. Which meant figuring out the damn cryostat issue. Which he couldn't do from a hospital bed. Or, as Mesa had so kindly pointed out, if he were dead.

Cavalon swallowed hard, annoyed by the agitation thrumming in his chest. He didn't know when tending to his most basic biological needs had started feeling like such a time sink.

Ford activated his nexus and a compact version of his clearance dossier sprung to life over his wrist. He held it up for the synthesizer to scan, and it beeped its approval, then got to work making whatever he'd requested of it.

Cavalon cleared his throat. "So, doc . . . I thought Jackin—er, Centurion North—had pulled you for intelligence team lead. How'd you end up in the medbay?"

Ford closed his nexus and picked up his tablet again. "With the extranet down, there's not much to be done on the intelligence front at the moment." He finished inputting something into his tablet, then glanced around the large medbay, humming with quiet activity. "You fill the role that's needed, even if it's not the one you planned for."

"You seem trained for it, at least."

"I was an infantry medic," he explained, "before the war."

"But then you got into intelligence?"

"For a time."

"And then?"

The synthesizer beeped and the completed cartridge dropped into the dispenser slot. Ford grabbed it and turned back to Cavalon with a wry grin. "And then I got tossed out here, where I'm arguin' with an animus who's pretendin' not to be a royal prince about how much epithesium he should ingest in a day."

Cavalon drew in a soft hiss through his teeth. "Yeah, yikes. Heard that jerk's a handful."

Ford slid the cartridge into a biotool. "That jerk's gonna save all our lives, if he doesn't kill himself first."

"Void." Cavalon frowned. "You all should make T-shirts."

Ford stuck the biotool to the inside of Cavalon's elbow and released the hissing shot. Cavalon gritted his teeth as a cool rush of liquid seeped into his veins. His lazy-ass royal Imprints scuttled to intercede, far too slow.

"A nutrient boost," Ford explained, "with some extra sodium and an add-in to encourage proper digestion. Void only knows what you've gone and done to your GI tract. You need to be stayin' on full rations for now. I'll make sure North knows."

Cavalon shook his head fervently. "No way, doc." He'd avoided the pack of anti-royalists roaming the halls up to this point. If they caught wind he was getting special treatment, he'd be getting the crap beat out of him again in no time. "I'm not eating more than anyone else."

"Aye, you are, in fact," Ford replied, and again the firmness in his tone gave no recourse. Not that Cavalon wanted to argue very badly. The nauseating hunger twisting in his stomach prevented him from summoning the will to keep fighting.

Ford pocketed his small tablet. "I'll be back to administer another boost in a couple hours. Get some rest."

"Hours?" Cavalon squeaked. "My shift starts—"

"You're takin' the day off, lad."

"But Jackin—"

"*Jackin* is the one who gave the order," Jackin's mellow voice cut in, and Cavalon turned to find him strolling up the aisle toward them. He stepped up and gave Cavalon's shoulder a firm grasp. "Seriously, kid, what the hell? Ever heard of a 'daily recommended dosage'?"

"I think *recommended* is the key word there."

"You know, for the smartest guy I know, you can be a real idiot."

"You're so mean to me, Uncle Jack."

"Do *not* fucking call me that."

Ford chuffed a laugh, then stepped away, giving Jackin a firm pat on the back on his way past. "Taggin' ya in, North," he said. "Try'n talk some sense into the lad?"

Jackin gave an amiable tilt of his head, watching the doctor go for a few seconds before returning his look to Cavalon. Any reserved congeniality slid away in an instant. "Epithesium? Cavalon? Really?"

"Void, how do you even know that?" Cavalon whined. "It just happened."

Jackin crossed his arms. "I know everything that happens on this ship, kid."

Cavalon sighed. Ford had stood there with his damn tablet and tattled on him, right in front of his face.

"And why were you even training?" Jackin chided. "You hit your weekly quota days ago. You know you can only afford so much exercise a week."

Cavalon sighed. He knew Jackin meant that in the sense of caloric currency, but he couldn't ignore the lingering implication that instead of training, he should have been doing his actual job. Time was currently their worst enemy.

"I know," Cavalon admitted. "I was only trying to jog my brain."

"Right." Jackin's brow furrowed. "The heat thing, still?"

He nodded. "Cryostat."

Jackin gave him a discerning once-over, then his gaze drifted up, unfocusing into the depths of the outpatient ward. He gave a few sharp, short nods, as if trying to convince himself of something. "We'll help in any way we can, kid," he said finally. "Just let Puck know and we'll make it happen."

"Yeah, I will," Cavalon said. As soon as he figured out what the hell he even needed.

Jackin's nexus band buzzed, and he swept it open.

His expression went flat as his light brown skin blanched, lips parting speechlessly.

Cavalon's heart sped, unsure what to make of that reaction. Jackin had nothing but a tight scowl on his face for pretty much six straight months.

Cavalon lifted a brow at him. "Sir, what is it?"

Jackin blinked a few times, then looked up and met his eye. "Excubitor's incoming."

CHAPTER FOUR

Adequin woke to Emery's high-pitched voice ringing through her nexus band.

". . . Repeat, Helm for Excubitor. You awake, boss?"

She tapped her nexus and cleared her throat, though her voice still came out thick and fractured. "Go for Rake."

"Sir, sorry to rouse you," Emery responded, "but we're decelerating from warp shortly. ETA to the *Typhos*: twenty minutes."

"Understood, Em. Fly safe."

"Yessir."

Adequin lay in the dark, staring at the dingy gray ceiling for a few minutes. When she finally gathered the will to get up, she took a quick shower, then replaced the bandages on her forearms.

A swell of nervous dread rose as she slid open her rickety wardrobe door. Her excubitor uniform hung inside, untouched over the last five weeks, the palette of orange and yellow badges of rank still pinned to the shoulders. She couldn't get past the idea of donning the uniform and acting the rank given to her by the military she actively worked to mutiny against. But she didn't really have anything else to wear. And more importantly, those aboard the *Typhos* would expect it.

So she channeled her Titan training, shelved the emotion, and focused on the procedure. She pulled on each navy-blue piece, tugging the jacket over her sore arms last. She took care to tuck the bottoms of the wraps up under the cuffed sleeves. Thankfully, the bruising had yet to creep its way onto the tops of her hands.

She tightened the top strap of the double-breasted jacket to ensure the discolored skin at the base of her neck remained covered. Appearance didn't concern her—the darkness of the heavy bags under her eyes would be plenty enough to make her look a wreck all on their own—but the strange bruising would cause concern and questions she didn't care to deal with at the moment.

Her heart thrummed in her chest as she paced the room and tossed the rest of her clothing into her ruck. It felt like it'd been years since she'd been to the *Typhos*. She should be relieved. The last five weeks had been difficult. Grueling, even. All the Sentinels they couldn't save— some missed by weeks, some days, some mere minutes . . . it weighed on her more heavily than she cared to admit.

Yet as much as she wanted it to be over, to be done with, to move on . . . she wasn't sure she was ready for what came next. She'd always known there would be a mountain of responsibility waiting when this phase was finally over. But the closer they drew to the *Typhos*, the more that "mountain" felt like the edge of a cliff.

The *Synthesis*'s personnel hatch let out a long hiss and cracked open with a rush of warm air. The gravity felt heavier, steadier, more secure. Like stepping on real ground after being spaceside for weeks.

Adequin squinted in the dank airlock as light spilled in from the hangar. The access ramp descended, and her gaze drifted over the mostly empty bay, large enough to accommodate a dozen ships the *Synthesis*'s size.

She stepped out, hesitating at the top of the ramp, her throat thickening as her eyes met Jackin's. His light brown skin flushed with a tinge of crimson and a restrained smile filled his face.

His wavy black hair had grown out some, trimmed shorter on the sides in a classic officer's cut. Less official was the full beard he'd maintained, which he'd let grow longer and now masked the worst of the burn scar that cut a path through it, a mirror of her own—though her Imprints had healed hers to nothing but a light discoloration. She'd watched his scar slowly heal along with each encrypted video he'd recorded and sent along with the *Courier* to keep her up to date on their progress aboard the *Typhos*.

It was a curiosity she still couldn't shake—that Jackin had *existed* for longer than she had. He'd been here six months while she'd been out there only five weeks. She couldn't quite convince her mind to accept it, despite having been on the other side of it for three years while aboard the *Argus*. No wonder Griffith had been so addled every time he returned. Disorienting didn't begin to cover it.

Adequin hoisted her ruck onto her shoulder and descended to the decking.

"Hey, boss," Jackin said, his tone unusually low and rough. His shoulders drew back, posture straight as he brought his fist to his chest in a proper salute. "Welcome aboard."

She inclined her head. "Centurion."

He extended his hand and she shook it, grip warm and firm, yet the gesture felt strangely hollow. Deficient.

"Good to see you safe, sir," he said.

"You too, Jack."

Jackin's eyes drifted over her shoulder as the rest of the crew began to disembark. His obvious relief came with a caveat of restrained agitation, and she already knew why. She was sure she'd hear all about it later.

"Welcome wagon's incoming," he said. "They'll pass out nexuses and show everyone to quarters. Puck's scrambling an orientation, not sure what time yet. How many newcomers?"

"Seventy-six," she answered.

Jackin opened his nexus and slid through a few screens. "Copy, seventy-six. We'll get everyone situated."

She eyed the tablet he had tucked under one arm.

His face fell as he caught her look. "I'd say no rush," he said with a heavy sigh, "but that's not really an MO we can entertain. If you need some rest, we—"

"No, I just woke up, I'm fine. Let's get it over with." She tapped her nexus to ping Emery.

"Here, sir," Emery piped seconds later, jogging halfway down the ramp before hopping off the side to stand between them. She slid a grin to Jackin, then saluted. "Centurion North."

"Oculus," he said with a regarding nod.

"Actually, it's circitor, now, sir. And the EX's private pilot, didn'tcha hear?"

Jackin's gaze swiveled to Adequin, dark brown eyes wide with incredulity. She might as well have told him they'd brought a Viator fleet back to join the uprising.

Adequin shrugged. "What can I say, she's a natural."

Emery beamed. "What can I do for you, sirs?"

"A team's incoming to show you all to quarters." Adequin checked the time on her nexus, now synced to the *Typhos*'s mainframe. "But we need to get acclimated to ship time, so only take a four-hour break. Then bring them back here to do arrival checks and a full inventory before turning out the cargo. Then get it turned around."

Worry creased Emery's brow. "We takin' the *Syn* out again, sir?"

"No, but remember rule number three."

Emery rocked back on her heels before swaying forward in a full-body nod. "Shit, right. Always keep your bird ready to fly," she recited.

"And make sure you get someone to take a look at those dorsal thrusters."

"Got it, sir."

"As you were."

Emery saluted, then bounded away.

Jackin turned an arch-browed look onto Adequin.

"After you," she said with a sweep of her hand.

Though Adequin remembered some of the *Typhos*'s layout from the couple days of stopover she'd had five weeks/six months ago, she let Jackin lead the way, following him out the wide bay doors and into the main hangar. The vast area remained eerily devoid of spacecraft, as far as hangars tended to go, and seemed to instead be used as a project staging area. Small crews worked in cordoned-off sections, some unpacking cargo crates, others disassembling machinery or sorting parts. The area had to be at least twice as large as the *Argus*'s had been, and this was only one of six primary hangars, not to mention the dozens of ancillary docking bays.

Adequin couldn't remember the last time she'd been on a capital ship. Ten years ago, at least, sometime during the Resurgence War. Regardless—the modern-day version of a capital ship was nothing like the *Typhos*; they simply didn't build them like this anymore. After the Viator War ended two hundred years ago, the System Collective's focus shifted from survival to expansion. The Legion started to commission more agile, efficient vessels to accommodate the changing needs. Behemoths like the *Typhos* had become a thing of the past. It was very likely the last of its kind.

"It's a bit of a walk," Jackin explained, and Adequin quickened her pace to catch back up with him. "Most of the lateral conveyance rails are shot. We're working on repairs, but it's not exactly high priority."

"Fine by me." After five weeks stuck on a ship the size of the *Synthesis*, she didn't mind an opportunity to stretch her legs.

They stepped out into the main halls and wound their way toward the bow. As they walked, they passed a formation of jogging soldiers in regulation training uniforms, an electrician working to repair a door control panel, and a pair of damage control specialists arguing the meaning of an error code. It felt normal, almost too normal.

And though every soldier they passed offered some variety of surprise, interest, or outright awe, every one snapped to attention. Jackin had clearly been running a tight ship. Her recurrent nightmares of returning to a lawless dystopian madhouse appeared unfounded.

They took a lift up a few levels, then proceeded into a narrower, less frequented passage that cut between sectors, coming upon a stretch vandalized by scrawled black graffiti. At first glance, she thought it was the old Sentinel nursery rhyme: *Sentinel, Sentinel, at the black. Do not blink or turn your back. You must stand ready to stem the tide, lest Viators come to cross the Divide.*

But her pace slowed as her eyes scanned the altered wording: *Sentinel, Sentinel, at the black. While we stood guard, they turned their backs. Think not of family, dream not of home. We'll die together, all alone.*

Jackin slid a discerning look over his shoulder at her, then slowed his pace to match hers. "We've got crews repainting," he assured quietly. "Though honestly, it's an endless cycle."

"Who's responsible?"

He shook his head. "Some of the crew aren't handling our proximity to the Divide all that well. Most have been pulled from gen pop, but diagnosing is an ongoing effort."

Adequin nodded her understanding. That'd happened a few times aboard the *Argus*, though with therapy and time, they'd recovered. It'd be even worse here, where they sat almost a million kilometers closer.

Down the hall, another message appeared, this one in a different handwriting, and a different type of paint entirely: *Sentinel, Sentinel, this ain't done. Grab your armor, get your gun. They tried to kill us, but you can bet . . . we don't forgive, we won't forget.*

Adequin swallowed past the tightness creeping up her throat. Two distinct feelings warred within her—one a dense weight of concern, the other a cool wave of invigoration. The soldiers had started to create a mythos around themselves. That could foster great inspiration and some much-needed camaraderie. But it could also devastate them if they fell short of their aim. Or if they fell apart before they even got that far.

Minutes later they arrived at Jackin's office—what would have been a praetor's when the *Typhos* had been in service two-hundred-plus years ago. The room was easily four times larger than necessary, with an oversized aerasteel desk accompanied by a trio of wingback leather chairs. Two worn gray couches sat to the right alongside a glass-topped credenza, complete with half-empty decanters and upended bar glasses. Centered on the back wall behind the desk hung an impressionist painting of the Meridian—the capital building on Elyseia—a monolith of sleek silver-blue glass that served as the modern-day seat of the System Collective, where the Quorum and Allied Monarchies assembled.

In general, the space felt far less austere than the offices aboard the *Argus*, which made sense considering the *Typhos* had been as likely to host diplomats or heads of state as soldiers. Though it'd certainly commanded many an engagement, the ship itself likely hadn't seen much action. If the dreadnoughts had been cannons, the *Typhos* had been the stronghold from which they'd been fired.

The door shut, sealing out the bustling sounds and hissing electronics of the rest of the ship. She tossed her ruck on a chair by the door. Jackin laid his tablet on the broad desk, then marched right back and pulled her into a hug.

Relief diluted the spikes of pain the embrace caused as Adequin tightened her sore arms around him. Tension sieved from her muscles like a damp rag being wrung out. This was why the handshake hadn't felt right.

"Where the hell have you been?" he asked, all strained formality gone from his tone, tinged with a fraction of a degree more relief than anger. "You were supposed to be back four weeks ago."

She sighed. No reason to delay the inevitable. "We restarted those outlier generators."

He let go and looked her over, black eyebrows pinching into a glare. "Void, Rake, we talked about that."

"We needed to check for distress calls anyway."

"There weren't any Sentinel ships stationed anywhere near those generators. We decided it didn't make sense to spend the—"

"No, *you* decided," she said. "We discussed it via courier messages delayed by days—weeks to you. It's impossible to communicate that way, Jack. It was hardly a conversation. So I made the decision to continue."

He ran stiff fingers slowly through the wavy hair on the top of his head and let out a heavy sigh. "It's more important for you to come back alive than to restart a couple more generators."

"There could have been more distress calls—"

He held up a hand. "All right. Let's not fight in circles this time."

She lifted her shoulders in a feeble shrug. "At least we're in the same room. It's more efficient than fighting in circles via weeks-long courier."

Amusement creased his eyes, and he gave a ceding incline of his head. "How are you, really?"

"Exhausted," she admitted. "We lost a lot of people, Jack."

"We *saved* a lot of people, Rake."

She held his gaze, letting the seriousness of his practical optimism sink in. In the quieter light of the gray-on-gray office, his eyes were more clearly bloodshot, the dark bags under them more apparent. Strands of ashy gray had crept their way into his black hair, flecking his beard, intent on climbing up to his temples next—all tangible indications of the burden she'd left him with.

"You look spent, Jack," she said.

He gave a wry grin. "It's almost like you left me here to babysit your rebellion."

Her gaze flitted down.

"No, hey," he urged. "I didn't mean it like that." He took her hand, and she ground her teeth as sharp bolts of pain shot up her forearms. Jackin didn't seem to notice. "You're the only one who could have done it. I know that."

She regretted not giving herself another shot of apexidone while she struggled to keep her voice steady. "How are things here?" she asked. "Last update I got would have been over a month ago for you."

Jackin licked his lips and nodded. "Right. Down to business." He swept his hand toward the absurdly high-backed, padded chair behind the desk.

She quirked a brow. "This's your office."

"Yours now."

She rubbed the back of her neck and reluctantly rounded to the other side of the vast desk. She gripped the cushioned leather arms and let out a tired sigh as she sank into the chair. If she'd resented the captain's chair on the *Argus*, she felt doubly so about whatever this one made her. Mutinous soldier. Insurgent hijacking a capital ship. Traitor inciting rebellion.

Jackin followed to her side of the desk and opened a holographic interface. He swept through a few menus, then slid the tablet he'd been carrying over the sync pad. A list formulated in the air over the console glass.

The *Typhos*'s computer system looked to be a couple of decades older than the *Argus*'s, which made sense, considering the *Typhos* had been decommissioned a decade before the *Argus* was even built. They may have appropriated most of their technology from Viators, but one thing humanity excelled at was building ships that could last.

Jackin leaned against the edge of the desk and scrolled for a few seconds, then let out a soft sigh. "There's a lot to cover."

"I see that . . ." She slouched deeper into the soft leather of the chair.

"I paged Puck, he'll be here shortly. We can get into more of the nitty-gritty with him."

"How's he been as optio?"

"Great," Jackin said. "Really great, actually. Everyone needed time to adjust, but he really stepped up. He's managing the day-to-day without needing my help."

Adequin nodded. Puck had always proven himself capable, but thriving under this kind of pressure took a certain kind of mental fortitude. It boded well that Jackin continued to think so highly of him after six months.

"Who'd you end up putting on IT?" she asked.

"Puck's actually been pulling both duties," he replied with a grimace. "He manages it, but it's too much long term. Hence this lovely, ancient operating system. He's only had time to maintain, not make improvements."

"One of the oculi I just brought back might be a good option as an apprentice, she's been helping me for weeks. She's smart, can think on her feet, doesn't get flustered easily."

"Great," he said, sliding open another screen. "Does she have a name?"

"Owen."

His fingers hovered over the display, waiting. "Owen what?"

"No last name."

He lifted a brow. "What's that about?"

"Honestly," she sighed, "I don't even want to know."

"Fair enough," he mumbled as he sent off a quick message. "I'll have Puck do an eval with her, see what he thinks." He closed the messaging screen. "With him on top of the daily grind, I've had more time to step back and focus on our bigger structural goals, and assess some of our bigger problems."

Adequin met his gaze. "Which are?"

"Well . . ." He crossed his arms and shifted higher up on the edge of the desk. "For starters, we have restless commanders. The instant the *Synthesis* blipped on sensors, every one of them put in a priority request to speak with you one-on-one."

"Pass."

He leveled a flat look at her. "I'd take it seriously. You've got a great base of support, but a few are actively, and openly, questioning why you're the one in charge."

"Why *am* I in charge?"

His eyebrows drew down, mouth pressing into a thin line. On anyone else, it'd be called outward defiance, but on Jackin it accomplished that and a lot more. It said that she was the one who started this, that she all but begged him to help, she made her bed and now no one else was going to be made to lie in it.

He expected a shrewd, capable leader. But she didn't know what that looked like on this scale. She'd been a Titan for over five years during the war, and knew all there was to know about small unit operations. She could crush an asset retrieval or an infiltration or an extraction in her sleep. But she had no idea how to coordinate the efforts of four thousand people, never mind keep them all alive, a step which objectively came first.

She breathed out a crackling sigh. "These soldiers don't see me as their leader, Jack. I haven't even been here."

"I think that's exactly why they do," he countered. "The oculi and circitors have done a frankly impressive job of deifying you."

She lifted a brow at him.

"Think about it," he continued. "They're stranded out there, you show up at the last second, save them from certain death at the hands of a force of nature that should be unstoppable, then disappear off into the Divide to save more."

Adequin sucked in a breath and pushed up from the confines of the chair. She crossed to the sitting area and grabbed the most whiskey-looking of the etched decanters. She yanked the stopper off and grabbed a glass.

The heat of Jackin's gaze lingered in her periphery as the liquid sloshed into the glass. She took a sip, and the warmth sieved into her tight chest, settling deep in her empty stomach, softening the pain-induced tremors by a fraction. She'd take it.

Jackin watched her in guarded silence as she crossed back to the desk and sat down. She eyed him as she took another slow sip. He didn't say anything, but blinked slowly, purposefully. She could practically see him adding "*the EX is day-drinking*" to his mental list of shit to deal with later.

Jackin cleared his throat. "The soldiers respect you," he said with forced evenness, "whether or not you choose to believe it. Their commanders, however—mostly legators, by the way—aren't biting quite as easily."

She gave a grim nod. She'd known most of the Sentinel commanders held that rank, which was why she'd bumped Jackin straight past it to centurion six months ago.

"Most only met you for the brief few minutes you were on-boarding their crew," Jackin continued. "They want a chance to talk to you directly, to see firsthand someone capable has the reins of this whole outfit."

"*Someone* does," she said evenly, taking a slow sip as her eyes grazed over him.

Confusion flitted across his face before his expression flattened and he pursed his lips. "Rake . . ." he warned.

"Yeah, fine, I get it," she relented. She didn't even know why she was being combative. "What do you suggest?"

"Though it'll be onerous, I think a forum might be the best approach. Otherwise you'll become the intermediary to all their stupid-ass squabbles. This way they'll be forced to gripe to each other face-to-face."

"Add it to the schedule."

He nodded, tapping to open the handful of requests and drop them into a single meeting for the following morning.

The door chimed with a short staccato bell, and Adequin glanced over the monolithic desk.

"Open," Jackin ordered, and the door complied.

Puck strode in, expression loose with his usual congeniality. His eyes fell on Jackin first, then his coltish frame stiffened as he registered Adequin's presence, drowning in the high-backed chair.

"Oh, shit. Sir," he stammered, then snapped a smart salute.

She swept open his personnel dossier. "Optio Amaeus Puck," she began, leaning forward in her chair, resting her elbows on the desk. "You've been granted the rank of centurion and all the rights and responsibilities the title carries."

Puck froze and his bronze skin blanched a shade. "I have?" His eyes darted between her and Jackin. "Uh, what about North?"

"He'll continue in his current role, but it's time to start the transition. I'll need my CNO sooner than later."

Puck's shock slowly drifted away, replaced with a toothy smile. "So, should we be calling you Praetor Rake?"

She gave a firm shake of her head. "Void, no. Excubitor will do just fine."

He nodded. "Copy that, EX."

"Sit."

He took a few quick steps and slid into one of the two wingback chairs in front of the desk. She tapped to update his rank in the system. She didn't know what functional good the bump would do in the short-term, but with so many unknowns, she wanted to do whatever she could to ensure a chain of command she trusted.

She expanded his dossier and glanced over his current absurd list of duties. "We'll need you to keep running tech until we can train an adequate replacement," she said. "Are you okay handling both a while longer?"

"Of course, sir," he agreed, tone steadfast, though his eyes were still wide. "Whatever you need."

"You seem surprised."

He gave a jittering shake of his head, as if trying to clear water from his ears. "Honestly, sir, I wasn't sure you'd trust me again, after what I did to get you off the *Argus*."

Adequin inclined her head. "Sometimes you need deputies who're willing to punch you in the face when you're being stupid."

Puck resisted a smile and Jackin shifted in her periphery.

"Regardless," she went on, "you've been Jack's right hand for six months. His trust is my trust."

Puck's mouth lifted in a flat smile, eyes slightly narrowed—a look filled with both pride and wary apprehension.

"Speak freely," Adequin encouraged.

"It's just . . . there are at least half a dozen officers from the other ships with more seniority," he explained.

"It doesn't matter. I want someone I can trust in this position," she continued. "You heard me already promote you, right?"

Puck's brow lifted at her suddenly casual tone. "Yeah, I heard, sir."

"So own it and shut up, please."

His lips twisted with a hardly suppressed grin. "Yessir."

With an unhindered sigh of strained effort, Jackin shook the bewildered look from his face. He rounded the desk and sat in the other chair beside Puck. "Now that . . . that's taken care of . . ."

Adequin readied herself with a deep breath, then nodded. "Go ahead."

Jackin began by diving into an overview of ship systems statuses. It'd taken four of their six months just to reconfigure crew accommodations, maximize food production, get the water recyclers up to speed, and ensure atmosphere and gravity stabilized to accommodate the new workload. He'd prioritized ship defenses after that, and pulled a few former gunners to evaluate the ordnance systems so they could get a better idea of how screwed they'd be if they ever had to actually fire their weaponry.

Puck reviewed their current team leads—Warner on security, Erandus on damage control, Eura on flight training, etcetera—before shifting into general population issues and overall morale. Which led to Jackin proposing a rededication ceremony to rename the *Typhos* in recognition of their new rebel force, or whatever they were now. Puck agreed; they needed to get her out in front of people, re-establish her as their leader, remind them what they were fighting for. Jackin insisted the impact on morale and solidarity would be immeasurable, and she hated more than anything that he was probably right.

"One bit of good news . . ." Puck said lightly, in a feeble attempt to end on a high note, "is that we've got a really decent group working the medbay. Mostly former rescue and squad medics, but they should be able to keep us all alive for a while. Though, like with most teams, some are better suited for forthcoming positions—defense, intelligence, statecraft—so we need to consider replacements for the long term." He frowned as he sat back with a sigh. "Unfortunuately, determining who to reclassify has been all but impossible. Most of the other commanders are keeping their soldiers' info close to the chest. It's like they think we're making an execution list to pass to the Legion."

Adequin exchanged a quick look with Jackin, then nodded grimly. "Let them keep it anonymous for now. We just need to know what everyone's capable of."

Puck nodded. "Understood, sir."

"And hell," she added, "maybe they'll be more cooperative now that you'll have a few more colors pinned to your shoulders."

Puck grinned and sat up a little straighter.

Adequin dismissed him with orders to prioritize the roster, and he left with a light bounce in his step.

She took the last sip of her whiskey then gave Jackin a forced grin. "What else?"

He closed out the screens. "I think we've covered everything that's pressing." He leaned back in his chair and crossed one ankle over his knee. "Tell me about your last run. How'd it go?"

"Last was the *Echion*. Thirty-eight people. The *Scyllia* and *Tauris* before that." For a grand total of seventy-six. For three ships that'd had almost eight hundred between them.

"What about cargo?" Jackin asked. "Were you able to get some of those food processor parts I requested?"

She shook her head. "We were short on time for all three, so our cargo pulls were limited. We did get some MREs, a couple atmospheric cycler filters, and some thermal control circuitry. Owen pulled a comms array module from the *Echion*, along with a few amplifiers. She said their ansible was newer than most, thought it could be useful."

Jackin licked his lips. "Tech's great, but we've got way bigger issues."

"Right," Adequin said with a heavy sigh. That whole eating thing they had to do. "How bad is it?"

"We reduced two weeks ago, and it's going down again tomorrow. We're lowering it as fast as we can, safely."

"What's the timeline?"

"Even with our processors at max output—and some *will* break down—it's looking like four weeks."

"Until?"

"Until we start making some hard decisions about who lives and who . . . doesn't."

She frowned. "What about hydroponics?"

"Our equipment's limited, and we can't really count on it. It's only just started to produce the last couple weeks."

"Really?"

He shook his head. "Their whole hydroponics ward dried up years ago, everything had to be ripped out and started fresh. They ate off food processors and MREs only."

"Void."

"We got it going as soon as we could, but it's not stable, or prolific. We can't count on it to make a dent in the truly colossal number of calories we need to produce."

Adequin sagged into the high-backed chair.

"We amassed so many people so quickly," Jackin explained, "and our resources haven't scaled at the same rate. Not nearly."

Adequin chewed the inside of her lip. Fucking math, always making terrible things even worse. She hated that having saved more people now felt like a burden. "I know our numbers have grown fast," she said, "but I'm surprised it's become such an issue so quickly."

Jackin shook his head. "It's not been quick. Remember for us, it's been six months. We've been lowering rations for over four months."

She sighed. Right. That whole time dilation thing.

"It'll be easier once we're through to Poine," Adequin said, trying to convince herself as much as Jackin. "We can find a home base, get some ground under our feet, get some supply lines set up."

Jackin ran a hand through his hair. "If we can make it inward in less than four weeks, sure."

She raised a brow. "How's the drive coming?"

"They're in the home stretch, but Cavalon's stuck. Has been for weeks."

"What's the problem?"

"I don't know, something to do with the cooling mechanism, maintaining superconductivity, melting the entire ship into an indiscernible hunk of aerasteel, etcetera."

"Okay, I'll talk to him. See if there's anything I can do."

Jackin gave a rueful shake of his head. "I'm trying to be patient with him, Rake, I really am. But we're getting down to it. If he doesn't figure this out in the next few weeks, we're all going to starve out here."

She let out a heavy sigh. "Understood. I'll go talk to him now."

Jackin sighed and scratched the back of his neck. "You'll find him in the outpatient ward."

She blinked. "The medbay? Why?"

"He passed out earlier. I guess he's been overindulging on epithesium."

Her eyes drifted shut as she pinched the bridge of her nose. "Void."

"He needs to scale way back on it. And he's fighting us on taking increased rations. I tried to talk some sense into him, but . . . it might be better received coming from you."

She eyed him carefully. "You guys been getting along?"

"Well enough."

She arched a brow at him. Jackin harbored some serious animosity for the Mercer royal family, though she still didn't know his reasons. "You're still holding it against him?"

Jackin gave a stiff shrug. "He's the grandson of a tyrant, Rake. It's hard not to hold it against him, at least a little."

"After everything he's done?"

"Listen, he's a good kid, I know that. It's just . . . it's complicated. We need him in order to survive this, and that's all that matters."

She flexed her jaw but chose to let it go. Jackin's ability to be cagey about his past was unmatched, and she was too tired for it at the moment.

She pushed up out of her chair. "All right, I'm on Cav duty."

Jackin nodded. "I'll send out the meeting notes to you and *Centurion* Puck. Where's *my* promotion by the way?"

The smile tugging at her lips annoyed her, but the amusement lightening his features was a welcome change from his seemingly permanent glower. She started for the door. "Empty promise, I'm afraid," she said, glancing back at him. "CNO's a higher rank than EX. I don't have the authority to promote you."

"I think we make our own rules now."

She sighed. "Yeah, I guess we do. Don't worry, you'll be CNO-and-then-some the second we drag this ancient rust bucket kicking and screaming through Kharon Gate."

Jackin chuffed a laugh. "Copy that."

CHAPTER FIVE

Cavalon rested his elbows on the workbench, staring down at the screen of one of six blurry tablets. His eyes refused to stay focused. Possibly because the vast majority of his notes—hastily typed while half-asleep in the middle of the night—were gibberish. More likely it was because it'd been hours since he had any epithesium.

The bay doors swooshed open behind him. He closed his eyes, set his jaw, and prepared for a fight. He knew Ford hadn't believed him when he'd promised to go straight to his quarters and rest. So naturally, the good doctor had tattled to Jackin again. One second they were pressuring him to finish sooner, and the next they insisted he worked himself too hard. It didn't compute.

"Animus."

His eyes flashed open, a wave of relief rinsing the tightness from his chest. That was not Jackin.

His gaze darted over his shoulder, and there stood Rake, amber eyes regarding him steadily. Her olive skin looked warmer, like she'd been lying on a beach for the last few weeks, made even more noticeable from the lighter streak that ran down her left cheekbone—scarring from burns she'd endured aboard the self-destructing *Tempus*.

Cavalon pushed away from the workbench, marched up, and wrapped his arms around her.

Though her posture remained stiff, her arms fixed around him and a latent tightness fled from his weary muscles. The last time they'd hugged, it'd been a hug for their lives, literally. Well, Rake's life. Drifting in the endless vacuum of space, no tether, no harness. Her only chance at not getting swallowed by the Divide to clutch onto him and hope he'd be strong enough to keep hold of her. To this day, he didn't know how he'd managed it.

"Shit . . ." He shook off his stupor and let go, shuffling back. "Uh, sorry, sir, I—" He gathered himself and took a deep breath. "Welcome back, sir."

Rake gave a nod and pushed some loose strands of brown hair out of her face as she adjusted the strap of a black duffle slung over her shoulder. She wore her full navy-blue excubitor getup—badges of rank on her jacket shoulders and everything. He wasn't sure why that surprised him.

"Cav?"

He blinked. "Yep?"

"You okay?"

"Yes."

She lifted a brow. "You're giving me . . . a look."

"Sorry," he breathed. "It's just been a while. Good to see you. Alive. Sir."

"I keep forgetting how long it's been for you guys."

He gave her a sheepish grin. "Feels different being on the other side of it, huh?"

Her eyes flitted down and a swell of regret beat hard in his chest.

He ran both hands down the sides of his face. "Shit. Void, sorry." Way to make her feel bad about not understanding both sides of the time dilation coin, while also bringing up her dead boyfriend. A boyfriend that to her, had only been gone for five weeks. At least he'd managed to find the most epically stupid thing he could possibly say and get it out of the way up front. "I'm absurdly tired," he rambled on. "It's not a great excuse, but—"

"It's okay," she assured him, and it sounded like she really meant it. Her gaze drifted over his shoulder. "That's quite an undertaking."

He glanced at the massive reactor orb. "Oh, that?" He waved a dismissive hand. "Just something Mesa and I've been toying with. Not a big deal."

"It's impressive. You should be proud."

He scratched his beard and let out a heavy sigh. "Only if I can get it to work. Otherwise it's nothing but a massive, useless mess of metal and cabling and metamaterials."

"You'll figure it out," she said in that easy, assured tone of hers that made him so sure it was the truth. He'd fucking missed that tone.

"I assume you're here to drag me back to the medbay?" he asked.

She shook her head. "Actually, I just came from there. I'd planned to break you out."

His lips parted, and he found himself briefly at a loss for words. "You . . . sorry, what?"

"I'd figured out a whole extraction plan." She grimaced as she hefted her bag up higher on her shoulder. "I was going to start by knocking over a tray of whatever looked the loudest or most hazardous. Then I'd have Emery call up from the hangar with a code fifty."

"What's a code fifty?"

"No idea."

He stared at her in stunned, openly amused silence. She was a little buzzed, if he wasn't mistaken.

"That's the point," she explained. "They'd all be so panicked trying to figure out what a code fifty is, they'd never notice you sneaking out the back door."

"I don't think the *Typhos*'s medbay has a 'back door,'" he said regretfully.

She shrugged. "Through the vents, then. As one does."

"Old times . . ." he said with a smile. She didn't smile back, but he recognized the glint of restrained humor in her eyes, throttled by years of Legion-issue repression. "Seems like a good plan," he admitted. "But you're the EX. Couldn't you have simply signed me out?"

She tilted her head. "What fun is that?"

He grinned broadly. He had no idea what the hell was happening. Time-dilated Rake was great.

"Want to take a field trip?" she asked.

His eyebrows shot up higher yet, and he blinked slowly back at her. He'd been so sure she was here at Jackin's behest—either to yell at him about taking care of himself, or to light a fire under his ass, or both at the same time, because why not? Or maybe to offer her help, however she could. She liked staying busy. But this was just too fucking weird.

He gulped, eyeing the strap on her shoulder. "Field trip, huh? I'd say it depends on what's in that bag . . ."

"Only one way to find out."

He chewed the inside of his lip, eyes narrowed at the duffle. Worst case, it was some kind of murder kit, and she intended to put him out of his long-standing misery. Best case . . . well, same, honestly.

Damn his curiosity. He gestured toward the exit. "Lead the way."

He grabbed his duty vest off the worktop as he followed her out, pulling it on over his sweaty shirt. Third shift had just started, and the corridors were mostly empty. Good for murderers looking to keep a low profile.

As he always did when venturing out into the ship, Cavalon tapped his nexus and activated the security interface. Puck had granted him limited tracking permissions so he could keep an eye on a few Sentinels' whereabouts—including Snyder and his two cronies who'd attacked him back on Kharon Gate. His nexus had been set to automatically buzz a warning whenever they came within a few corridors, but Cavalon preferred to be proactive. Though it'd take some serious balls to assault him when he had the EX as an escort.

Cavalon watched Rake carefully as they walked, looking for any indication of where she might be taking him. His gaze landed on her hands, which constantly moved, tugging at the cuffs or collar of her jacket, fingers twitching or stretching.

He didn't *actually* think she was going to kill him. At least he was 99 percent sure, but the Divide had a strange effect on people. Evidently a result of its unnatural nature—the collapsing mass of the universe held at bay by the output of that ridiculous network of dark energy generators the Viators had constructed. But Rake had spent five years aboard the Sentinel vessel that'd sat closer to the Divide than any other. If she was going to lose it, surely she already would have.

They headed starboard, then up to a level Cavalon had never been on before. Judging from the low-light mode and thinner atmosphere, it wasn't a deck frequented by anyone else either. Finally, Rake paused at a wide door at the end of a corridor.

"Nexus," she said, holding a hand out.

He hesitated only briefly before realizing it was an order. He fumbled his nexus band off his wrist and passed it to her, rubbing over the exposed flesh where the band had rested. He couldn't recall the last time he'd taken it off. To his surprise, Rake slid her own off as well, and tossed both on the floor beside the door.

"Oh, void," he mumbled. "You've had it, right?"

She arched a brow at him.

"This is turning into one of those 'where no one can hear you scream' things."

She shook her head as she tapped her clearance into the control screen beside the door.

It slid open. Cavalon followed her in a few steps, stopping in his tracks as his gaze slid up the high-ceilinged walls, covered by massive, arcing observation windows. His lips parted and he traipsed straight up to the glass. The thick, armored shutters had already been retracted, revealing a dense smattering of stars so bright, he had to squint. As his gaze drifted left, the pinpricks of light dispersed, slowly fading to black, stretching toward the emptiness of the Divide. He hadn't seen a clear view inward since they first set foot on the *Typhos* six months ago. It was weirdly reassuring to see something still existed out there, even if it was only unreachable starlight, a hundred million light-years away.

He glanced back to find Rake waiting patiently. She stood beside a wide table draped with a heavy canvas dust blanket. More sets of covered furniture dotted the stately room, easily four times as long as it was wide, leveraging the advantage of the view. Unlit glass chandeliers dotted the high ceilings, each a dramatic assemblage of crystal hexagons suspended in a crescent formation.

He looked back at Rake. "Where are we?"

"The Lanrish Salon. For entertaining dignitaries. Your great-times-eight or whatever grandparents might've spent time here."

He wondered if that generation had been as loathsome as his grand-father, or if that particular trait had been curated through all the selective breeding that'd happened in the last two centuries. It didn't bode well for him either way.

"This way," Rake said, then headed away from the windows, toward the back of the room. Cavalon followed.

Rake led him into a small galley-style kitchen. A few appliances punc-tuated the two long countertops against either wall. She set the duffle on the counter and started emptying the contents. Cavalon hovered in the doorway, too stunned to properly react.

She arched an eyebrow at him. "What's that look?"

"Honestly . . ." He heaved a sigh. "This is just a dream come true. Rake in the kitchen."

She stopped unpacking, and the murderous glower she leveled at him sent a nostalgic lance of terror through his chest. How he missed it.

"So you want to be an oculus again, then?" She returned to her un-packing.

He tentatively stepped up to join her. "Ouch. EX coming in hot with the threats."

"I don't know . . ." she said, the edge of frustration gone from her tone. "Is it a threat? Might be a relief at this point."

He scoffed a nervous laugh, choked by a tight strain in his chest. "Yeah, I'd happily go back to mopping in circles if you want."

She pulled a knife out of the bag and slid it across the steel counter. Then she passed him three small, honest-to-the-void, *onions*.

"Chop these," she ordered. "Try not to cut your fingers off."

He lifted one of the onions and sniffed it, and the pungent odor sent his eyes and mouth watering. He hadn't seen real produce in over a year.

"Define 'chop,'" he said warily.

She sighed and grabbed one of the onions. With her own knife, she sliced it in half then peeled away the papery outer layers. She cut a thin chunk free, then turned it and sliced it the opposite way, resulting in a tiny pile of half-centimeter-sized chunks.

"Etcetera," she said.

He nodded. "Got it." He took the onion back and got to work.

Rake stepped away, hunting through the cabinets. She gathered a va-riety of implements including metal bowls, a shallow baking dish, and a couple of large spoons, then returned to stand beside him. She took a crinkling packet out of the black bag and emptied the dusty contents into a bowl. A canteen came out next, and she poured a seemingly arbitrary amount of water into the mix, then stirred for a long while. She finally dropped the dough out onto the counter and kneaded it.

Cavalon's eyes burned, the spicy aroma growing stronger as he reduced more and more of the onions to tiny bits. He was still working on the second onion when Rake pressed the dough into the baking dish and set it aside, then took four small carrots from the bag, and started chopping.

He'd only just finished with the last onion by the time Rake had produced a bowl full of chopped carrots, potatoes, and spinach. She dug into her bag and brought out a small assortment of resealable packages. She tore one open and sprinkled some into the mix.

"How much garlic, you think?" she asked, grabbing another packet.

"Uh, I don't even know what unit it's measured in."

"You've never had to cook once, have you?"

He scoffed with feigned offense. "I may have had a sheltered upbringing, but I did pick up a thing or two, thank you very much."

She sighed. "Let me guess, you took a minor in culinary science?"

He laughed. "No, but good guess. There was a guard who liked to cook in her spare time. And because I was an annoying, clingy, bored kid, I hung around and bugged her during off-hours."

"Oh yeah?" She slid him an arch-browed look.

"Yep. Deveraux. A fresh-faced new recruit at the time, so she had yet to acquire the guards' traditional aloof demeanor. They housebroke her pretty quick, don't worry."

"What'd she teach you?"

"Well, not how to chop, clearly."

"Clearly."

"Honestly, I was so bad at everything, she quickly demoted me to taste tester."

Rake dumped his onions into the mix. "How'd your grandfather feel about that?"

He shook his head. "As long as I was with the guard, Augustus didn't give a shit what I was doing."

"It had to be strange growing up that way, with chaperones around all the time? Were you close to them?"

"I dunno if you'd call it 'close.' There were a few I knew better than others—in particular the ones who went to university with me when I was sixteen, including Deveraux. They were the ones who followed me from school to school . . . and from bender to bender, dragging me out before I could drown in my own vomit."

Rake frowned as she sprinkled more powered garlic into the veggies.

"But that's kinda what I thought friendship was," he admitted. "So, yeah, I'd say I considered them friends, or at least allies." He flashed her a stiff grin. "Which made it even worse when they cuffed me and locked me up and beat me when I resisted, then dragged me off to the edge of the universe to die. In the end, they were all loyal to Augustus."

"Are you sure that loyalty was willingly given?"

He licked his dry lips and met her eye. "I guess . . . no, I can't be sure."

"Sometimes, it's too dangerous to stay loyal to what you believe in. I wouldn't assume their friendship wasn't real, at least in some respects. They might have had no choice."

Heat radiated in his chest. She had a point. It wouldn't surprise him in the slightest if Augustus had dug up some blackmail on them to ensure loyalty. But he also knew that for every one guard that might have harbored genuine affection for him, there were a dozen that fell somewhere between mere tolerance and outright loathing. The further he got from that life, the more plainly he could see it for what it'd really been.

He cleared his throat and decided it was well past time to deflect. "I'm surprised you know how to cook yourself, Miss Enlisted-at-Sixteen. The Legion must have fed you most of your life."

"We do get leave, you know. Well, Sentinels don't, so it's been a while. Regardless, I learned before I enlisted."

"Oh, fun. More Adventures of Young Rake on Seneca-IV, right?"

She nodded as she went to start the oven.

"Except Rake wasn't her name then, was it?" he asked. She'd admitted as much when they were about to die aboard that first dark energy generator. But the Divide had tried to swallow them up before he could get her real name.

"No, it wasn't," she replied plainly, with no apparent inclination to elaborate.

He leaned a hip on the counter and scratched the back of his neck. "I can't imagine the aforementioned shitty parents were responsible for this kind of life skill?" he ventured.

"In a way, they were. When things got . . ." She shook her head as she poured the mix of vegetables into the baking dish. "Let's just say, there were periods of time when I needed to provide for myself. There was a pub in town, and the owner would pay me to wash dishes or run errands. They taught me a few things before the pub got shut down for 'health code' violations."

"You say that with air quotes?"

"There were no violations—no worse than anywhere else in town.

They just couldn't keep paying the extortion fees the Saxton Guard collected every month."

"I mean, wildly negligent governmental oversight is why you're paying taxes, after all."

She gave a sidelong eye roll.

"Why couldn't you keep hanging out with the pub owner even after it closed? No other kitchens on Seneca-IV?"

She shook her head, tucking some loose strands of hair behind her ear. "They died shortly after. A bombing during a riot."

"Oh, shit. Sorry. That's horrible."

"I kept trying on my own for a while, but I never quite got it right. Eventually, the Saxton Guard buckled down, and stealing the produce from the greenhouses got too risky."

"Uh, did you just admit to larceny?"

She lifted a shoulder in a vague shrug.

He narrowed his eyes at the baking dish. "Where'd you get these veggies, anyway?"

"Appropriated them from the hydroponics lab."

He laughed. "Appropriated is just a fancy word for steal."

"This is 'my ship,' right? I should get some perks."

"Yeah, you should," he agreed. But he didn't like the degree of sarcasm she'd injected into "my ship."

He silently watched her finish the pie and put it in the oven, his amusement sliding away as a dense pressure built in his chest. Something was off about all this.

Not her being forthright and open and even bantering with him—all of which was weird for entirely different reasons. It was the underlying vibe she gave off, like an asterisk marking the whole encounter—some unnamed caveat existed that Cavalon was too distant from her to understand.

It didn't feel like an act, but the emotion behind it felt forced. Like it was taking every effort she had left to put forward this guise of congeniality.

By the time the veggie pie finished baking, they'd exhausted all avenues of food-related small talk. Rake took the dish out and cut them each an overlarge slice, then they sat atop the counter, noshing it down with the easy, uncomplicated silence of delicious food consumption.

As Cavalon ate, a wave of dizziness swept over him, chills rushing across his skin as the food settled in his stomach. He wasn't used to the extra calories and his body was wholeheartedly appreciating the shit out of it.

"So," he began over his penultimate mouthful of pie. "You said you never got the recipe quite right. How's this attempt compare?"

"Still shit, unfortunately."

"Ah, well. Maybe someday."

"Practice makes perfect."

"For the record," he said, shoving the last forkful in his mouth, "this tastes nothing even remotely like shit."

"You would know."

He gulped down the bite. "Exactly."

Rake set her empty plate aside and pulled the small duffle bag across the counter toward her. She took out a half-full bottle of whiskey, then angled it toward him. He held up his hand to say no thanks, but she dropped it back down before he could refuse.

"Sorry," she said, regret deflating her tone. "I forgot."

"No worries."

"Mind if I do?"

"Not at all."

She inclined her head. He did his best to moderate his expression as he watched her take a few long drinks. Her shoulders loosened, breaths a bit too shallow as her eyes glossed over. She licked her lips and didn't cap the bottle.

He eyed her for a few long moments, then leaned back to rest against the overhead cabinets. "I still can't imagine young Rake as an apprentice chef."

"I was hardly any kind of chef. It's the only thing I know how to make," she admitted. "I only kept making it because Hudson used to gush over it. Said I'd missed my calling. He was one of those painfully optimistic types."

Cavalon gave her a sideways grin. "Right, your surrogate uncle." The one who'd enlisted her at sixteen, saving her from Seneca-IV. "Am I the only one here that knows about him?"

She shrugged as she took another drink. "You, and everyone who overheard us on comms. Mesa, Puck, Jack, and . . ."

She thumbed one of the two pairs of dog tags she wore around her neck. Cavalon bit his lip. He knew exactly who they belonged to; he'd sat there in the sweltering heat of the dark energy generator and watched while Rake had pulled them off Griffith's body.

She hadn't said a word about him since he'd died. Cavalon continued to assume she wasn't ready to talk about it. Maybe she needed to. But with him? Not likely. Jackin, maybe. Mesa? Cavalon wasn't sure. And he didn't know if he had the social currency to push her into it. Or for her to forgive him if it was a step too far.

So like the coward he was, he changed the subject. "Speaking of how you've been enlisted half your life," he began, "how're you handling the whole mutiny thing?"

"Fine," she murmured, her sullen tone unsettling to his ears.

He licked his dry lips. He'd been afraid of not having the currency to talk about Griffith, why'd he think the thing she'd uprooted her entire belief system for would be better?

She sighed and the metal pendants jangled as she dropped them to her chest and picked up the whiskey bottle again.

"Sorry," he said quickly. "I know the whole thing's probably still raw."

"It's not that." She exhaled a hard breath. "Not really. I knew what I was doing when I started it. Just trying to determine how I fit into things now, after being away from it for six months." She took another drink. "But I'll figure it out. I became who I was despite the people who raised me, I'll become whatever's next despite the Legion."

He stared back at her, lips parted, entirely unsure what to say. It was another of those casually wise things she loved to throw out, so nonchalantly, like it'd been any other random thought that'd passed through her brain. But it was also a somewhat alarming way to phrase it. She had become who she *was*? Who'd that make her now?

Maybe she didn't even know. Maybe that was the whole problem.

He set his empty plate down and cleared his throat. "You know, I think I know how you feel. I've been struggling with that myself."

She glanced at him. "Yeah?"

"I became who I am despite my upbringing. Despite Augustus." He leaned his shoulder into hers. "With a little help from a renegade excubitor . . ."

She offered an acquiescent head tilt.

"But I also know I can do better," Cavalon continued. "Not only get past it, but rise above it. Figure out how to be a better man than he could ever pretend to be."

"Damn. Where'd you get those rose-colored glasses?"

He gave a grim smile. "Really not sure, actually. Guess it's just . . . encouraging to have something to live for, for once."

The bottle sloshed as Rake set it back onto the counter. "Well, I'm glad you're in good spirits, but you still look like death."

"Thank you. I've been working on my figure."

Her jaw flexed as she leveled a flat look at him.

"Rations keep going down, it just takes some getting used to," he explained. "I wasn't helping the transition with the overindulgence of epithesium either."

"We need you strong."

He shook his head. "Doctor Kellar already tried. I don't want special treatment."

"Kellar?"

"Ford? He and Jackin seem pretty chummy. I think they might have known each other, pre-war."

She wiped her brow with the back of her hand. "Well, you need to get over your martyr complex. It's not up for discussion. You can either take the extra nutrients willingly, or I can arrange to have it done by force."

He smiled. "Kinky . . ."

The look she trained on him made him instantly regret every stupid comment he'd ever uttered. He frowned, eyeing the hard lines around her bloodshot eyes, her flushed cheeks, how she held herself slightly crooked like she had a hitch in her back. No matter how hard it'd been aboard the *Typhos* the last six months, he couldn't imagine what she'd gone through restarting those generators over and over again. She'd lost a lot of people. It had to have taken a toll on her, one he couldn't begin to understand.

"Okay," he agreed quietly. "I'll eat the extra rations."

After a time, she cleared her throat, though her voice still came out crackled and dry. "I'm sorry, Cav. I really didn't arrange this to rail on you. You don't need to be babysat anymore."

Cavalon caught her eye and pressed his lips into a thin smile.

"Just do me a favor," she continued, "and try not to starve yourself to death."

He gave a light chuckle. "You know, when you came and found me, I figured there was going to be a *lot* of railing, honestly. I assumed you were planning some big speech about honor and discipline and duty. Try to remind me what we're fighting for."

She scoffed. "Who do you take me for? That's the opposite of what you need right now."

His chest lightened, some of the strain giving way. He gave a short nod.

"If we get so caught up in survival, we forget to live . . ." She gave a rueful shake of her head. "What's the point?"

His head bobbed up and down. "Damn. Yeah." He looked down, gripping the edge of the counter as a thought careened out of the back of his brain. His mind raced so fast, he could hardly keep up with it. "Wait . . ." he breathed, the word dying out on his tongue.

Rake lifted a brow at him. "What's wrong?"

"Forget to live . . ."

"What?"

He didn't respond, eyes defocusing as he stared off, letting his mind lay out the plan for him.

"Cav?"

He pivoted to face her. "I've been so worried about containing it, I never thought about just *exposing* it. It's damn old-school . . ." He scoffed a laugh. "But it might actually work."

"Wait, what are we talking about?" she asked.

"The cryostat."

"This is the thing you've been stuck on?"

He nodded fervently. "And it'll be a cinch to implement—starfighter launch tubes run directly under that wing of the hangar. I just need to open a pathway below the divertor cassettes. So long as it's a hermetic seal, it'll expose the cryostat to hard space without exposing the rest of the components."

"Exposing it to space is enough to cool it?"

"No, no, the supercritical helium does that."

"Oh, well, obviously," Rake deadpanned.

He pressed his fingers against his eyelids as a mess of jumbled ideas and schematics and computations fought for his attention. It didn't take long for the thought-deluge to stagger and stall out as the mathematical implications made themselves known. Even on a day when his brain wasn't a frazzled mess, he'd need a computer to run these numbers.

"I'll need calculations, shit . . ." He glanced at his nexus-less wrist. "What time is it?"

"Probably around 2300."

"Damn." He really didn't want to wake Mesa simply to theorize, especially if it didn't pan out. He'd already presented her with a half-dozen duds over the last week.

"What's wrong?" Rake asked.

"I need to run some simulations to make sure I'm right."

"You need a coder?"

He nodded fervently. "Preferably one that knows their way around applied mathematics."

"Not sure on the math part, but there's a newbie we picked up along the way that knows her way around computers—was great with Viator systems, and has experience with the reactors."

"Yes, brilliant, great, point me in her direction."

"She should be offloading the *Synthesis* about now, in bay A5. Emery'll introduce you."

"Perfect, thank you." He made for the door, then faltered. He spun and paced back, gripping Rake's hand. "Thank you. Not for the idea, but for . . ." He swept his other hand out to the dirty dishes around the small galley. "This. I needed it. Really. And sorry to leave you with the mess."

"No worries." Rake held up her whiskey bottle in a toast. "It's good to see you, Animus."

His chest swelled. "Yeah, about that—I thought promotions were supposed to come with perks. When's that part coming?"

She cast him a bitter smile. "Let me know if you find out."

He gave a wary smirk and dashed out the door.

CHAPTER SIX

Cavalon skirted past a group of jogging soldiers as he half-sprinted down the corridor, filled with a rare assuredness. Unlike the dozens of others, this solution *fit*. He felt strangely positive that this absurd plan of Rake's would actually work, and the reactor would not explode, and the jump drive would suck up the solar power it needed, and they'd have unlimited jump travel to go wherever they wanted in the universe. Once they got the stupid thing through Kharon Gate, at least. If he didn't truly think he was incapable of it, he'd call his current mindset optimism.

The *Synthesis* sat alone in bay A5, its cargo and personnel hatches open and bustling with oculi offloading crates and personal effects. The Viator-turned-Drudger-turned-Sentinel vessel reminded Cavalon of a time he at once felt nostalgic for, and yet wanted nothing more than to forget forever. A time he held accountable for forming him into a functional human being, but one marred by loss, death, and betrayal.

He approached the underbelly of the *Synthesis* just as Emery stepped out of the personnel hatch.

"Holy shit, boss!" A broad grin spread across her face as she half-jogged, half-skipped down the ramp toward him. She threw her thin arms around his neck, lifting up onto her toes to grip him in a fierce hug.

"You really are my boss now, huh? Mister Animus?" She dropped away and stepped back, crossing her arms and setting her jaw in a smug grin. "Though, ya know, I was promoted."

His mouth dropped open. "You were?"

Her eyes narrowed.

"I mean—you were!" he corrected. "Congrats, Em, really. Circitor?"

"Yep. Watch." She spun toward an oculus standing beside a collection of crates on the far side of the ramp. "Hey, Landus! Go help Martinez with the warp drive assessment."

The oculus nodded and scurried off.

Emery grinned back at Cavalon. "See? They gotta do what I say. Fuckin' lemmings."

He chuckled.

She jutted a thumb over her shoulder at the belly of the ship. "Rake let me fly this thing onto the Divide. Can you believe it?"

Cavalon swallowed, giving a shallow head shake. He really couldn't.

"I'm 'a natural'—her words."

He smiled. "That's great. We're going to need more ace pilots."

Emery beamed.

"I really wanna catch up, Em," he said, "but I need a rain check—my brain's onto something."

"That saving our asses thing?"

"Yeah, that. Rake said you picked up a coder she trusts?"

"Computers?"

"Yeah. They know any math?" he asked.

"Oh, for sure. You're gonna love her—she's as big an entitled dick as you are."

Cavalon followed as Emery led him to the open cargo hatch, bustling with soldiers clumped in various groupings, trying to figure out how to use the ancient cargo lift drones.

"Yo, Owen!" Emery called over the chattering oculi.

A woman stood up from the other side of a cargo lift mechanism, and Cavalon's remaining levity melted from his face as recognition sunk in. Owen Larios.

Her hazel eyes regarded him evenly, a sheen of sweat glistening on her light brown skin. Her wavy dark brown hair had grown, now gathered into a braid that ran past her shoulders. Her duty vest hung open, a narrow sandy-brown oculus badge pinned to the left arm of her long-sleeved navy shirt. She strapped her vest closed as he followed Emery closer.

Cavalon's gaze locked on to the only confirmation he needed—the white scar behind her left ear from when she'd lost her footing trying to climb over the southern wall of the manor.

His mind warred with it, trying to fit together two pieces of separate puzzles. He'd last seen her almost a year ago on Elyseia, in the stale dustiness of the relief bunker in the eastern wing of Mercer Manor. With a pained grimace of pity and probably a little worry etched into her normally soft features. Mere weeks before the Mercer Guard shackled him and escorted him out to the Divide to die.

He blinked a few more times, and she didn't vanish, didn't prove herself a time ripple or a figment of his addled mind. It really was her.

Owen gave a half smile, not looking nearly as surprised as Cavalon felt. She'd never worn her emotions on her sleeve quite like he did.

Emery shifted uncomfortably, her smile wavering. "Um, shit. Do you guys know each other?"

Owen nodded, then crossed the few meters and hugged him. He hugged back perfunctorily, still dazed. He didn't think he'd ever hugged or been hugged so much in one day before. This one felt different than the first two, though. More tentative, more procedural, more packed with history and outright disbelief.

Owen stepped back, and Cavalon's gaze darted furtively over her once again. With an effort, he shelved his hesitation. "Owen. Good to see you."

He almost scoffed at his own asinine greeting. It lacked in every perceivable way, not even beginning to cover everything that needed saying. But with Emery standing there gaping and all the oculi padding around nearby, he couldn't bring himself to let his full reaction loose.

Owen stepped back into a sweeping bow. "Your Highness."

Cavalon pressed his fingers deep into one temple and groaned.

Emery gave a nervous half chuckle, staring between them, expression a blend of confusion and curiosity. "Uh, Cav here needs some computer help," she said. "EX sent him your way."

Cavalon gave a stiff nod as his cryostat realization resurfaced, flooding his chest with anxious relief.

He knew it could work, it had to, and now that he'd conceptualized it, he wouldn't be able to rest until he'd either disproven the concept or made it work. And he needed someone—someone who was apparently Owen—to get that proof.

"Computers are what I do," Owen said pleasantly. "How can I help, my liege?"

"Void," Cavalon cursed, clearing his throat. "Right, okay. Um, it'll be easier to show than tell—reactor bay's down the way." He looked to Emery. "If your CO authorizes it, that is."

"All yours, Animus. You kids have fun." She gave Owen a bright, slightly tense, smile then started back toward the personnel hatch.

Cavalon stared at Owen, who watched Emery's retreat with way too much interest. He clenched his jaw. He recognized that look.

"This way," he prompted, tone stiff. He started the trek across the wide docking bay toward the main hangar and Owen kept pace beside him. Once they were clear of the ship, he maintained his brisk steps, turning a flat look onto her. "Owen . . ." he growled.

"Cav."

"She's way too young for you."

Owen scoffed. "One: Fuck off. Two: Since when are you all judgmental?"

"Not judgmental. She's my friend—and you're an asshole."

"Sure you aren't just jealous?" She waggled her eyebrows at him.

Cavalon rolled his eyes.

"Because you know," Owen went on, "she couldn't do enough talking about you . . ."

"She told you about me?"

"She didn't give your name, if that's what you're worried about." Owen waited till they'd passed a group of chatting oculi before continuing. "But how many civilian astromechanical engineers too smart and snarky for their own good end up out at the Divide? That's not hard math, even for a *simpleton*."

Cavalon set his jaw. "I called you that *once*. And I was super wasted."

She held a hand over her heart. "And to this day, the memory slays me."

He threw a hard glance over his shoulder. "She's a teenager, for void's sake."

"She just turned twenty, actually, so lay off it." She gave a proud smirk. "See, I know more about her than you do."

Cavalon pushed an aggravated breath out his nose as he continued marching toward the exit.

"Besides," Owen went on, "I'm only five years older, or uh . . . wait, how old am I?" She scratched the back of her head, seeming truly unsure. "I honestly don't even know the date right now. Can you believe that time dilation shit? Oh, of course you can, Mister Gravitational Tempology."

He sighed. "I always forget you're younger than me."

"It's because I seem so mature, right?"

"Mm-hmm," he hummed.

"*You* certainly seem to have grown up in the interim . . ." She kept up with his swift pace as she drew her shoulders down, expression flat with mock seriousness. "With this whole-universe-on-your-shoulders glower and gray-ass beard. You're looking more like your old man every day. I half-thought you were him at first."

Cavalon swallowed past the bitter lump at the back of his throat. Just like Owen to mention one's dead father as casually as giving an update on the weather. "Yeah, well," he grumbled. "This shit'll age you. I haven't exactly been having a blast since I left the Core."

Owen laughed. "I see what you did there—*blast*. Hah."

His traitorous lips twitched at the corners, but before he could consider enjoying the accidental joke, his gaze darted to the vacant decking around them. He took Owen by the elbow and pulled her toward the base of a thick bulkhead column, tucking into the corner, shielding them from the traffic of the hangar.

He leaned in, voice barely a whisper. "Why the hell are you here, O? What's going on?"

A fraction of her unmitigated snark faded. "Whoa, Mercer, relax. You think I'm a spy or something?"

"No, void. That's not what I meant."

"Damn, CJ . . ." She gave a wistful sigh, hazel eyes drifting over him. "You really need to get over this doom-and-gloom attitude." She reached up, her cool fingertips pushing at the outer corners of his eyes, stretching the skin back against his temples. "It's giving you wrinkles . . ."

He jerked his head to shake her off and her hands dropped. "I'm being serious, O."

She rolled her eyes.

"I know it's part of the whole Larios tradition to offer recruits for service," he said, "but I thought that was just some ceremonial fanfare bullshit."

"Ceremonial fanfare? Maybe. Bullshit? Definitely. But it does help to redirect attention from one's galactic monopoly on munitions manufacturing to have some of us out actually using said munitions."

Cavalon exhaled a heavy sigh. As with each of the five royal families who ruled the most populous systems in the SC, the Larios family had its own corporate exploits. Where the Mercers had a sweep on genetics and biotechnologies, Larios focused on military-grade weapons and defense tech of all flavors. And anyone who thought that made the System Collective a thinly veiled corporatocracy would be exactly right.

Owen nudged him, then pinched the collar at the base of her neck like she was tightening a necktie. "Besides, I think I fill out the Legion uniform quite well, no?"

"Please tell me that's really why you're here. And it wasn't Augustus."

Her eyes flitted to the deck, the smirk at her lips flattening with guilt. "Sorry, man. I can't do that."

He glanced at a group of passing oculi, then edged them farther toward the base of the column. "What the hell happened?" he hissed.

Owen lowered her voice. "What the hell do you think? Remember when I helped you build the fucking bomb you used to destroy your grandpa's cloning facility?"

Only the command circuitry portion—but that seemed beside the point. "Two, actually," he mumbled. *Also* beside the point.

"Well, guess who found out?"

"Shit. And he got you sent out here? How?"

"He told my mom some bullshit story that I organized a denuclearization rally on Cautis Prime. I don't think she believed him, but what's a middling Larios supposed to say to Augustus fucking Mercer? 'Nah, man, I trust my kid more than you? Please go ahead and ruthlessly murder my whole family now'?"

"Void . . ."

"Anyway—he suggested I 'learn to respect the family traditions' with a couple-year stint in the Legion. I was supposed to do basic training at Legion HQ, but we flew straight past it, ended up at the Divide. I don't know if my family even knows."

"Well, shit." He rubbed the back of his neck. "I'm really sorry, O. Damn. I never wanted to implicate you. I really thought I covered my tracks with that."

"Honestly, you probably did . . ."

"What?"

Her bottom lip jutted out and she hunched her shoulders. "It might have sort of, kind of, been my own fault. I told Gusty I helped."

"You admitted it?" he hissed. "*Why?*"

"To try and take some of the heat off you!" she hissed back, then held her hands up placatingly. "I was only trying to help. It's not like it was the first time we did something that fucking stupid. I knew he'd be pissed, but not so pissed that he'd . . ." She took a deep breath and lowered her voice considerably. "Disown you then try to get us both murdered by criminal soldiers."

Cavalon growled out a groan as he dragged a hand down the side of his face. Why? Why the hell would she do that? He bit down on the inside of his lip as the word for it clawed at the back of his mind, sending guilt pooling into the pit of his stomach.

Loyalty. Ugh. Owen was too smart to have admitted involvement directly to Augustus's face without realizing the severity of the repercussions. It'd been an oversight, certainly, for her to assume the old man would take it for anything other than explicit betrayal.

Damn. Owen either actually gave a shit about him, or she had a death wish—which knowing Owen, wasn't likely the case. She'd always relished life, even when they were kids. If she wanted to get herself killed, there were about nine thousand more direct ways than weaving herself into the outskirts of Augustus's machinations.

He didn't know what to make of it; he couldn't even wrap his head around it. Maybe Cavalon's various dependencies had skewed his perceptions of his relationships more than he realized. He'd never considered he might have a single trustworthy friend back at the Core. And maybe he didn't, now that Owen was out here too.

"Hey," Owen said, nudging him back to focus. "Shut your brain off about it. We're here now, let's just make the best of it."

There it was, that unbridled optimism. Even out at the farthest fringes of the universe, Owen intended to live life to its fullest.

"Besides," she went on, "you seem to be doing well for yourself, *Animus* Mercer."

He managed a weak shrug.

A shit-eating grin spread across her face. "And yet you still need the help of a little-ole middling Larios?"

Right, that thing that was going to save them all. He willed his brain to stay focused. "Yeah, yeah," he said. "I'll show you."

He led her into the aftward corridors, swiping his clearance to grant them access to the reactor bay.

"Bloody hell," Owen breathed, her gaze drifting up the twenty-meter-tall orb as they approached the workbenches. "You built this?"

"Mesa and I did, yeah." He started shoving sweat-crusted towels and empty water bottles off to the sides, clearing room over the holographic terminal glass. "She's another animus, a Viator-tech expert. She's off-shift or she'd be here giving me hell about throwing a new coder into the mix without having them properly vetted."

Owen's gaze shot over to him, eyes wide. "Wait, Mesa? Mesa Darox?"

"Uh, yeah."

"The Savant?"

"Uh . . . yeah. Shut *up*, you do not know her. No way."

Owen shook her head. "No, I don't, but I've read her work."

"Her work?"

"You're kidding, right? She's written dozens of essays for the *Altum Cultural Review, Illium's Xenologic Journal,* a bunch of others. There's basically an entire xenotechnology minor based on her work at Altum Institute."

"There . . . is?"

A rueful smile crept onto Owen's face. "Just like you not to have any idea who you're friends with."

Cavalon frowned, scratching his beard absently.

Owen gripped his shoulder. "So, what are we looking at, bud?"

"Right." He took a minute to organize his thoughts, starting from Rake's accidental statement. He did his best to explain the initial problem to Owen, giving a quick summary of the approaches he'd already considered and dismissed, and why. When he proposed his new idea, he was pleasantly surprised to see the way her eyebrows slowly rose, eyes brightening with silent approval.

"Shit, yeah," she said when he was done. "That could work."

"Could, or will?" he asked, picking at the edges of his fingernails.

She shook her head. "The practical part's on you. But it sounds solid, honestly."

"You think you can get a simulation of it? I just need you to break out a new instance to test it on, or Mesa'll kill me."

Owen turned to the workbench, opened a few reactor system screens, and started tapping through them. He watched with unfettered curiosity as she effortlessly navigated through the Viator system.

"Stop it," she grunted, not looking up.

"What?"

"You're staring."

"Well, sorry, but you're acting like you were raised on Viator code."

She waved a dismissive hand. "I had a lot of time to kill on those dark energy generators while the grunts were dumping hydrogen into the machine or the EX was out fixing the hull."

He drummed his fingers on the workbench. "You worked closely with Rake, then?"

"*Excubitor* Rake, yeah." She arched a brow at him. "You always so casual with your COs' names?"

"I never really learned to be a proper legionnaire," he admitted. "Not that Rake didn't try to beat it into me. After everything we went through, it just seems pointless to be so formal all the time."

She scoffed. "Well, aren't you Mister Fancypants."

"Not fancy. I owe her my life a few times over. That kind of thing, you know . . . inspires loyalty."

"Yeah, I know how that feels." She cast a furtive glance around the empty reactor bay, but lowered her voice anyway. "You know, she showed up to the *Asteria* and rescued us instead of our escape vessel that'd already left? With our legator, optio, and more than half our circitors aboard."

"Why?"

She shrugged. "I guess because we had more people than they did. Couldn't make it to both in time, so she had to pick. Though we still barely made it out of there. Never seen someone fly like that before . . ."

Cavalon nodded. That story didn't surprise him in the least; in fact it felt like textbook Rake. Regardless, the thought still managed to collide with his vast capacity to worry. He had a long way to go in learning the Legion's "rules," but he could safely say that wasn't protocol. Not that they were really part of the Legion anymore. But he had to wonder what the other commanders aboard the *Typhos* would think if they found out she'd picked a bunch of oculi over a ship full of officers.

"That's why I volunteered to stay aboard the *Syn* and help instead of coming back here," Owen went on. "I wanted to work toward repaying her, at least." She glanced back at the screens. "And if I can help with this too . . . more points in the good karma with the EX column."

"Yeah, I get that."

Owen returned her focus to the screens, looking over each system one at a time. He swept his clearance a few times to allow her access deeper into the system.

"I can do it," she announced finally. "I'll only need a few hours, but if you want an accurate simulation, I think we're going to need specific measurements on the paths you plan to use. Otherwise it's nothing but one big guess."

"Yeah, okay," Cavalon said, nodding fervently. He opened the scheduler on his nexus and began typing a message. "I'm updating Mes, she'll get it when she wakes up. We'll need to take a field trip outside to get readings on those venting paths. The *Typhos*'s hull diagnostic system is shit—found that out the hard way when I took an EVA team to pilfer some of the thermal shielding."

"*You* led an EVA team?"

He flashed a grin. "I'm a spacewalking expert, thank you very much."

She sighed. "Well, if you're going to go fuck around in a vacuum, might I suggest you get some sleep first? You look like actual death, man."

"I feel like actual death, so that tracks."

She gave him a flat stare.

"Yeah, yeah, it can wait till morning. It'll be best to have Mesa's rested brain on it too. Let's make it 0700."

"I'll be here with bells on."

"I'll send a request to Centurion North and make sure your work duty's assigned to me."

"Em too?"

Cavalon sighed and forced a smile. "Of course."

"Thanks, Lord Cav. You're the best."

"I'm aware."

"If you're done with me for now, *sir*, I should get back to offloading the *Syn*."

"Yeah, yeah, carry on."

She gave a cheeky salute, then started to head back toward the door. "Oh, by the way," she called back. "Epically shitty circumstances and all, but it's good to see you."

"You too, O." Cavalon watched her disappear into the corridor. The bay doors sealed shut, leaving him alone in the reactor bay. The dense hum of electronics buzzed in his ears, a cool wave of relief sending goose bumps down his sweat-slicked skin.

This was it; he could feel it. In just a few days, the jump drive would be ready.

CHAPTER SEVEN

Seventeen years ago in the Outer Core, a sixteen-year-old Adequin darts through torrents of acid rain. Each step gives off a thick squelch as her knee-high boots thud deep into dense mud.

She ducks into the Legion tent through two large flaps. Inside, thick vinyl walls dampen the downpour to a soft murmur. The quiet weighs on her ears, a soothing blanket of white noise. Shaking the water from her hood, she drops it back, then tugs her respirator down to rest around her neck. Her eyes dart desperately to find him.

Standing at a desk in the back, Circitor Hudson Rake cuts an imposing figure. Modestly tall, broad shoulders, a freshly shaven square jaw, auburn hair shorn close to his scalp. The paradigm of a proper legionnaire. He could have walked right off one of the recruitment posters peeling from the walls inside the old municipal building.

From his outward appearance, she has no reason to believe he'll be any different than the other dozen recruiters who'd come through, making their rounds through the Outer Core colonies. But she knows too well—appearance is meaningless. It can be crafted, honed, and wielded, just like any other weapon.

But there's something different about him, something in the way he holds her gaze; his steel gray eyes are more receptive than the others. He sees more than most, or maybe he *looks* for more. She knew the second she laid eyes on him, as surely as afternoon rain would fall across the Redwind District, as surely as the Saxton Guard would hand out their weekly corporal punishments, as surely as not going home gave her a higher chance of surviving the night: This is it. The recruiter who will say yes.

Yet she hesitates. Questions if she's being reckless, if her calloused-over emotions are interfering with her sense of logic. But there's a limit to what one can endure and not risk hating themselves for their own negligence. Inaction can be just as dangerous as action.

She grits her teeth and banishes all reluctance, stepping up to his desk.

His brow drops. His fair-skinned cheeks ignite with a rash of crimson— apparent fury, though she clutches to her resolve like it's the final breath of clean air through an expired filter.

It's the fifth time she's come this week. She's a damn headache, he says. The stubbornness of the young, he says. If only she were eighteen, he says.

Then finally: He needs time to figure out the paperwork, he says. This one he whispers as he's throwing her out for the fifth time, in between shouting at her to get lost, gutter rat, or he'd call the sheriff to haul her off. A guise for the sake of the other recruiter who watches with a harrowing display of apathetic disinterest.

After seven of the longest days of her life, she returns at midnight to learn the fruits of his efforts. Sheets of rain beat out a hollow rhythm on the roof of the olive-drab tent. He passes her a simple leather folio. She stares at it—an entire past and future contained in a file thinner than her hand. She thumbs through it eagerly, her heart pulsing out a rapid cadence, straining against her ribs.

She's his niece, now. *Adequin Rake.* He's offered his name to protect her.

Yet a bitter mass twists deep in the pit of her stomach. She's both relieved and overwhelmed. She doesn't understand how someone could risk their career for a person they've only just met. She cannot grasp why.

She will always wonder what cascade of events led to him being assigned this post, to joining the recruitment efforts, to enlisting in the first place, to being raised a man who observed, listened, and acted, in that order. What life would she have led if any of those steps had been missed, for any of a thousand reasons?

For now, it doesn't matter. For now, she's sixteen, standing in a Legion tent with the very first person she'll count amongst those who saved her life. For now, she barely manages a thank-you, clutching her new identity to her chest like a life vest.

She steps out of the tent, angling her hand to shield the unforgiving rays of sun tearing a path through the cloud cover.

But that's not right. The sun shone a mere handful of days on Seneca-IV, and this day had not been one of those precious few.

Her eyes adjust to the brightness.

Across the muddy thoroughfare waits a man who cannot be there; he belongs to a different time. Yet there he stands in his tailored dress blues, the rays casting his brown skin in a warm glow. Sweat slicks her collar as she tries to step toward him, but she can hardly move. The air has grown thick and superheated, like swimming through oil.

The corners of his eyes wrinkle as his gaze lands on her. "Aevitas fortis," he calls in his baritone rumble, and the words resonate in her chest.

Before she can answer, the sun arrives.

Swelling outward from its depleted core, it burns through the atmosphere, a blaze of fire blanketing her in a fraction of an instant. She doesn't fault it. It's a necessary process. The only way certain elements can be created. Hydrogen into helium into carbon and so on until iron is all that remains.

Her hands clench to fists and through the molten haze appears a wavering, flame-soaked version of herself in the years to come, in a cave on a mountain on a planet on the fringes of the Outer Core—Paxus. Where she finds the will to lower her rifle, because she cannot shake the feeling this Viator breeder does not want to live for their own reasons. There is a strange lack of hubris in the way they implore her.

The breeder's face remains unnervingly steady. Their slate-gray, segmented carapace is oddly beautiful even in the harsh light, stippled with a stark contrast of maroon flecks. A gleaming trail of Imprint tattoos not unlike her own tracks up the hardened shell of their left arm, a tessellated pattern of dark steel and bronze squares.

"Without us, you will perish," they repeat, as if they still need to convince her, as if the decision isn't already evident in the resigned dread lining her expression.

Her shoulder drops, the barrel of her rifle along with it.

The breeder's wide head tilts, each of their four glossy black eyes unblinking as they absorb her decision. It looks strangely like shock.

Her haggard voice climbs up out of her throat and she speaks the Viator words for, "Leave, now. Never come back."

Two of the breeder's four eyes blink. Maybe they wonder if they misheard, or if it's a trick. Maybe they wonder why. She wonders why herself.

The breeder's armed guards step forward, boots shuffling across the dusty rocks. They grunt encouragement, reach out, usher the breeder toward the exit, to safety, away. Their footsteps echo across the hard stone of the cave. The breeder's lingering gaze finally falls away, and they're gone.

A swell of heat surrounds her, charring her skin—the flames of the star. Her fingers loosen and her rifle falls from her grip. She drowns in the swells of mass and gravity and fusion as an anthem of stardust engulfs her.

Adequin woke pouring sweat.

Her nexus buzzed against her wrist, willing her awake with a series of gentle pulses. She rubbed the heels of her palms into her eyes. Afterimages of blazing starfire danced across the backs of her eyelids.

The adaptive lighting sensed her movement, beginning its gradual fade up to simulate a rising sun. She checked the time—0630, almost midnight to her. Even with her room VI's sleep-wake program assaulting her with early morning UV light, it'd take some time to get switched over to ship time.

The sheets stuck to her skin as she pushed to sit up, swinging her legs over the side of the couch. Her feverish head spun with the effort. Pain lanced down her injured arms, flushing any remaining grogginess from her mind.

Her new quarters, or—as officers' rooms were more accurately named aboard the *Typhos*—her *stateroom*, was many grades more comfortable than her room on the *Argus* had been, and light-years more than her accommodations aboard the *Synthesis*. So much so, she'd found it difficult to fall asleep, despite her exhaustion. The sheer depth and width of the mattress alone had been daunting enough, then there'd been the soft sheets and broad pillows, all further conspiring against her. She'd finally given up and taken to the couch.

Her nexus buzzed again, and she gritted her teeth as she silenced it.

With an effort she stood, showered, then replaced the healing gel bandages on her forearms with dry wraps, relishing the relief the pressure of the tight bindings garnered. She ran a quick comb through her damp hair, doing her best to tie it into a tight bun, though her fingers shot with jolts of fiery pain with each tiny motion.

Minutes before 0700, she stepped up to the imposing door of the CIC. She inhaled a deep breath, then laid her hand against the access pad. The door slid open.

Inside, dozens of viewscreens and terminal consoles lined all four walls. Every station sat dark and deactivated—likely unused for decades, if not centuries. A single strip of light glowed to life, recessed in a trench crowning the room. The only other light came from beneath the rim of the large, square command table dominating the floorspace. The tabletop was a single flat piece of holographic glass, designed to allow for a variety of briefing or survey modes.

Overlapping, corrugated black foam lined the upper walls and ceiling, creating an angular cap around the room. The more compact and acoustically sound, she supposed, the less shouting of orders would need to be done. She had to wonder what battles of the Viator War had been waged from this very room. And if more were yet to come.

She stepped up to the faintly glowing war table and leaned her fists on the top. She let out a wide, strained yawn that scraped against the back of her throat.

Behind her, the door whizzed open. Jackin swept in, a tablet tucked under one arm, carrying a mug of coffee in each hand. His hair was combed, posture straight, dark brown eyes bright and well-rested. He'd always been a morning person.

"Morning, boss. How you feelin'? Get some rest?" He passed her one of the coffees.

She took it, warming her fingers on the piping-hot mug. If only she had some whiskey to cool it down.

"Thanks, Jack," she said. "Yeah, I slept some."

"Those staterooms are comfortable, right?"

"Yeah."

He scoffed and shook his head. "I know that look."

She closed her eyes and sighed. He rested a hand on her shoulder, and she flexed her jaw as the gesture sent spikes of pain down her sore arm.

"You could let yourself enjoy it," he said, clueless to her pain. "Just a thought."

"Is Puck coming?" she asked.

"No," he said, leaning a hip against the edge of the war table. "He has about twelve thousand things to do. Besides, I didn't want it to seem like we were trying to shore up by throwing our entire command team in front of them at once. I'm hoping this can feel more like a round table and less like us imposing our will."

"Probably a good call," she admitted. She took her first sip of the still-too-hot coffee, dull and bitter with synthesization, but also full of caffeine, and that was all she cared about. She'd just as soon mainline it if Jackin would let her.

"Speaking of Puck," Jackin said. "Since you went all rogue with the promoting yesterday, we're gonna need to figure out who to bump to optio at some point soon."

"What about Eura?" Adequin asked. "She was Griffith's second for years."

His lips pinched. "She's really the only pilot we've got that's worth her salt."

"We could transition Emery into that instead."

He rubbed the nape of his neck, shaking his head. "With no formal flight training?"

"You think my efforts were subpar?" she chaffed.

"I'm sure they weren't, boss, but really, how many times has she flown? And only ever the *Synthesis*."

"Fair enough," she conceded, twisting the mug in her hands as she considered other options. If they followed proper chain of command, then the *Typhos*'s former centurion would be the appropriate choice. But the old man had passed away only a few days after ceding command to her six months ago, leaving his former optio as the senior-most officer of their original crew. "What do you think about Beckar?" she asked. "He was optio for the *Typhos* for over five years, right?"

Jackin chewed his bottom lip, gaze distant as he gave a shallow nod. "Yeah, that'd actually be a smart move. Beckar's support outweighs the others by a large factor. The *Typhos*'s crew makes up almost a quarter of our population, and they still hold most of the primary ship function roles."

"And they're all loyal to him?" she asked.

Jackin finished a quick sip of his coffee and shook his head. "Nothing to suggest otherwise so far. We've actually been trying to discourage loyalty based on origin ship, but it's been hard to stamp out entirely. In this case, it'll work in our favor." He took a contemplative sip of his coffee, bobbing his head slowly. "Yeah, I like it. Besides, it could go a long way if they see us starting to put some non-*Argus* folk into leadership roles. Extend a laurel, or whatever."

"I think it's an olive branch."

He shrugged.

"You think Beckar will be up for it?" she asked.

"Yeah," Jackin said with a fervent nod. "He's still unreasonably grateful we managed to save them. He'd been toeing the old man's line for years; I think he's just relieved to have a functional command structure to get behind. Let's see what you think of him this morning, and we'll go from there."

"Sounds good," she agreed.

Jackin checked the time on his nexus. "As for the meeting, keep in mind that those with the most crew behind them are Legators Ashwell and Korovich. So as with Beckar, their support will be more meaningful in the long run." He rubbed the nape of his neck, brow knit. "Let's just say they have some . . . *challenging* personalities. Just try to be receptive, and patient," he encouraged, his words tinged with anxiety. "We need as many of them as possible to walk out of here feeling good about having you at the helm. Try to remind them who you are, what you've done. It wouldn't be a bad idea to pull out the war hero card."

Adequin took another drink of the awful coffee, burning her tongue again. She set the mug down with a sigh. "Okay, yeah. I'll try. Anything else?"

He shook his head, but his gaze quickly went distant. He scrubbed a hand slowly over the scarred side of his beard.

Adqeuin chewed the inside of her lip, suddenly aware of the heavy silence in the room. "Jack? What is it?"

He hesitated for a few long moments, then cleared his throat. "I had a chance to review some of the action reports from the *Synthesis.*"

Meaning he stayed up way too late or got up way too early to read every single action report from the *Synthesis.*

"And?" she prompted.

He licked his lips, then met her eye from under a lowered brow. "I'm not sure Emery realizes the importance of impartial reporting."

"What do you mean? She was a great second."

"Sure, but she likes you too much. She clearly tried to make some very dangerous situations sound . . . normal."

"Well, news flash, dangerous situations *are* normal around here."

He crossed his arms. "You know what I mean."

"I don't."

"The *Asteria.*"

Her jaw tightened.

"You went to the dreadnought and not the escape vessel," he explained, as if every second of that rescue wasn't burned into her memory.

What he left unsaid was that protocol clearly dictated the escape vessel as priority. There had been officers on that ship, the highest ranks of their crew, including their legator and optio. But fewer people. *Far* fewer people. And there had only been time to save one.

"Both options were shitty," she argued.

His lips pressed into a grim line and he shook his head. "I'm not saying you should have picked A over B. I'm saying you should have gone with C."

Her eyes flitted over him in confusion. "What?"

"You should have left."

"Left?" she croaked, then pushed up off the table to face him squarely. "Save neither?"

"The Divide was still collapsing nearby—you were less than ten thousand klicks from it, for fuck's sake. So in that situation, yes, *neither.* To ensure your own safety and that—"

"Void, this again?" she groaned.

"—of your crew. Yes, this *again*, Rake. I can't believe we're back to it either, honestly."

She rubbed a stiff hand down the side of her face, shaking her head.

"You saved *hundreds* more after that," he went on, shoulders rigid. "If you'd have died at the *Asteria*, those hundreds would be dead right now too. As well as you and your crew. Not to mention the dozen dark energy generators you wouldn't have been able to restart after that. We still don't know how it's collapsing, but that could have expedited its arrival at the Core by decades, maybe centuries."

Adequin gritted her teeth. "I don't really need reminders of the many ways in which I could have gotten even more people killed. What's your point?"

"My point is that your decisions don't happen in a void. You have to think further ahead than the immediate. Not every choice is best made with a knee-jerk reaction."

"You weren't there," she growled. "You don't understand the cost."

"Trust me," he snapped, fixing her with a flint-eyed glower, "I understand. I'm making decisions here every damn day that risk lives. It doesn't matter whether you're flying flashy missions at the Divide, or trying to decide if—or, with every passing day, *when*—the three hundred soldiers we have in the psych ward will need to be sacrificed so the rest of us can survive another week."

Adequin gaped, a rash of heat strangling the air from her throat—at once stung by his criticism and horrified by that suggestion.

"You wanted me to keep judging your actions, remember?" he said evenly.

"There were ninety people aboard the *Asteria*," she seethed. "How can you say it wasn't worth it?"

"Because it's objectively not. You survived, which even by Emery's lenient account, was damn lucky. But luck doesn't make it the right call. It just as easily could have gone lateral."

"But it *didn't*."

"*It doesn't matter*," he said, rounding the table toward her, a feverish glint in his eye, tone equal parts anger and desperation. "You're accountable for thousands of people. Risks are required, but they need to be measured. Worth it."

"You're making people into numbers again, Jack."

"Right now, people *are* numbers!" he shouted, fist pounding hard against the top of the war table. "*Flammable* numbers. One wrong move, and this whole pile of kindling could go up. One bad decision, and it's all over." He took another step toward her, his fierce glower sharpening. "If you have to give up a dozen lives for the sake of a thousand, you do it. *Especially* when one of the lives at stake is your own. Don't throw away everything we've built over the last six months."

She ground her teeth, fists clenching. He held her gaze, jaw firm, shoulders drawn back.

An electric trill cut through the deadened silence, and it took

Adequin's incensed mind a few moments to realize it was the door chime. She glanced at the sealed door, then blinked the haze from her eyes and refocused on Jackin.

He blew out a strained breath. "Look, I'm sorry," he said, his tone laced with a thick sincerity that somehow only fueled her frustration. "I didn't mean to get into all this before the meeting. Just . . . consider what I'm saying."

She forcibly released her clenched fists, nodding through the anger stiffening her neck.

"Ready?"

She nodded again.

With a rushing hiss the door slid open. Boot scuffles and prattling chatter wafted in—already brimming over with petty arguments. She let out a long sigh.

An hour later, Adequin had internally tallied every available route to an airlock.

She hadn't done as much talking in the entire five weeks she'd been gone as she had in the last hour, and her throat had gone dry and raw from the effort of constantly keeping them on track. Even in her by all counts equable mental state aboard the *Argus*, she'd had very little patience for this kind of bureaucratic bullshit. Now she could hardly stand it.

Legator Ashwell stood opposite Adequin across the wide war table, flanked by a half-dozen supporters. The angular cut of her short blond hair masked half her perma-scowl. Her four hundred soldiers made her second only to Beckar in terms of crew count.

Legator Korovich was next in line with three hundred and fifty. He stood back from the table, arms crossed above his paunch, shoulders slouched, brow wrinkled with chronic distrust.

Then there was the amicable Beckar, standing at Adequin's right with his square chin and likable demeanor. He'd been almost *too* pleasant, his subservient attitude edged with a quickness to defend her against the others. Which relieved her—the more he strong-armed for her, the less she'd have to throw her weight around. It also made her want to punch him, right in that symmetrical face of his. And she couldn't really say why. She didn't know what she'd done to garner that kind of loyalty, and for some reason, that infuriated her. She'd been MIA for six months, and they'd spoken all of maybe ten words to each other in their lives.

Jackin was the one they should look to; he was the one who'd been calling all the shots. He must have worked hard over the months to ensure they saw him as a conduit, enacting her will. But she didn't know why he'd bothered. Blind, reckless loyalty was how unfit people were put into power. She didn't want to become a lesson for the history books.

Six other commanders stood near her and Beckar in an effort to imply their allegiance. Like children segregating themselves in the schoolyard. Only a handful hovered between the groups, unwilling to make an inadvertent political statement based on proximity.

Adequin glanced at Jackin, who stood off her left shoulder. He hadn't said a word yet. He offered a supportive grimace, encouraging her to hang on to her sanity a while longer.

"All I'm asking," Ashwell growled from behind her blond curtain, "is what the hell are we even doing? What's the endgame?"

"Survive," Beckar said simply. "First the Divide, then the Legion."

"Why do we need to survive the Legion?" Korovich groused. "We work for them, last I checked."

Beckar leveled a look of strained tolerance at him. "You heard from HQ lately, Frank?"

Korovich's rigid scowl deepened.

"He's right," Adequin said. "Consider how we've been treated out here—meager food and supplies, no leave, no chance at advancement, or redemption, for that matter. Forced to live so close to the Divide, we're slowly losing our minds. Leaving us with no FTL capabilities, all to keep watch for a Viator threat that will never come."

Korovich shook his head adamantly. "You don't know that."

"I uniquely do," she said simply, causing a rare moment of silence to fill the CIC. She let it rest for a beat to allow the reminder of her implied clout sink in. The war hero angle was just about all she had going for her, as Jackin had so politely pointed out.

Not that there was even any truth to that. Only a few people from the *Argus* knew she'd let that last Viator breeder live, and that the System Collective's claims of xenocide had been a fabrication. That everything she was renowned for was a lie.

Beckar broke the silence first. "If you want to be official about it, Frank, think of it this way: Praetor Teign issued a withdrawal from the Divide. We weren't on the list. None of us."

"It could have been a miscommunication," Korovich said, scowl tightening. "You know how well comms work out here."

Adequin shook her head. "Not one of the dozens of ships we rescued received a withdrawal order," she countered. "That can't be an accident."

Beckar gave an emphatic nod. "They wanted us dead out here, and they'll want us dead when we go home too. To me, that degree of disregard means we're no longer under their command."

"So that means we're under *hers*?" Ashwell spat. "Just because her ship happened to be the central hub doesn't make her the boss."

"She does outrank us all by a healthy margin," Beckar pointed out.

Adequin sighed. Her favorite part so far had been all the times they went on talking about her like she wasn't even there.

Ashwell crossed her arms with a huff. "She only outranks us because Lugen threw a pity rank at her."

Adequin's pulse spiked—not at Ashwell's brash insubordination, which was another matter, but at the mention of Praetor Lugen. Her CO— former CO. Former mentor, former friend. She'd thought.

Their brief chat aboard Kharon Gate so many weeks . . . *months* ago had left her with more questions than answers. He'd seemed honestly surprised they hadn't been recalled, yet offered no definitive recourse, remaining as cagey as ever. No matter how much responsibility he'd given her and trust he'd put in her over the years, he'd always held back. Always had something to hide. And now she might never have a chance to continue that conversation.

"Rank *should* be taken into account," Korovich argued.

"Should it?" Ashwell sneered. "In the same breath, we're being told we're no longer Legion. So which is it?"

One of Beckar's defenders cleared her throat. "We've got more pressing matters than scrapping our entire regulatory structure and starting from scratch."

"That's kinda the definition of mutiny—"

The argument escalated, and it took only moments before a handful of doppelgängers popped into existence around the room, causing even more bouts to erupt.

Adequin sighed. Great. Throwing flashes of the future into the mix always made impossible situations easier.

After a minute, the bickering swelled to the point she couldn't even keep track of who was on what side, never mind which of the commanders were real and which were time ripples.

She pinched the bridge of her nose to try and press away a burgeoning migraine. Hanging her head, she let her eyes go unfocused on the soft blue-white surface of the war table.

Then her breath stilled, an icy chill rushing through her veins. A new voice joined the din—one she'd recognize anywhere. A baritone rumble that resonated in her chest.

She looked up to find Griffith standing across the war table, his hands braced as he looked down at a readout. The glow shone up from the lit worktop, highlighting the faded *Volucris* tattoo at the base of his neck. The doppelgänger lacked the thick, trimmed beard he'd had since they first came to the Divide over five years ago, replaced with a dusting of black and gray stubble delineating his square jaw.

She stared, completely aghast, unable to move as she watched him argue with an even more haggard duplicate of Korovich.

Jackin's hand pressed between her shoulder blades. "Rake . . ."

She swallowed. Heat burned behind her eyes. Her callused fingers drifted up to her collar, and she pressed at the edges of Griffith's dog tags. Her thumb slipped and the metal cut into the edge of her nail. She glanced down, a single drop of blood pooling at her cuticle.

When she looked back up, he'd vanished.

No one else reacted. They carried on debating, ignoring every doppelgänger as a matter of course. This was daily life aboard the *Typhos*. And none of them had known Griffith.

The deluge of arguments filled into the empty space around her, electrified and staticky like super-charged air. The topic had rounded back to her, to her worthiness, her virtue, her prowess. Some felt she was the most qualified regardless, that she'd served the entire Resurgence, had been a Titan for five years, had been Lugen's right hand, and had more experience around high command than the rest of them combined.

Others disagreed. Said it didn't matter. She hadn't been on the *Typhos* for the last six months, enduring what they'd endured. She wasn't one of them.

Yet somehow, not one mentioned how they'd all be fucking *dead* right now if she hadn't defied Lugen's order to return to the Core. If she hadn't risked the people she cared about the most to restart that first dark energy generator. If she hadn't tortured herself over the last five weeks to continue restarting them, over and over again, pouring her literal blistering flesh, blood, and tears into those damn machines. She'd spent so much time and energy and pain saving them—to what end?

"Quiet!" Jackin's gruff tone cut through the din. The arguments cut off as if severed with a blade. Every pair of eyes turned toward them.

Adequin glanced back at Jackin, who stood with his arms crossed high over his chest, jaw set. He didn't move a muscle, but the rallying glint in his eye said all it needed to.

Adequin turned to the momentarily cowed commanders. Her breathing slowed and with an effort, she unclenched her jaw. "If you think I want to be in charge," she said, her voice a steady, low growl, "then you don't know me. What wars we served, what missions we've carried out, what ranks we had . . . Ashwell's right. We're no longer Legion. None of that matters." She let the words hang in the air for a few long seconds. "What does matter is that I started this. So I'm going to finish it. You can join us. Or not."

Her gaze drifted over each of them, taking an account of the varying degrees of apprehension. Even Ashwell had the courtesy of looking diffident.

Jackin cleared his throat and moved to stand beside Adequin. He gave her the briefest, hesitating sidelong glance. "Those who don't want to join," he added, tone conciliatory, "can stay at Kharon Gate. After we've cleared the *Typhos* through to Poine Gate and moved on, you can send emissaries to confer with the Legion."

Ashwell's razor-sharp stare hit them both. "That's basically saying stay or die."

"Then so be it," Adequin snarled, and for a welcome change of pace, Ashwell's face fell completely slack.

"Why make people wait?" Korovich asked, oblivious to Adequin's threat. "We should let those who want to leave go now."

"Not going to happen," Adequin said, jaw set. "We severed Kharon Gate's connection to the Legion extranet six months ago for a reason. They think we're dead, and we have to keep it that way as long as possible. That means waiting till the jump drive is ready, so we can disappear into the Drift Belt the second we're through Poine Gate."

This apparent news caused a small surge of murmured discussions. Why it'd taken them this long to think it through that far, she'd never understand. Maybe they were just used to blindly following orders.

Someone beside Beckar spoke up next, "We can't let people relieve themselves of duty without repercussions."

"Sure we can," one of the neutralists countered. "We've essentially pressed them into service."

"Then we keep the defectors with us," another suggested. "Prisoners of war until we're more established."

"No," Adequin asserted, and they all settled down again. "We're not going to keep feeding people who aren't willing to fight. You join us or you stay at Kharon, those are your options."

Frustrated murmurs rose, and Jackin hedged a tense look at Adequin. He raised his hands to quiet them, and again affected his placating tone as he amended her gruff take. "Before we leave Kharon Gate, we'll vouch for anyone staying behind—Rake can use the Titan prius statute to issue a personal statement directly to Praetors Teign and Lugen."

Korovich glowered. "You really think that will make a difference when it's from the lips of a traitor? We'll still look like mutineers."

Adequin flexed her jaw and shifted her glare to him. "We can always tie you up and make sure you have plenty of conspicuous bruises so you can say we forced you."

Jackin let out a heavy sigh. But strangely, quite a few of the commanders seemed more impressed than offended. Ashwell among them.

"You have until the jump drive's ready to decide for you and your crew," Adequin said. "Though I suggest you give them some say in the matter, or you might have a mutiny of your own on your hands." They stared back at her silently, and she swept her gaze across them, unblinking. "Now get the hell out of my war room."

A few glowers and frowns remained, some heads hung low and properly cowed, others seemed genuinely torn, but they all remained blissfully silent as they filed out.

Jackin stood back with his arms crossed, expression unreadable as he watched them leave.

When the last had gone and the door sealed shut, Adequin let out a quavering breath and leaned on the table with both hands.

For a few long, quiet moments, she stared at the empty space where Griffith had been.

"How was that possible?" she asked finally, her low voice cracking.

Jackin gave a heavy swallow, loud in the dull silence of the insulated CIC. "It's just another possible future . . ."

"One in which he lived long enough to be standing here, strategizing at this war table?"

"Yeah . . ."

Meaning there was a way she could have saved him.

A vise closed around her rib cage. She locked eyes with Jackin, and he held her gaze, lips pressed into a frown, eyes rounded with empathy. He was only trying to manage *her* reaction. Not having a reaction of his own.

Adequin cleared her dry throat. "You don't seem very shaken, Jack. He was your friend too."

His lips twitched with unsaid words, but his wavering look radiated with guilt.

"Shit," she cursed. "You've seen him before?"

His gaze drifted down. "Only a few times."

She leaned on the table again, sucking in a sharp breath.

"Rake, don't think into it too much . . ." Jackin's voice faded, overtaken by a high-pitched ringing in her ears.

If they'd seen him before, that meant there were futures he was still a part of. Which meant there were pasts in which he'd lived, in which they'd found a way to reverse his condition. Or maybe simply where she hadn't made him take that last trip on the Divide in the first place, and he'd never gotten sick. Where he'd still been aboard the *Argus* when the Divide had collapsed.

There were so many moments she could have gone wrong, where she could have lost the thread. It was impossible to say which had ensured his death. For all she knew, this future could be the only one in which she'd failed.

Jackin's hand on hers tugged her focus back to the comfortable warmth of the CIC, the acoustics softening every motion, deadening every breath. She eyed her hand, pressed flat against the glowing war table, a tendril of the branch-like black veins creeping onto the top of her wrist. Jackin folded his fingers around her palm, unaware of the bruised, raw flesh hidden by her uniform.

She didn't need to meet his eyes to imagine the pity. She jerked her hand away and marched to the door. "I'm going to go check on the reactor."

"Rake, wait—"

With a rushing hiss, the door sealed shut behind her.

CHAPTER EIGHT

Cavalon palmed his way across the matte-gray aerasteel hull of the *Typhos*. He never thought he'd see the day he'd actually enjoy the feeling of zero-g. It was honestly all too comfortable—the weightlessness sifting the aches from his joints, nothing but the crisp, dense sounds of his own smooth breaths in his helmet, and whomever he allowed on comms. Out here, every movement became orderly, meaningful. He was in complete control of his fate. And with fourteen EVAs under his belt, he'd had plenty of time to grow used to the idea of being only two minutes and a fraction of a centimeter from certain death at any given moment.

Now that the Divide had settled into its new border, there were no more unnerving flashes of sharp white light igniting as stray matter was purged from the universe. It made it a hell of a lot easier to forget how screwed they'd be if this new plan didn't work.

"How's it goin' out there, boss?" Emery's voice crackled over the staticky suit comms, patched in from the maintenance control station inside.

"We're almost there," Cavalon assured, eyeing the faded yellow demarcation tape a few meters ahead. Though for once, he wasn't the one holding them up.

He craned his neck to look over his shoulder, following the lifeless snake of the tether connecting him to Owen. Her pearlescent suit shimmered as it caught the beam of his helmet light, a stark white stain against the inky outward side of the *Typhos*'s massive hull. The ship's exterior illumination array had long since fallen to disrepair, putting the outward side of the hull in perpetual dark, while the aggregate light of the universe cast a radiant white halo along its edges.

Owen hesitated, gripping the hardware connecting the tether to her tandem harness with both hands like it was the hilt of a blade and she wasn't sure if it was better to leave it in or rip it free and risk bleeding out. Cavalon watched with barely contained amusement as she purred out a crackling groan, trying to summon the courage to let go and pull herself along the hull after him.

He wasn't sure why he found it so damn amusing to see her squirm. Maybe just that strange human instinct to inflict newcomers with a trial by fire. Part of becoming a Sentinel was realizing you had no fucking idea how to do anything, but adapting anyway. It was reassuring to see Owen as uncomfortable earning her stripes as he'd been.

Growing up, she'd always been beyond fearless: curious, hungry for adventure, with an endless trove of bad ideas to get them in tons of trouble. She'd been the kid always getting hauled off and reprimanded by the Mercer Guard for "endangering the prince's life." Cavalon had never, not once, been less afraid or more physically adept at something than Owen. Not that he'd earned any bravery medals his first time on an EVA. It'd been almost an hour and she hadn't tried to take her own helmet off, so she was already doing better than he had.

"How's it going, O?" he encouraged.

"Swell," she chuffed, the anger of her subsequent breaths enough to keep the comms activated, transmitting a few more seconds of her huffing and puffing. "Why am I here again? Just to torture me?"

"This is the last one," he assured. "Promise."

"You could have fucking brought any one of your trained EVA pals to do this."

Gum chomping announced Emery's forthcoming participation on comms. "You're doin' great, babe," her high-pitched voice assured. "It's seriously impressive you haven't hurled in your suit yet."

Owen audibly gulped.

"Trust me," Cavalon said, airy reassurance in his tone, "these people will find a way to make you save the day in zero-g in no time. You'll be thanking me for the practice."

"I literally hate you," she grumbled.

"Hey now, you're the one who wanted more EX karma, remember?"

"Yeah, but not like this, bloody void. I signed on as a damn code monkey."

"Might I remind you both," Mesa's crisp tone interjected from inside with Emery, "that your suits do not contain an infinite amount of oxygen. Not to mention the inherent dangers of operating in a vacuum. I suggest focusing on the task and continuing your petty quarrels another time."

"Sorry, Mes," Cavalon crooned. His HUD lit, highlighting the approximate outline of one of the dozens of starfighter launch tubes off the starboard quarter. "And look at that, we've arrived. I've got eyes on maintenance access for hatch 114."

"Copy 114," Emery piped.

"Orienting . . ." Cavalon tapped the wrist of his suit and the shallow orange holographic nexus screen spread out above the white fabric. He opened the guidance module, then spun until it indicated alignment. "Oriented."

"Copy oriented," Emery said. "Reference one marked."

With one hand, Cavalon grabbed the long handle bar outside the access hatch, then took hold of the tether with the other and hauled Owen to his position. She approached, hands stiff and outstretched as if reaching for a life preserver, then clasped either of Cavalon's shoulders in a viselike grip.

He chuffed a laugh. "Do you think you're going to fall or something?"

"Shut up, dude," she whined.

"Grab the rail," he said, doing his best to cover his glib tone with calm patience.

Owen reluctantly transferred her death grip onto the rail. Cavalon tapped at the nexus on her wrist to bring up the guidance module.

"See, I'm nothing but a warm body right now," she grumbled. "You could have brought an empty suit."

"An empty suit certainly would have complained less."

He ignored the fierce glare he knew came from beneath her visor and stayed focused on her suit's nexus, ensuring the orientation had synced properly.

"Stay," he said, holding up both hands in placation. "I'll be right back."

"Not if I drop-kick you in your stupid head and send you plunging off into the Divide."

He sighed as he worked his way to the other side of the launch tube. "For starters, you can't drop-kick someone in zero-g. Also, we're tethered together, remember?"

"I'm pretty sure I can at least figure out how to unhook a damn tether."

"I dunno, your history with ropes isn't great. Don't forget the manor wall climbing incident of 208."

"Fucking void, Mercer—"

"Now, children," Emery scolded. "You're upsetting Mesa again."

"All right, I'm here," Cavalon said as he arrived at the opposing maintenance panel. "Orienting."

"I mean, what are we even doing?" Owen asked while Cavalon tapped away at his nexus. "Manual measurements? How is this a job?"

"Yeah, yeah, I know. But unlike everywhere else in the universe, Sentinels don't get to have drones to do the dirty work."

"Or even just functioning hull diagnostics, apparently," Emery pointed out.

"Apparently," Cavalon agreed. "I'm aware of how stupid it is, O, but it doesn't make it any less necessary. Besides, we like to do things the hard way here at Sentinel HQ. You've been around a while now, you should have gotten the gist."

"Yeah," Owen grumbled. "I'm reading it loud and clear."

"And oriented," Cavalon announced finally.

"Copy . . . that . . ." Emery mumbled, voice fading into concentration. "All right. We're golden in here, we should have everything we need. Now, please don't murder each other on the way inside?"

"No promises," Owen growled.

Cavalon activated the airlock controls and the hatch cycled, blaring out a pressurization confirmation.

Owen tore her helmet off a fraction of a second later. She glowered down at her boots, drawing in a few poorly controlled breaths. Sweat glistened on her light brown skin as she yanked her hair from its tie and ran her fingers through the thick waves.

Cavalon unlatched his own helmet and tossed it on the rack. He offered a wide grin. "How ya doin', champ?"

She started to tear her space suit off her body like it was on fire. "You're such a dick."

"That's Lord Dick to you."

Mesa appeared in the corridor, arms folded primly across her chest. Emery bopped into the door frame in front of her. "This outing was a great idea, boss," Emery said.

Owen let out a soft growl and shot daggers from across the airlock, but Emery didn't seem to notice.

"I cross-checked with the measurements in the system," Emery went on, "and they're all a minimum of fifteen meters off, one way or the other."

Cavalon wiped his brow and inclined his head to Mesa. "Looks like your pointless redundancies weren't so pointless this time around."

Mesa narrowed her eyes. "Thank you?"

"With those three sets of reference points," Emery said, "we should be good to go ahead with the rest."

Cavalon stepped past Mesa and Emery out into the relative coolness of the empty corridor. The lengthy passage had once been home to an escape pod cluster back when the *Typhos* hadn't belonged to the Sentinels, and thus had been allowed to have things like escape pods. Now it felt like a ghost town of airlocks, with dozens of escape hatches lining the corridor along the farthest reaches of the starboard beam, each hatch offering no escape other than a fairly permanent one.

Owen padded out to join them as she aggressively retied her hair into a single braid.

"Okay, team," Cavalon began, and they followed loosely behind as he started down the corridor back toward the reactor bay. "Now that we have the measurements, we need to get the simulation going, but

I'm feeling confident about the outcome. If we coordinate this right, we could have this sucker ready in the next couple days. We should start collecting what we'll need to implement it."

"Which is?" Emery prompted.

"Well, plenty of aluminum to feed the fabricator, but we'll also need to scrounge up a healthy dose of ammonia. Puck said we could pull some oculi from maintenance if we needed, and I think that time's come. Emery, you mind taking point on that?"

"Of fucking course," she piped, a soft spring lightening her step.

"Mesa," he said, slowing a step to fall in beside the Savant. "We're going to need our B-team to do a hermetic check of the launch tubes in question."

"I have already submitted the work order," she assured him.

He flashed her a grin. "You're the best."

"I am aware."

Emery smiled. "So, we're really gonna have a self-powered jump drive in this thing soon?"

Cavalon bit the inside of his lip and exchanged a look with Mesa, who seemed equally unable to suppress the satisfied smirk tugging at the corners of her mouth.

"That's the idea," he said.

"Though, it is not that it will be self-powered," Mesa corrected, "but rather that we will have brought its source of power near to it."

"Right, yeah, exactly!" Emery skipped a few quick steps to catch up and gave Cavalon and Mesa congratulatory pats on the back.

Even Owen relented, a fraction of her grudge against Cavalon sliding away long enough to look impressed.

"That's exciting!" Emery continued, her enthusiasm at once tiring and contagious. "You guys really should be more excited right now. Why aren't you more excited?"

Mesa sighed. "We are simply too exhausted."

"We're excited on the inside, Em," Cavalon assured her, jealous that she had the capacity to have so much damn energy. He missed unlimited epithesium.

An echo drew Cavalon's gaze to the long hallway in front of them. He hesitated, steps slowing.

Halfway down the airlock-lined corridor, a group of a dozen soldiers rounded the corner.

Cavalon's brow creased. There shouldn't be any foot traffic in this secluded corner of the ship. This corridor led nowhere.

His confusion transformed to dread as his eyes focused on the man at the head of the pack—thinning black hair and a perpetually disaffected sneer. Snyder. The men and women behind him were a mix of oculi and circitors, all offering equally embittered scowls.

Cavalon cast a cursory glance at his inept nexus, but saw no notification. He must have missed the warning—maybe it'd triggered when they were still off-ship and the signal hadn't made it through the hull. But as Snyder drew closer, Cavalon caught a glimpse of his empty wrists—of all of the soldier's empty wrists—all devoid of a nexus band. They'd finally figured it out.

As the group approached, Owen slid a confused look to Cavalon. "What the hell is this?"

"Oh," Cavalon sighed, "just wait for it."

Emery shimmied aside to eclipse herself behind Owen, tapping something into her nexus.

Snyder came to a stop in front of them, crossing his arms over his chest. His pasty complexion had yellowed and taken on an almost slimy sheen. Reduced rations had done him no favors.

Over Snyder's shoulder stood McCalla, the tall woman who'd helped Snyder kick the shit out of Cavalon on Kharon Gate. The old scars covering the left side of her jaw and neck complemented her frigid glare. His third former assailant stood at the back of the group, a thickset man with an overgrown mop of brown hair named Fulton. Cavalon didn't know any of the others. Each wore a small square patch on their shoulder, though it was no badge of rank Cavalon recognized.

"So it's true," Snyder said, and to Cavalon's intense displeasure, he glared right at Owen. "A deckhand said he spotted a Larios disembarking."

"Void, not this again," Emery seethed.

"Why hello, Miss Flos." Snyder inclined his head. "Thanks for joining us again."

Her sneer didn't fade as she curtsied, her form both accurate and remarkably graceful. Owen cracked up laughing.

Cavalon eyed the disgruntled pack behind Snyder. "You made a few more friends since we last spoke," he said. "Or I guess I should say, since you last violently assaulted me. Did you need some backup this time since you can't throttle me with hijacked Imprints anymore?"

Snyder shrugged. "They just wanted in on the fun. Pretty damn easy to find like-minded folks when half the people on the ship were screwed over by your gramps."

"Half?" Cavalon scoffed. "You underestimate him."

"Ohh," Owen exhaled with an air of dawning realization. "This is about Gusty?"

"What isn't?" Cavalon grumbled. Even on the fringes of the universe, his grandfather found ways to make his life miserable.

"Mercer might be the Allied Monarchies' ringleader," Snyder snarled, "but you Larioses are no better."

Owen crossed her arms and gave the kind of disaffected eye roll only someone raised a part of the Allied Monarchies could accomplish. Emery sidled up beside Owen, and Cavalon caught a glimpse of her fiddling with something at the back of her belt . . . something that looked suspiciously like the black hilt of a Legion-issue knife. Jackin had issued a strict no-weapons policy aboard the *Typhos*, but Cavalon wasn't sure Emery'd gotten the memo since yesterday. More likely she simply didn't care. Regardless, Cavalon had no intention of letting her get herself in trouble with that knife.

He nodded toward the row of black Sentinel Imprints lining Snyder's right arm. "You know, I outrank you now, Circitor." He opened his nexus. "If you want to try something, go right ahead."

But as the screen loaded, a flash of red light caught his eye and he glanced down to find a warning: "Imprint Control System Offline."

Cavalon's lips parted as he met Snyder's contemptuous smile. How the hell had they hacked Imprint controls?

Time to take the situation more seriously. Four against twelve wasn't great odds, but Cavalon had been training hand-to-hand for months, and if he called on the full strength of his royal Imprints, he'd be able to take at least half of them on his own, probably more.

As he sized them up, his gaze stuck on Snyder's shoulder and the badge pinned to it—a small black square intersected with five lines that met at a white diamond in the middle. Something about it raised a twist of bitter familiarity in his gut, though he couldn't place it.

"What's with the club patches?" he asked.

Snyder lifted a thin eyebrow. "I'm surprised you don't recognize it. The OCR."

Cavalon growled a sigh. Good fucking void.

The Outer Core Refugees were a fledgling expatriate movement comprising those thrown out of the Core by Augustus's thinly shrouded eugenics laws. They had no discernible mission statement—sometimes they wanted the Allied Monarchies board to endure the same election procedure as those that sat on the Quorum, sometimes they wanted every member of the five royal families burned at the stake, and sometimes they wanted to pull the plug on the entire structure of human government to live as lawless barbarians.

That very lack of focus ensured that for over forty years, they'd never become more than a slightly itchy thorn in the System Collective's side and a scribbled footnote in session notes at Allied Monarchies' board meetings. Every decade or so, they'd earn an uptick in membership after finding some charismatic new leader, who'd eventually screw it up by handing the SC everything needed to pin some terrorist plot on them, discrediting any ground the OCR had made in the meantime while their new leader was quietly executed. And repeat.

Emery and Mesa exchanged brief glimpses of confusion, but the humor had fled Owen's face entirely. She knew all about the OCR. The last jackhole to take the reins had set off a bomb on Viridis that'd killed her uncle and three of her cousins. It wasn't their deaths she cared about—Cavalon knew from experience that branch of the Larioses were all massive pricks—but it'd come too close to home for comfort, too close to threatening her own family, who she actually *liked*, weirdly.

"OCR, huh?" he said, refocusing on Snyder. "So you've taken it upon yourselves to begin a Divide chapter?"

"Yes, actually," Snyder replied.

"Can I join?"

"Very funny."

"I'm actually not kidding. I could be your inside man."

Snyder's rigid sneer didn't falter.

Cavalon sighed. "Okay, I don't know the secret passphrase, I get it. I'm truly sorry Gramps is such a raging tool; that's actually something I'd love to address once we're back at the Core. But the only way any of us are ever going to get there is if you walk away right now and let us get on with our day."

Snyder crossed his arms. "Just like a Mercer to assume nothing's more important than what he's doing. We all have posts too, you know. You're not the only one with responsibilities."

Emery snorted a laugh. "Most of your lot's in sanitation, last I checked."

Cavalon quirked a brow. "Yeah, there's no way building an engine aboard this stranded vessel is more important than ejecting all our shit out an airlock."

McCalla's fists clenched as she stepped forward. Cavalon eyed Snyder's honed glower and took a moment to wonder why he'd felt it was a good idea to start antagonizing them. One didn't dissuade an angry bear by poking it in the damn face.

Cavalon gritted his teeth, angry with himself for falling back on old instincts. They were just such easy targets.

"I would like to take this opportunity," Mesa announced, her crisp tone sharp in the echoing corridor, "to remind you all that inciting physical altercations is considered grade three misconduct and as such, is subject to a range of nonjudicial punishments as seen fit by the acting chief of security."

"What're they gonna do?" McCalla growled. "Dock our nonexistent pay?"

"We're not here for you, Darox." Snyder held up a hand to placate Mesa, but it seemed to have the opposite effect.

Mesa's shoulders drew down, her normally soft features taking on a hard edge. "And I suppose you believe that means I will stand idly by?"

A brief glimmer of hesitation shone in Snyder's eyes before his asshole scowl overtook it. "Look, it's your choice, Savant. Doesn't bother me either way."

"Very well," Mesa said, her tone surprisingly even. "If it is to be a fight, let us proceed."

Snyder blinked at her.

Mesa made a casual oscillating motion with one hand. "We are very busy. I do not have time to continue discussing it."

Emery snorted a laugh. The anti-royalists all stared, blank-faced, at the Savant provoking them.

Mesa turned to Cavalon, rolling her large eyes and giving a soft shake of her head. "I shall do it, then." In a single, smooth movement, Mesa swiveled, drawing her elbow back as she pivoted forward. She jutted the heel of her palm into Snyder's breastbone, sending him crashing back into his friends, then leapt after him.

A swell of amusement bubbled in Cavalon's chest, barring air from his lungs as he hacked out a laugh, choked by disbelief.

He tore his gaze from the whirlwind of navy-blue limbs that had once been Mesa while his Imprints slid up his arm, and he barely dodged an incoming fist from Fulton.

McCalla went for Owen, who seemed to have teamed up with Emery, but Cavalon couldn't keep tabs on the others for long as he caught a glimpse of Snyder disengaging from Mesa's path of destruction to head straight for Cavalon.

His tired Imprints took their sweet time sliding into formation, and he endured the full force of Fulton's fists to his gut twice before they arrived to shield him. On the third hit, Fulton hissed, recoiling as his knuckles met the hardened grid of Imprint squares.

Cavalon kept one eye on Snyder's approach while sidestepping a wildly telegraphed punch from Fulton. His chest and triceps buzzed as clusters of his Imprints split off to other areas, grinding as they locked down into his muscles. He threw an Imprint-powered fist straight into

Fulton's temple. Fulton dropped, collapsing to the deck with a satisfying thud.

Snyder took a large step over his unconscious ally, fury evident in the hard scowl and flush of crimson on his pasty cheeks.

Cavalon rushed into Snyder's guard, throwing out a punch, but Snyder leaned back and Cavalon didn't have time to course correct. He missed Snyder's cheekbone and his knuckles cracked hard into the side of his nose instead. Snyder growled, stumbling back. Cavalon grimaced. So much for another one-punch KO.

Snyder wiped the blood spilling from his nose, then lunged at Cavalon.

Cavalon retreated, but stumbled as his feet dragged, a sudden weight of fatigue saddling him like a wet blanket. He ducked too late, and Snyder's fist struck high on his cheek. His vision fractured, granting a moment of peaceful unconsciousness as he tilted, awake again just in time to feel jolts of pain as he hit the floor.

Snyder was on top of him a second later. With one hand, he pinned Cavalon by the neck, palm crushing his windpipe. He delivered a punch straight to Cavalon's cheek that twisted his neck back, slamming his chin hard into the floor.

Cavalon grimaced and spat out blood. He gasped for breath, sight spinning. Snyder's elbow drew back again.

Cavalon clenched his teeth to brace for impact, but Snyder hesitated. He threw a glance over his shoulder as one of the OCR automatons flew past and crashed into another, sending them both sprawling to the floor.

Cavalon blinked the sweat from his eyes as he traced the source of the thrown body, finding the last person he expected to see—mostly because he still wasn't used to her being on this ship.

Rake. Rake with her shoulders swelled, jaw clenched. Rake with fuming rage in her eyes like he'd never seen before, full of a wrath that could not have been caused by this brawl, however asinine it was.

Warner and a handful of his MPs fanned out behind her, shouting orders to stand down while they began to subdue the OCR goons. Rake discarded another of the soldiers like she was tossing out a gum wrapper, her glare fixated on Snyder, still straddling Cavalon.

Snyder's mouth dropped open. Rake radiated fury as she stalked toward them, then grabbed Snyder by the back of his collar and hauled him off Cavalon. Snyder cried out as she wrenched his arm behind his back, then pinned him facedown to the floor.

Cavalon grunted as he twisted, dragging himself along the floor a few meters so he could lean against the wall. He spat out thick globs of blood, breaths heaving.

Jackin appeared, looking equal parts bewildered and livid as he dodged a stray punch from one of the few loose anti-royalists. Mesa swept a leg under the woman before she could try again, then helped Jackin cuff her.

A few meters away, Owen crouched beside Emery, inspecting her split lip with a display of honest concern that sent a strangely pleasant rush of relief through Cavalon's chest.

Rake leaned a knee into the small of Snyder's back and twisted his arm tighter. Snyder groaned, his pasty face flushed with frustration. Rake's grimace stiffened as she leaned in. "What exactly made you think this was a good idea?" she growled.

Snyder's jaw flexed, and even through the pain of Rake's rough handling, had the balls to say, "There's two of them now. I couldn't resist."

Rake's scowl wavered slightly as she looked up, gaze landing on Cavalon before swiveling to Owen. Realization flattened her features. Owen frowned, glancing down and scratching her cheek slowly.

Cavalon wiped some of the blood from his chin. Owen hadn't told Rake who she was, apparently. Hopefully she hadn't outright lied about it. That wouldn't go over well.

Rake returned her fury to Snyder, yanking his wrist higher up his back. She leaned to hiss into his ear, barely audible. "Surely you didn't forget what I told you back on Kharon Gate?"

Snyder groaned, water welling from his eyes, mixing with the sweat rolling over his bruising nose. "That you'd personally end me."

"That I'd personally end you *if* . . ."

"If I laid a hand on one of your soldiers . . ."

". . . Ever again," she finished.

Snyder honed in on Cavalon, pure hatred in his eyes. "Especially him," he croaked. "Your pet royal."

Cavalon dragged a hand down the side of his face. Bloody void, it was like Snyder had a death wish.

"What do you think *end* means?" Rake's voice grew low, difficult to hear over the MPs continuing to cuff the others. "Especially here, now, like this? When we're reducing rations every week, struggling to keep people alive?"

Snyder didn't respond, pain creasing his pallid face.

Confusion flashed across Rake's eyes as she spotted the square patch at his shoulder. She ripped it free from his uniform and turned it over in her hand. "What is this?"

Snyder didn't respond.

Rake leaned harder into his back. "Don't fucking make me repeat myself."

"OCR," Snyder gritted out through clenched teeth.

Rake stared at the badge in her open palm for a few long moments. She looked up at the anti-royalists Warner had lined up down the hall. Some shifted uncomfortably, their looks obstinate despite being cuffed, on their knees, and beyond neck-deep on Rake's shit list. Only McCalla and Fulton had the good sense to appear intimidated.

Then Cavalon realized—the rest hadn't been aboard the *Argus*. They hadn't had a chance to amass respect for Rake as the others had. But she'd still saved their lives; that had to count for something.

Rake's hard gaze landed on Cavalon, and he wiped a warm droplet of blood from his lip. It was impossible to read her flat stare, but he was fairly certain he didn't like where this was going.

She threw the patch aside and looked back down at Snyder. "This is strike two," she growled. Relief twitched across Snyder's face, then she got to her feet, gripping Snyder by the scruff of his vest and hauling him up off the floor. "We're not doing strike threes."

Snyder's feet shuffled uselessly against the floor in a feeble attempt to stop her as she dragged him down the corridor. Straight toward the nearest escape pod airlock.

Cavalon's wide eyes shot to Emery and Owen, then Mesa, then Warner. They all stood watching, unmoving, stunned.

Jackin took off after her. "*Rake*," he warned.

"Rake," Cavalon implored, his voice a dry croak as he scrambled up off the deck, muscles burning with fatigue. "Rake, wait!"

She didn't so much as turn her head in acknowledgment of either of them. She threw Snyder into the airlock, then punched the controls and the door sealed. Jackin rushed up behind her, too late. With a few quick flicks of her wrist, Rake canceled the equalization and opened the outer doors.

Blood rushed to Cavalon's head, filling his ears with a deadened weight. Rake's shoulders swelled as she turned, squaring off with Jackin, barring him from reaching the controls.

The commotion faded away as Cavalon focused inward, staring down at the glimmering white fabric covering his arms. He'd forgotten to take his suit off.

He dashed into the neighboring airlock, clambering to pull a helmet off the shelf and onto his head. His right hand fumbled at the seals as his left tapped at the airlock controls, shutting him inside.

Once upon a time, Rake had patiently talked him through the stages of a vacuum-related death—Snyder might have ninety seconds, though with no suit at all, maybe only a minute. Still plenty of time. Cavalon tried not to think about what the hell had happened to the calm, tolerant, practical Rake who'd told him that.

He hooked the retractable tether to his harness as the airlock sounded a warning, then relieved him of weight. The outer doors slid open and the pitch-blackness of the Divide greeted him.

His gaze darted out into the crushing darkness, but without any kind of exterior illumination, he couldn't tell how far Snyder had gone.

He activated his helmet lamp, shining the beam out into the void. His pulse throbbed in his throat. Snyder couldn't have gone that far—the lock had at least partially equalized before Rake had canceled it. He caught movement in the corner of his eye and spun. Cool relief flooded his veins.

Snyder's pasty skin illuminated in the soft light shining out from the neighboring airlock. His fingers had stiffened into a mangled claw, locked in an immobile grip at the edge of the hatch frame.

Cavalon tapped his nexus to choke the retractable tether to six meters, then pushed off the narrow platform toward Snyder. He reached out, hooking both arms around Snyder's waist just as the tether pulled taut, yanking them both back along the same trajectory. He guided them back into the airlock and activated the controls, cradling Snyder in preparation for the return of gravity. He stared blankly at the man's swelling skin, beet-red and bubbling as they endured the ten-second eternity of pressurization.

The airlock siren blared. Snyder's swollen skin deflated in an instant, but had taken on a polished sheen and already started to bruise. Cavalon lowered him to the floor.

The inner airlock door opened. Cavalon pulled his helmet off and tossed it away, heart still frantic in his chest. He took a tentative step back as Emery and Mesa rushed in, engulfing Snyder in a thin metallic heat blanket. Owen stood in the door frame tapping her nexus, opening a line to the medbay.

Out in the corridor, Rake shouted at Jackin. He gripped her wrist as if trying to bar her from interfering with the rescue attempt. But if Rake had really wanted past, Jackin wouldn't have stood a chance.

"His pulse is steady," Mesa announced.

Seconds later, Snyder coughed. He twisted, sneering with pain as he began to regain consciousness.

"Hey, dickwad," Emery crooned, tightening the metallic sheet around Snyder's shoulders. "Welcome back."

Jackin let out an audible sigh of relief, then let go of Rake. She glowered as she shoved him aside and stalked off.

Cavalon almost tripped on the threshold as he stumbled out into the hallway. "Rake!" he shouted after her.

She didn't slow.

Jackin watched her go, pushing stiff hands through his hair. His gaze darted from Mesa and Emery tending to Snyder, to Warner and the MPs still watching over the cuffed OCR soldiers, who all stared on in various states of dismay. Jackin had a mess to clean up.

His look landed on Cavalon. "Go," he ordered, but Cavalon had already taken off after her.

CHAPTER NINE

Cavalon scurried to catch up, but Rake had made it quite a ways down the hall. She turned sharply into the next intersecting corridor.

When he arrived at the corner, she'd already unlocked access to a maintenance hatch and disappeared inside. The joke was on her though, because Jackin had given Cavalon unlimited clearance months ago, so he could pilfer whatever he needed from the bones of the ship at any hour of the day or night, and stop waking him at 0200 to grant access.

Cavalon yanked off his suit's glove and set his palm on the pad to unlock the door, then sprinted to catch up.

"Rake!" His shout echoed harshly off the narrow aerasteel walls, lined with pipes and ducting and cabling conduits. The temperature climbed.

Rake hadn't moved faster than a purposeful walk, yet she continued to outpace his desperate, tired jog. His muscles cramped, strength waning, unable to handle the constant fluctuations of adrenaline. His body cried out with fatigue, willing him to stop, to rest, to find some water, some epithesium, a mattress, or maybe just a cryogenic chamber in which to wait out this entire disaster. But he kept on, willing his body to function a little longer.

When he finally caught up, his hand had barely come to rest on her shoulder when she halted and spun, thrusting a palm into his chest and shoving him back.

He caught her wrist. On instinct, he tried to twist her arm to spin her into a hold, but she threw her weight forward and jammed her shoulder hard into his chest, freeing her wrist. She seized his shoulder with one hand, then struck him in the stomach with the other.

His breath left him completely—half from disbelief and half from the brutal impact. His body recoiled, sending cramping waves of pain through his torso.

He ground his teeth, a spark of unbridled anger stoking in his chest. Copper filled his mouth as he unconsciously summoned his Imprints.

Stance wide, elbow high, his Imprints bored into his muscles as he put the full force of whatever measly amount of strength he had left into the punch. His knuckles cracked against her jaw.

She fell back into the wall, hitting hard against a stack of pipes. She dropped to one knee, hand going to her split lip as blood dripped down her chin.

"Oh shit," Cavalon croaked, throat bone-dry. "Are you okay?"

He stepped forward, hand out in offering, but Rake rebounded to her feet. She threw a jab with her off-hand that hit hard against his rib cage, and he stumbled. Her right fist followed up, the blow hitting him square in the meat of his stomach. A bitter, hot wave of nausea flooded his mouth, a white glare spreading across his vision.

Through the haze, he threw out a wild punch. She raised her arm to block the swing and his forearm cracked hard into hers.

Rake cried out and Cavalon's breath stilled.

Her glower vanished, pain overwhelming her fury. She staggered back and collapsed against the pipes, buckling to the floor, clutching her arm to her chest in agony.

Cavalon froze, confusion wracking him. He'd put a fair amount of strength behind the hit, but not bone-breaking strength.

"Shit, what happened?" He slid to his knees beside her. His breaths heaved as a flood of guilt overwhelmed him—what the hell was he doing? Fighting Rake? This was ludicrous.

She didn't respond as she slowly coiled into a fetal position, eyes clenched tight.

Cavalon swept open his nexus. "I'm calling the medbay."

"No," she barked, the single syllable hard enough to stop his fingers in their tracks.

"What? Why?"

"It's fine, it's just some—" She grunted and sat up, bracing heavily against the wall, still cradling her arm. Her breaths began to slow. "It just hurts. It's fine, really. They can't do anything."

"Why not?"

She licked her bloodied lips, shaking her head. "It's Imprint-related. They wouldn't know how to deal with it."

"Imprint-related?" he asked, but he knew she didn't intend to elaborate. He edged closer, eyeing her nestled arm. "Let me see, at least."

Her jaw firmed as she fixed a stony glare on him.

"Or I'll call a real doctor," he threatened.

She finally jerked her head in the barest sliver of a nod.

Grimacing, she slid one arm out of her jacket. She wore a tank top underneath, her exposed upper arm and shoulder marred with swaths of maroon, purple, black, blue, yellow, green—every color bruise he'd ever seen, all mixed together in a horrifying watercolor of contusions. Long tracks of blackened veins stretched like forked lightning over the marred flesh.

"Void, Rake . . ." he muttered, giving his beard a slow, astonished scratch. His gaze drifted to her forearm, cocooned in a white wrap. He reached out and took her wrist, and she winced as he started to unwind the bindings.

Underneath, he found more of the same horrific bruising, but joined by clusters of open sores, each one a tiny, bloody crater surrounded by raw skin. Some were partly scabbed over, where others looked brand-new. He'd likely reopened some when he struck her arm.

"This is from the dark energy generators?" he croaked out.

She gave a shallow nod. "I guess human skin's not made for having Imprints taken off and reapplied so many times."

A nauseating wave of culpability crushed down on him, and he closed his eyes, pinching the bridge of his nose. "I'm so sorry. Void . . ." he muttered. "I should have helped you restart them."

"No. What you were doing was—*is* just as important. We needed you here."

He nodded aimlessly. "Please see one of the docs about this," he urged as he retied the wrappings, her damaged skin warm on his cool fingertips. "I know you think they can't help, but at least let them make sure it's not infected." He decided to take her silence as agreement, then sat back against the wall beside her and scrubbed his hands over his face. "Fuck. I'm sorry I hit you."

She shook her head. "It's my fault. I started it."

He leaned his head back and stared up at the ceiling. "Let's just blame the Divide. It certainly seems to make everyone else unstable."

Her chin bobbed slowly, and she remained silent for a few long moments. "I should have known Snyder wouldn't let it rest with you," she said, tone quiet but hard. "I should have dealt with him on Kharon after the first incident. I was too lenient."

"Well . . ." Cavalon said, scrubbing a hand through his disheveled hair. "By definition, your Sentinel army comprises a bunch of miscreants. They're gonna be assholes sometimes."

She sighed.

"Listen . . ." He took a breath, thinking through what he meant to say for a few moments. "How you choose to deal with your rebellious rebels is your decision. I'm not going to question that. But I'd like to think I know you, at least somewhat, at this point. And that . . . that wasn't you."

She stared down at her lap for a long time, then wiped blood from her chin with her knuckle. "Remember I told you about that pub owner who died?"

Cavalon blinked a few times, then blew out a slow breath as the realization hit him. "Void. That bomb was delivered by the OCR?"

She nodded. "There was a huge group of them on Seneca-IV. They constantly harried the Saxton Guard, and innocents got caught in it all the time." She forced a long breath out her nose. "It's a huge part of what made it such a dangerous place to live. The Saxtons were tyrants, but they didn't kill random civilians. Outright, at least. That bomb was the first time the OCR had hit so close to home. For me, at least."

"That's terrible, Rake," he said. "I'm really sorry."

"I know it's not an excuse, but when I saw those damn patches . . . I felt like I had to do something. Stop it before it was too late . . ." Her voice grew distant and she slouched into the wall.

"Well," Cavalon began, "I think it's safe to assume Snyder's not going to try anything for a while. The others might be a different story."

"They won't be leaving the brig anytime soon," she growled. "Unless Jackin plans to depose me."

Cavalon nodded. From her tone, she didn't think that'd be such a bad idea.

Rake stared at her ruined arms. "If he'd threatened anyone but you . . ." She gave a regretful shake of her head, her words as sincere as they were caustic.

A creeping realization nagged at the back of Cavalon's mind. Rake might regret what she'd done on a broad level, but it'd come up against the boundaries of her willingness to lose him. It both flattered and terrified him. It was too reminiscent of that cold calculation he'd been so aware of—and so afraid of—when he'd first joined the Sentinels. When saving people became a game of math and logic, individual lives stopped mattering. Snyder's continued existence meant a chance, however fractionally, that he'd end Cavalon's.

Rake bent her knees and leaned her elbows on them. Hanging her head, she sat in silence, bloodshot eyes unblinking.

Something bigger was going on; he could feel it in the air between them, see it in the neurotic, practiced way she endlessly thumbed that extra set of dog tags around her neck. This wasn't just about him, or Snyder, or the OCR, or the Sentinels.

He was such an idiot. He'd known something was off, but then he'd gotten distracted by his revelation with the cryostat and forgotten all about it. Rake had needed help, and he'd ignored it.

"There's more going on here than you're letting on," he said, voice barely a whisper. "But if you don't talk to me, I can't help."

She stayed silent for a few long moments, sighing lightly over the soft jangle of her necklace chain. "I saw something earlier in the CIC," she said finally. "A time ripple of Griffith."

Cavalon sat back, pressing both hands to his face and blowing a loud breath into them. He willed the ulcer twisting in his stomach to relax. "Shit, Rake." He dropped his hands. "I'm sorry. We should have told you."

Her gaze flitted to him, disbelief narrowing her eyes. "Bloody void," she growled. "You've seen them too?"

"I have . . ." he admitted reluctantly. "I'm sorry we didn't warn you. We see so many people, all the time. Duplicates, of course, but we saw you and Emery, and the rest of the *Synthesis* and *Courier* crews, and tons of people we've never met who probably died on the other ships." He chose not to mention how often he'd seen her former aide, Bray, as well as Griffith's friend Lace, both lost in the *Argus*'s demise. "Ripples are everywhere, all the time. You kind of stop seeing them after a while, you know?"

She ran her hands down her face, giving a reluctant nod.

"One thing that's always consistent," he added carefully, "is that if we see Griffith . . . we don't see you."

She met his gaze, expression stiff and unreadable.

"So, yeah, there's clearly a future in which he survived . . . but you didn't. And I'm really glad to be in a version that has you in it. One thing I'm sure of more than anything is that we need you."

She let out a crackling sigh, folding her arms over her knees and staring down for a few moments.

"Sir, maybe it's not my place . . ." he began. "I'm not sure where that line is anymore, honestly."

She shook her head. "Me either. Go ahead."

"You haven't had two seconds to pause since we left the *Argus*. And now you're back, and Jackin's got things as well in hand as they can be, considering. I get it. You're waiting it out—treading water until the next disaster arrives to give you something to fix. So you can push it aside again."

"Push what aside?"

"You need to grieve him."

Her brows knit, look drifting down.

"Take the time," he continued. "Mourn Griffith. And the *Argus*. If you rush headlong into the next problem, it's going to fester."

She picked at the edges of the wrap at her wrist. "I didn't try to space Snyder to create a problem."

"I'm not saying that—I know you did that to protect me. I do appreciate that, Rake." He leaned forward to catch her eye, and she gave a short, reluctant nod. "As much as I don't want you to kill people for me," he added, "it's nice to know you're willing."

She offered a small, bitter smile. "I know. And I know you're right about Griffith . . ."

"But?" he prompted.

"I just . . . I don't know how. To grieve him. I've never lost anyone I cared about . . . like that. Hudson's the nearest, but that felt so different."

"Because he went MIA?"

She nodded. "I never saw a body; they never even let me look at the mission reports. I never had any idea what happened to him. I accepted it in time, but it took years."

"That, I understand," he said, then heaved out a sigh. "When my grandmother went missing, I was in denial for years. Then my father . . . well, that went even less well."

"What about your mother? You never mention her."

He scratched the back of his neck, slicked with sweat in the balmy passage. "I never knew her; she died when I was a baby. I was pretty much raised by my father and grandmother. Even as a kid, I got into it all the time with Augustus, and my grandmother served as a buffer. After she was gone, my father tried to fill that role." He gave a grim shake of his head. "Despite his best efforts, Augustus and I kept clashing hard, which is why I went to university for so long. Then when my father died, well . . . things careened downhill from there. You know how that mourning process went. Building nukes to blow up clone factories. The epitome of healthy grieving."

"So it really was a response to that . . ." she began, honest curiosity in her tone. "You blame Augustus for your father's death?"

He glanced down, kneading the palms of his hands in turn. He hadn't really intended to bring up his father. He'd never even admitted this much about it before. But if it was what Rake needed, he had to find the balls to talk about it. There were plenty of other festering emotional wounds he could keep buried.

"I wouldn't say I *blame* Augustus," Cavalon began, voice cracking. "Blame implies I don't know for a fact he's responsible."

"If you have evidence, why not turn him in?"

He scoffed a bitter, dry laugh. "Careful there, a bit of your optimism is showing."

She sighed and gave a lazy roll of her eyes.

"You know it wouldn't matter if I did," he went on. "Let's not forget who we're dealing with."

She stayed quiet for a few moments, then cleared her throat with an effort. "Back at that first generator . . ." she began, bracing her elbows on her knees again, "Griffith made me promise to live. To find a way to go on. I feel like I'm failing him."

"You seem pretty alive to me."

She shook her head. "I've survived. I'm not sure that's the same thing."

Cavalon's chest tightened. She wasn't wrong. But admitting he'd had the same kind of thoughts circling his head for months wouldn't really do much for the optimistic progression he was pushing for. Time to switch tactics.

"You know, when I first met you . . ." He scoffed a laugh. "Frankly, you scared the shit out of me."

She tightened down on her despondency long enough to give him a flat stare.

"Still do—don't worry," he assured.

She pinched the bridge of her nose.

"But mostly," he went on, "I was impressed. The way you could walk into a room and command respect without saying a word. The only other person I'd ever met that wielded that kind of power so naturally . . . well . . ."

Her hand dropped from her face. "Gramps?"

He nodded. "And for obvious reasons, I never endeavored to be like him. But with you, I felt like I finally had someone to look up to again, like I had with my father. How he'd quietly shirk Augustus's bullshit, find ways to work within a broken system. My grandmother was the same way. All three of you, natural leaders, in your own ways. But what Augustus never had an ounce of—and that they did, and you do, in tiring, endless spades—is compassion."

Her rigid expression loosened somewhat.

"Augustus is the one thing we'll always have to look to," Cavalon went on. "A guidepost, if you will. If we're working against him, we're headed in the right direction."

"A lodestar," she offered.

He smiled and stared at her for a few seconds, a sliver of the haunted look gone from her sweat-slicked face. He'd gotten through to her, at least fractionally. It was the equivalent of using a cottonball to stanch a gaping gunshot wound . . . But for now, he'd take it.

"Exactly," he said. "An egomaniacal, sociopathic lodestar."

She gave another almost-smile.

"It's up to us to show them how it should be," Cavalon continued. "What the difference is, what we're fighting for, and how to change it. That's not what that thing with Snyder was. You know that. But I get it. You try so hard to find your way out, but end up lost in it. Like getting pulled under a wave and not being able to tell which way is up."

Her head bobbed lightly, gaze unfocused. "Yeah."

Cavalon's heart sank as he leaned back against the wall. He could see now why he'd avoided real friendships for so long. It felt like he had a knife twisting in his chest, all because Rake was hurting. And he couldn't figure out a way to fix it.

After a few moments, she pressed her face into her hands and let out a long sigh. "I'm sorry, Cav."

"There's nothing to be sorry for . . ." He shifted, turning toward her. "Just remember our lodestar. Well, *ridding the galaxy of* our egomaniacal, sociopathic lodestar, to be more specific."

"Right." Rake smiled warily, then pushed some of the sweaty hair from the sides of her face. "They went after Owen as well?"

"Yeah . . ."

"That explains why she wouldn't give me a last name."

He nodded. "Larios. She's like, fortieth in line, or something like that."

"Not quite as high-profile as Prince Cavalon?"

He gave a wry smirk.

"So you knew her before?" Rake asked.

"Yeah. We were friends growing up. Remember I told you someone helped me build the command circuitry for the revenge nukes?"

She quirked a brow. "No. I think you skipped that detail."

"Oh, uh . . ." He forced a grin. "Well, someone helped, and it was her. She's only here because she admitted to Augustus what she did, and her family had her shunned as punishment. So she's not a traitor, is what I'm trying to say. Well, she is, but not to us. You can trust her."

"I do."

"You do?"

"She volunteered to help with the generators, no questions asked. Caught on fast. Took her less than a couple days to figure out how to remotely connect our nexuses to the Viator networks. She's smart as hell."

He flashed a toothy grin. "Just like your last royal, right?"

"Meh," she mumbled with a casual shrug.

"Hey now, be nice or I won't finish building that star for you."

For what he was pretty sure was the first time since she returned, a real smile broke across Rake's lips. It disappeared as she winced in pain, holding her fingers up to the split in her lip.

"Sorry," he hissed, ". . . my bad."

"I don't remember you having such a mean right hook."

"I've been training with Jackin."

Her eyebrows rose. "Jack?"

"Yeah. He's a good teacher. Patient. Which I need."

She licked the trickle of fresh blood from her lip, gaze distant.

"Warner too," Cavalon went on. "Puck and Mesa, sometimes. It's been a bit of a group effort. Everyone pitching in when they can. As we do."

"Well, they've done well," she said. "Sorry I couldn't be here to help."

"I mean, now that I can say I've taken down the EX, I've got pretty much all the fighting clout I'll ever need, right?"

She leveled a flat look at him.

"Also, I'm pretty sure that makes me EX by default." He leaned, nudging her lightly with his shoulder. "That's how chain of command works, right?"

Her lips lifted in a smile, though it didn't reach the rest of her face.

He slumped against the wall, tension knotting in his shoulders. He was doing it again, turning everything into a damn joke. He'd just *hit* Rake, multiple times; it wasn't something he should be taking lightly, whether or not she'd started it. He knew she'd forgive him, but treating aggression with callousness hit a bit too close to childhood for his comfort.

His lips opened and he hesitated, though he didn't know why he was holding back at this point. She'd always been honest with him, and had proven herself nothing if not trustworthy. He'd been taking so much from her, and never made an effort to give back.

A memory stuck in the back of his mind, one that fit nicely with that newfangled optimism of his. Something his grandmother had often said when he was a kid . . . that if your intent was true, it was never too late to change things.

"Will you tell me a story, sir?" he asked.

Rake stayed silent for a few moments. "What do you want to hear?"

His brow lifted in surprise. He'd expected at least *some* resistance.

He dug into the very shallow reserve of courage he kept stored away for days when he might be suddenly expected to save the universe. "Tell me about when you and Griffith first met?"

She let out a long, crackling sigh from the back of her throat, rubbing her face a few times. He was positive she was going to tell him to fuck off.

But then she shimmied back, slouching into the wall beside him. "It was 214 AV, on Tartarus-II . . ."

CHAPTER TEN

Adequin stepped into the *Typhos*'s medbay, dreading the antiseptic stench. But the waft of air that greeted her smelled clean and refreshing, and felt at least ten degrees cooler than the corridor outside.

She hesitated just inside. Cavalon had threatened to halt work on the reactor unless she promised to visit the medbay. To be fair, she'd only said she'd *visit*, not be seen by a doctor. Guilt prevented her from fleeing. Cavalon had managed to dig her out of a dark place yesterday. She owed it to him to follow through. Besides, she'd never hear the end of it once Jackin found out, so she'd end up doing it one way or the other.

She dodged the gazes of a few milling lab coats as she worked her way toward the intake desk. To her right, a long corridor of beds stretched out, only a handful occupied. Snyder lay on the first bed inside the arched entryway.

She crossed her arms tight as she approached the foot of his bed. A half dome of green-tinged glass covered his torso, his chest raising and lowering at a mechanically constant rate. His face and neck and hands were red and marred with bruising.

With a clanging swish, a curtain drew closed between them.

"No visitin' hours yet, lass . . ." a deep voice grumbled.

Anger spiked in her chest as she turned to face the offender, a modestly tall man in his early fifties. His thick, ashy white hair sprung irritatingly right back into place as he pushed a hand through it. His gaze caught on her badges of rank and his casual disregard perked up.

He put his fist to his chest in a fluid but formal salute. "Aye, Excubitor, sir." His thick brogue sounded much like the Northern Cautian accent her former chief mechanic Lace had, but with the dial turned up to eleven. "My apologies. Didn't see you come in, sir."

"I didn't catch your name."

"It's Kellar. Circitor Ford Kellar."

"Right . . . Jackin has you earmarked for intel?"

He inclined his head. "Ready whenever you need me, sir. Not that I mind my current post."

Rake glanced back at the central intake hub. "Well, we appreciate it. We're short on skilled physicians."

"Aye. Been trainin' up some folks, though. We'll have a healthy graduatin' class before you know it."

"Good to hear."

"Is there somethin' I can do for you, sir?"

She glanced at the drawn curtain. "That circitor, he was brought in yesterday?"

"Aye."

"How's he doing?"

"All right, sir. Mostly skin and tissue damage, decompression sickness. No radiation exposure s'far out, so we can be glad for that. Can't say he'll be gettin' cleared for duty anytime soon, but he'll make a full recovery."

Adequin nodded, picking at the raw edges of her cuticles. "Good to hear."

"I'm actually glad to see you, sir," Ford said. "I keep gettin' requests from your former crew to ambush you for a checkup."

She sighed. "Well, thanks for . . . *not* doing that."

He offered a hesitant smile. "I know better than to try and sneak up on a Titan. Though, I guess I kinda just did, eh?"

She gave a reluctant nod, and he watched her carefully for a few drawn-out moments.

"Well," he continued, "now that I got you trapped, how about we see to that checkup?"

She licked her dry lips. "Not sure about a checkup, but there is something I need looked at."

He nodded in response, then tilted his head to indicate she should follow. He led her past the central hub, into a small, private exam room. He sealed the door, and Adequin wrung her hands as she leaned against the edge of the exam table.

Ford lifted an eyebrow. "Got into a bit of a scrap there, sir?" he asked.

Her fingers drifted to the split on her lip from Cavalon's surprisingly effectual right hook. "Yeah, it's fine. It's not why I'm here."

He stood patiently, arms crossed loose over his chest. "Let's hear it, then."

With a heavy sigh, she unstrapped her jacket and shouldered out of it, letting it drop onto the padded table behind her. The crisp air chilled the bare skin of her upper arms. She picked at the hem of the nanite gel wraps covering her forearms, awaiting his response.

Ford stared, expressionless at first, eyes drifting over the blackened veins and dark bruising covering her shoulders and upper arms. After a long moment he scratched his chin slowly. "I see . . ." He took a step closer. "May I?"

She grunted her consent.

He lifted her left arm and began to unwind the bandages, callused fingers working lightly around the soreness of her wrists. She'd have called it the gentle, practiced touch of a career doctor, but she knew he'd only been an infantry medic briefly. Though, much like Jackin's records, most of his time before and during the early years of the war were unaccounted for. Maybe he'd been some kind of secret spec-ops doctor. She wondered if he'd be as cagey as Jackin about the sealed part of his record.

"Where'd you get these bandages?" Ford asked.

"The cargo of the *Messino*." She winced as a section of the wrap stuck when he peeled it away.

"Sorry," he said, grimacing in apology. "I thought they looked familiar. It's not exactly standard-issue stuff."

"That was your ship?"

"Aye," he replied. His lips twisted as he concentrated on peeling away another viscid section of wrap, caked with half-dried blood. She bit the inside of her cheek, trying to ignore the sharp stings of pain as he pulled it free.

"If they're not standard," she said, "how'd you get them?"

"About a year ago, a few pallets of high-grade CHM stuff came in with one of our restock shipments."

She tilted her head, giving a contemplative nod. CHM supplies in general weren't an oddity. Culloden-Hale Medical Group was operated by the Cautian royal family, and the Cullodens had been the ones centuries ago to adapt the Viator biotool technology for human physiology. They were still the primary provider of medical equipment and pharmaceuticals for the Legion, the System Collective, and most private facilities. But she had no idea why they'd send high-end supplies all the way out to the Divide.

"I assume it was a clerical error," Ford explained, seeming to notice the confusion etched on her face. "Never saw a thing like it before, or since."

He finished unwrapping both arms, and she resisted the urge to scratch as the fresh air pricked at the raw flesh. Ford took a step back, expression twitching with a grimace of mixed pity and alarm. He really didn't seem the type to overreact, which made his evident concern that much more intolerable.

"How long's this been goin' on?" he asked.

"I started noticing it after the third or fourth time. A little over four weeks ago, give or take."

His eyes lifted, brows arched high in question.

"It's from using the Viator neural networks," she explained. "I had to connect to one aboard each of the dark energy generators."

He scratched at the gray scruff lining his jaw. "And how's that work exactly?"

"Not sure I can help with 'exactly.' All I know is it appropriates your Viator Imprints, then uses their link with you to create a neural connection to the computer. The process pretty much felt the same as getting them applied. Whatever that entails."

His throat bobbed with a heavy swallow. "That works to explain the mess it's made of your forearms, but what of the rest?"

"Not sure. It's been slowly spreading up my arms since it started."

He let out a long breath. "Have you tried taskin' your Imprints to heal it?"

She cringed. Even the thought of asking them to move sent bolts of pain down her arms. "Yeah, I tried. They won't go anywhere near it, it's like my forearms are null space. They don't even register it as viable flesh anymore. The squares that used to occupy my right arm by default won't return—they stay along the back of my neck now."

Ford sighed. "For the lesions, I assume you've tried a tissue-knitting cartridge?"

"A few times, yeah. Shot just hurts like hell and nothing happens."

He gave a rueful nod, then stepped to grab a biotool off the counter. Tapping to activate it, a beam of green light fanned out and he dragged it along each of her arms. It beeped and his eyes traced over the readout.

He set the biotool down, bringing a draft of heat toward her as he stepped close. He ran his thumb gently against the inside of her elbow, tracing it up her arm and shoulder, then across her collarbone. He pressed against the edge of the bruising at the base of her neck, sending a spike of pain down her arm. She winced and exhaled a groan.

"Sorry," he rumbled. "Well, it's warm, and the skin's moist. I'd be more worried if it was showin' signs of decay. I think it'll heal, given time."

"You don't sound very sure."

He shook his head. "I'm no Viator Imprint expert, sir. I've no training in them. Honestly, I've not seen anything like this. I'm not sure what we can expect."

She licked her lips slowly and nodded.

"We should do a weekly checkup to keep on top of it. For now, I'll synthesize a topical ointment that should expedite the healing."

Ford tasked the synthesizer to start on the ointment, then pulled a few supplies from the cabinet. He carefully cleansed each of the wounds, doing a far better job than she'd been able to do herself over the weeks.

When the ointment was done, he applied a thin coating, then started to re-dress her arms in dry gauze.

"Those wraps are great for burns and bruising," he explained, "but you need'ta use regular gauze to cover 'em for a few hours after you've applied the ointment. Sleep with 'em clean and uncovered if you can. Let's try the ointment twice a day to start. Feel free to come back here and I—er, we can apply it for you, if you prefer."

He finished with the gauze, then used a low-power version of the biotool's cauterization mode to seal the ends in place. She tilted her head as she watched him work. She'd never thought to use a biotool that way before.

"You need'ta try and not use your Imprints." He rested against the edge of the table beside her. "At all, if possible, for at least a few weeks. The ointment'll help close the wounds, but the deeper tissue and muscles need time. So you need to sit as quietly as possible for the next short while. No training, no drills. Lotsa water. Get as much rest as you can." His gaze drifted over her. "Can you do that for me, sir?"

She arched an eyebrow at him in a leery glare. "Yeah . . ."

He tilted his head. "Sorry, sir. Just wanna make sure we're on the same page. North warned me you might not be the most cooperative patient."

She clenched her teeth. "Well, you can 'warn' *North* that I'm a big girl, and he can fuck off."

Ford gave a broad smile. "Is that an order? 'Cause I'd be more than glad to deliver that message."

She resisted the amusement tugging at the corner of her lips. He had one of those annoyingly contagious smiles.

"I'll not use my Imprints," she assured him, "unless it's an emergency."

"Sounds like a deal, sir. I'll have the rest of the ointment sent up to your stateroom once it's done." He pushed away from the exam table and headed for the door. "I'll grab you some more gauze to take with."

Ford left, and the door stayed open in his wake. He headed straight across the central hub to a stack of unpacked crates on the far wall. He opened the top crate and dug around inside.

A few seconds later, Jackin approached. Ford threw him a smile and Jackin's eyes were bright with response, but Adequin was too far to hear what they were saying. Ford passed Jackin a packet of gauze, then pointed to Adequin's room. Jackin started toward her, and she forced her gaze off into the corner. As if not looking somehow meant he'd go away.

Jackin rapped on the door frame. "Gauze delivery . . ."

Her cheeks heated as she looked over at him. His brow furrowed, dark brown eyes tracing up and down her exposed arms. She grabbed her jacket and pulled it on, covering the worst of it, though he'd already seen plenty.

"Void, Rake." He gave a sorrowful head shake. "Why didn't you tell me about this? I had to find out from the kid?"

"I wouldn't have told him either, but he punched me in the forearm."

Jackin froze. "Cavalon punched you?"

"Relax. We worked it out."

"Well . . . shit, okay. It'll heal, at least. Ford says you need to keep from using your Imprints for a while, though."

"Yeah, yeah, I know."

Jackin eyed the few doctors milling about outside, then sidled up to the exam table, lowering his voice considerably. "I took care of the Snyder thing."

She lifted a brow. "Took care?"

"All the witnesses were taken straight to holding and we cleared up any misunderstandings. They all understand what happened." He leveled an even look at her. "The facts are clear now."

"What facts?" she scoffed.

"That Snyder tried to kill you, and you were defending yourself."

Her pulse beat loud in her ears.

"That he'd loaded up on quill, and because of your . . ." His wounded look flitted down to her wrapped arms. "Because of your injuries, you weren't able to use your Imprints to defend yourself. So when he pulled a knife, you had to shut him in the airlock to stop him. A malfunction triggered the outer seal to release."

Adequin stared back at Jackin, unblinking, unable to form a response.

"Emery had a damn knife on her for some reason," Jackin grumbled, letting out a strained sigh. "She's already gone on record saying Snyder disarmed her and turned it on you. There'll still be rumors, there's nothing we can do about that. But we've established the official record early, at least."

"Jack," Adequin croaked, unsure whether to be horrified or thankful. "Why would you do that?"

His gaze heated, sharp and unforgiving. "Remember what I said before?" he growled. "One wrong move, and this whole pile of kindling will go up in flames."

Her nails dug into her palms.

"I had to snuff it out," he continued. "You gave me no choice."

"Well, void, Jack—that was some shrewd scheming. And a damn fast response time."

"Would you rather I'd sat on it and let it fester for a few days?"

"Just curious how a former navigations officer learns how to incident manage like that."

He stared, expression deadpan.

"Though, shit," she continued, "for all I know, you could have been a fixer for the Ninth during that mysterious gap in your service record."

"Void, Rake." He crackled out a weary sigh. "That shit's a myth and you know it."

She hadn't meant it seriously, but by the way his expression flattened, unblinking, too steady, she almost felt she'd hit on something. There were long-standing rumors of an undeclared ninth command component of the Legion, dedicated entirely to carrying out dirty work for the System Collective's various political messes. Even as a Titan, she'd never learned whether there was any truth to it. But she didn't even care. She was sick of trying to piece together Jackin's past from fragments of his reactions during his carefully devised responses.

"It may have been a ruthless fix," Jackin gritted out, "but I had good reason."

"And what's that?"

"I give a shit about you, okay? I was trying to protect you." He swept a hand out behind him. "To protect all of this. I don't want to see this ship revolt against you. Is that what *you* want?"

She ground her teeth. "Of course not."

"Then stop acting like it. For all our sakes." Jackin yanked a small tablet from his belt and dropped it on the exam table beside her. "I wrote you a script for the dedication ceremony. I suggest you stick to it."

Her brow creased. "Dedication ceremony? When?"

"Night after next, assuming all goes well with the reactor. Mesa seemed confident it'd be ready the day after tomorrow."

A lightness rose in her chest. They could have a working jump drive on the ship in less than two days.

But any hope extinguished quickly, replaced by a swell of guilt. She'd tried to kill one of her own soldiers yesterday, and if it wasn't for Cavalon's quick response, she would have been responsible for his death. And now, because of the lie they'd built, Snyder's service record would be blackened by assault of a commanding officer, maybe attempted murder. Not that service records really mattered anymore.

Jackin watched her agonizing, and his scowl faded a sliver. He stared down, hands on hips, boot tapping out a nervous rhythm on the floor. His mouth pinched with suppressed words, but he only gave a single shake of his head, then left.

Two days later, Adequin arrived at the stifling hot reactor bay.

Cavalon and Emery milled about up on the scaffolding, while Mesa and Owen worked at the primary computer terminal. Around the bay, a dozen other soldiers attended various tasks—some packed diagnostic equipment, some cleaned workbenches, others doted over a mess of cabling that disappeared into the floor on the far side of the reactor orb. Two oculi guided another as they steered a gantry into place, hoisting a large, arcing piece of the reactor's shell in its grip.

Adequin leaned against the wall near the entrance and watched, not wanting to distract them when they were so close to finishing. She could have arrived fashionably late to give them some leeway, but she'd completely exhausted her willingness to sit in that high-backed praetor's chair, reviewing the backlog of incident reports and fielding the endless stream of messages from the other commanders. She was running out of creative ways to dodge meetings.

The door behind her slid open, bringing a waft of cooler air that chilled the sweat on the back of her neck. Jackin stepped up beside her. He crossed his arms and stared out across the bay.

"Not quite ready," she said, and he nodded, not meeting her eye. He hadn't exactly *ignored* her for the last two days, but their exchanges had been perfunctory at best. "How'd the meeting with Puck go?" she prompted.

"Fine," he replied curtly, then shook his head and some of the formality dropped from his demeanor. "He doesn't see a way around it. The second we've relayed through Poine, the *Typhos*'ll try to connect to the Legion extranet."

"So we keep the array deactivated?"

He nodded. "For the foreseeable future, yeah. I also asked him to look into how those OCR thugs hacked the Sentinel Imprint control system."

"Good," Adequin said, "have him earmark that for later."

Jackin quirked a brow.

"It doesn't seem like a bad idea for us to have a way to selectively disable them once we get back to the Core. We don't need the Legion to have any more advantages than they already do."

"Yeah," he sighed out in a crackling grumble. "Fair point."

She glanced back at the bay doors. "Where is Puck, anyway?"

"He's going to . . . not be in the same room as all of us when we start this thing."

"You don't trust Cavalon?"

"I do. But I also understand what we asked of him."

She blew out a soft breath. She had to agree; it was a lot. Maybe too much.

They fell into silence. Mesa's soft chatter and Cavalon's boot scuffs cut over the whining bursts of an impact driver echoing off the walls.

Adequin eyed Jackin in her periphery. "That's why I did it, you know."

Jackin glanced at her. "Did what?"

"Lost my temper on Snyder."

"Tried to kill him, you mean?"

She cleared her throat. "Yeah." She kept her gaze trained on Cavalon. "We can't risk him. He's too important."

Jackin scratched the scarred side of his beard and shook his head. "I know that. But there's another way. One that doesn't involve untried capital punishments."

"I know."

They watched the others work in weighted silence for a long stretch until finally, Jackin spoke again. "You ready for tonight?"

She blew out a sigh. The dedication ceremony. To say she wasn't looking forward to it would be such an irresponsibly drastic understatement. "Ready as I can be," she mumbled.

"Listen," he said, a serious warning in his tone. Adequin's gaze drifted to him, though he still stared off at the reactor orb and didn't meet her eyes. "I picked up your slack in that meeting with the commanders— hell, since you stepped foot on this ship again, but this dedication is all you. Don't screw it up."

She exhaled through clenched teeth, nodding stiffly. She hadn't intended to *purposefully* screw it up; then again over the last two days she hadn't spared even a minute of thought over what she was going to say. She supposed she should at least read through the speech Jackin had given her.

Finally, Emery dismissed all their oculus assistants, then threw a broad grin over her shoulder. "Sirs, we're ready!"

Adequin and Jackin headed for the workbenches as Mesa and Owen approached. Adequin caught Cavalon's eye as he rounded the scaffolding, and he gave a nod of acknowledgment, pale cheeks pink and glistening with sweat. He slid down the ladder and joined them.

Mesa brought up a series of screens over the glass worktop. She and Cavalon ran down a checklist, reviewing diagnostics and spooling up subsystem after subsystem. With each activation, Cavalon grew more outwardly agitated, knuckles going white against the countertop. Then, for a few silent moments, he and Mesa shared a look of barely perceptible agreement.

Mesa leveled her overlarge eyes at Adequin. "Excubitor, subsystems are operational and functioning within expected standards. We are prepared to activate the reactor on your authorization. Do you have any questions before we proceed?"

Adequin leaned both hands on the workbench. "Does this mean the jump drive will be ready as well?"

Mesa shook her head. "Not immediately, no. Once the reactor is activated, we will need to run evaluations to ensure proper interaction with the jump drive components. Also the mass must be monitored, for a time. It is best if we ensure stability and output levels before placing a load on the photovoltaic bridge."

"How long will it need monitored?" Adequin asked.

"The star should settle into its full maturity after approximately fifteen hours. I would like to monitor its stability for an additional fifteen hours after that, during which we may run any required function tests."

"Understood," Adequin said. She didn't like the idea of waiting even longer, but she'd rather they be careful. Thirty hours wouldn't make or break them, even with their current food issues.

"The hydrogen has already been injected," Mesa said, "so we are ready on your order."

Adequin nodded. This part, she was familiar with. "Go ahead."

Cavalon moved to a new set of screens and opened a menu. He cleared his throat, eyeing Mesa, then Owen. Each stood behind their own set of screens, hands hovering. Emery watched from over Owen's shoulder.

"Everyone keep eyes on the cryostat," Cavalon warned. "If we have to pull the plug, remember to throttle the fuel cycler first. Last thing we need's this bad boy goin' supernova on us."

Adequin exchanged an apprehensive glance with Jackin.

"Initializing . . ." Cavalon lifted a finger to the holographic screen, then tapped a small white box.

The reactor produced an innocent clicking noise, followed by a dense pulse of electronic thrumming. In an instant, the air of the room heated, and Adequin's skin pricked with more sweat.

Every gaze except Mesa's and Cavalon's drifted to the massive orb, which looked exactly the same as before. Unlike those aboard the dark energy generators, they'd built no observation window into the exterior shell. Whatever was happening inside was only visible to the diagnostic instruments, and to anyone smart enough to understand what the numbers meant.

"Coil heat is elevated," Mesa warned, "6.4 K and rising."

Cavalon wiped his brow with the back of his hand. "O, how're those pipes looking?"

"Transferral's still developing," Owen replied, stony glare locked on her screen. "Eighty-six percent. It'll work."

"5.5 and lowering," Mesa updated.

"Ninety-six," Owen said, giving a firm nod. "That's our top floor."

A few long moments later, Mesa said, "4 K. Temperature is stabilizing."

Owen smiled across the workbench at Cavalon. "Told you. It's working, bud."

Cavalon's cheeks were ghost white as he gave a disbelieving nod. "How're the divertors holding up?"

Mesa nodded. "Vertical target flux is steady at ten megawatts."

A grin tugged at Cavalon's mouth. Apparently that was a good answer.

After a few more minutes they'd all quieted down, watching their readouts with clenched jaws, eyes unblinking.

"Reactor stability is excellent," Mesa reported finally, and a wave of relief rolled across the group. "All subsystems nominal."

Adequin gripped Cavalon's sweaty shoulder. "Good work, Animus."

He beamed at her. "Thanks, sir."

Adequin thanked Mesa as well, then Emery and Owen for whatever part they'd played over the last few days. The others traded bewildered, yet exultant handshakes and hugs, much the same haggard elation they'd exchanged when they'd restarted the first one six months ago. This one might not be saving them from immediate death and helping to stop the universe from collapsing . . . but its task felt equally important.

Adequin checked the time on her nexus. Thirty hours would be 1900 tomorrow. The minutes couldn't go by quick enough.

That evening, Adequin stood in her stateroom staring at a garment bag with an arch-browed glower. She'd never been a fan of dress blues. The forced formality seemed the way of a bygone age, not the practicality of open war she'd been used to for much of her career. So she'd been disappointed to learn that someone aboard the *Typhos* had found a cache of Viator War–era officer's blues, and now intended to inflict the spoils of their artifact-hunting expedition on her.

She glanced at her nexus. The dedication ceremony was due to start in less than an hour. Despite how frustrated she was with Jackin right now, she also—quite annoyingly—found herself eager to earn his approval. If putting on a two-hundred-year-old costume would assuage him, she'd happily oblige.

So she showered, then tried to emulate Ford's patience as she applied the ointment and wrapped her arms. Though it eased the pain somewhat for a few hours after application, she hadn't seen any improvement, for either the open sores, or the veins and bruising, which continued to climb onto the tops of her hands and across her collarbones. She hoped the design of the dress blues could hide the worst of it.

She unzipped the garment bag, revealing a multitiered hanger draped in various pieces of navy-blue fabric. It looked like the great-uncle version of their modern dress uniforms, with more bronze buttons, hooks, and accents.

She lugged the bag across the room and hung it beside the floor-length mirror on the wall. She donned the slim-fitting pants and had started tucking in the undershirt when her door chime sounded.

"Centurion North," the artificial voice of her room's VI announced.

"Let him in," she instructed. She glanced back as the door slid open.

Jackin stood in the door frame, hands slid in his pockets, looking irritatingly smart in his own dress blues—the same overstated affair of navy and bronze as her own, only with slightly fewer colors on the sleeve.

He hesitated, eyeing her bruised arms warily.

"Coming in or not?" she asked as she pulled her jacket from the garment bag.

He stepped in, and the door shut behind him. He leaned against the wall beside the mirror, and she gave him a discerning once-over, using him as a template. There were still a lot of pieces in that bag she wasn't quite sure what to do with.

The jacket was pretty standard—closing with a panel down the front, buttoned off to one side. Bronze piping lined the seams, and the shoulder pads resembled hardsuit spaulders but were made of stiff brown leather. A single darker navy layer wrapped around his shoulders and dropped off his right hip, hitting just below the knee. The extraneous piece removed any pretense of practicality.

"Is a whole ceremony really necessary?" She tugged into the narrow sleeves of the jacket. "Can't we just push out a notification to nexuses?"

"Yes, it's necessary, and no, we can't."

She drew her jacket closed and started to fasten the first of a dozen bronze buttons, each embossed with the Legion logo—a four-pointed star intersecting a hexagon. "You know," she cautioned, "by most standards, renaming a ship is bad luck."

"They already renamed most Sentinel ships anyway," he replied. "The *Argus* was the *Rivolus* during the Viator War."

"Yeah, and look how that turned out."

He gave her a flat look. "We need to disassociate ourselves from the Legion, but we still have to use their supplies and ranks and uniforms. Renaming one of their capital ships as our own is the most overt thing we can do, for now."

"Yeah, I know. I just don't know why I have to stand up in front of everyone to announce it."

"Partly because you threw someone out a damn airlock the other day."

Adequin huffed a sigh as she tugged on the stiff boots. She returned to the garment bag and pulled out a piece of darker navy fabric, full of tiny hooks and sharp corners and strange angles.

She frowned as she eyed Jackin's dark navy layer, trying to discern how it worked. She turned it over in her hands, becoming less and less sure which way was up.

Jackin exhaled a soft sigh and stepped forward, taking the formless piece of fabric from her. He hooked the narrowest strip to her left shoulder, then draped it across her chest and tight around her right shoulder before drawing it down her back and around the front again. He pinned the angular front piece in two spots—one high on her right shoulder, the other on her right hip, and the asymmetrical tabard fell into place.

"Thanks," she murmured. He stepped to the garment bag and took out the spaulders. "Any updates on Snyder?" she asked, voice thin and quiet. "I saw him briefly in the medbay the other day, but Ford wouldn't—"

"He's fine," Jackin said, equally quiet. "He'll need better skin grafting once we can get access to some modern medical equipment. But he'll recover."

He stepped close to attach her shoulder pads, and she picked at her cuticles, gaze going unfocused on his chest. "Thanks, Jack . . . for taking care of that. I didn't intend for it to become a mess for you to clean up. I clearly didn't think it through."

He cast a quick glance at her from under his lowered brow, then refocused on attaching her spaulders and didn't respond.

"I know I haven't been the leader you hoped for," she continued. "I'm sorry. I just need some time to reorient."

He shook his head. "I don't get it. I've seen you seize command before without even flinching. The *Argus* was on the brink of mutiny when you arrived, and you whipped things into shape within a couple weeks. I know you're capable of this kind of command, and you should too."

"That was command of two hundred, not four thousand. And two hundred people I let die, last I checked."

He blinked slowly, then his eyes sharpened. "I see."

Warmth crept up her neck. "See what?

"You think you're going to get them all killed again."

Her gaze flitted down. "Yeah," she admitted.

"If you don't cut out this self-pity bullshit," he said, tone hard, "that's exactly what's going to happen."

She gritted her teeth. "I'm trying, but I didn't ask for this."

His lips parted, brow flattening. "You didn't ask for this?" he said, voice thin with disbelief. "You *specifically* asked for this, Rake. You wanted mutiny, and you're getting it. This is what it looks like."

She glared, posture going stiff.

"Void, Rake," he cursed, pacing away a few steps, hands on hips as he turned back to face her. "You made a decision that makes every one of these people a traitor to their government. Do you even realize that?"

"Of course I do."

"So if they don't die out here via the Divide," he went on, his abrasive tone rising, "or catastrophic engine failure, Drudgers, starvation, or void-only-knows what else, then they'll die back at the Core at the hands of their own government." He pushed a stiff hand through his wavy hair, shaking his head. "Do us a favor and figure your shit out, before it gets us all killed." He stalked toward the door. "Don't be late," he grumbled, then left.

Adequin watched the door slide shut, frenzied pulse racing, bruised arms and shoulders aching with the rush of blood.

Well, that'd fucking backfired.

Though she couldn't reason out why she continued to bother. She'd tolerate his insubordination to a point, but in the end she was still his commander, and he owed her a degree of respect. She'd always thought they'd been more than just comrades, but this was looking less and less like anything resembling friendship. If Jackin wanted to be nothing but a judgmental second, so be it. She was tired of trying.

Jaw clenched, she turned to the mirror, yanking to adjust the angles of fabric draped around her shoulders. A nodule of truth nagged at her, one that no amount of roughing up her wardrobe could change. Because regardless of how mad she was, Jackin was right.

She'd started this, and she owed it to everyone to figure out how to guide them in a way that wouldn't get them all killed, whether on this side of Kharon Gate or the other. She already knew exactly what held her back, and it wasn't nearly as simple as mourning Griffith and the *Argus* as she'd let Cavalon believe. She'd buried it, let her training instinctively suppress it. Because what she really wanted out of all this was vengeance.

She'd been out of commission for weeks, saving more Sentinels, yes, but effectively treading water. There hadn't been an opportunity to exact the revenge she felt she needed. She was stuck in a holding pattern it was impossible to escape from, striving to undo something that'd already been done.

She couldn't let herself become consumed by it. She loved Griffith,

and she always would, but that was the past. This reactor led to their future. She had to put what'd happened at the Divide behind her.

That meant letting go—of Griffith, the *Argus*, and the thousands of
other Sentinels they'd lost. That meant embracing what she'd been too
scared to become, the role she'd gladly let Jackin hold in her stead for the
last six months—the responsibility she'd so desperately wanted to avoid.
Whether she wanted to or not, she had to become the leader of this
rebellion.

CHAPTER ELEVEN

Cavalon paced a nervous trench through the communal living area outside Emery and Owen's bunk rooms. He sipped on the bitter heat of his approved daily ration of coffee and tugged at his too-snug collar. He hadn't put on a suit since his last formal Allied Monarchies' affair over two years ago, and he'd never intended to again. Though these musty ancient dress blues felt more like playing dress-up.

Emery sat on a short couch with her knees tucked up, fingers filing through a worn packet of gum as she counted under her breath. Their other bunkmates had either already left for the ceremony, or didn't exist. The *Typhos* had once accommodated over ten thousand, so they weren't exactly short on living space.

Emery folded a piece of gum into her mouth, then pocketed the remainder inside her duty vest, smoothing over the front as she strapped it closed. Only those of animus rank and higher were required to wear the old suits.

Owen stepped out from a bunk room, hair rumpled and arms stretching high overhead.

Emery smiled over at her. "Mornin', sunshine. Was just about to wake ya."

Owen creaked out a yawn. "This getting turned around to ship time bullshit is . . ." She rubbed a knuckle into her eye. "Bullshit."

Cavalon chewed the inside of his cheek as he kept up his short orbit around the small arc of worn furniture. Maybe he had time to run down and check on it one last time. "How long do we have?" he asked.

"Twenty minutes," Emery replied.

He ground his teeth. Definitely not enough time. He huffed out a breath, continuing his loop.

Owen slumped against the door frame, narrowed eyes tracking him as he paced. "Dude, can you . . . not?"

"What?"

"Pace frantically?"

He halted, leveling a disgruntled look at her. "I'm not 'pacing frantically.'" He swept his flat hand in a drifting arc away from his chest, as if smoothing out a sheet. "I'm excising the pent-up anxiety from my body via repetitious physical exertion. It's fucking cathartic."

Owen stepped around the couch and slid the coffee out of his grip.

"Take it down a notch, man," she said slowly, half-tempering, half-annoyed. "Remember that whole food rationing thing? I don't think your reduced caloric intake can afford this much anxiety."

He heaved out a breath. "I'm sorry, okay? I built a fucking star in the basement and now it's just sitting down there with fucking *Erandus* watching over it—"

"I know, I know," she purred, dragging a placating hand down the side of his arm. "You left your baby alone for the first time; it's tough on every new parent."

He frowned, toes twitching in his slightly too-small costume boots as he fought the urge to pace again.

Owen took him by the arm, leading him to sit on the couch beside Emery. "Take a seat. Try to relax." She took a sip of his coffee, and her face contorted into a tight grimace. "Ugh. This shit's somehow worse than what we had on the *Syn*."

She went to the sink in the corner of the room and poured the coffee out. Cavalon tried not to lament the lost caffeine. Besides, she was right. He wasn't sure his body could handle any more blood pressure.

A clanging knock sounded, and Cavalon looked over to find Warner standing in the open door frame, looking rather trim in his cleaned and pressed uniform.

Emery practically squealed as she swung her legs up and vaulted over the top of the couch. She charged Warner, grasping him in a hug. An honest-to-the-void *smile* broke the man's normally gruff mask of inscrutability.

"Welcome back, Em," he rumbled.

Cavalon quirked a brow. "What is . . ." He scratched at his beard with both hands. "Happening?"

Emery released her hold on Warner and looked back at Cavalon. "You okay, boss?"

He shook his head. "You were *both* at the escape pods the other day," he accused. "Or did I imagine that?"

"No, we were," Warner replied.

"So how is this a reunion?"

"That was different," Emery explained with a frown. "That was all serious and bad and stuff." She shared another smile with Warner. "We didn't get to say a proper hello."

Warner quirked a brow. "This gonna work as a proper hello?"

"Oh, hell no," Emery said. "A *proper* hello will require at least half a bottle of something."

Warner nodded his agreement, sandy brown eyes smiling along with his whole mouth . . . Apparently Warner's teeth were very white and very straight. Cavalon fixated on the strange sight, unable to look away.

Emery shoved Warner's shoulder. "What're ya doin' here, Mister Big Shot Security Man? Figured you'd be busy prepping for the ceremony."

Warner sighed. "I am. Here on business, I'm afraid." He glanced at Cavalon. "To escort the animus."

Cavalon glowered at Warner. "You tracking my nexus?"

Warner crossed his arms. "I wouldn't need to if you'd have stayed in your quarters as instructed."

Owen picked up her duty vest from the back of the couch and shrugged it on, then offered a hand to Cavalon. "Ready, bud?"

"I guess." He took her grip, and she hauled him to standing. She faced him squarely, then licked her fingers and went to swipe a strand of his hair off his forehead. He dodged and tried to push her away, but she slipped aside, cackling as she mussed his hair up even worse.

"O!" he whined.

"Void." Warner let out a low chuckle. "You weren't kidding when you said those two are like siblings."

Emery snickered.

"I wouldn't know," Cavalon gritted out, glowering as he locked his elbows to hold Owen firmly at arm's reach. "Are siblings *the worst*? 'Cause then, yeah."

"Aw," Emery crooned, "let him be, babe."

Owen relented, pushing his hands aside as she stepped away. "Fine." She fought her smirk into a frown as she padded over to Emery, then whined, "He's such a baby, though."

Emery hooked her arm into Owen's, and the two headed for the door.

Warner stepped aside to let them pass. "You two go ahead," he said, "I'm escorting princeps in last. EX's orders."

Cavalon frowned. Though he couldn't say it was the worst idea ever.

Emery's face fell as her eyes scanned Cavalon's dress blues. "Oh. Gotcha."

She gave a somber wave and left as Owen offered a mocking salute. Cavalon glared.

After failing to make small talk with Warner on the painful ten-minute walk, Cavalon arrived at hangar bay E1. A hum filled his ears, the quiet chatter of thousands.

The Sentinels stood in loose square formations of two or three hundred each, likely gathered by origin ship. What had to be every single one of the hundred-some armored MPs stood on guard around the vast hangar, each clutching a shock baton.

The gathered crowd faced the far bulkhead, on which hung a large tapestry embroidered with the Sentinel logo: two angular C shapes turned against each other, the negative space creating a blocky S fracturing a hexagon. At the foot of the banner stood a small raised platform, home to a podium and a small table topped by a navy-blue pennant and a dark glass bottle, reminding Cavalon why it was they were even there—to rename the *Typhos* in honor of . . . whatever they were now.

During his princely upbringing, he'd been made to attend more ship dedication ceremonies than he cared to remember, so he was aware of most of the traditions. The Legion had adopted the ancient Elyseian version—ceremonial liquid broken against a bulkhead, the raising of the pennant followed by the call of the first watch. A simple process that should get him in and out in short order, and back to staring anxiously at the reactor's diagnostic readouts.

Cavalon looked out over the crowd to find a place to stand.

"This way, princeps." Warner overtook him, eyes laser-focused into the nearest crowd, as if an assassin might leap out any second. When Cavalon didn't immediately follow, Warner gripped his elbow and hauled him forward.

"Relax, buddy," Cavalon said, then lowered his voice. "They can murder me now, I already finished it. Mesa knows how to push the go button."

Warner didn't even have the goodwill to look annoyed, his gaze staying sharp on the crowd as he towed Cavalon down the long main aisle.

As they passed, Cavalon waved at Emery and Owen, who stood amongst a few others from the *Argus*—Eura and two of her oculus friends from the *Tempus*, along with Erandus's blond pal, Murillo. Owen gave one of her well-aren't-you-just-a-special-fucking-flower eye rolls.

Warner gripped his elbow harder and dragged him on.

Head low and shoulders hunched, Cavalon followed the rest of the way willingly. But he didn't have to like it. It was too reminiscent of his life as a royal: being isolated by design, separated because someone had given him a rank and a few more colored badges and a fancy suit. He tried to remind himself that unlike his royal heritage, he'd *earned* that rank and those colored badges and the fancy suit.

Yet he couldn't shake the feeling it was all temporary. Proving his mettle had become a constant, looping background task to maintain, or risk his worth becoming null. After all, the closer they got to a functioning jump drive, the closer they got to not needing him. How many colossal astromechanical undertakings could one rebel army possibly need? His only other use was as a geneticist, and he wanted nothing to do with that. His ancestors had done enough meddling in the human genome for the whole of their species's existence.

Soon it'd come down to the basics: soldiers, ships, guns, food—which all required money. Money he had, he supposed, in the form of his inheritance and a few well-placed investments, *if* he could get his hands on it. Plenty to fund an army this size, at least for a while.

He'd more than gladly bankroll Augustus's eventual demise, but what use could he really offer the Sentinels beyond that? Maybe some keen insight into his shithead grandfather, and how—and how quickly—more Drudger clone "Guardians" could be printed. He supposed he could offer inside information on the five royal families. How deep the corruption of the Quorum really went. Much to his chagrin, his steel-trap brain was privy to the dark secrets of more than a few royals and senators, which surely could be exploited somehow, maybe leveraged as blackmail.

The thought of descending into some kind of political advisory role caused his entire body to break into a cold sweat, and he half-stumbled while walking.

He could only hope Rake would get sick of him before that time came. That outdated knowledge wouldn't make a dent in what they were up against anyway.

Cavalon almost ran square into Warner's back as he came to a dead stop at the head of the central aisle. Cavalon's chin rose, eyeing the massive Sentinel flag looming over them.

In front of the platform, a collection of higher-ranking officers stood chatting in small groups. Mesa stood out, her lithe Savant frame making her easy to spot, along with the fact that she'd somehow gotten out of the vintage dress-up party. It was possible they hadn't had one small enough to fit her.

Puck, on the other hand, had the opposite problem, his suit easily a few centimeters too short in both sleeve and inseam. It didn't seem to bother him in the slightest as he grinned down at Mesa, well over a head taller than her, and half a head taller than most of those around him.

At least Cavalon wouldn't be completely alone amongst the chattering Sentinel commanders, a fate akin to physical torture.

Warner nudged him and gave an encouraging grunt. Cavalon excused himself past a couple of haughty-looking legators to stand beside Mesa. She acknowledged him with a steady incline of her head and Puck flashed a welcoming grin, but Cavalon hardly registered it as he stared at the *centurion* badges on his former CO's shoulders. In his focused haze knuckling down on the reactor, he'd totally missed that promotion on the bulletins.

Warner settled into a post at the end of the aisle with a good vantage of the surrounding crowds. His keen gaze drifted, both unreadably indistinct and hyperfocused, a practiced look Cavalon recognized all too well after almost thirty years of being followed around by the Mercer Guard.

Some of the officers on the other side of Puck shuffled suddenly, moving aside to let Jackin pass in front of them, his light brown skin flushed with exertion or frustration, maybe both. His black hair had been combed back, and he'd given the sides a trim since Cavalon had seen him last, along with a bit of a beard tidy, which exposed the long scar reaching down his right cheek and under the high collar of his jacket.

Jackin nodded to Cavalon, Puck, and Mesa, then took up a spot beside the officer in front of Cavalon, a man with coppery-blond hair and a square face—Beckar, the *Typhos*'s former optio. Jackin leaned in and whispered something to Beckar, who gave a short nod.

A hush fell across the crowd, and Cavalon's gaze mechanically drifted to the front.

Rake had stepped onto the side of the short stage, her back straight, chin level, doing the dress blues a great deal more justice than anyone he'd seen yet. She paced to the podium and set a small tablet on the clear glass top.

She looked out across the crowd, her gaze hard, yet oddly curious, like she was trying to gauge their collective merit just by staring at them. Cavalon wasn't sure what to make of it, but he was fairly certain public speaking wasn't an inherent trait of a Titan, so he assumed this would be interesting.

Jackin folded his arms tight over his chest while his foot began to tap. He stared at Rake with barely concealed distress, like she might nuke the place.

Rake rapped the top of the podium with a knuckle, then cleared her throat. The sound system sent the crackling noise echoing out over the crowd. The silence somehow grew quieter, and thousands of soldiers stared as Rake looked down at her tablet.

"Good evening . . ." She cleared her throat again, not looking up. "I'm Excubitor Adequin Rake, and it's my . . . pleasure to welcome you to this dedication ceremony. I've not had a chance to meet all of you yet, but I . . . look forward to working with you as we begin this journey together."

Jackin's stiff shoulders slackened, and his boot slowed as Rake continued her banal recitation.

"The SCS *Typhos* was commissioned in 106 BV at the Astraeus Shipyard in the Cautis System. It served the First under five different praetors, traveling hundreds of thousands of light-years across every sector of the galaxy. It acted as a symbol of humanity's strength and unity for eighty years before being decommissioned in 25 BV. In 1 AV, it traveled to the Divide to become the fourth Sentinel outpost.

"This evening, the *Typhos* will be brought out of retirement, renamed and rededicated as we prepare it for its next tour of duty in service to the Sentinels. Which, as many of you have likely surmised, means I have some good news to share." She finally looked up from the tablet, gaze drifting aimlessly across the crowd. "Earlier this afternoon, the reactor project was completed."

A steady rise of murmurs and confused hesitation filled the hangar as the words sunk in, then a staggered belt of cheering applause erupted across the room. Cavalon winced, the roar of thousands reacting in unison an onslaught to his eardrums.

The officers around him and Mesa turned to harass them with praise, and heat bloomed in his cheeks. Beckar shook his hand first, with an almost too-firm grip, then he blindly exchanged handshakes while others clasped his shoulders or offered pats on the back. Mesa received a similar deluge, and Puck grinned ear to ear, gripping her shoulder and rocking her back and forth gently as if trying to coax some show of self-pride out of her. Her thin lips did manage to press out a smile, but it seemed more a reaction to Puck's exuberance than the others' appreciation.

Another hush fell across the crowd as Rake raised a hand to quiet them, dampening the show of collective optimism in a matter of seconds.

"Tomorrow," Rake said, "we'll be activating the jump drive for the first time. As we journey inward . . . it's possible we'll encounter resistance. The *Typhos*'s engines are old, and we may need to defend ourselves while the drive spools between jumps."

Cavalon noted how she didn't specify what *kind* of resistance that could be. Many Sentinels likely believed rogue Drudgers were their biggest concern.

He glanced out across the attentive crowd, wondering how many of them erroneously thought they'd be going home.

"Which is why," Rake went on, "all operations, navigation, weapons, and defense systems posts are on-call until further notice. The watch schedule on the network has already been updated. See your CO if you have further questions . . ."

Rake paused as she stared straight down, her fingers stiffening around the tablet.

Jackin's boot started up a nervous rhythm.

Rake's chest heaved as she let out a sigh. Her shoulders drew down. "I'm sorry."

The two words echoed out across the hangar, and she discarded the tablet onto the podium top.

"I know I haven't been here. I've not been the leader you need. That you deserve. I'm trying."

Cavalon's breaths slowed. He was quite sure it'd never been more silent anywhere in all of human history. Even Jackin's foot tapping had been shocked into stillness.

Rake hung her head for a few long moments. "We've all lost so much the last few months. So many people. People we cared about."

Heads bobbed and downcast looks were exchanged, but silence still permeated the hangar.

"I don't know what solace it might offer," she went on, "but I do, truly, know how you feel. I couldn't save most of my crew. Including . . . someone I loved."

A dull ache pulsed in Cavalon's chest. It hurt to see her this exposed, in front of so many. Though it was a smart move.

One of the crueler aspects of his upbringing had been rigorous training in public speaking. Rake was adopting a classic tactic: seeding an authentic connection with the crowd. It inspired trust, faith, and proved one worthy of listening to—and rallying behind. This was just a really intense, really sincere version of that. A very Rake version. He doubted she'd even consciously deployed it.

Judging by the unblinking, captivated stares of every single person in Cavalon's view, it was working, tactic or not. One glance at Jackin's fixed look of shock, and Cavalon was fairly sure it wasn't part of *his* plan.

"I need to heal from that loss," Rake said. "We all do. I'm trying to find a way."

Tingling relief coursed through Cavalon, and his back straightened a little. That was what they'd talked about after the Snyder incident—that if she could grieve the *Argus* and Griffith, maybe she could find her way back to that tough but fair and honest compassion. Get herself back on track.

"I question every day whether I made the right decisions six months ago," she continued. "Whether I could have done something to change the outcome of all this." She gave a tight, bitter smile. "Here on the *Typhos*, our many time ripple friends like to remind us of those possibilities, quite often."

Nervous, conceding chuckles rumbled quietly through the crowd. Cavalon found himself nodding along as well. One of his primary motivations in getting the drive done was the promise of getting rid of those damn ripples. They would only need to make the first of their two required jumps toward Kharon Gate before they'd be free of them.

"I can't say if this is the best of those possible futures," Rake went on. "Maybe there's something I could have done differently . . . I'll never know. But we're all familiar with making mistakes. We all did something, of one kind or another, to end up out here. Some worse than others, maybe." Rake's jaw flexed as she glanced down, shaking her head. "I'm likely the worst of that list."

Cavalon froze, heartbeat catching in his throat. Jackin's jaw slackened, looking briefly horrified before he caught hold of his reaction, and his boot started bouncing harder.

Cavalon exchanged a dismayed glance with Puck and Mesa, then folded his arms tightly over his stomach as he reined in his own nerves, because she *wouldn't*, would she? Tell four thousand tired, frustrated, hungry soldiers she'd let the last Viators of the Resurgence War go free? That if the Legion didn't nuke them the second they traveled through Kharon Gate, that real, live, breathing Viators might?

Cavalon stared up at the ceiling and silently begged every pantheon of supreme beings he didn't believe in for her to move on.

"But we're only human," Rake said quietly, and the strain fled Cavalon's chest, sending out an almost dizzying wave of relief. "We can let those mistakes tear us apart," she continued, "or we can use them to grow stronger." Vigor slowly built in her voice, each word firmer than the next. "Those mistakes brought us together. And now we're being given a choice on how to use that. We survived, despite everything working against us. Unlike our fallen comrades, we have a chance at getting home . . . But home's not safe. Not yet."

Cavalon chewed the inside of his lip, darting his look to those around him. The other Sentinel commanders didn't seem all that surprised, but the purr of the crowd suggested the masses weren't as in-the-know.

"We all know that's true, on some level," Rake said. "That if the Legion cared about us, if they wanted us alive, we wouldn't be here now, like this. With two-thirds of us dead. And not a rescue ark in sight."

The temperament of the crowd altered yet again, mournful gazes hardening with anger. Cavalon had to give her credit, it was frankly impressive how easily she'd roped them all in—intentionally or not. She gave the slightest yank of the emotional leash and they all readily followed.

"So we can go back to the Core, back to the command who left us to die . . ." She paused, glancing at the massive Sentinel flag looming over her. "Or we can make our own path. Make this sacrifice worth it by turning this shitty situation into a solution. Into something more. Our comrades' deaths can be senseless tragedy . . . or they can be kindling."

That final word prompted another rolling mood shift, and Cavalon watched with a fair amount of awe as shoulders dropped, postures straightened, and chins rose.

"Because things back at the Core aren't as peaceful as the SC would like us to think. And we have reason to believe it will only be getting worse."

Her amber-eyed gaze landed right on Cavalon and his anxiety flared. Heat flushed his skin as a realization struck him, deep in the meat of his gut like an untelegraphed right hook: He was *already* her political advisor. Shit.

"We've all heard 'need to know' before," Rake went on, looking back out over the crowd. "And by any interpretation, this is information the Legion wouldn't want me to share. But I don't want to keep you in the dark, or throw you away at the edge the universe. I want you to help me stop what's coming before it's too late. And to do that, you need to know what's really going on.

"For years, the System Collective has been deploying measures to legally impose genetic discrimination and oppression. It's been happening slowly, maybe even since the end of the Viator War. This is most clearly evidenced by the Heritage Edict. For decades, this law has been quietly stripping those with mutagen defects of their citizenships, deporting them from Core worlds to unratified colonies, where they may not get representation in the Quorum for years, if ever."

Cavalon glanced out over the crowd, their expressions a medley of concern, confusion, frustration, or outright anger. In front of him, Jackin shifted his weight, shoulders tensing as he folded his arms tight over his chest.

"The System Collective was created to unite mankind in the face of an alien enemy," Rake said, "but now it's being used against us—to control the population and manipulate its citizens for personal power and wealth. And now, the SC has passed a new directive—the Legion Personnel Welfare Act. They've commissioned a fleet of Drudger clones and intend to replace every operations arm of the Legion with them."

Murmurs rose before being replaced by hushed silence.

"They do this under the guise of ensuring our safety," Rake went on. "But in doing so, they've made a critical oversight. This legislation severely curtails the Legion—an entity meant to be equitably guided by our elected representatives in the Quorum—and instead places the entire militaristic force of mankind under the control of a single man. Of a single monarch, of a single planet. One who certainly doesn't have humanity's best interests at heart."

A rising undercurrent of anger swelled, bringing more murmurs and heated glares. Even Cavalon found himself growing furious, and he'd already known all of this, and then some.

"We've been waiting in the wings out here," Rake continued, "some of us for years, some for a decade, some longer. Wondering if the people we swore an oath to protect would ever need us again. And they do. Just not at the Divide.

"Yes, we could return to the Core and throw ourselves at the mercy of an institution that left us to die, and who, in all likelihood, believes we already have. Or . . . we ready ourselves. We establish a base of operations, gather resources, make connections, and become what the people will need to stand up to the tyrants trying to control them.

"Today, I've asked each of your commanders to come to a decision. About whether to stay with the Sentinels aboard this ship, or to remain at Kharon Gate and attempt to return to the Core, and to the Legion."

Cavalon glanced over his shoulder. From the sudden exchange of confused looks and hushed conversations, he didn't think many of the soldiers had gotten that update from their commanders. Or been asked their opinions.

"No one will be forced to do this," Rake assured them, holding up a hand to quell the rising voices. "Though your commander will speak for your vessel, you as an individual will be given the chance to withdraw at any time from now until we arrive at Kharon Gate. Because this, by every definition, is mutiny. We need everyone to understand that, and fully accept it. And it will not be easy. In fact, it's going to get a lot harder before it gets better.

"But as you make your decision, I'd ask you consider the judgment of your commander, but also keep in mind your comrades who will continue on without you. As well as the ones you've already lost."

Rake let the thought sink in, then looked at the bottle and pennant on the table beside her.

"That's how the Legion dedicated vessels," she murmured. "We're not going to be using any of that . . ." Her brow furrowed as she glanced out

across the crowd. "There's no one clear way to do this. We're all from different backgrounds, different lineages. However, five hundred years ago,
every sect of humanity unified to form the System Collective under the
guidance of the Culloden family of Cautius Prime. Thousands of years
before that even, the ancient Cautians had been the first to champion
peace between human factions."

Rake tapped something on the podium, and the amplification transferred to her nexus, following along with her as she paced to the back of
the stage, toward the base of a towering bulkhead column.

"The Cautian rite for launching ships is simple . . ."

She took a small switchblade from her pocket and flipped it open. She
held out her other hand, then sliced the blade across her palm, drawing
a thin line of blood.

She reached out and pressed her hand against the bulkhead. "I pledge
my loyalty to this vessel, to see it through calm and storm, to protect it as
it will protect me. I solemnly swear to bear true faith and allegiance to
my fellow soldiers and commanding officers, to carry out the responsibilities of my posting, and to defend humanity against all enemies, from
without or within."

Rake paused for a few long moments, then lowered her hand. A swath
of red stained the silver metal. She turned back to face the crowd.

"Commanders, please come forward."

Beckar gripped Jackin's shoulder, then slipped out of the crowd of officers and marched toward Rake. A handful immediately followed, then
a dozen or so trickled in behind them. One woman with angular blond
hair shifted grumpily, then murmured, "Eh, fuck it," and took off after
the others. A nervous paunch-bellied man scuttled after her, taking up
the rear of the line.

Rake gave an appreciative smile as Beckar approached. "Optio Theo
Beckar, repeat after me . . ."

Rake produced a biotool and sterilized the knife, then passed it to
him. Beckar cut his palm, held it against the bulkhead, and repeated
Rake's words. The next stepped forth, then the next, each pledging their
loyalty in blood and oaths, until a half-meter-square swath of metal was
slick with red.

Cavalon gulped. He was going to feel extra bad if his reactor blew up
the ship tomorrow.

The officers cauterized their palms, and one by one filled back in
around Cavalon and the other junior officers.

Rake returned to the podium. "I know many of you heard about the
assault the other day."

The impressively still silence returned again. Jackin's foot started up its tapping and Cavalon's gut turned. That was not the topic he'd expected her to segue into.

"To come home to find you splintered . . ." Rake said, head shaking slowly, "and to find people I care about in danger from the very soldiers they're trying to protect . . ."

Cavalon glanced down, really hoping the heat in his cheeks wasn't as obvious as it felt.

"I won't tolerate it," Rake said, in that same simple way she'd used so many times to make Cavalon believe he was capable of anything. Now it was being employed to deliver the universe's most definitive threat. "Please know that."

She paused, gaze scouring the crowd to let the sentiment sink in.

"But if you have grievances, tell us. Talk to us, please." Her tone shifted lighter, more agreeable. "We continue to follow the protocols of the SCL because it's what we know. It's a structure to hold us up—it's ordered and simple, and gives us a path to follow. But we're not the SCL. We will be making changes, because we can do better. And we want your help figuring out what better is. So we can be as strong as possible."

She glanced up at the looming Sentinel flag behind her.

"As we leave the Divide, we become the last of our kind. But we'll take up the mantle given to the order when it was first commissioned in 1 AV. The Sentinel's original credo: to protect mankind from the return of threats unknown. Those threats may now be coming from within, but we *will* continue to protect our species, and do so with the Sentinel name. Which brings me to our final order of business . . . to rename this vessel . . ."

Her chin lifted as she looked overhead to the beams of truss lining the massive ceiling.

"This capital ship, which was a hero of the Viator War, yet sent out to pasture—to *die*—out here, just like we were." She returned her look to the crowd. "In ancient Elyseian mythology, the Typhos was a colossal biomechanical beast of unknown origin. It terrorized the skies of the Elyseians' origin world, able to command and take direct control of its vassal ships, even when halfway across the planet. That made it a fitting name, given the *Typhos*'s purpose during the Viator War. But we no longer need a name that extols a past filled with unending war. We need a name that will inspire us to look forward. To look toward what's to come."

Cavalon's heart sped as her eyes landed on him. She gave the barest of nods, then scanned the crowd again.

"The SCS *Typhos* will henceforth be known as the *Lodestar*."

Cavalon grinned.

The crowd roared its approval as fists took to the air and boots stomped. Cavalon joined in as the mood infected him. High highs and low lows—just as the Divide intended. He prayed to the void this ridiculous perpetual jump drive of his would actually work, and not fail miserably, causing this high to plummet them into disaster.

CHAPTER TWELVE

The following morning, Adequin arrived at the CIC. This time, she was the one with too much energy—nervous energy, unfortunately.

Jackin stood at the war table, sifting through navigation screens. A crew of six technicians worked at stations on the far side of the room. Beckar hunched in quiet conversation over the shoulder of the comms operator. Coordinating their exodus from the Divide would make quite a trial by fire for his bid for optio. A bid he wasn't even fully aware of, as far as Adequin knew. If he handled himself well, she'd be hard-pressed to come up with a reason not to offer him the post.

She headed toward Jackin. "Morning."

"Hey, boss," he replied absently, not looking up from the screens. "I've got the coordinates prepped."

Adequin nodded. Normally, navigation would be covered by one of the operators, but Jackin was their fastest navigator, and time could be their cruelest foe at the moment.

"It'll be easier to see more precisely where we're at once we've made the first jump and can relay a direct signal to the crew at Kharon Gate. Right now it's kind of a shot in the dark."

"Because there's nothing out here to orient us?" she ventured.

"Just like old times," he agreed.

"We on track?"

He nodded. "Cavalon and Mesa's team worked through the night with Beckar and the CIC techs to make sure the drive's playing nice with the computers."

"What's the report?"

"Old and shitty, but functional."

"I'm starting to think that should be our motto."

His lips pressed thin in a dampened smile. "Beckar's working on getting the operators up to speed. Should be ready in fifteen or less, assuming the eggheads are still on track, which they were as of an hour ago."

Adequin took a step toward him, crossing her arms as she leaned against the edge of the table. "I know you're pissed at me," she said, keeping her voice quiet in the deadened silence of the insulated room, "but I'm going to need your help with this. I don't know the proper calls for jump nav."

Jackin met her eyes, gaze steady. "Yeah, I know, boss. Beckar and I will guide you through it." He shook his head, edging closer as he lowered his voice. "I'm not pissed at you, Rake. It's just . . . the last six months have been tough. I think I got it in my head that you'd return with sunshine and rainbows, and everything'd be easy again." He rubbed the back of his neck. "But that's too much to put on you. That's not your fault."

She gave a small grin. "To be fair, I didn't *not* bring sunshine back with me . . ."

An incredulous smile stretched across his face. "You really gonna swoop in at the last minute and claim credit for that?"

She shrugged. "You said yourself he'd been stuck for weeks. And within a couple hours, I'd fixed him."

"You did, indeed. How'd you do that, by the way?"

"He's just . . ." She let out a heavy sigh. "You know, an extrovert."

Jackin quirked a brow.

"He needs to feel real connections with people to stay energized," she explained. "Or even just to function."

Jackin scratched his beard and gave a rueful shake of his head. "And we had him locked in a hangar with the same few people for six straight months."

"He just needed a change in perspective."

Jackin crossed his arms as he sat against the edge of the table. "Well, I'm glad we got you back so we can have him at full power."

Her eyes narrowed with glib admonition. "He's not a drone with a dead battery."

"Of course not. More like a really lifelike AI."

She scoffed a laugh. "*There's* my cynical second. Emery's great but . . ." She let out a long breath. "One can only handle so much cheerful optimism."

He smiled. "You're welcome. It's the Myrdin in me. We're raised to second-guess the shit out of everything."

Adequin's lips parted, her response stalling out in her throat as she wondered if she'd heard him wrong. "I didn't know you were from Myrdin," she said, disbelief pitching up her voice.

The corners of his eyes wrinkled with a mix of amusement and regret. "I'm sorry, Rake."

She raised a brow, keeping her voice low. "That it took me almost six years to learn that?"

"Yeah." He kneaded the back of his neck with one hand, letting out a heavy breath. "And for everything else I never told you. Everything you've had to glean over the years. You've always been transparent with me, but I haven't returned that. I'm sorry for that. Really."

She watched him carefully, still stunned, searching his eyes for some indication of emotion, but his visage was as stoic as ever.

"That stuff you said during the dedication, about 'need to know,'" he went on, ". . . you're right, it can be dangerous. But for me, coming up through the Legion the way I did . . . need to know was almost always a good thing. A safety net. A way to keep people from getting hurt."

She nodded. "Yeah. I get that."

"Just know, what I said before stands. I do *want* to share more with you."

"We're as far from the Core as we can get at the moment. Why can't you?"

He glanced at Beckar and the others, still working quietly across the room. He shook his head slowly. "I told Bach. About a year ago."

Adequin blinked slowly. It must be worse than she'd imagined. Griffith would have told her otherwise.

"I didn't *plan* to tell him," Jackin clarified. "It just . . . came out." His look went briefly sheepish and he lifted a shoulder. "There may have been whiskey involved."

A pained smile twitched at the corner of her lips. "Sounds like Griffith." He'd loved to ply friends with whiskey.

"I knew, logically, he was safe out here," Jackin continued. "Especially since he was out with the *Tempus* most of the time. But it didn't matter, I was a wreck regardless."

"Why?"

"I felt so guilty, knowing what he knew could get him hurt—if or when he returned to the Core." He met her gaze again. "I just don't think I can deal with that guilt again. Especially not with you."

She licked the dryness from her lips. "I understand, Jack," she said finally. "Really. What I said before stands too. When it's safe, you can tell me. Or not. I trust you." She gripped the side of his arm. He gave a grateful nod. "And, I'm sorry I went off book with the speech."

He wiped a hand down the side of his face. "Eh, yeah. But honestly, I'm glad you went rogue. It was very . . . you."

She cast a tired smile.

"That's all I want, you know," he said quietly, sincerity lacing his tone. "I know you think I'm trying to force you to be something you're not," he said. "But it's there, Rake. You proved that last night. Everyone else knows. You just don't see it yet."

The strain under her ribs twisted. She really did wish she could be even half the leader Jackin saw in her.

Beckar crossed the room toward them, a barely contained, closed-lipped smile stretching across his well-proportioned face. "Sorry to interrupt, sirs, but Engineering gave the all-clear."

Adequin shared an expectant glance with Jackin, and they followed Beckar to the opposite side of the large war table.

Jackin reopened his screens, then passed a clone of his navigation display to Adequin. He lowered his voice. "Call for jump prep."

Adequin gave a grateful nod. "Begin jump prep."

"Copy, prep," Beckar responded. "Galen, bring the drive online."

"Initiating," Galen answered. "And we're live, sir."

Beckar stepped up behind Galen and stared over her shoulder. "Is that estimate right?"

"Afraid so, sir."

Beckar looked up at Adequin. "Old-timer's feelin' tired this morning, EX. Spool time's fourteen minutes."

Jackin let out a low whistle and Adequin grimaced. Even on the oldest, largest ships from the Resurgence War, she'd never heard of a jump spool longer than five minutes.

Beckar seemed to catch Adequin's worry. "After a few jumps, we can get some coordination between Command and Engineering and get that number down."

Galen gave an agreeable nod over her shoulder. "A little greasin', sir, bet we can get it down by two or three minutes."

Adequin nodded her thanks. "Understood."

"Nav's next," Jackin prompted.

"Navigation on-screen," Adequin said, and Beckar complied, relaying the order. A large three-dimensional map expanded over the war table.

"Lock coordinates," she ventured, and Jackin nodded his approval.

"Setting coordinates," Jackin confirmed, tapping at his screen for a few seconds. "Coordinates locked. We can cross-check systems while we wait for spool."

"Beckar, cross-check."

Beckar nodded and delivered a series of orders to his operators, who busied themselves with their screens for the next few minutes.

Meanwhile, Beckar stood staring at the spool status screen with his fingers linked in front of his stomach, knuckles going white as he alternately flexed the fingers of each hand.

Jackin leaned on both fists against the top of the glowing war table, jaw skimming slowly as he stared at the map. Adequin chewed the inside of her cheek, wishing Cavalon were there to crack enough inappropriate jokes to adequately fill fourteen agonizing minutes.

She could only imagine the tension they were enduring in Engineering about now. Down there with that three-hundred-year-old jump drive linked, somehow, to that jury-rigged-as-shit reactor. She tried not to think about the hundreds of ways in which this could go wrong—how they could get crushed in the folds of space-time, or maybe ignite into what would more or less amount to a mini-supernova, incinerating the ship in a fraction of a second.

Though strangely, a third possibility felt even worse—that it just might not work at all. Her stomach turned at the thought of being stuck at the Divide for more endless weeks while everyone slowly died. At least if there were a catastrophic system failure, it'd be over quickly.

After a few excessively long minutes, Beckar's hands dropped and his back straightened.

"Spool's complete," Galen confirmed. "Panel is green, sir. Jump is a go."

Beckar nodded. "Stand by for jump."

Adequin exchanged a look with Jackin, the relief evident in the smoothing of his rumpled brow. He gave a single nod.

She pushed all theoretical catastrophes from her mind, then cleared her throat. "Execute." That call she knew, at least.

"Executing . . ."

The seconds lingered, filled only with soft beeps, fingers padding on controls, and held breaths.

Then at once, Adequin's head spun, vision flickering white. She shifted her weight to shake out the disorientation, as if within a fraction of a heartbeat, she'd aligned a different direction. Dead silence rang in her ears as they waited.

An eternity later, a high-pitched ding pierced the lull. The map over the war table rebooted.

Beckar leaned over Galen's shoulder. "Jump . . . complete," he said warily, not sounding like he believed himself.

"Sensors are clear," the technician at the defense station announced. "No contacts."

Adequin eyed Jackin. "Confirm arrival coordinates."

"Copy, checking coordinates," Jackin said, already busy flying through menus. Finally, he let out a stilted sigh. "We have a signal lock on Kharon." A broad smile stretched his face. "Coordinates confirmed. Successful jump."

A weight lifted from Adequin's chest as the CIC erupted into cheers. She shared an exuberant handshake with Jackin that felt almost as underwhelming as the one when she'd first returned. She thanked

Beckar, shaking his hand while the operators stood from their stations to exchange congratulations in varying degrees of relief and excitement.

One more jump and they'd be at Kharon Gate.

Adequin turned to the war table and opened a line to Engineering. "*Typhos*, er . . . *Lodestar* Actual for e-deck."

"Go for e-deck," Emery replied, an edge of tension in her tone. "We need some good news down here, sir."

"Coordinates confirmed. We have a successful jump."

"Thank the void," Emery muttered.

"Sirs . . ." Beckar rumbled, the caution in his tone causing Adequin's stomach to turn. "We're getting a low voltage warning."

A series of alert beacons lit, and the active workstations erupted in a flurry of alerts. The operators rushed to slide back into their chairs. Beckar calmly relayed a series of orders.

"Em," Adequin called into comms, "what's going on down there?"

"Uh, we had a slight malfunction, sir. Kinda fiery."

"Is everyone safe?"

"Yes, sir, everyone's fine."

"What's going on?" she demanded.

Emery hesitated.

"Circitor . . ." Adequin warned.

A soft sound rumbled across the mic, and a few seconds later, Cavalon's voice rang over the line. "Sorry, sir, Cavalon here. I need a minute to confer with Mes. I, uh . . . I'll come up to the CIC. Give me ten minutes."

Adequin exchanged a wary look with Jackin. If Cavalon had something he'd only say in person, no way it was good news.

"Belay that," she said. "I'm on my way to you." She didn't wait for Cavalon's acknowledgment as she made for the door, glancing back at Jackin. "Stay here, prep the next coordinates. I'll see what I can do to get things going from down there."

Jackin wiped his brow with the back of his hand. "Yes, sir."

Adequin descended to the engine deck, mind racing as it worked hard at conjuring up a list of worst-case scenarios. She was pleasantly surprised to find no gaping holes in the side of the ship when she arrived.

Sweat stuck her jacket to her back as she entered the sweltering engine room. It stank of scorched rubber. Much like the hangars, the massive chamber featured high ceilings intersected by long aerasteel beams. A network of walkways allowed access to various components of the multi-tiered drive. On the bottom level many stories below, a handful of workers shouted orders back and forth as they milled around one of a dozen large, shed-like modules covered with venting and ducts.

On the far side of the chamber, Mesa, Owen, and two others stood atop a portable lift, working to remove some large piece of warped metal. Erandus stood a ways off with a few others from damage control. He shouldered out of the straps of a portable fire-suppression system, setting it on the deck while he debated something with his subordinates.

Adequin scanned the room and spotted Cavalon and Emery crouched at the foot of a wide duct that stretched up and disappeared into the ceiling overhead. The access door had been removed and set aside, its edges charred with black soot.

Cavalon glanced over as Adequin stepped farther into the room. He grimaced and stood from his awkward hunch, then marched to meet her. He wore a pair of thick work gloves, sleeves pushed up past the elbow, sweat glistening on his forehead, grease and soot staining his pale cheeks.

"What's going on?" Adequin asked. "Is it the reactor?"

"The reactor's fine," he assured, pushing his damp blond hair off his forehead. "It's the photovoltaics bridge I built to feed the solar energy into the jump drive. A neutrino capacitor overheated. The drive's built to gather a nice, slow, endless trickle of solar energy, not for an adrenaline shot directly to the heart. I accounted for it, but clearly not by enough."

"Tell me it can be fixed."

"It absolutely can, yes."

She exhaled a sigh. "Good."

"Fairly easily, actually," Cavalon went on. "Mesa can start on it right away, though it's going to take at least a week or so to fabricate the components and get it reinstalled . . ." His brow furrowed as he scratched the back of his neck.

"It sounds like there's a but?"

He cast a furtive glance back at the others, then took her elbow and guided her farther away, ensuring they were out of earshot. "We're going to need more ceronite," he said, voice barely a whisper. "Normally it'd only need to be recycled every few months or so, but the fluctuation caused a calculation error, and it blew through our entire reserve."

She eyed his soot-covered face. "Blew through?"

"It, uh . . . ignited, a little. Turns out ceronite burns with a nice magenta flame." He tried to say it lightly, but his voice broke on the last few words. He looked down. "I should have been more careful. Run more simulations, maybe."

"Hey, no." She gripped the side of his arm. His focus landed back on her. "This isn't your fault. It's a three-hundred-year-old jump drive that hasn't been maintained in two hundred years. There were bound to be issues."

He nodded, lips pressed thin.

"So, ceronite . . . as in the metamaterial that fuels jumps?"

"Yeah." He wiped the damp hair from his forehead with the back of his hand. "We already used every ounce of what we had to top off the tank on this thing. Viator War–era jump drives aren't all that efficient, it turns out."

"Can we make more?"

He maintained his rueful expression as he scratched both sides of his beard and shook his head. "We don't have the manufacturing hardware we'd need, even if we did have the composite materials, which we definitely don't. I mean, if you gave me enough time and endless resources, sure, I could probably figure it out. But we don't have either of those things, last I checked."

"There's a handful of surviving dreadnoughts," she suggested. "We could double back and see if we missed any while we were loading up supplies."

He continued to shake his head. "There's no way a Sentinel ship would have it. The only thing it's used for is jump drives, and last I checked the Legion wasn't really keen on giving us travel opportunities."

She scratched her jaw. "How'd we have any to start with?"

"The Drudgers had stocked it on the *Synthesis*. Void knows why."

"Shit. So . . . if we can't fabricate it, and there's no chance of finding it at the Divide . . ."

He gave a rueful nod. "Then we have a hundred-million light-year errand to run."

"You're kidding," Jackin said, every fiber of his tone a statement.

Adequin bit the inside of her lip and shook her head.

Jackin stared at her from across the expanse of the war table, the glowing top casting his blank-faced stare in a wash of blue-white light. With the jump drive out of commission, they'd dismissed Beckar and the operators for the time being, and now stood alone in the CIC.

Jackin cleared his throat. "You want to take a team inward on the *Synthesis*—a Drudger vessel—to go find an abandoned ceronite manufacturing plant?"

"I don't *want* to. We have to."

He scoffed a bitter laugh. "No way, Rake."

"Yes way, Jack. It's the only way we can get this drive working again."

"Yeah, yeah . . ." He waved one hand dismissively, wiping his brow with the other. "I get that it's necessary—and we'll get to all the ways in which that's going to be a huge fucking problem in just a minute. What I'm concerned with is why in the void you think *you're* going to be commanding this mission."

She rounded the table toward him. "There's no one here even half as trained as I am in this kind of asset retrieval. I'm the only choice."

"You're the commander of this ship."

"For all of five days."

"You *just* got back."

"*Exactly.* The crew's not going to miss me being gone another few weeks. They're still used to you and Puck, it won't cause a major upheaval. Besides . . ." She lightened her tone and gave his arm a playful jab. "You're the one that said all the dashing off on dangerous missions is what endears me to them." She flashed a wary grin.

Jackin growled as he pushed away from the table and paced back and forth a few times. He ran stiff hands through his hair then came to a stop, facing her squarely. "If you leave this ship, you could come back to a mutiny of your own."

"At least there'll be a ship to come back to."

"You really don't believe anyone else could get this done?"

"I'd like to, but we're not there yet. We don't have enough time to train a team, or even vet the people we have. Most of these soldiers came out of low-grade units, and it's safe to say they haven't received much in the way of training since."

"Not everyone's a Titan, you mean."

"This is what I'm trained for, Jack."

He let out a heavy sigh.

She licked her lips slowly, watching his jaw clench and eyes dart as he fought some internal battle.

"Fine," he said finally, though his scowl remained.

Tension lifted from her shoulders and she gave him a grateful nod.

"Just promise you'll come back in one piece," he said.

"You know I can't do that."

"Lie to me, then."

She swallowed past a lump. "Okay. I promise."

"And you're not doing this alone—you need a team."

"Of course."

He threw open a nexus comms menu. "Who're you thinking?"

"Well . . . I don't like it, but I think I should take Cav."

He arched a brow at her. "This'll be dangerous. You willing to risk him?"

"We can ask him if it can be anyone else, but my guess is he'll want to be there to make sure we're getting what he needs. And I'll need him if we have to troubleshoot alternatives on the fly. It's not like we'll have open comms back to the *Typh*—er, the *Lodestar* to ask questions."

"All right," Jackin agreed with a sigh. "Who else?"

"Another pilot's probably a good idea."

"That pretty much leaves Emery and Eura, assuming you want to only take people you've worked with previously."

"That'd be ideal. Eura might have more experience, but Emery and I are used to working together. That'll make it easier."

Jackin nodded and added Emery to the contact list.

"I'm open to suggestions on an operative," she said. "Someone who's a decent shot. I was thinking Warner, but I'm guessing losing him would be hard for you guys."

"Yeah, that's not ideal. Especially if we're in for another few weeks of waiting—unrest could spike again. What about Circitor Murillo? She's got a rep for being an ace shot, and I bet Warner'd vouch for her."

Adequin tilted her head. "Yeah. Good idea."

"What about cyber?"

"Well . . . Puck would be ideal, but it's your call if you think you can stand to lose him. Do you think Beckar's ready to step up and take his place?"

Jackin scratched his beard for a few long moments, gaze distant. "Yeah. As long as I'm still here, we're safe to lose Puck."

"It's not that I don't want you there, Jack . . ."

His look refocused onto her. "I know. So, it'll be you, the kid, Emery, Murillo, and Puck . . . How about some oculi to run interference?"

She shook her head. "The smaller we keep the team, the better. Fewer variables to manage. Especially considering no one's been trained in small unit ops."

"Okay, if you're sure. That only gives you two pilots."

"Puck can fly in a pinch."

"Okay." Jackin hit the final button to summon the list to the CIC. "They're on their way."

CHAPTER THIRTEEN

Cavalon clawed his fingers through his beard as he stood between Emery and Murillo in the oppressive silence of the CIC. Rake, Jackin, and Puck stood on the opposite side of a broad, glowing stretch of holographic glass. He'd never found a table so intimidating before.

Puck had just finished digging through the *Lodestar*'s database and brought up a depressing three-dimensional map. A sea of small white dots represented hundreds of star systems in the Drift Belt, and amongst them hovered a single, glowing purple orb—SCR-929-6.

"The *good* news . . ." Puck broke the somber quiet warily, "is that this is only a five-day warp from Poine Gate. And there ain't shit else in this sector, and never was. Even if this factory isn't abandoned, which it sure as hell should be, we shouldn't encounter anything else out there for a few hundred light-years in any direction."

Puck opened his mouth as if to continue, then seemed to think better of it. He was going to leave the *bad* news unsaid—that there very clearly wasn't a single other hit anywhere in the Drift Belt. The next closest was in the Lateral Reach—weeks away, even by relay course.

Cavalon didn't know the specifics of their time constraints, but he'd gleaned enough to understand that a trip all the way to the Reach would not be an option. It'd be hard enough just to get through Poine Gate, make it the five-day warp to hopefully find this factory abandoned, intact, and unguarded with a stash of ceronite left behind, and return before the Sentinels had starved. This single planet—so remote, it'd never even been given a name, only a designation in the System Collective Register—was a wild shot in the dark, and their only hope.

Rake had managed to soften the blow of the bleak outlook with an impressive display of unwavering confidence. They only needed to plan the operation, then execute it to the best of their ability. Simply reach out and take what they needed. The universe was theirs to mold to their will.

Cavalon exhaled sharply. If only it were that simple. His participation had primarily consisted of actively suppressing his default state of unbridled defeatism.

He'd been so focused on the reactor, he hadn't ensured the connection systems were as solid as they could have been. After realizing the solution to the cryostat, he'd rushed the rest, pacified by the prospect of finally, after six long months, being fucking *done* for once. And now, in all its hundred-million-light-year-journey glory: his punishment.

He clamped his eyes shut, pushing the doubt and guilt aside. In the last six months, he'd invented a perpetual jump drive and built a star *twice*, for void's sake. Yes, the drive needed fixing, and yes, technically that was his fault. But it wouldn't have even existed in the first place without him.

He agreed with Rake's assessment that he should come along—they had one shot at getting this, and they had to be 100 percent sure they were coming back with enough of the right thing. So he could more than make up for any past mistakes by being useful and competent on the mission.

Emery gnashed at her gum while scowling at the map. "If this stuff's used in every jump drive in the galaxy, why's it so damn hard to find?"

Cavalon cleared his throat. Time to be useful. "The SC's been centralizing ceronite production for decades."

"Why bother?"

"Publicly, quality control," he explained. "In reality, they want to limit jump abilities. Then they can tax and toll the shit out of spacelanes, force stopovers at certain stations, jack the prices on ceronite and acium alike. Plus, the slower people can travel, the easier it is to keep an eye on what they're up to—and modern jump engines are hard to trace. It'd probably be easier to find some closer to the Core, but not without SC officials climbing up our asses. We're actually lucky to be looking for it this far out." He frowned at the map. "Though I would have expected a few more hits than this."

"Well," Puck said, tone leery, "keep in mind, this is the information available on the *Lodestar*'s mainframe. Which was updated in 1 AV . . ."

Cavalon licked his dry lips. Right. So only about 224 years out of date.

"What about Kharon Gate?" Murillo asked. "Wouldn't their network have more updated maps?"

Jackin shook his head. "For spacelanes and jump points, yes. But Apollo Gates don't keep strategic asset information on the mainframe. It's only accessible when connected to the Legion extranet. A holdover from the Viator War, when gates were swapping hands every few days."

Puck looked about to speak again, then only shifted his weight, folding his arms over his chest.

"Centurion," Rake said. "Speak freely."

Puck ran a hand over his shaved head. "So, obviously it won't be safe to hang around Poine Gate once we're through—we'll be lucky enough to get out of there without them catching on where we came from. But once we get to 929, I might be able to safely hack into the extranet, assuming there's still a Legion ansible in-system."

Jackin grimaced. "Sounds like a good way to get a bounty on your ass."

"Hey, now," Puck said with feigned offense, "remember who you're talking to." He cracked his knuckles. "I'm a pro. No flags here."

Jackin's knit brows didn't seem at all convinced.

"Besides, it's a last resort only," Puck assured him. "So we don't feel like we're going into this with only . . ." He eyed the agonizingly blank map. "*One* option."

Cavalon lifted a hand warily. "What about our magic 4D Viator star chart fluid mapping thing?"

Rake leaned both fists on the top of the table and gave a mournful shake of her head. "Currently, the atlas only shows the Divide. We'll see if it updates once we're in the Drift Belt, but we have to assume it won't." Her gaze swung to Puck. "Will you need anything to do that kind of hack?"

"In the way of special equipment, no. Though if you've been squirreling away anyone with a keen insight into Legion intelligence efforts, now'd be the time to speak up."

Rake looked to Jackin with a high-browed glance. "He's the only former intelligence we've got, right?" she asked.

Jackin gave a reluctant nod. "That I know of."

Cavalon quirked a brow, and it took him a moment to realize they were talking about Ford.

"Can medical stand to lose him?" Rake asked.

"I'll confirm," Jackin replied, "but I'm sure they can make it work."

"And you trust him?"

He gave a single nod. "With my life. We worked together for almost a decade—he's solid."

Cavalon chewed on the corner of his lip. That confirmed his theory that the good doctor and Jackin had known each other from "before," but in classic Jackin style, he'd left out anything that might even remotely resemble specifics.

"All right," Rake said, looking to Emery. "Add Circitor Ford Kellar to the roster."

"Yessir." Emery tapped at the holographic screen in front of her.

"Okay, team's set," Rake said. "Itinerary is a sixteen-hour prep, warp to Kharon Gate, relay from Kharon to Poine, warp five days to 929. If it's a bust, we risk connecting to the Legion extranet to gather more intel, then regroup. What other issues does that raise?"

Emery cleared her throat. "Well, sir . . . we've avoided relaying inward this long for a reason. How'll we avoid getting blockaded by the Legion stationed at Poine Gate?"

"By owning it," Rake replied, her flat tone so matter-of-fact, it caused Cavalon to do a double take.

Jackin crossed his arms and voiced Cavalon's disbelief. "Seriously?"

She held up a hand. "Hear me out. When we spoke with Poine six months ago, they were already on skeletons. It's not likely they've stationed *more* people there since—if anything, it'll be less. They'll be at worst complacent and bored, and at best depressed and exhausted. Either way, they won't be ready for a strike team to drop in on them."

Puck lifted a brow. "Strike team?"

She nodded. "We'll have Warner pull a squad of his best people. They'll take the *Courier* through right after the *Syn*, and we can act as a distraction while they board."

"Couldn't we just snap-warp away?" Murillo asked.

"Technically, yes," Rake replied warily, "but that doesn't set us up very well for a return trip."

"Or cover our tracks," Puck added. "Even if Kharon closes the path right after we relay, Poine would be able to see where we came from."

"Right," Rake agreed. "And on the way back, we'll need control of Poine in order to re-establish a connection with Kharon. So we have to take it one way or the other. I'd rather get it secured before we leave than have to deal with it on the way back."

Cavalon's brow furrowed. "While Warner and the team's boarding, what'll stop the crew on Poine from sending for help?"

"I can throw out a signal jam easy enough," Puck offered. "It won't last long, but assuming our boarding team's on top of it, we should have time."

Rake nodded. "Then we leave a crew there to service what little traffic comes into that gate, and keep up the guise. If things are anything like they were six months ago, I don't think the Legion will be expecting regular check-ins."

"And if our team fails to take it?" Jackin countered.

"That's why it's critical we go in separate ships," she admitted, a hint of regret in her tone. "They're as much a distraction for us as we are for them. Whether they succeed or not, we'll have to continue on to the factory."

"But then how do you plan to get back here?" Jackin asked.

She shook her head. "If it comes to that, we'll have to figure out negotiating with the Legion. We won't have a choice. Just keep things buttoned up here so we can be ready if it comes down to fighting our way back through."

Jackin gave a tight-lipped nod. "'Course, boss."

"Any other issues?" Rake asked. Silence and head shakes provided her answer. "Then let's talk logistics."

"Is the *Synthesis* our only viable ship?" Murillo asked.

Jackin nodded. "Its armaments and defense systems are light-years better than the *Courier*. And those are the only two ships we have that are safe to take through an Apollo Gate."

Cavalon scratched his beard. "Is the *Syn* cleared for atmospheric entry?" he asked.

"Yeah," Jackin replied, "though there's no telling what condition those systems are in."

Rake turned to Emery again. "Everything good on your arrival checks?"

"Yessir, though I don't think any groundside systems are on the checklist these days."

"Okay. Pull a team to give its landing gear and launch engines a once-over. Won't do anyone much good if we end up stranded planetside."

"On it," Emery said, pulling up another screen.

Rake looked at Cavalon. "What kind of supplies are you going to need for the ceronite? Assume the factory won't have anything useable."

Cavalon blew out a long breath. All this standing around trying to think of ways to be useful to the conversation, yet he hadn't bothered to think ahead about his actual *job*. "Well, some transport canisters—we can just use the empty ones from the *Synthesis*. A space suit will do the job of a radiation suit. I'll need a chem classifier, and something to test oxidation. Nothing else major, I can grab it all myself."

"Okay, good." Rake turned to Emery. "Em, have the quartermaster start pulling stuff to fit us out. Every flavor of grenade and gun we have, breaching kits, recon probes, codebreakers, kinetic barriers, if we have them—you get the idea."

Emery gave an enthusiastic nod. "Copy, arming us to the teeth."

"Should we scrounge up some civvies?" Murillo suggested. "In case mercs or routers have taken up planetside? They tend to have itchy trigger fingers when legionnaires show up."

"Good idea," Rake replied, throwing a quick glance to Emery, who was already nodding her understanding. "And if we have time, we should burn the serials off the armor and weapons. It's all old enough to pass as salvaged, but let's make it look stolen just in case."

Cavalon watched as they delved into every grimy detail of the mission: what medical stocks to bring, how much food, what kind of repair components they might need, how much acium to store for the warp drive. Though he wished he could offer more insight, logistics wasn't his forte. The others had far more experience and training, and he was happy to sit by quietly and soak up that experience and training for future use.

"Any other questions?" Rake asked finally.

Cavalon let out a heavy sigh. Only about a million. Starting first and foremost with: What happened if they failed?

But when everyone voiced a round of "no, sirs," Cavalon joined them.

"Jackin, you'll give Ford a full update?" Rake asked.

"Will do, boss."

"Everyone else know what they need to do?"

This time it was "yes, sirs" and Cavalon nodded his agreement, mind spinning as he endeavored to formulate a clearer, overly cautious list of what he needed to pack over the next few hours.

Rake swept the map closed with a flick of her wrist. "We leave at 1500 tomorrow."

CHAPTER FOURTEEN

Adequin stepped aboard the *Synthesis* and let out a contented sigh. She'd spent the last sixteen hours dreading her return to the confines of the foul-smelling, dingy ship. Yet now that she'd arrived, she felt nothing but relief as her scope of leadership shrank.

She made her way to the helm, clutching the atlas pyramid under one arm. Mesa had corroborated the possibility of it connecting to a new set of data beacons once they arrived inward. Even if they didn't need it strategically, they'd at least be able to glean some valuable cartographical information—not the least of which being where the hell in civilized space they could safely settle once they got the *Lodestar* through Poine Gate.

In the cockpit, Emery sat in the copilot's seat running preflight checks, and Owen worked at the starboard-facing defense station.

"A ship of four thousand and not a pack of gum amongst them?" Emery said. "Yeah *right*."

Owen sighed. "Relax, babe."

"They're holdin' out on me," Emery grumbled, then threw a look over her shoulder. "Oh hey, welcome aboard, boss."

"The *Courier* is loaded up," Adequin said. "We almost ready?"

"Yessir," Emery replied. "On track for departure at 1500."

Adequin dropped her ruck on one of the crash seats beside the doorway. "Owen, we'll be underway soon, you'll want to clear out shortly. You still helping Puck with system updates?"

"Uh, yep," Owen stammered, her voice wavering up an octave. "Helping Puck is what I'm doing." She kept her unblinking eyes steady on her screen as she cleared her throat. "Just making a couple tweaks to the stealth system."

"Tweaks mean improvements, I hope?"

Owen flashed a grin over her shoulder. "That's the idea, sir."

Adequin gave a grateful nod. They could use all the help they could get. "Thanks, Oculus."

"No problem, sir."

"Ford and Cavalon are in the hold getting their supplies secured," Emery said.

Adequin set the atlas pyramid on the dash between the pilot terminals. "Either of you seen Murillo?" she asked. "Or Puck?"

Emery gave a swerving shake of her head, then exchanged an expressionless glance with Owen.

Adequin narrowed her eyes, about to ask what the hell was going on when bootsteps approached behind her. She turned to face Jackin as he dropped a ruck inside the door.

Adequin stared at the bag, blinking slowly for a few seconds. Her gaze drifted up as he crossed his arms. Emery and Owen suddenly became very focused on their work.

Adequin cleared her throat. "What's going on . . . ?"

Jackin tilted his head back toward the hallway. "Let's talk."

Adequin's pulse sped, sending bolts of pain down the bruised skin of her arms. She marched past Jackin, down the hall, and into the captain's ready room, a narrow affair barely large enough to house a small terminal desk, fronted by a backless bench.

She forcibly peeled her fist open to palm the door control, and it sealed shut behind Jackin.

"What do you think you're doing?" she growled, rounding on him.

"I'm taking Murillo's place," he replied calmly, his tone as steadfast as his expression.

"Excuse me?" she fumed, heat clawing up her neck. "Who's going to run the damn ship?"

"Puck's staying."

Her shoulders stiffened as she struggled to force calm. "He can't stay—I need him!"

"We're bringing Owen in his stead."

She scoffed. "Oh we are, are we?"

Jackin inclined his head. "Puck cleared her personally."

"That's putting a lot of damn faith in a civilian royal who's served less than *two* months."

"Well, void, Rake," Jackin cursed, and some of his infuriating composure slipped away as his dark brown eyes sharpened at her. "I recall a certain someone who risked all our lives—multiple times—on that *exact* premise just six months ago."

She clenched her jaw. She'd been so stupid. This had been his plan all along. He'd accepted her bid to lead the mission far too easily. She'd been so heartened by his apparent belief in her, she'd let it blind her.

"Cavalon trusts her," Jackin went on. "That should be enough for you."

"I'm not pissed about the swap, Jack," she forced out, frustration wavering in her voice, "I'm pissed you lied to me. That you went behind my back to find a way to fucking babysit me."

"That's not what this is."

"Bullshit." Her Imprints shuffled along her bruised shoulders but hesitated at her neck, refusing to rush down her injured arms.

Jackin eyed her collar. "You gonna hit me, Rake?"

"Do I need to?" she growled. "I give you a lot of lateral, but amending calls behind my back? This is taking defying orders to a new level."

"You wanted me to keep questioning you—this is what that looks like."

"Questioning my calls is one thing. That doesn't mean you force my hand when you think I'm wrong." She stalked toward him, lowering her voice and edging her tone toward pleading. "You want to do what's safest for the crew? They need you here—*I* need you here."

He glared. "Void, Rake, *you're* the one that should be here, not me!"

"Why? So I can sit on my hands while my crew starves around me? You really think I want that?"

Disbelief flatted the anger from his creased brow. "And you think *I* want that? You're not the only person who cares about saving lives. I can't sit by and watch everyone wither away around me for another month; I had my fill the last six. You were here all of five days, and you couldn't handle it. How do you think I feel?"

Despite the hot blood coursing through her veins, urging her to rebut him, she knew he was right. She wasn't being fair. But her anger only triggered more waves of pain in her arms, inciting her anger in turn. An endless cycle of fury and agony she couldn't control.

"I knew there'd be no changing your mind," Jackin went on, "so I didn't even bother to ask. But I'm not letting you leave without me this time, Rake. I swore to Bach I'd stick by you—"

She gaped at him.

"—but I couldn't do that the last six months," he continued, the anger in his tone growing weaker, taking on an edge of desperation. "And I was wracked with guilt that entire time, wondering if you'd die out there. Wondering if I could have stopped it if I'd only listened to him and been there to make a fucking difference like he asked me to."

Her clenched fists loosened, shoulders dropping.

He met her eyes steadily. "I intend to make good on that promise. Things are in order here. Puck can handle it, and he's got Beckar to help him. Stop pushing me away, and let me help you."

She wet her lips. "What do you mean you 'swore to' Griffith? When did that happen?"

He rubbed the back of his neck. "Not long before he died."

"What the *hell*, Jack? What'd he say?"

His gaze fell, chest swelling as he hunted for the words. Then Emery saved him.

"Uh . . . Helm to EX?" Emery said warily.

Adequin tapped her nexus. "Go for Rake."

"Sir, we're all green up here, got the go-ahead from the *Courier* as well. Ready to depart when you are."

"Copy. On my way." She closed her eyes and took in a few breaths, forcing her pulse to return to a semi-normal resting state. This operation required her full focus. She didn't have time to get emotional. Or worry about the past.

"I'm sorry, Rake," Jackin said, fierce sincerity in his tone. "You're right. Maybe I should have just told you I intended to come. I didn't think you'd . . ." He shook his head, the muscles in his jaw working. "Believe my reason. It's not only about keeping a promise to Bach. I'm just . . . pretty shitty at expressing how I feel."

"I know you care about me, Jack." She exhaled a steadying breath, and her voice came out thin and frayed. "I just wish you'd also trust me."

His gaze fell. She didn't wait for his response, turning and leaving him alone in the ready room.

She alternated grinding her teeth and cursing under her breath as she headed back to the helm. Though frustrating beyond measure, she knew the real source of her anger wasn't because he'd lied or swapped her crew around behind her back, or even because he'd kept Griffith's apparent dying wish from her.

It was because with them, Jackin would be in far worse danger. Or far more *direct* danger. Life aboard the *Lodestar* might have a finite time-line, but at least they were shielded from all the other dangers the galaxy had to offer. Especially in the Drift Belt, where anything resembling law and order was either a thing of the ancient past, or had never existed at all. At the fringes of the outer arms of the galaxy, Drift Belt systems were frequented by mercenaries, marauders, and routers—elite black market smugglers who operated more like organized crime families. And of course Drudgers—both the run-of-the-mill, dim-witted kind, and possibly even some of the elder Mercer's organized, mind-controlled clone Guardians.

Yet a twinge of relief warred with the guilt. Relief, because she actually did want him there, with her, helping her—no matter the risk. She felt stronger with Jackin by her side.

As she stepped back into the cockpit, she forced the thoughts aside, making room for her training to take over, automatically vanquishing the emotions and honing her thoughts to refocus on the next few steps.

Disembark. Warp to Kharon. Relay to Poine. Don't get shot down by the Legion. Don't strangle Jackin.

Twenty hours later, Adequin stood before the broad viewscreen over the *Synthesis's* dash and watched as Kharon Gate ignited with a blaze of fiery yellow-green light.

After a few blinding seconds, the burst settled into a vaguely spherical, churning mass. The chartreuse glow hovered between three massive prongs stretching out from the triangular face of the tapered station.

Adequin glanced at Jackin, who stood to her right along with Ford, then to her left at Cavalon, Emery, and Owen, their expressions a medley of anxiety, awe, and exhilaration.

The station operator's voice crackled over comms. "Gate Command for *Synthesis.*"

"Go for *Synthesis,*" she replied.

"Gate is stable and ready, sir. Relay course: one node—Poine Gate, Soteria Cluster, Drift Belt. Please confirm."

"Confirmed," Jackin replied.

Emery threw a bitter grin at Adequin. "Only place we can go, after all."

She gave a relenting nod. Poine Gate was in fact the only direct connection to Kharon. They could plot a longer relay course, but each node along the way would be notified of their passing—and of their unverified transponder code—and increased the chances of someone catching on that they weren't entirely on the up and up. Luckily, Poine was by far the closest to where they wanted to go anyway.

"Relay set," the operator said. "Cleared for departure. Good luck, Excubitor."

"Thanks, Circitor. *Synthesis* is on approach." Adequin tapped to connect to the *Courier.* "*Courier,* that's a go. Give us thirty seconds to deploy the jamming signal, then wait another thirty and follow us through."

Warner's dry rumble crackled over comms. "Copy sixty seconds. See you soon, sir."

Adequin dismissed the comms panel. "Stations, please."

Everyone slid into their seats—Jackin in the copilot's chair to the right, with Ford at the defense station behind him, and Emery at the sensor suite over Adequin's left shoulder. Cavalon and Owen strapped into two of the four crash seats beside the door.

Adequin buckled her harness and flew them toward the brilliant orb of green.

She held her breath as they approached. She'd last relayed over five years ago and hadn't missed the unsettling feeling in the slightest. To some, it felt like falling asleep, to others more like an internal pause, as if their hearts stopped beating momentarily. To Adequin, it'd always felt far more formidable. Dark and vacant, as if in that fraction of a moment she no longer existed anywhere in time or space. Then subsequently turning up alive and unscathed on the other side of thousands—or in this case millions—of light-years . . . it felt like an affront to existence.

Adequin shook away the hesitation and refocused. "Prepare for relay."

Jackin tapped his menus. "Comms disabled."

"Sensors disabled," Emery added.

"Shields and cloaking disabled and queued," Ford announced.

"Ready for relay," Jackin said.

"Copy. Relay incoming." Adequin stared at the slow, billowing pulses of teracene before them. Narrow, arcing limbs sprouted off, swaying gently as if drifting aimlessly in a calm sea. Glints of light licked up around their nose as the mass engulfed them, and the *Synthesis* relayed.

Adequin's eyes snapped open.

A pressure swelled under her ribs, dread saddled by a relentless weight of corporeal responsibility.

A docile beep drew her gaze to the *Synthesis*'s dash. The screens flickered, resetting. She squinted at the viewscreen, at the endless cloud of yellow-green surrounding them.

Jackin's hands already moved over his menus. "Relay complete. Report."

Ford and Emery voiced a round of affirmative system checks.

"Orienting," Jackin announced. "Ford, deploy when ready."

"Rolling out jamming signal," Ford confirmed.

Adequin's fingers twitched over the controls, but she closed her fists and forced patience. Her instinct was to steer them off on ions to put some distance between them and the gate. But the best shielding they had at the moment—from scanners or weapons locks—was the churning ball of teracene. So for now, she needed to leave them floating in their own relay backwash.

She wiped her palms down the sides of her pants. If she'd been wrong about Poine still being on skeletons, and the Legion had for some reason stationed more troops there, she couldn't say she relished the idea of leaving Warner and his MPs behind to field a fight they were likely to lose. But she knew she didn't have a choice. It'd be the lives of four thousand for the lives—or at least freedom—of a dozen. The kind of math Jackin wanted her to do. But not the kind she had to like.

"*Courier's* through," Ford said.

Adequin squinted at the viewscreen, into the gauzy veil of chartreuse light. A distorted glint of steel darted away as the *Courier* sped out of sight.

"That's sixty seconds," Jackin announced.

Adequin nodded. Time to embrace the role of "distraction."

She engaged thrust and spun them starboard. She started to call for shields, but the words died in her throat as Ford beat her to it. "Shields up," he announced. "At one hundred."

"Shields?" Cavalon croaked from over Adequin's shoulder. "But they won't fire on us . . ." The squeak in his voice made it half a question, half self-assurance.

"We're in a Drudger ship," Emery pointed out.

"But with a Legion transponder."

"Which is even more suspicious."

"Cloak spooling," Ford said. "Can't deploy till we're clear of the tera-cene . . . Huh . . ."

Jackin threw a look over his shoulder to Ford. "What?"

"Sensors, please confirm," Ford said.

"Confirmed," Emery replied. "Short-range sensors are clear, sirs."

Adequin's eyebrows rose. "Even docked?"

"I don't see anything at either set of airlocks, other than the *Courier*," Emery confirmed.

Adequin flexed her jaw, eyeing the indeed empty sensor screen after Jackin passed it across the dash to her. So far on the edge of the galaxy, Poine was definitely not any kind of travel hub. But it was standard procedure to keep at least a few ships stationed at a gate for tracking down rogue vessels or responding to distress calls. Then again, that'd been the case for the gates at the Divide as well.

"All right . . ." Adequin said warily. "Let's wait it out. Keep us dark on comms until we get the signal from Warner."

"Aye."

A glint of light caught Adequin's eye, and her gaze shot to the atlas pyramid, resting innocently on the dash between her and Jackin. Its etched grooves radiated with soft white light.

Hope swelled in her chest. "Cav?" Adequin jutted her chin at the atlas pyramid. "Can you . . . ?"

"Yep," he piped, followed by the clatter of his harness as he unbuckled.

He bounded up and grabbed the pyramid. She unlatched her dog tags to pass him the medallion key, and he disappeared behind her.

Moments later he cleared his throat. "I don't see any change, sir," he said, regret in his tone. "Still only shows the Divide."

"All right," she said, "let's keep an eye on it."

"Will do."

Ford's throat cracked in a confused grumble. "Sir, I'm not gettin' a thing comin' in or out of Poine—network, data, comms—nothin'. It looks like their array's deactivated."

Adequin looked at Jackin, whose grimace of relieved concern mirrored her own. She quelled her nerves and swept open the sublight controls. She ramped the ions to a quiet velocity and steered them gently out of the relay mass into clear space.

Poine Gate loomed large on the viewscreen. A flat wash of white illuminated the scaled, matte-black hull, and it took Adequin a few disorienting moments to realize the source of it—starlight. Because they were now ninety-three million light-years closer to stars.

The *Courier* sat docked at the starboard airlocks, which were devoid of the usual demarcation and collision guides. The exterior illumination array was inactive station-wide, and observation windows were dark. It looked too much like Kharon Gate had when they'd found it abandoned six months ago.

From the starboard bow of the main hull, a narrow beacon of light erupted. Its trail swept slowly across the *Synthesis*'s nose three times.

"That was fast," Ford said, the concerned tone rattling low in his throat.

"Comms up," Jackin announced.

"—*Synthesis*, do you read?" Warner's voice rang over comms.

"Loud and clear, Warner," Adequin replied. "What's your status?"

"Sir, uh . . . There's no one here."

Adequin blew out a heavy breath. "Yeah, we were starting to wonder."

"My team's doing a full sweep as we speak, but no one's in either control room, and everything inside is in standby mode. The logs have been redacted, just like on Kharon."

Abandoned, yet the gate had been left on. Which was a good thing—as the only direct connection to Kharon, if Poine had been turned off, they'd have been stuck at the Divide.

Jackin pushed a stiff hand through his hair. "Void . . ."

"At least they left it on for us . . ." Emery said, her voice thin with strained optimism.

"But why the hell did they?" Cavalon asked.

Jackin exchanged an anxious glance with Ford.

"Doesn't matter," Adequin said, shaking off her own unease with an effort. "Warner?"

"Here, sir."

"Proceed as planned. Have your team occupy the gate, and don't act like they're home if anyone shows up, unless it looks like they're going to KO the gate. Only turn the comms array back on long enough to ping Kharon and send Puck the update."

"Copy that. They won't tip their hand unless they have to. Good luck, sir. We'll keep the lights on for you. Figuratively speaking, that is."

"Thanks, Warner. Stay safe."

Adequin closed the connection. She was grateful they hadn't had to take Poine by force, but she wasn't sure the uncertainty of finding it abandoned was any better. In any other circumstance she'd say it felt like a trap, but she couldn't piece together how anyone would have even known to set one.

"Coordinates locked," Jackin said. "121 hours to SCR-929."

Adequin steered them clear of Poine Gate and accelerated to warp.

Adequin woke on the fourth day and stood before the grimy mirror in her quarters, replacing the bandages around her forearms. Though the bruising hadn't improved, the painful sores had gone from detrimental hindrance to itchy, agitating annoyance, thanks to Ford's relentless checkups. The amount of shame-inducing judgment the man could pack into a single ashy-browed glower was downright impressive, and effective enough Adequin had remembered not to use her Imprints for four whole days.

"Good morning, *Synthesis*," Jackin's morning-voice chirped over the intercom system. "We'll be decelerating from warp in less than ten minutes and edging right into our solar swing-by. Pack it up or tie it down if you care about it, and you may want to take a seat for the next forty minutes or so until we reach velocity."

Adequin chewed her bottom lip as she finished securing the wraps. That meant they were within fifteen hours of arrival and on track for their clandestine approach. Making use of the slingshot had been Jackin's idea—decelerating from warp early, straight into a path aligned with 929's orbit. The interference from the star would mask their presence in-system, and the naturally altered trajectory would offer the stealthiest approach available to them in the decidedly not-stealthy *Synthesis*.

Once they reached velocity and could confirm their slingshot trajectory, they'd power down anything nonessential—no engines, no nav, no electronics whatsoever except life systems and the bare-bones, ancillary scanner Ford and Owen had cooked up over the last few days. It was the only way to travel faster than their ions could carry them while staying out of warp speed so they could still scan for contacts, errant signals, or automated defenses as they approached 929-6—though it'd be testing the limits of the *Synthesis's* inertia dampeners.

Adequin knew it was overkill. They were plotting for threats they weren't likely to find—this system had never been populated, and the factory had been on its last legs even two hundred years ago. But they had exactly one chance to do this right, so she intended to execute by the book.

"Boss," Jackin's voice rang over her nexus.

She tapped it open. "Here."

"Meet me at the helm?"

"On my way."

She made her way to the cockpit, where Jackin stood alone in front of the pilot's chair. The atlas pyramid rested on the dash beside him, its mazelike grooves still faintly glowing from within. Over the last four days, Adequin had checked it every few hours, but there'd still been no change.

"There a problem?" she asked.

"Nope." He slid open a holographic menu. "Just thought you'd want to see this."

With a static flicker, the viewscreen erupted into a wash of amber light. Adequin stepped toward the dash, squinting until the ship's cameras filtered the input.

SCR-929 loomed the full height of the screen, a molten jewel of amber light girded with a halo of golden rays and accented by curls of plasma—coronal loops that jutted up from the fringe like the tines of a crown. Warmth crept into her cheeks as she stared it down, unblinking. It'd been so easy to liken their mini-stars to the real thing. But she'd simply forgotten.

Unlike the reactor version, the mass of it didn't notably spin or seethe, no flares of light erupted off the edges every few seconds, and no tumultuous storm of plasma churned just under the surface. This was its steadfast, primal forebear, and their attempts to recreate it now seemed at best naive and at worst insolent, akin to taunting a god.

A vision played in her mind's eye: the Divide rushing toward the star, the chromosphere stretching away first, dragging the corona along with it until the plasma of the core pulled free. The sheer mass of it straining to fight, but ultimately defenseless until a final symphony of static white consumed it—the Divide erasing it from existence.

The last few months snapped into focus, the enormity of what they'd done to stop the collapse weighing against her. More than five years since her banishment . . . she'd forgotten what it was they were trying to save. What would have happened to the mass of the universe if they'd died out there?

She sensed Jackin's gaze burning against her and turned to meet his look. The soft light from the viewscreen shone warm across his light brown skin, a fragment of hope glinting in his eyes. One corner of his lips lifted in a half grin. "Been a while, eh?"

She gave a stiff nod. "Yeah." She looked back at the star for a few long moments. "Thanks, Jack."

"Sure thing, boss," he said quietly.

Fifteen hours later, their analog approach to 929-6 had been as quiet and uneventful as predicted. Adequin manned the copilot's seat on the right while Jackin initiated their deceleration from the pilot's chair. As before, Emery occupied the port-facing sensor terminal, with Ford at starboard. Cavalon and Owen bickered quietly about something in the crash seats at the back of the room.

The daylight side of 929-6 covered half the viewscreen, a dull gray orb shrouded with thick, dreary cloud cover. Despite its lackluster appearance, the sight sent Adequin's heart hammering into her throat. She knew it was only an image, but an image of a real planet, real ground, its distance from her measurable in kilometers, not tens of millions of light-years.

Jackin seemed to be having a similar reaction as he sat mute unblinking gaze locked on the screen. From the paleness that'd crept into Ford's cheeks, it'd been a good while since he'd seen a planet as well.

Jackin pushed a hand through his hair, refocusing with an effort, then guided them into orbit. Once they were settled, Adequin ordered Emery to deploy their small army of survey drones, and they settled in for a wait.

Adequin had just started to doze off when the dash beeped out a lukewarm tone. She sat up straight as a holographic screen materialized. A preliminary survey alert had returned.

Cavalon and Owen got up and stepped to stand between the pilots' chairs. "What's it say?" Cavalon asked.

Adequin blinked at the list, unsure what to make of it. "Jack?"

"Yeah . . ." He rubbed his temple and stared at the readout on his own screen.

"What does CDN-34 mean?" Adequin asked.

Jackin and Ford shared an uneasy look, then Ford cleared his throat. "It's the preliminary classing, sir. Contaminated: Decaying Nuclear. With a recheck timer of thirty-four years. It means the atmosphere's no longer viable. It's radiative."

Adequin arched a brow. "You sound worried."

"It means it's uninhabitable, sir."

"Couldn't it have always been that way?"

"Not accordin' to our records. And, not in the way you're thinkin'. It's not naturally radiative, it's *been* irradiated."

Cavalon crossed his arms, brow furrowed as his blue eyes narrowed at the cloudy orb. "From some kind of battle?"

"Could be," Jackin answered. "But there's been no sign of wreckage so far, orbital or surface."

"No battle would mean what?" Emery asked. "Someone killed a planet on purpose?"

Ford shook his head. "Hard to say without more data."

"For now, it doesn't matter," Adequin said. She almost didn't want to ask her next question. "What about the factory?"

"I gave one drone the coordinates," Emery said. "It should have gone straight there to check it out."

Jackin gave a rueful nod as he dug deeper into the results. "That area's showing as null—natural land formations only. So the factory's either been destroyed, or our intel about the exact location was wrong."

"Well . . . shit," Cavalon grumbled. "So, now what?"

Adequin blew out a long breath. "We wait for the complete survey to come back," she said, injecting as much assuredness into her tone as she could muster. "Emery, send out a modification to the drones' parameters—make sure they're scanning as deep as they can. I want to ensure we're not missing anything subterranean."

"Copy that, sir," Emery responded and turned back to her terminal.

"In the meantime," Adequin said, glancing to Ford. "Let's get started on plan B. Try to find that Legion ansible."

"Aye, sir." Ford waved Owen over, and she dragged a stool up to sit beside him.

"And Jack," Adequin said, spinning in her seat to face him. "Check the atlas one more time?"

"Yessir," he rumbled.

She went to unlatch the medallion from her neck, then stopped. Jackin picked up the burnished gold pyramid, and she hesitated, lifting a brow.

"What's wrong, boss?"

"When'd it stop glowing?"

Jackin tilted his head, brow creasing. Before he could respond, klaxons blared. Adequin winced as piercing shrieks cut a sharp staccato beat into her eardrums.

"Proximity alerts starboard," Ford shouted over the din.

The dash erupted to life with a wash of crimson. Adequin spun to face the array of holographic defense screens that'd materialized, eyes darting over the surge of information.

"Shit," Ford grunted. "They're already on us. Raising shields."

"Copy shields," she replied. "Emery, switch sensors to ship-to-ship."

"On it, sir."

"Looks like Drudgers," Ford said. "It's some kinda Viator battle-cruiser, though not one I recognize offhand—tryin' to get a read on it."

"How'd they sneak up on us that fast?" Emery growled.

Adequin ground her teeth. "No idea. Jack, pull us from orbit."

He didn't respond. Adequin spun to look at him and froze. Her heart hammered loud against her ribs as she stared at the vacant pilot's chair. The buckled harness rested limp against the back of the empty seat.

"The fuck . . ." she growled, digging her nails into her armrests as she darted a look over her shoulder. "Where the hell did Jack go?"

"Rake!" Cavalon shouted.

At the terror in his voice, she abandoned her hunt for Jackin and homed in on Cavalon. He stood a couple of meters back, arms raised, eyes wide as his gold and bronze royal Imprint tattoos darted in short, aimless bursts around the bare skin of his forearms.

"My Impr . . ." he mumbled, but his voice evaporated from his throat, as if the very sound waves were stolen from the air before they could reach her ears.

Cavalon's fingers drifted to his beard as a speck of black materialized high on his pale cheek. The dot grew outward, decaying the skin around it, revealing sinew underneath. The muscles withered next, a white slice of raw bone stark against the crimson before vanishing itself, until his jaw had disappeared entirely. Across his body, more black specks appeared, growing outward as more layers peeled away.

Adrenaline crashed through her. She pawed at her harness buckle and threw the straps off, rushing toward him. But by the time she reached him, nothing remained.

Cavalon was gone.

Owen gaped, her hazel eyes large and round, lips parted in disbelief. Ford and Emery sat twisted in their seats, staring at the empty air where Cavalon had been.

Adequin stood frozen as her thoughts reeled, unable to fathom what she'd just witnessed.

The only explanation her addled mind could grasp was that Cavalon had somehow been a time ripple. And Jackin too. Surely the real Jackin and Cavalon were somewhere else on the ship.

Then the reality of where they were in the universe crashed down on her—they were way too far from the Divide for that to be a possibility.

Maybe the real versions had never boarded to start with. Maybe they'd been time ripples all along, and now the universe had caught up with them and had decided to rip their doppelgängers from this space-time, one layer of flesh at a time.

No. It made a modicum of horrifying sense, but it didn't sit right. She looked back at Jackin's still-buckled harness. This was something else entirely.

"Boss!" Emery shouted.

Adequin snapped from her stupor. Emery stared, face slack, eyes wide and unblinking—her horrified look directed at Adequin's arms.

With a blinding swell of pain, Adequin's Imprints surged to life. They broke from their default locations, sliding into her back and legs, then crashing down into her sore arms. Unused for over five days, they tore across her bruised flesh anew, reopening every half-healed sore that remained, tearing deep, each path a trail of burning lava through her tender arm muscles.

Her knees buckled, and she braced herself on the headrest. But as she stared down at her own feet, dread descended. Tiny specks of black began to form down her legs.

Emery darted forward, palms out, reaching as if she intended to snatch Adequin out of the strange physical state, but her grasping hands went straight through her.

Everything went black.

CHAPTER FIFTEEN

Briefly, she lingers. A diffusive, subsonic thrum surrounds her.

The vibrations lash free, belting out like a cosmic roar, resonating into the hazy gloom. She can feel space between the light, can reach out and touch it, thread her fingers through it as if it were blades of grass.

Then, a spark.

Electrostatic, violent regeneration—a sudden magnetic adhesion of molecules. Each fiber knits, cell by cell.

Systemic pain welcomed Adequin back to consciousness, the only sure evidence of her mortality the endless waves of pain firing down her bruised arms. She gasped for air and it slid, thick and barbed, down into her lungs. A foul, acidic smell lingered, a briny taste coating the back of her mouth.

A dry groan crackled from her throat as her mind tried to account for her body.

Her hands cramped, fingers dragging against an unrelenting surface, cheek heavy against cold metal. Her ribs ached, her muscles spasmed, insides twisting, forcing her to remain facedown while her stomach crawled its way back down her throat. Each heartbeat sent out hot pulses of pain.

Then she remembered she had eyes she could open.

Her eyelids fluttered. She blinked away the haze clogging her vision and a sideways room came into view. A gray aerasteel wall lingered just out of reach.

"Rake!"

It took her a moment to relate the panic-ridden voice with a person in her memory. Cavalon.

Her gaze shot up, sending her head reeling and stomach lurching. With an effort, her eyes focused.

Across the room, Cavalon knelt beside Jackin. Jackin faced away, hunched on all fours, body heaving as he expelled the watery contents of his stomach. The atlas pyramid lay at the base of the wall beside him, doused in a glossy red liquid. Jackin's hands and arms and stomach were covered with the same substance, and the smooth metal floor under him had been smeared with it.

Adequin stared for a few drawn-out heartbeats, unblinking. The lingering acidic scent gave way to iron. To the scent of blood. Jackin's blood.

Her muscles jerked into action. She got her knees underneath her somehow, feeling like a colt just learning how to prop itself on flimsy legs. She steeled her lurching stomach and pawed her way across the cold floor toward them.

Cavalon gripped Jackin's waist to cushion the fall as Jackin collapsed to one side. He rolled onto his back, clutching his stomach, hands burned and raw and covered in blood.

Insides still screaming, Adequin sat up onto her knees and lifted Jackin's abraded hands from his stomach. An oozing slick of crimson stained his upper abdomen—a strangely uniform, triangular-shaped lesion that'd fused clean through his vest. His eyes were clamped shut as his neck swelled with tiny red and white blisters. Tracks of blood ran from his nose and ears.

He broke his hands free from her blood-slicked grip and grabbed at the wound again. He let out a groaning mewl, inflaming the twisting ache in her chest. She clawed at the straps of her jacket and yanked herself free of the sleeves.

"Hold his wrists," she instructed.

Cavalon complied, peeling Jackin's hands back and pinning them to the floor.

Adequin balled up her jacket and pressed it hard against the wound. Jackin growled, writhing and breaking free of Cavalon's grasp, painting trails of blood across Adequin's hands and the wraps covering her forearms as he pawed at her.

"Jack, stop," she pleaded, voice weak in her throat.

He bared his teeth, eyes still clenched shut.

"I need you to relax—I'm going to staunch the bleeding, but you can't fight me."

He groaned out something unintelligible.

She clamped one of his bloody hands in hers and leaned into his ear, trying to ignore the fresh trickle of blood that gathered at his earlobe before spilling down his neck. "Jack, it's Rake. You with me?"

His writhing slowed, his trembling hand tightening over hers.

"It's going to be okay." She focused on her breath, striving to keep the panic from swelling, to keep her voice steady and reassuring, as unrepresentative of her real feelings as she possibly could. "I need you to concentrate on breathing, only breathing. You have to compartmentalize it. That's an order, Centurion."

He grimaced out an approximation of a nod. She reformed her jacket to cover the wound, pressing firmly. He groaned and balled white-knuckled fists hard against the floor.

"Shit." Cavalon sat back onto his heels. He huffed out a few ragged breaths, eyes round. "Rake, you're okay," he breathed, voice frayed. "I—you were . . . I could see your, like . . . *insides*."

She licked her chapped lips, chin bobbing in an unconscious nod. "I saw the same thing happen to you on the *Syn*."

"Void . . ." He angled his furrowed brow down at Jackin. "I don't feel great, don't get me wrong, but what the hell happened to Jackin?"

"I don't know," she muttered.

Cavalon heaved in a breath, his pale cheeks ghostly white. He wiped both hands down the sides of his face, leaving a slick of Jackin's blood in his blond beard, though he didn't seem to notice. "Where are we?"

She craned her neck, eyes scanning the four walls—not a difficult feat in a space only a few meters square. A double-wide door on the far wall was the only facet of the otherwise featureless room.

"Holding cell," she answered.

"Right, but Rake . . ." he breathed. Reluctantly, she met his haunted look. "How did we get here?"

Dread crushed against her chest at the anguish in his tone. One term came to mind, which she refused to utter, because it wasn't a real thing.

Jackin's lull broke, and he let out a pained groan, shifting beneath her. She gnawed on her lip, moving one hand to his cheek to try and settle him. He just needed to fucking pass out already.

"They must have boarded the *Syn*," she said. "Gassed us, maybe, through the vents, and we lost consciousness. Then they took us prisoner."

"No," Cavalon said with a firm shake of his head. "We didn't get gassed—you know it. You watched me disappear just like I watched you appear."

She shook her head.

"Did you feel it too?" He leaned in, childlike wonder in his tone. "Like you were being reformed from the inside out?"

She kept shaking her head, but her silence and glassy stare gave him his answer.

Cavalon pressed both palms to his face before letting out a dark, low rumble of laughter.

"Void, Mercer," she seethed. "Why the hell are you laughing?"

"Remember at that first dark energy generator, when the Divide was trying to swallow us? You joked about wanting teleportation as your superpower."

She hung her head and sighed as he continued his throttled chuckle, pushing his hands through his sweat-slicked hair.

"We didn't *teleport*," she growled.

"It could just be person-sized Apollo Gate tech. Why not?"

Adequin ground her teeth. "Because of physics? We can't even take certain ships through Apollo Gates, let alone individual human bodies."

Cavalon scoffed a laugh. "Reconstituting physics is basically my new job description, so . . ."

"Viators never had tech like that during the war," she argued.

"That you *know* of."

"We'd have known."

"Well," Cavalon said, crossing his arms, "it's real unlikely Drudgers suddenly got smart enough to invent teleportation, so I think we have to accept this one at face value."

She flexed her jaw, trying to ignore the warmth of Jackin's blood seeping out around her jacket.

"Besides," Cavalon continued, "this isn't even the first time this *year* we've stumbled on major Viator tech we had no idea existed. And it makes sense, think about it—where's Emery, Owen? Ford? Why only us?" He held up his forearm, flashing the tidy line of gold and bronze squares at her. "My Imprints were freaking out before it happened. They must act as an anchor."

Adequin glowered. "Then why the hell's Jackin here?"

Cavalon jutted an accusatory finger at the bloody, discarded atlas device. "He was holding that when it happened, right?"

Her heart sunk into her chest, pushing out a few hard thuds against her eardrums. She focused in on Jackin's raw palms, recalling the strange triangular shape of the wound on his stomach.

Jackin convulsed, turning aside to retch up more watery, green-tinged liquid. Adequin kept pressure with one hand while she lifted the other to the side of his face. His skin was scorching.

She wiped spit from the corner of his mouth as fresh blood seeped from his nostrils. It caked into his beard and trickled across the scar that cut up his right cheek from the last time she'd sat hunched over him, tending to his injuries while the *Tempus* had tried to self-destruct around them. A vise clamped in her chest at how ghostly pale his light brown skin looked.

"Call for help," she said, her voice cracking.

Cavalon blinked at her, incredulous. "You really want to *ask* them to come kill us?"

"They would have just blown up the ship if they wanted us dead. Jack needs treatment. Now. Or he's going to die."

Cavalon's pale face went even whiter, and he stared at the pool of blood gathering on the floor around Jackin's midsection.

"Swap me," she demanded, and Cavalon jerked into motion. He crawled closer and pressed his hands against her blood-soaked jacket, keeping the pressure as she stood and skirted the few meters to the door.

Her Imprints cut hard pricks of pain into the bruised skin of her shoulders. She pounded on the door. "Hey! We need a medbay!" she shouted into the dense metal, her sharp tone echoing through the small room. "A biotool, a transfusion kit—something! Please!"

For endless minutes she kept pounding, then shouted in Viator next, repeating her mantra plus a few dozen choice expletives and a handful of threats. The guttural language grated against her dry throat. It'd been a long time since she'd spoken more than a word or phrase at once. Though most Drudgers at least understood the human tongue, they almost exclusively spoke Viator. Maybe it would pique their interest if they realized she could speak their language.

She inhaled a deep breath, closing her eyes to refocus. Her entire body ached, and her injured arms were killing her, but she needed to be ready to engage, if it came down to it. Fighting Drudgers was always a toss-up; they were highly predictable, but physically formidable. And without a weapon, the element of surprise, or much room to move, she'd be outmatched with any more than two or three at a time. Having Cavalon and Jackin to safeguard presented even more challenges.

She eyed the bloody atlas pyramid. It'd make a decent bludgeon, but she had no doubt there were security cameras perched in every corner. They might not be willing to come inside if they thought she was preparing for an attack. Besides, as far as ideal weapons went, it was pretty much the definition of lousy. Drudgers sported the same carapace plating as their Viator progenitors, but genetically enhanced with metallic compounds, creating a hardened, natural armor. A blunt instrument like the atlas pyramid would have to be deftly plied—directly to the temple—to be of any use at all. What she really needed was a knife, where the thin blade could fit between the plating segments. It would have been part of their weapons loadout, had they left the ship by standard means.

She steeled herself, jaw flexing, letting the reality of the situation force her battle-adrenaline into check. Though her instincts pushed her toward martial solutions, the quickest way to get Jackin aid was to convince them to help him. Even if she could take them out, Jackin could die before she could find a trauma kit, never mind the medbay. Though many Viator vessels shared similar layouts, from this holding cell alone, she had no idea what class of ship they were on, and there hadn't been time to get a clear read before they were forcibly extricated from the *Synthesis*.

She took a breath, deciding it best, for now, to ignore how they'd been kidnapped by technology she'd never heard even a whisper of a rumor about.

She continued pummeling the door. With an effort, she altered her approach from threat and malice to pleading petition.

After a handful of minutes that felt like an eternity, an alarm blared. Metal groaned and thunked within the wall, and the door bisected.

Adequin took a step back as two Drudgers stalked in, rifles raised. One fixated on Cavalon, the other on her.

She held up her hands, palm-out in submission. "Please," she said in Viator. "My comrade needs help. I can do it, but I need supplies."

A third Drudger stepped between the two riflemen and came straight for her. It shoved her away from the door, then spun her to face the side-wall and slammed her against it. The cold metal of a pair of mag-cuffs locked down around her wrists, securing her hands behind her back. She winced as pain threaded up her wounded arms.

She craned her neck to find Cavalon in a similarly compromised po-sition—on his knees, forehead against the far wall, cuffed by a fourth Drudger. A fifth stood over Jackin, gazing down at him as he writhed, struggling to keep Adequin's jacket pressed to his own wound.

Adequin's Drudger escort twisted her, shoving its taloned hand to her chest to pin her back against the wall. It angled a plasma pistol up under her chin and stepped closer.

She grimaced, holding her breath as its pungent, earthy scent filled her nostrils. It narrowed its overlarge eyes at her—the same size and shape as the Viators' primary set of eyes, but instead of inky voids of black, they contained unsettling, overlarge versions of human irises, much like their Savant counterparts, but to a far creepier effect. Of the two mash-ups Viator geneticists had devised a millennium ago, Drudgers had received the bulk of their looks from their progenitors. Their edges were rounder, and they were slightly shorter, slightly stockier, but at first glance, they looked almost no different. This Drudger was clearly young from its light-gray carapace, which glinted with metallic reinforcement even in the dim light.

The Drudger appraising Jackin grumbled in Viator, "Aros, what of this one?"

A sixth Drudger stepped through the door frame—Aros, presumably.

Its darker, aerasteel-gray coloring pegged it as older than the rest, though still not quite middle-aged. It hung back in the door, clutching its plasma rifle in both hands. "Take the defective one," Aros instructed.

Two more Drudgers marched in and gruffly picked up Jackin by the shoulders and ankles, eliciting a groan of pain.

"Careful," Cavalon bristled. The one that'd cuffed him snarled, and Cavalon hunched, eyes downcast.

Adequin's heart sped as they hauled Jackin out of the room. "Where are you taking him?" she demanded, looking straight at the elder Drudger, Aros.

Aros honed its coppery-hazel eyes onto her. "Sanook, keep it quiet."

Her young Drudger captor, apparently Sanook, responded, gripping her by the shirt. Its short talons tore into the cloth and scraped against her skin. It pressed the muzzle of its pistol harder against the bottom of her jaw.

She sucked in a deep breath and reined her emotions in, sealing them behind a flinty facade. Showing them her worry would only motivate them to use Jackin as leverage. Leverage to elicit what, she couldn't say. The fact that they hadn't shot them the second they'd arrived meant these Drudgers weren't just marauders out hijacking ships. They wanted something.

Her eyes darted, taking stock of the six Drudgers, though she could sense even more lingering in the hall. They all wore HUD nexuses—a thin piece of metal adhered to the temple which extended a small, one-way holographic screen in front of one eye. Maybe for squad coordination, or simply as a means of communication and information sharing, like their own nexus network.

What she knew for sure was that they were all armed. Unfortunate, but not a deal breaker. The more concerning issue was that each had Imprint tattoos visible—some along their arms, others along the backs of their necks, trails disappearing under the collars of their dark gray jumpsuits. The shapes and colors of their Imprints were almost as varied as the shades and patterns of coral and teal markings on their segmented skin. Two, including her guard Sanook, had square Imprints, like hers and Cavalon's, but they were a bright, polished white. The one guarding Cavalon had long, narrow, evergreen rectangles. Aros's were matte-black and rounder, or maybe small octagons.

Aros grumbled something under its breath, then addressed one of the guards waiting in the doorway. "The curanulta," it instructed, jutting its narrow chin at the atlas device.

Adequin's brow twitched. They knew what it was, or at least what to call it.

One of the riflemen scooped up the bloody device. Sanook loosed its grip on Adequin long enough to yank the medallion chain free from her neck, along with her dog tags. And Griffith's.

Sanook passed the chain off to the rifleman with the atlas. Shoulders tensing, her fingernails scraped against her bindings and her Imprints buzzed across the back of her neck, ready to help her offer the cuffs a stress test.

Taking a legionnaire's dog tags was bad form, even for a Drudger, but they didn't seem to care as the rifleman disappeared out the door with the atlas and chain in its greasy hands.

Now she not only had to take out all their captors, find Jackin, stabilize him, and haul him to the hangar or an escape pod, but she had to hunt down and retrieve that necklace.

Aros turned toward Adequin. Sanook stepped aside, keeping a hand on her, pistol raised, while giving Aros a clear angle to glower at her.

"What happened to the crew of the *Fusion?*" Aros demanded in a guttural, semi-approximation of the human tongue.

She cleared her throat. "I'd translated it to *Synthesis,* actually."

Sanook gave her an admonitory jostle, slamming her back into the wall. She winced, shoulders cramping as pain threaded up her bruised arms.

Aros's thin lips parted in a snarl. "That is our contractors' ship," it said, switching to Viator, a language it was clearly more comfortable with. "We will know what you have done to them."

Adequin focused on maintaining her expression, staring back at Aros with a clear, flat look. She had no intention of admitting to having slain the former crew of the *Synthesis,* whether or not they'd had justifiable reasons. "*We killed them all*" seemed like a bad answer, no matter how she framed it.

So instead, she lied. "I don't know what you're talking about," she said, forcing her gaze straight and breaths steady. "It was for sale on Erasmus Station. We purchased it legally. You can check the registration."

With a growl, Aros marched forward, shoulders tight with barely restrained frustration. Aros shoved Sanook aside. The younger Drudger dropped back to stand beside the door, but kept its pistol trained on her.

Aros bared its teeth, sending a putrid scent into her nostrils that forced a hacking cough from her lungs. "That is a lie," Aros snarled. It spun her around, slamming her chest into the wall, then gripped her wrapped forearm, eliciting shooting lances of pain.

She clenched her jaw and hissed out a breath, unable to keep her facade in check. Its talons slid against her raw skin as it yanked up the sleeve of her T-shirt, revealing her bruised bicep, lined with black veins.

"These injuries," Aros snarled, its voice low and grating, "are from excessive Imprint re-application."

She bit through the pain, clearing her throat with an effort. "Yeah, thanks. I figured that out a little too late."

Aros's grip firmed, and it twisted her arm. Blinding pain obfuscated her senses as its rough grip wrenched against her skin.

Aros leaned into her ear. "Which networks have you been accessing?" it demanded.

Pain ignited her anger, and she bared her teeth, hissing out a response in Viator, "I was fixing their fucking generators!" She selected the most vulgar of Viator expletives she could remember off the top of her head. Aros didn't seem to care as its hold loosened and it dropped her arm.

It turned her around, pinning her by the neck to the wall. It remained uncomfortably close, near enough its hot breath stung the side of her neck. "*What* generators?" it asked, but from its calculated tone, it knew exactly what generators.

"At the Divide," she replied.

"You *humans* were at the Divide?" it scoffed, spitting out the word for humans like it was an old piece of food that'd been stuck between its teeth.

Adequin grimaced. "We're Sentinels," she began, forcing evenness into her tone. "It's a unit of our armed forces that's always stationed out there."

"Sentinels are criminals," Sanook recited.

She glared past Aros at Sanook. "Yeah, and some are *murderous* criminals."

Sanook's eyes went to slits.

Aros's top lip curled in a silent snarl. "And what was your crime, *Sentinel*?"

She swallowed blood-tinged saliva, pinching her lips together in a bitter grimace. "You'd laugh if I told you . . ."

Aros's shoulders swelled as its fists balled. Adequin pressed herself against the wall, bracing for impact.

But Aros froze and Sanook suddenly stood up straight. Practically in unison, they lifted a hand to their nexuses on their temples, gazes going distant. A minute passed with nothing but inward stares and the growing stench of Drudger odor in the small, warm cell. She managed to edge a look at Cavalon, who remained cuffed on his knees by the bloodstain

Jackin had left behind. His face was a stoic mask of indifference. He was holding it together well, all things considered. Hell, he might be better at this than she was. With Augustus in his life, he'd likely logged more hours being interrogated than any Titan ever had.

Another Drudger marched in, brandishing a biotool in its taloned hand. It passed it off to Sanook, who approached Adequin.

"Rake!" Cavalon shouted a warning, blue eyes round with terror, and his captor shoved him hard enough to send him toppling to the decking.

Her Imprints cut into her skin as she tried to twist away from Sanook and the biotool, sliding against the cold cell wall. "What is that?" she demanded. Strength flooded her muscles, but her bindings proved their worth, and she could do nothing but squirm fruitlessly against the metal restraints. "Wait!"

Sanook ignored her as it injected the cartridge straight into the side of her neck.

She gritted her teeth. A cool wave rolled under her skin as the injection flowed down her neck, blanketing her chest with ice. Her vision spun and she strove to hang on to consciousness.

But the feeling passed moments later, and her sight righted itself, head clearing into sharp focus, heart thudding relentlessly against her ribs. It felt like they'd injected a wave of iced adrenaline.

"Shit . . ." Cavalon breathed. He'd stopped struggling against his guard and lay stock-still on his side, staring at Adequin's arms.

She craned her neck to look down. In a slow, downward cascade, her blackened veins grew fainter and fainter. She froze, staring in awe. The bruising remained the same, but the veins had completely disappeared. In a matter of seconds.

What the hell had they given her?

She'd be more worried if she didn't feel so damn *great*. It was like a lingering fog had been lifted, one that had been saddling her for weeks. Her muscles felt light but strong, the tight ache gone from her now-loose joints. And her silver and copper Imprints willingly slid all the way to her elbows. It still ached as they shifted across her bruised skin, but they were willing to move past her shoulders again. Maybe she could break out of these cuffs after all.

With a turn of its hand, Aros gave a silent instruction. The Drudger guarding Cavalon yanked him to his feet. Sanook grabbed Adequin by the back of the neck and shoved her out into the hall. They stepped into formation with a handful of other Drudger guards, Aros at the lead. She forced a look back to ensure Cavalon followed behind.

"Where are we going?" Cavalon squeaked out as the procession pressed forward.

Adequin repeated the question in Viator.

Aros glared back at them, letting out a short hiss. "The sovereign awaits."

CHAPTER SIXTEEN

Apparently the sovereign did *not* await, because the decadent room their interrogators dropped them off at was devoid of any kind of greeting party.

Adequin eyed Cavalon as they waited, cuffed and on their knees at the foot of a terraced dais. At the top, a long bench was backed by a wooden panel, carved with a mazelike design and framed with a border of triangles.

Three pairs of statuesque Drudgers guarded each of the exits—one at the top of the dais and two along the arcing wall behind them. Each stood armed with an etched bronze shock staff, clad in metal armor that seemed more ornamental than practical, with sculpted edges and a geometric design flash-printed into the metal.

Adequin kept her gaze focused on the nearest pair of guards, while her mind's eye plagued her with echoes of Jackin's pained cries. She could still feel the heat of his fresh blood on her fingertips, now dried and crusted under her fingernails.

She drew in a breath through clenched teeth, forcing the memories aside. Jackin had been wounded, she couldn't change that. She needed to concentrate on what she still might be able to fix.

She'd have to find some way to come to terms with the sovereign, which wasn't an easy feat when Drudgers were involved. Drudger penance tended toward one of two styles: outright execution or indentured servitude. They didn't generally take well to payoffs, even if she had something to barter, which she definitely didn't. It'd be a lot easier to strategize if she knew what the hell they wanted from them.

Cavalon unsubtly cleared his throat. "Uh, Rake . . ." He kept his chin straight and spoke without moving his lips. "What's going on?"

Adequin cast a furtive glance at the guards behind them. "Their sovereign has requested an audience," she whispered.

His eyes darted, though his expression remained placid. "What the hell is a *sovereign*?"

"It's a shitty translation. The word means more like . . . an orienteer, kind of. Like a societal helmsman."

"Explain?" he squeaked.

"It was a Viator thing," she explained, "a title that shifted between them fluidly based on the primary needs of the unit—military or civilian. It was their way of maintaining some semblance of leadership in an otherwise flat society."

Cavalon sighed. "Right. Because they didn't segregate."

She gave a shallow nod. It was a structure that required a great deal of faith in one's species. That kind of unmitigated trust was something humanity had yet to scratch the surface of. By their very nature, she wasn't sure they were capable of it.

"But if they don't segregate," Cavalon whispered, "how do they justify having something called a *sovereign*?"

She shook her head. "Again, it's a misnomer, but we were taught to translate it to that. It's not what you're thinking—sovereigns were only seen as leaders because the others agreed it was so. They helped determine the will of their people to guide the group. The others respected them as an overseer, but if the sovereign fell short or their needs changed, they just picked a new one."

"And everyone was okay with that?"

She shrugged. "It worked for them for thousands of years. Drudgers don't usually adopt it, though it's not unheard of."

Cavalon's jaw flexed, sweat slicking his blond hair to his forehead. Adequin could sense the anxiety rolling off him in waves, but he kept his chin up, shoulders back, chest out, and did a surprisingly good job of keeping it in check.

Adequin's knees had just begun to ache from prolonged kneeling when the entrance at the top of the dais slid open.

Two Drudgers marched in, the first carrying a bladed staff, the other a short plasma rifle. They both wore gunmetal gray armor similar to the guards, but with more decorative flourishes and a muted-teal cloth tabard that hung off either hip.

But as the door slid shut behind them, Adequin froze. Adrenaline coursed through her veins, her instincts seizing her muscles with a panic she didn't know the source of. She strove to keep from fidgeting against her bindings. Something was wrong.

Her eyes drew to the two newcomers. They were too tall, too thin, and the pieces of carapace visible under their armor lacked the metallic sheen of the guards. The taller one with the rifle came to a stop in front of the bench. It stared down at her and Cavalon with two sets of glossy black eyes.

Adequin's breath scratched against the back of her throat. Not two Drudgers. Two Viators.

The shorter one with the staff stepped forward, pausing at the edge of the dais. Warmth swelled in Adequin's cheeks.

She'd recognize *that* Viator anywhere, with their weathered, slate-gray carapace, stippled with stark flecks of maroon. Pleated skin creased their forehead as they stared with some manner of curiosity.

It was the face that'd haunted her dreams for five years. She could practically smell the dank mustiness of the cave walls in Paxus as her mind pulled forth memories she'd been trying so hard to forget.

Adequin looked from the breeder to the other Viator, a guard of some sort, who stayed back beside the throne-like bench, rifle clutched in both taloned hands. They stood half a head taller than the breeder, with deep, charcoal-black skin that conveyed an age of at least eighty—sixty or so by human standards. The narrow skin folds on the guard's face tightened in what could have been mistaken for a scowl. But she'd never been very good at reading Viator expressions.

She knew that face as well—the one from the recording they'd found aboard the *Synthesis*. The one giving instructions to the Drudgers they'd killed. The one who'd set them on a course to restarting dark energy generators.

Her mind warred with it, just as it had when they'd first seen the recording. And she didn't want to believe it any more now than she did then. But she couldn't ignore it this time; this time it was staring her straight in the face. Literally.

The breeder's gaze drifted over Adequin with an evaluative steadiness. A pattern of dark steel and bronze Imprint tattoos ran up the hardened shell of their left arm. Their trimmed talons clicked as they reaffirmed their grip on the staff, Imprints remaining static.

That the Imprints didn't move seemed an item worthy of note, and Adequin focused on that minor detail to keep her panic in check.

Cavalon let out a gritty squeak, then whispered, "Rake, are they . . . ?"

With an effort, Adequin cleared her throat. "Yeah."

Cavalon's composed facade melted, and he slunk back, shoulders and chin dropping as he sat back on his feet.

Adequin flexed her jaw, a knot of sympathy twisting in her gut. He'd never been in the same room as a Viator before, probably never even in the same galactic sector as one. The engagements of the Resurgence War had been confined to the Outer Core—occasionally leaking into the fringes of the Perimeter Veil and the Lateral Reach. But the Legion had ensured it'd never gotten remotely close to the Core.

The pleated skin of the breeder's forehead flattened, and they made a diffident hand motion.

To Adequin's right, one of the Drudger guards marched toward them, armor clanking in the otherwise silent room. Cavalon flinched as it passed behind him, but it continued on to Adequin.

Its taloned fingertips scraped against her wrapped forearms as it grabbed at her wrists. Seconds later, the cuffs fell away with a clatter.

Adequin's panic-stiffened muscles kept her frozen in place, and she peripherally eyed the guard as it returned to its spot beside the door.

The breeder's gaze tilted. Two of their four black eyes blinked. "Stand," they said in Viator, and if Adequin didn't know better, she'd say their tone conveyed invitation much more than instruction.

Did she know better?

They'd never been taught to read Viator emotional cues—mostly it'd been implied Viators had no emotions other than scalding indifference or outright hostility. But she'd watched enough recon footage and spied on enough conversations to have intuited a few things. Yet she still didn't know if she could fully trust her instincts.

Adequin bit back a groan and with an effort, got up off her aching knees. She rubbed at where the bindings had chafed her wrists as she straightened to her full height. Though the shot they'd given had invigorated her, her insides still ached from . . . whatever means had brought them here, and she still felt a little like she'd been chewed up and spat back out.

The breeder descended the dais. They stepped up to her, a good fifteen centimeters taller, and stared her straight in the eye. "Welcome to the *Presidian*."

Adequin blinked, stunned into silence.

"I am called Kaize."

She swallowed over a hard lump. "Rake."

"Rake." The single syllable grated its way from the back of Kaize's throat.

Cavalon exhaled a creaking breath, a barely throttled whimper.

"And this one?" Kaize asked.

"Bray," Adequin replied, injecting every bit of will she had into keeping her expression unreadable, and the lie hidden from her already-turbulent vitals. "My aide," she explained, and fully intended to leave it at that. Old war pals or no, there was no way she was going to admit who Cavalon really was.

"The corruption in your arms . . ." Kaize said, continuing in the Viator tongue. "Have you sensed improvement?"

"Yes," Adequin replied with a slow nod.

"Adaxorine works swiftly."

She blinked while she searched her memory for the word. "An antibiotic?"

"Yes. You bore a Viator infection."

Adequin's brow creased.

"There are virulent bacterial strains known to thrive in the sealed warmth of our neural network machines," Kaize explained. "We inoculate our young against them. We have not seen a human case in many cycles, but the symptoms are axiomatic."

Adequin traced her fingers along her wrapped forearm. "I'd thought my Imprints had turned against me."

"Much the opposite, legionnaire. They have been quarantining the infection, reducing blood flow to your forearms and cleansing the blood that returns. The bruising and veins on your upper arms are proof of the bacteria beginning to break down those barriers. You would have died had it reached your heart."

Adequin stared, unblinking, at a loss for words. She dismissed her shock with an effort, then inclined her head slowly. "I suppose I owe you my life, then."

The thin skin folds on Kaize's forehead puckered. "And I, you."

A chill tore down Adequin's spine. She wondered when they were going to get around to discussing the war-ending, traitor-making elephant in the room.

"Though in a way," Kaize continued, "I suppose it was more than one life you gave."

Adequin licked her dry lips, holding Kaize's inky-black stare for a few long moments.

"This is very much *caelestis*, is it not, legionnaire?" Kaize said.

Adequin's mind raced to translate the word, but she was coming up short.

"The will of the universe," Kaize explained. "To burden us with the same task, then to see that we share oxygen again, after being separated by so many cycles and light-years."

"Caelestis," Adequin agreed, the new word strange on her tongue. She assigned the definition to memory, not able to come up with an accurate one-to-one translation. Other than maybe one. But she didn't believe in fate.

"When we convoked the *Fusion*," Kaize said, "we expected to bring aboard the captain of our missing contractors. The summoner is not designed for human physiology. Your Imprints have mitigated damage to you and your aide, but I must apologize for the state of your elder kinsman."

Adequin let loose a long breath from the confines of her strained chest, unable to do anything but blink at the Viator apologizing to her. She took a second to right herself before responding, though her voice still wavered. "Is he okay?"

"Our technicians are looking into it."

"Can I see him?"

"Not presently."

Adequin bit the inside of her cheek and nodded reluctantly.

"May I ask why you have commandeered the *Fusion*?" Kaize asked.

Adequin gulped. "Your contractors attacked our relay gate and one of our ships. They were . . . eliminated in the process."

Kaize rolled their wide head on their thick neck, eyes slitting as they dragged a disdainful look between the four Drudger guards standing post at the doors behind Adequin. "I knew the brutes would find a way to use it maliciously. I apologize for any difficulties they caused you and your kinsmen. Under ideal circumstances, I would have never given them something as powerful as a curanulta."

"But they needed it as a key into the generators?" Adequin surmised.

Kaize's chin raised in a nod. "Yes. The dilachia carthen, where you acquired the infection. May I ask which sites you visited?"

"To my knowledge, all of them."

The larger pair of Kaize's eyes rounded.

Adequin cleared her throat. "When we found the curanulta and realized what your contractors were supposed to be doing, we did our best to continue the work. We restarted every surviving generator at the Divide—at least, the Legion-occupied section of it. Three alpha generators were destroyed, maybe more. But all the betas survived."

"I see . . ." A fleck of curiosity narrowed Kaize's eyes, and they were silent for a long while before they spoke again, tone slow and even. "It is very much caelestis there was someone both perceptive enough to realize what needed done, and selfless enough to attend it. I understand it very nearly reached the Apollo Gates' empyrean curve?"

Adequin gave a soft nod, though she was still working over the translation of the last words. She'd not heard that phrasing before—empyrean curve—but it must refer to the configuration of the Apollo Gates at the Divide. Though to Adequin's knowledge, they didn't sit along any kind of preconceived line. If *empyrean* meant they were supposed to mirror the shape of the universe, they'd been doing a poor job the last three-thousand-plus years; until the beta generators had been restarted, the Divide's arc had been far wider than any imaginary line one could create connecting the gates.

"If you mean the Divide's relay gates," Adequin replied, "then yes. Very nearly." By light-years maybe, but cosmically speaking, centimeters.

Kaize angled their look at Adequin's wrapped forearms. "And you risked your own flesh, and certainly your life many times over, in the process . . . Thank you."

Adequin clenched her jaw and stared at the Viator *thanking* her. She'd wake up any second now.

"Tell me, legionnaire," Kaize went on, "why have you left your post?"

Adequin hesitated, drawing in a slow breath as she turned to Cavalon. Things had been too weird the last few minutes, and she wanted to gain his support for admitting the truth, but one look at his ghost-white face reminded her that he didn't have any idea what they were saying. He could read some Viator—maybe most, at this point—but not speak it. For all he knew, they could just as well be negotiating to trade him for the ceronite as swapping recipes.

"Hey, it's okay," she assured him, tone low. "It's going well."

He stared at her, unblinking, not appearing even minimally assured.

She returned to Kaize, taking a deep breath as she considered her options. She didn't want to start this relationship—or continue it, she supposed—with lies. And she didn't want to give Kaize any reason to turn against them while they still held Jackin's life in their hands.

"We're trying to leave the Divide," she admitted. She shook her head. "It's complicated, but . . . our people abandoned us out there. Now we're trying to return to the galaxy, but we've run out of a metamaterial for our jump drive. A team of us have come to find some."

"Ceronite?" Kaize asked.

Adequin inclined her head, mind churning to remember the exact Viator translation for it. "Ceronite," she repeated. "Yes."

Kaize's chin raised. "As you may have noticed from the planet you were orbiting, your kinsmen have made a fine point of razing our former manufacturing facilities."

Adequin glanced at Cavalon, recalling what he'd said about the SC's efforts to consolidate ceronite production. Apparently that included scouring outer worlds for every last trace of it.

"I am afraid you will find it difficult to come across here," Kaize said. "You will likely only find it somewhere in your central worlds."

Adequin clenched her jaw, trying to keep the stab of dread from showing on her face. "We can't reach the Core before our people at the Divide will starve. Are there no other factories left?"

"Not that are known to us. Ceronite acquisition has become problematic for us as well, as we continue restarting the dilacha carthen." Kaize made a soft ticking noise, gaze drifting up. "If your kinsmen only knew what a hindrance they are to their own continued existence . . ."

Adequin's brow creased, and it took her a moment to connect the dots. The Legion only occupied a small section of a theoretically all-but-endless network of generators, all around the edges of the universe. Of course Kaize would have had to contract out some of the work.

At that, Adequin forcibly canceled the thought from her brain as the scope threatened to overwhelm her sense of logic. Feeling inconsequential to the universe had become pretty run-of-the-mill the last five years, but she'd grown no more desensitized to the scope of the Divide's construction than when it'd first been posed to her after they realized what the generators were.

"How long have you been restarting the dilacha carthen?" Adequin asked.

Kaize's taloned fingers clacked as they drummed against their staff. They didn't seem as though they intended to respond, but finally said, "It is a wheel that always turns. A cycle that never ends."

"You should have told us," Adequin said, her voice quiet in the otherwise silent room. "We could have been helping you restart them all along."

The thin folds of skin on Kaize's forehead creased deeper. "Your kind would not have allied with us, even for their own sakes—they have too much reckless pride. And we could not have come out of hiding to present the issue without causing mass panic at best, another war at worst. Then to trust your kinsmen with knowledge of that technology afterwards?" Kaize's grip firmed on the staff. "No, it is untenable. Drudgers, despite their many weaknesses, are at least loyal."

Adequin let out a shallow sigh. That was a fair assessment, so she found it difficult to refute.

"We learned long ago there would be no possibility of lasting peace with humans . . ." Kaize's thin lips turned down. "This technology is dangerous, and we must keep it from those who would use it irresponsibly. I trust you will conceal its presence from your kinsmen, to the best of your abilities."

"Of course," Adequin said, and though her wavering voice may have projected some degree of dishonesty, it wasn't a lie. The second she'd realized what the generators did, she'd wanted nothing more than to strike the knowledge from her own mind and hide it from humanity forever.

The door at the top of the dais swished open. Aros walked in, clutching the atlas pyramid in its taloned hands. It passed the atlas to the charcoal-skinned Viator beside the bench, along with the chain containing the medallion and dog tags. Aros gave a perfunctory bow, then left.

The Viator guard marched down the steps and handed the atlas to Kaize, who gave a chin-lift nod of appreciation.

Adequin stared at the atlas, the gold geometric facades still stained with swaths of Jackin's dried blood.

"We have liberated it," Kaize said, their tone that of explanation, though Adequin didn't follow.

"Liberated?" she asked, repeating the word, positive her internal translation of it was incorrect. Maybe more like unlocked.

"We did not trust our contractors enough to leave it open to its full capabilities," Kaize said, then held the atlas out toward Adequin. "You will need it as a passkey to the Arcullian Gates, as well as the updated maps to guide you there."

Adequin's lips parted, opening and closing a few times in speechless confusion. "Arcullian Gate?"

"If you intend to acquire ceronite and return to your kinsmen at the Divide, you will need a quick, discreet way into and out of the Core."

She blinked. "And you're giving us a quick, discreet way?" she asked, her voice cracking at the edges.

Kaize gestured out with the atlas again, and Adequin took the device. Kaize pressed the chain with the triangle medallion and dog tags into her other hand. "Please ensure it does not fall into the wrong hands."

Adequin managed to croak out, "I will," before her throat went bone dry. Her balmy fingers closed around the cold metal chain.

"Your kinsmen aboard the *Fusion* have retreated out of orbit and are not responding to our attempts at communication," Kaize said. "We ask that you visit our bridge to persuade them to land in our docking bay, so your wounded kinsman can be safely transferred."

Warmth flooded Adequin's face. Jackin was well enough to be transferred. And to be called "wounded" and not "dying" or "a corpse."

Yet she hesitated. She had to—one weirdly peaceful conversation could not override a decade of training. Could she really willingly drop her team into the docking bay of a Viator battleship?

But if it was all a trap, it'd be an unnecessarily elaborate one. Considering the guns they had on this battlecruiser, they could outlast their shields and destroy the *Synthesis* a hundred times over. The ship itself was certainly not worth salvaging.

Adequin inhaled deeply, forcing the paranoia down. "You're okay with us keeping the *Fusion*?" she asked.

Kaize's facial folds thinned, eyes narrowing in an almost discerning look. "We needn't pretend I am doing you any great favor by bestowing that derelict vessel."

Adequin pressed out a flat smile, confusion bubbling in her chest. Kaize had made a joke. A Viator had made a joke.

She glanced at Cavalon to share in her disbelief, but his distant look reminded her he had no idea what was going on.

At Kaize's silent instruction, two of the Drudgers standing guard at the doorways marched forward, falling into an escort formation around them. One lifted Cavalon to his feet and released his bindings. Cavalon rubbed his wrists, staring between the Drudgers with slack-mouthed confusion. Adequin secured the medallion chain around her neck while they led them toward one of the back doorways.

Adequin paused in the threshold and turned back to Kaize. "Thank you. I know you didn't have to do this."

"It was not a difficult decision, as far as decisions go," they said, gaze drifting over Adequin. "You made a considerably more difficult one, those many cycles ago. I have made a choice to emulate that. It is a shame your kinsmen have hidden what you have done. Rectitude left unseen bears the danger of inconsequence. It should be an example for your kind, not a regret."

"I know," Adequin said, heat flushing her cheeks. "But they weren't ready for it."

"I understand," Kaize said. "Just know, legionnaire, that we are not interested in more wars."

Adequin gave a shallow nod and turned to go, guilt beating in her chest as she tried not to think about how she was on her way to start one.

Aros and Sanook joined the two armored Drudger guards, escorting Adequin and Cavalon from the chamber through a maze of empty hallways. They'd either cleared the corridors for the sake of their visit, or possessed a complement barely large enough to maintain a ship this size. Adequin got the feeling it was the latter.

As they walked, she did her best to convey to Cavalon what she and Kaize had discussed, and his utter terror faded to barely restrained terror. She was sure he heard the words, but less sure he was currently capable of processing them.

They finally came upon a broad, double door at the end of a wide corridor. Aros guided her forward, while Sanook kept Cavalon back.

Adequin made to protest, but Aros growled, "The aide stays," then dragged her on.

Still clutching the atlas pyramid, she threw a helpless glance at Cavalon as Aros pressed her forward. The wide doors slid open, and she stepped inside.

She took a deep breath, her thoughts automatically deferring her worry over Cavalon and Jackin, sliding straight into reconnaissance mode. She'd just been brought aboard an active Viator bridge. And despite any confusion about their status as an adversary, the Titan in her couldn't help itself.

The room was at least twenty meters in diameter with terminals lining almost every wall. A glow of white holographic light drew her eye to the center, where a globe of three-dimensional maps hovered over a sunken dais, which brought the center of the array to eye-height. Though massively more complex, the map system's structure and design matched their atlas menus almost exactly.

Aros gripped her shoulder harder and pressed her toward the far wall. The dim room relied on the holographic array as the main source of light, though a few strips of red running lights dotted the decking and stairways.

Her eyes quickly scanned the dozen inhabitants. Mostly Drudgers in simple gray jumpsuits, though at least two had the height to be Viators. Most pretended to ignore her, but a few of the lighter-skinned ones snuck looks as Aros shuffled her past. For some, it might have been their first time seeing a human.

Aros led her up to a wide terminal on the back wall. A comms menu had already been opened. The operator standing by tapped at the screen with its taloned fingers, and a video call interface expanded.

"Go," Aros instructed.

Adequin pressed the call button. "*Synthesis*, this is Excubitor Adequin Rake aboard the *Presidian*, please respond."

She waited, boot tapping against the metal decking.

"Em," she said, hoping the casual tone might encourage them. "It's safe, I promise. Accept the call."

Seconds later, a staticky image appeared. The interference cleared away as Emery leaned over the dash, staring slack-jawed at the camera. "Boss . . ." Her round eyes darted, taking in the room behind Adequin. "Shit . . ."

"We're all right, Em. We're free to go, but we need you to dock. The *Presidian* will send landing clearance."

Emery leaned in, her face distorting with the wide angle of the camera, then whispered, "Blink twice if this is a trap."

Adequin sighed. "It's not a trap." She hoped. "We're safe; we just need a pickup. But have Ford prep the medbay for Jackin. Stomach wound—maybe burns. Transfusion kit."

Emery's stiffened awe deflated, and she frowned. "Copy that, boss."

"See you soon, Em."

Aros closed the connection, then swept a taloned hand toward the door.

When they exited the bridge, Cavalon and the rest of the escort were no longer waiting for them. Aros kept a hand on her shoulder, guiding her forward through the maze of halls. She stayed quiet, actively suppressing her Imprints' rising desire to spread into a combat formation. With her crew en route, if it *was* a trap, now would be when they'd toss her in a cell and throw away the key.

Eventually they rounded a corner into a wide corridor that, if Adequin's memory of Viator battlecruisers served, led directly to the primary hangar. A small cluster of armed Drudgers waited to one side. Amongst them, Cavalon stood clutching Jackin under one arm, struggling to hold him upright.

Adequin slid out of Aros's grip. She jogged up to them, taking Jackin's other arm over her shoulder. He sagged into her. A flood of relief warmed her chest—that he was even alive, let alone conscious. But her stomach twisted at how pallid his light brown skin looked. Both of his hands had been encased in gauze mitts. They'd done away with his shirt entirely, and medical mesh wrapped his midsection, only partially obscuring the streaks of old scars covering his back.

"Shit, Jack." She struggled to keep the atlas pyramid tucked under one arm, securing her other hand around Jackin's waist. From the weight he leaned into her, he needed the help. "Are you okay?"

"Just peachy, boss," he groaned. A layer of sweat coated his scalding skin, and his eyes stayed clamped shut. Dried blood still stained his ears and nose.

A buzzing click of sliding Imprints startled a surge of adrenaline into her system. Her eyes darted to Cavalon first, then Aros, then the Drudgers, though no one seemed to be priming a strike. Then her gaze fell on Jackin's right arm, which Cavalon had gripped in both hands at the elbow to help keep him standing.

"Holy shit," Cavalon muttered.

Three lines of glossy white Imprint squares ran along Jackin's right arm, the stark color contrasted against his light brown skin. A few scuttled out of their default alignment—a row running from the top of his hand to halfway up his forearm before bifurcating into two lines up his bicep. They curved onto the top of his shoulder, then disappeared behind his back. The rest were busy at work: white squares darting from under the edges of the mesh around his abdomen, buzzing as they scuttled over the wound.

Adequin stared, lips parting in shock. Though an objectively drastic solution, it actually made a lot of sense. Imprints were one piece of Viator tech they'd never had to adapt for human physiology, because the nanites did that part for them. Though the Imprints couldn't make up for the lost blood, they'd expedite the healing and be able to reach any internal issues far quicker than anything else available outside of a proper human medical facility.

The fact that they had a Viator Imprint machine on board was more surprising than anything they'd encountered yet. There were only six in use by humans—one controlled by each of the five royal families, and one by the Legion, reserved for Titans and the upper echelon of the Vanguard. Each had a limited number of uses before they'd run out of whatever nanite-metamaterial cocktail made them work. Adequin had no doubt the SC had a round-the-clock task force of scientists dedicated to cracking that mystery.

Jackin's jaw flexed with a throttled a groan, and she tightened her grip on his waist as his sweat-slicked skin threatened to slip out from under her. She didn't envy him. Getting Imprints applied was a horrible, painful process, and to have that pain on top of the wounds he'd suffered . . . she couldn't imagine.

Aros and the other Drudgers suddenly stood up straight, shoulders squaring off perpendicular to the hall. Adequin craned her neck to find Kaize and the Viator guard rounding the corner behind them, followed by four of the armored Drudgers. Aros nudged Adequin forward, and with Cavalon's aid, she hauled Jackin toward the hangar.

The *Synthesis* sat docked in the nearest of a dozen empty berths in the multitiered hangar. Instead of the personnel ramp, the wide cargo ramp lowered and two armor-clad figures marched out. It took Adequin a moment to recognize them as Emery and Owen—decked out in full combat gear and shouldering the biggest rifles they had on board.

Owen stuttered to a stop halfway down the ramp. She lifted the visor on her helmet and stared past Adequin. She slapped Emery on the shoulder, and Emery halted. They mumbled an exchange, then Emery backpedaled a half meter before Owen grabbed the edge of her chestplate to stop her.

Adequin glanced back at the imposing retinue behind her. She had to wonder if Kaize had decided to come see them off for the sole purpose of startling her crew. Not that she could say she wouldn't have done the same.

Ford appeared to have no such reservations as he slipped between Emery and Owen and rushed down the ramp. He jogged straight to Jackin and held a hand to the side of his face. "Shit, he's warm. North, you with me?"

"Yeah," Jackin said, voice groggy. "Here."

"Bloody void," Ford muttered, then looked to Adequin, searching for answers.

"They gave him Imprints to stop the internal bleeding," she explained. "I think they're still working on the gut wound. But I'd start a full scan to see what's been addressed. I don't think he's had painkillers."

Ford's brow drew down as he stood to his full height, shoulders tense and jaw firm. He turned the glare onto Kaize and their retinue.

Adequin's heart kicked as Jackin let out a whimpering groan. "Ford," Adequin said, half-order, half-warning, then let her tone soften. "Please, just take him."

Ford's glower broke and he gave a curt nod. "All right. Here we go, mate," he breathed. He hefted Jackin into his arms, then carried him into the ship.

Adequin exchanged a strained look with Cavalon, then turned to face Kaize. "Thank you," she said. "Those Imprints likely saved his life."

Kaize tilted their head. "His condition is our fault. It is the least we could do."

Adequin passed the atlas to Cavalon, and he reluctantly started up the ramp, eyeing her over his shoulder.

"And thank you for letting us keep the curanulta," Adequin said.

"Put it to good use saving your people."

"I will."

"Farewell, legionnaire."

Adequin started up the ramp, then paused a few meters up. "Kaize?"

They stared back expectantly.

"It's not legionnaire . . . it's Sentinel."

Kaize lifted their chin in a nod. "May caelestis continue to favor you, Sentinel."

Adequin gave a grateful nod. Emery and Owen fell in behind her as she ascended the ramp into the belly of the *Synthesis*.

CHAPTER SEVENTEEN

Cavalon dropped the bloodstained atlas pyramid onto the dash of the *Synthesis*. It was like when he was a kid, and they'd come out with battle-damaged versions of action figures, complete with scuffed armor, split lips, and bloodied scowls. At least, that was the only correlation his over-whelmed mind was willing to make at the moment.

After they'd boarded the *Synthesis*, Rake had gone straight to the medbay to help Ford, while Emery flew them out of the maw of the *Presidian* as quickly as humanly possible. They now orbited a nearby moon, awaiting Rake's instruction. Which left Cavalon, Emery, and Owen in the cockpit sharing uneasy glances, feeling like the kids left to figure out how to make themselves dinner while the adults dealt with a crisis.

That whole situation had been way, way too much. How Rake had kept her shit together enough to be a functional, well-spoken, productive person, he'd never know.

How he'd kept *his* shit together enough to stand there mutely and not internally collapse, he *did* know, unfortunately. He'd homed in on the same thread of detached lucidity he used to call on after he and Augus-tus had a particularly contentious bout, and he'd be subsequently forced into a round of "therapy," or what Cavalon more accurately referred to as reconditioning. He'd only gotten through it without attempting to murder the therapist by retreating into himself, mechanically spouting the words he knew they wanted to hear, and pretending he was watching it all through an entertainment feed and not his own eyes. Little did he know the technique would serve him again when faced with meeting *actual living Viators* in person.

Admittedly, it felt a little irrational to be proud of himself for simply not falling apart at the seams and for standing like a houseplant while Rake did the legwork, but he had to take whatever morsels of self-pride he could these days.

Owen flung off her harness to turn and gape at him. "What the actual fuck just happened?"

Emery closed a handful of flight screens, then shouldered out of her harness and spun to kneel on her seat, gripping the back of her headrest, green eyes burning with terrified curiosity. "Did you . . . *teleport* onto that ship?"

Cavalon gulped, heat scorching the back of his neck. As much as he'd pressured Rake earlier on calling it like it was—she'd been right.

Saying it out loud was too overwhelming. "I mean, I don't have another explanation for it . . ."

"Bloody void." Emery sat back on her feet with a sigh.

Owen gave a breathy scoff. "Sorry, but who the hell cares about the stupid teleportation? Were those fucking *Viators*?"

Cavalon's shoulders lifted in a weak shrug. "Only two of them."

"Oh, well, if it's only two of them," she mocked, then her sassy demeanor fell away to gruffness again. "Of a supposedly *extinct* species. All of whom wanted us all very, very dead not that long ago."

"How did you get out of there?" Emery asked. "Did Rake have to trade all our firstborns or something?"

Cavalon sighed, too tired to roll his eyes. "No. It was just a . . . misunderstanding."

Owen squeaked out a dry laugh. "A misunderstanding? How's that exactly?"

"When they saw the *Synthesis*, they thought we were their missing Drudger crew."

Emery's face paled. "The ones we killed at Kharon Gate?"

He nodded.

"Well . . . shit." Emery chewed on her bottom lip and started peeling off her combat armor. "Were they pissed?"

Cavalon gave a weary shrug. "They spoke Viator the whole damn time, I only partly understood what happened. It didn't seem like they really cared about the Drudgers." He threw a forlorn look at the atlas pyramid. "I mean, they gave us that shit back, after all."

Emery and Owen slid edgy looks at the bloodied device, like it was some beloved ally that had been taken hostage and might have turned traitor.

"So those Viators were sending Drudger crews out to restart dark energy generators?" Owen asked.

"Yeah," Cavalon replied, "and doing it themselves, apparently."

Emery quirked a brow, piling armor onto the dash. "If they're restarting generators, then what the hell were they doin' in the Drift? The Divide's not exactly nearby."

Cavalon shook his head. "I don't think they *were* here. They must have had a trigger to warn them when our atlas, or the *Synthesis*, arrived back inward. They were upward of the Perimeter Veil just a few days ago."

Owen shook her head. "The Veil? Even if they saw us the second we relayed through Poine, they never could have made it far enough to meet up with us in five days. It'd take *way* longer than that to get down here from the Veil."

"I know," Cavalon sighed, "but I swear that's what it said."

Emery turned a discerning glower onto him. "What *what* said?"

"There was an open bulletin on a console near the hangar."

"And you *read* it?"

"Yes . . ."

She quirked a thin brow. "You can read Viator?"

"Yeah, I mean . . . yeah." He gave a helpless shrug.

"Since when?"

He glowered. "Since six months ago when you all expected me to build a fucking star from scratch using blueprints and code written in their damn language. Why's everyone so surprised I'm capable of learning?"

Owen gave him a consoling pat on the back. "That's not normal learning, dude."

A menu on the dash beeped, then Rake's voice crackled through. "Rake for Helm."

Emery yanked her chestplate off, then shook her limbs out. She tapped the call open. "Emery here, sir."

"Stay in orbit for now, but keep it rigged and ready to go. Have Cavalon bring the curanulta to the medbay, please. Stay patched in; we're going to have a meeting."

"Copy that, sir." Emery tossed the battle-damaged atlas at Cavalon and he caught it awkwardly.

"Thanks," he mumbled, then headed out the door.

Cavalon shuffled into the *Synthesis*'s small medbay. Across the room, Jackin lay on the half-reclined exam table. He appeared conscious, though tired as hell, with heavy bags under his dark brown eyes. A transfusion kit hung on a rail above the bed, feeding a line of blood into his arm.

Beside him, Ford sat on the edge of a stool, though with his tall frame, it was more of a lean. He held a biotool, staring down at it earnestly.

Rake hovered at Jackin's other side, his dried blood smeared up her wrapped forearms and bruised biceps, and staining her gray T-shirt. Strands of brown hair fell around her sweat-slicked face, more streaks of blood on both cheeks. Battle-damaged Rake.

Cavalon squeezed his eyes shut, fighting back flashes of Jackin aboard the *Presidian*, in those terrifying few moments before Rake arrived to calmly manage the situation: Jackin hunched on all fours, retching an inhuman, green fluid out onto the cell floor. Jackin with blood draining out his ears while he croaked out a guttural cry and extracted the blistering hot atlas pyramid from his own stomach. Jackin crumpling, writhing, slick with blood. Damn his fucking flawless memory.

Cavalon opened his eyes. Jackin squirmed on the exam table as Rake held him down and injected something into his arm. The veins in his neck swelled with stifled pain. His new glossy white Imprint tattoos slid across his light brown skin as they rushed to maintain multiple tasks.

Battle-damaged Jackin was too much, too scary. Cavalon didn't like seeing him laid up like this. Jackin may have harried him daily for the last six months, but he'd also been supportive and patient and appreciative, if broadly aloof and distant. And Cavalon knew why. Jackin hated Augustus, as everyone in their right mind did. He'd kept himself at a distance because of it, and Cavalon couldn't blame him.

A normal person might wonder when they last saw someone they cared about this grievously injured, but for Cavalon, the answer was far too simple: never. Before his grandmother had disappeared, she'd never taken ill, and before he died, neither had his father. And that's exactly where the list began and ended. His eyes drifted to Rake. Where it *had* begun and ended. Now he had all these damn people to worry about. What rational person leaves a life of luxury and safety to get themselves into one of the most dangerous situations in the universe *then* decides to start giving a shit about people?

"Cav?"

He looked up to find Rake approaching.

"You okay?"

He blinked a few times. "Yeah," he croaked out. "Sorry, I'm still processing. That was a lot."

"Yeah, it was," she said, keeping her voice low. She gripped his arm. "We just need to focus for a little bit longer, figure out where we're going. Then we'll talk it out—you and me, okay?"

He gave a shallow nod.

"Besides me, you have the most experience with the atlas," she said. "I need you here for this."

"I'm here," he said, tone firm.

She gave a grateful nod, then crossed the few meters back to Jackin's side.

Cavalon firmed his grip on the hard edges of the warm atlas pyramid as he forced himself toward the foot of the exam table, trying to ignore how much of Jackin's dried blood still stained his own clothing.

The biotool beeped, and Ford sat up straight.

"Will I survive, doc?" Jackin quipped, his voice a dry, hoarse croak.

"You better," Ford mumbled. He scanned the readout and the furrows in his brow smoothed slightly.

"Ford . . ." Rake prompted, a hint of warning in her tone.

"Aye, apologies—internal bleeding looks to be fully repaired. They musta given him some kinda clotting agent. The stomach wound is deep, but his Imprints've built up a few layers of tissue already. It'll take a day or two to fully seal, and muscle work beyond that." He clasped Jackin's shoulder in a light grip. "I'd say you have a couple weeks' worth of recovery ahead'a ya."

Jackin grimaced down at the glossy white Imprints shuffling around his bandaged torso.

Rake squeezed his other shoulder. "I know your instinct right now is to fix the worst of it, but your Imprints draw on your body's energy to work. You'll exhaust yourself if you let them go on too long. They'll need breaks."

Jackin frowned. "I don't know how to stop them."

"We'll work on it," Rake assured him. "Don't worry for now."

"What the hell caused all this?" Ford asked.

Jackin shook his head. "They didn't tell me shit. They just took me straight to the Imprint machine, and I, uh . . . I'm missing some time after that."

Ford looked to Rake, but she shook her head. "I wasn't with him. But it sounds like it was a side effect of how we . . ." Her gaze drifted to Cavalon. He gulped. "*Arrived* on the ship."

Ford blew out a hard sigh.

"We need to figure out our next steps," Rake said, then looked to Jackin. "Are you up for it now?"

"Yeah," Jackin said with a grimace. "Let's get on with it before these Imprints run me dry."

She leaned to tap open a comms menu on the terminal above the counter nearest Jackin. "Em, you still there?"

"Yessir."

"Owen as well?"

"Here, sir," Owen replied.

"All right." Rake cleared her throat. "Despite recent complications, the mission objective stands: acquire ceronite. We need a new source."

"Sir, we did check," Owen warned, "and there's no Legion ansible in system."

Ford nodded. "We can hop to the next system and look, but it could take a while to find a functioning one out here. Even then, I can't say what our chances would be in finding another ceronite factory."

Rake inclined her head. "I did get some insight into that aboard the *Presidian*."

Ford and Jackin stared at her, mouths round with unsaid words.

"Just like Cavalon had warned," Rake continued, "the sovereign claimed the SC has centralized production to the Core, commandeering any remaining stores and destroying outer-sector factories."

"Wait, I'm sorry—" Jackin practically choked on the words, sliding into a short coughing fit. Ford rubbed his back, offering a bottle of water, but Jackin ignored it. He cleared his throat with a concerted effort. "Sorry, boss, but are we believing things Viators tell us now?"

Rake gave a rueful grimace. "Jack, it was . . . *the* Viator."

Jackin's face fell, the shock flattening his lined brow. "Void . . ."

"Shit, boss," Emery mumbled via comms.

"What're y'all on about?" Ford asked, clueless expression darting between Jackin and Rake, but they both ignored him.

"Yeah, what's that mean exactly?" Owen asked, voice wavering with forced steadiness.

"It means . . . they're not the bad guys," Rake said. "At least, not at the moment."

Ford choked out a disbelieving scoff, but held back comment.

Jackin's bloodshot eyes went to slits. "You really believe they can be trusted?"

"I do," Rake said with steadfast assuredness.

Jackin's shoulders slumped against the reclined back of the exam table. Eventually he gave a steadfast nod and said, "Okay, boss."

Ford eyed Jackin's reaction, disbelief crossing his visage before he slid a mask over it.

"So . . ." Cavalon began, not wanting to worsen the mood, but somebody had to do it, "now are we gonna talk about how it's physically impossible to get to the Core and back in time?"

"Yeah," Emery put in, voice pitchy through the comms speaker. "I ran some quick estimates, and the fastest relay course from here to the nearest Core system is six weeks, and that's using every gate available. If we need to avoid Legion nodes, it'll take even longer."

"I know," Rake said. "But there may be another way."

Jackin lifted a brow. "How's that?"

"Their sovereign said they 'liberated' our atlas," Rake explained. "They said if we use it to find something called an Arcullian Gate, we can reach the Core in time."

"Right . . ." Cavalon murmured, recalling Rake's attempts to update him on their walk to the *Presidian*'s bridge. "But what's an Arcullian Gate?"

"I don't know." Rake inclined her head to the battle-damaged atlas device in Cavalon's hands. "Let's find out."

Cavalon laid the pyramid on the small instruments table at the foot of Jackin's bed. Rake swept the medallion over the top.

A globe of crisp white holographic screens erupted from the peak, stretching over two meters in diameter. Jackin lay just outside the orb, his light brown skin looking even more blanched in the glow of the screens.

Cavalon frowned at the displays. Nothing looked different—it was still set to their default layout, which showed a mostly empty, three-dimensional view of the Divide, with tiny, widely spaced blips indicating Kharon Gate, the *Lodestar*, and the few remaining Apollo Gates and Sentinel vessels dotted along the new border of the universe. The border Rake had built.

Rake backed out of the map view and opened the primary menus. Half the screens morphed into a slew of categories and selections.

Previously, the menu had two options: map and file repository. Now there were dozens and dozens. Cavalon slowly took in the labels, his mind working overtime to translate the Viator symbols. A whole column was dedicated to different default map views, with a few empty slots that looked like savable presets. The central column was all settings categories, then the third was home to things like queries, filters, comms, and one akin to "routes" or "thoroughfares." At the bottom there was a selection he thought said something like "body census" though he really, really hoped his translation was wrong on that one. The ability to show light-years' worth of up-to-date star charts and ship locations was scary enough; all the way down to living beings was too much.

"Void . . ." Jackin croaked. Ford stared in silent awe.

Rake craned her neck to look up at the highest reaches of the extensive menu. "I guess that translation should have been more like . . . *unlocked*, not liberated."

"I don't know . . ." Cavalon said, tone reverent as his eyes drifted over the new layout. "Feels pretty liberating to me."

He shared a look of mildly daunted amusement with Rake, and she gave a relenting tilt of her head. She began opening menus and submenus, setting some aside by sliding them around the arc of screens to the unused portion of the globe behind her. She saved the new layout, then opened a menu labeled with two symbols Cavalon thought meant "query."

A wide, multilayered Viator keyboard expanded in front of her. She started to hunt down symbols, then palmed the keyboard and threw it aside. In its place, a square outline appeared. With one finger, she drew the symbols and they formed as glowing holographic glyphs in the air. Each shrank down after she completed it, lining up below the box until she'd drawn six. She submitted the request. The results splayed out beside the keyboard, and she tapped the top option.

The menu screens slid away, and the entire orb erupted with holographic light. Cavalon squinted as his eyes adjusted.

The interior of the globe now brimmed with tiny dots of light—white, blue, red, green, indicating stars, planets, moons, asteroids, and hell— probably ships. The Divide had been like looking at a blank canvas that had yet to see a single stroke of the cosmic brush. They really were fucking alone out there. No wonder it drove people to madness.

Cavalon stepped closer to one of a hundred tilted discs of amber light. At the center sat a slightly larger white globe, surrounded by six pricks of blue, each with its own thin line indicating its orbit. He touched the white dot with a finger, and a mini holographic placard sprung to life beside it. 20318, four terrestrial planets, two gas giants, and a handful of other orbiting objects. Below that, a list of elements and minerals, but he was too overwhelmed to bother translating it.

He looked up to find Rake similarly investigative. She'd brought up information on a half-dozen amber discs around her.

Rake took a step back, bringing her hands together then thrusting them out, as if ripping a piece of fabric in two. The edges of the holographic orb flew outward, a wash of sharp-edged light melting against the walls of the room. The atlas filled the small medbay, wall-to-wall, with the cartographic light of the galaxy.

"Yeah . . ." Jackin drawled, eyes glittering with reflections of simulated starlight, "let's go with 'liberated.'"

"Well," Ford rumbled, "seems we can safely say we don't need'ta figure out hackin' the Legion extranet for maps . . . *ever* again."

Emery's voice crackled over comms. "Guys, what the heck's goin' on down there?"

Ford paced to the comms terminal. A video feed of the helm blipped into existence above the console, showing Emery in the pilot's seat with Owen hovering over her shoulder.

"What the . . ." Emery exhaled.

Owen leaned in, squinting. "That's *our* atlas?"

Cavalon stepped to examine one of a dozen tiny pulsing symbols composed of two offset crescent moons facing away from each other. Each was highlighted in bright orange. "These glyphs—what do they mean?"

"That's the query I put in," Rake said. "The Arcullian Gates."

Ford scratched his jaw. "Might they simply be undiscovered Apollo Gates?"

"I wondered that," Rake said, "but they have a specific word for Apollo Gates."

"Arc'antile," Cavalon recited.

She slid him a curious glance, but didn't comment.

"There's three showing in this view alone," Jackin said. "There must be dozens more across all the other sectors."

Cavalon shook his head. "No way we just *missed* a couple dozen Apollo Gates."

"We could have, if they weren't connected to the other gates," Owen offered. She squeezed in beside Emery, who slid halfway off the seat to give Owen room to cram in toward the camera. "Only way we found most of the ones we did way back when was because the other relays had the network listed in their databanks. If they weren't on those lists, it'd make sense that we never stumbled across them."

"The question is," Ford said, "is there one close enough?"

Rake lifted both hands and pinched her fingers. The maps responded, moving the view through space as she dragged her hands back in a cycling motion. Cavalon's sight reeled, and he had to look down at his boots, light-years and light-years shuffling past meter by meter as she clawed through space.

"Here's the closest to where we are now," she said finally, and Cavalon looked back up. "Only two systems away."

"And where's it connect?" Jackin asked.

Rake tapped the orange glyph. The gate icon glowed, then dozens of thin white lines spiderwebbed out from it. Cavalon gaped.

The answer was . . . everywhere.

The lines forked to each star system and relay gate visible, all the way up to where the map disappeared into the walls of the medbay.

"Shit," Jackin mumbled.

"It's . . ." Cavalon began, eyes scanning the supposed "available routes." "Wait, what *is* this?"

"These can't be right," Ford said, stepping away from Jackin's side to glower at the display. "There's an exit point for every damn star system in the sector—gate or no gate."

Owen let out a low whistle. "So these Arcullian Gates can drop us practically anywhere in the galaxy, even if there's no return gate?"

Emery sighed. "Guess this explains how our Viator friends got to us so damn quick."

Rake chewed on her bottom lip, amber eyes darting across the impressive web of connections.

"Well, damn," Jackin sighed. "That's incredibly dangerous. You could easily get stranded."

Rake nodded her agreement. "We'll need to be really careful."

She formed a triangle with both hands before swiping her arms out to zoom in. She swiveled the view, then narrowed in on the *Synthesis*—represented by a glowing purple triangle orbiting a blue sphere. She tapped the nearest orange glyph and it calculated the route.

"The gate's only a few hours' warp away," she said, then looked to Jackin. "It's a risk, but I think it's worth taking. None of our other options get us back to the *Lodestar* in time."

Jackin gave a stiff nod of reluctant agreement.

"Sir?" Cavalon asked.

"Go ahead," Rake said.

"It's, uh, all fine and good to find some super secret back door to the Core, but, what the hell are we gonna do once we get there? We can't exactly fly a Drudger ship into a Core system and expect a casual reception."

"Yeah . . ." Owen chimed in, tone reluctant. "I made some tweaks to our transponder and ship systems to keep us quieter, but that won't stand up under Core surveillance. And even if we get that far, the second we land this thing anywhere populated, local Guard will come down on us, asking a billion questions."

Rake's chin bobbed, and her gaze went distant. "Which means we're going to need a new ship," she said, almost to herself. She pulled the tie from her hair and ran her fingers over her scalp a few times. "I'll gladly entertain any ideas."

Emery frowned. "I think all my discreet, wealthy, generous contacts have dried up since I came out to the Divide."

"Your sarcasm doesn't help, babe," Owen muttered.

"Well, I'd imagine you royal types have some contacts to bend," Emery countered.

"Yeah," Cavalon sighed. "That's one way to get us all arrested and/or blown to pieces."

"Probably the latter," Owen said.

"They're too high-profile," Rake agreed. "We can't risk exposing them."

Ford slid a discerning look to Jackin, then lowered his voice. "You could . . ."

Jackin scrubbed a hand over his mouth and let out a long breath.

"I don't know if you have a choice," Ford said, rebutting Jackin's unspoken rejection.

Rake looked at them expectantly. Ford sat down on his stool, arms crossed, seeming like he wanted no part of the conversation.

"Jack?" Rake prompted.

Jackin cleared his throat. "I know some people that might be able to help."

"Who?"

"Corsairs."

Rake's high-browed look fell flat. Emery or Owen made an indiscernible noise through comms.

Cavalon scoffed. "Routers, really? Is that a good idea?"

Jackin's expression remained flat as he kept eye contact with Rake. "They're the most well-connected smugglers in the galaxy. If anyone outside the government and the Legion has access to ceronite, it's them."

Ford nodded. "And to avoid customs and checkpoints, they're our best shot. They've got to have a cleaner ship than this."

It took Cavalon a second to realize he meant *logistically* clean—able to clear security checkpoints without a second glance—and not physically clean, though honestly, both applied.

Rake assessed Ford seriously. Ford glanced at Jackin, who looked back at Rake, his visage stern and unreadable.

Cavalon picked at his nails. What Ford said was true, but that didn't begin to cover how dangerous the idea was. Yes, the Corsairs were known as one of the more morally upstanding router clans, but that was a damn low bar. All that meant was they'd probably not sell them into indentured servitude on sight, depending on the origin of Jackin's relationship with them.

Corsairs could maintain higher standards than other routers due to their influence and wealth. Nowhere near the affluence of, say, a royal family, but pretty high as far as bands of criminals went. That would only make it more difficult to find a way to come to terms, considering how little they had to barter with. Not that Cavalon had any experience smuggling black market goods into Core worlds . . .

"And you know these people?" Rake asked Jackin. "Trust them?"

"Yes. We'll have to come to an agreement, but once we do, they'll hold up their end of it."

"Except we don't have much in the way of cash or collateral to bargain with," Emery pointed out.

Cavalon glanced at the view of Emery and Owen, still crammed together on the pilot's seat. "Money's not an issue," he said, then looked back at Rake. "Or it doesn't have to be. If you can get me to an Outer Core bank."

Rake shook her head. "That's a huge risk; surely Augustus has eyes on your accounts?"

Cavalon gave a light scoff. "You think I keep it all in accounts he knows about? Besides, I've got offshore accounts I can route it through if needed."

She gave him a flat look. "Sure, but let's keep in perspective who we're talking about. Let's not underestimate him already."

He frowned. She wasn't wrong. There wasn't much, if anything, that could be trusted when it came to his grandfather. He was still pretty sure he could get it out safely, though he'd have to pull some pretty complicated shenanigans, and they didn't have that kind of time.

"We don't need money," Jackin interjected, and a heavy quiet fell over the room. He winced and pressed a hand to his stomach.

Rake's brow creased deep. "You need to focus on getting better."

"Trust me," Jackin said, his tone flat, though his eyes looked pleadingly up at her. "It's not a problem."

Rake bit her lip, then nodded. "Okay. Then tell me where we're going."

Four hours later, Cavalon slouched in his crash seat in the cockpit, awaiting deceleration from warp. For the ninetieth time, he tugged his harness straps down to keep them from chafing his neck.

Rake sat in the pilot's seat, silent and stoic since she'd been forced to leave Jackin and Ford in the medbay. The still-bloody atlas pyramid rested on the dash in front of her.

Owen drummed a finger rhythmically on the rim of her starboard-facing defense station, while Emery shifted in the copilot's seat. She chewed rather loudly on her poor bottom lip—a new neurosis caused by her tragic lack of gum.

"How's Centurion North even know where to send us?" Emery asked. "Aren't routers, like . . ." She scratched at her hairline. "Notoriously hard to track down? Isn't that kinda their whole thing?"

Rake gave a stiff shrug. "He had the coordinates memorized, so they must have some kind of permanent base."

"Yeah," Cavalon put in, "Corsairs are one of the few router clans who maintain a legitimate front to mask their shadier dealings, so it's likely they have an established headquarters. Most routers only rent berths in central Core territories during certain trade cycles, then migrate their flagships out to cheaper locales in the off-season. But Corsairs are pretty well established, so that's probably not the case."

Owen slid him an impish grin. "Care to share with the class how you're so well-versed in router operations?"

He held his fingers to his chest and huffed an offended scoff. "Due to my princely education, of course."

"Mm-hmm," Owen hummed, returning her focus to her terminal.

Emery peeked at him past the edge of her seat back, eyes wide with a slightly hedged version of the same ogling treatment she'd given him on Kharon Gate when she'd first learned he had Imprints.

A bleep from the flight console drew everyone's focus to the dash.

Rake swept away an alert. "Decelerating from warp," she warned.

Cavalon's stomach dropped as they slowed to cruising speed. He sighed in relief as he unbuckled his harness, rubbing the sore skin on either side of his neck.

"Shields at one hundred," Owen announced. "Cloak active."

Cavalon paced to stand behind Rake, squinting at the viewscreen as a sliver of black blotted out a narrow portion of the starry backdrop.

"Is that it?" he asked, pointing out the thin band, only visible by the light it blocked.

Rake shook her head. "Maybe. Emery—sensors?"

"Nothin' on sensors," Emery responded. "Visual shows a faint ping, but claims it's a refraction anomaly."

Rake engaged the ion engines. The flat line grew larger but no easier to see as they sped toward it.

"Spotlight," Rake ordered, and Emery flicked it on. "Bringing us around."

Rake steered them in a wide arc. The face of the structure canted into view—a simple, massive triangular framework of black aerasteel. The three facets were constructed of immense, overlaid scaled slabs, a seemingly common ancient Viator design motif. That comforted Cavalon in a way he couldn't quite account for.

He used to feel exactly one way about mysterious, untested ancient Viator technology: terrified. Now, he found his terror throttled by a confusing medley of awe, respect, and . . . gratitude. Just like the dark energy generators, this piece of terrifying technology might help them save the Sentinels.

Rake continued arcing around the structure, and their spotlight caught the inner side of the triangle, lined with a glittering metallic border. A smattering of stars shone through the triangular opening at the center.

"That's . . . it?" Owen asked, sliding an arch-browed look at Rake.

Emery exhaled a light scoff. "It looks like they forgot to build the rest."

Cavalon's chin bobbed as he unconsciously agreed. He took a step closer. Something struck him as familiar, and he finally realized what it was: the metallic border. It was comprised of alternating gold, silver, and copper triangles.

"Trecullis," he muttered, and at Owen's questioning look, he added, "That's what Mesa called the entrance to the dark energy generator."

"It looks similar," Rake agreed.

"You think this tech is that old?" Emery asked, a hint of worry edging her tone. Worry, because three-thousand-year-old technology at the edge of the universe was one thing. Three-thousand-year-old technology sitting in their own backyard was another entirely. Like with the dark energy generators, it called into question their entire understanding of when Viators had arrived in the galaxy. He really wished Mesa were there to cite some obvious counterpoint that would make it all dry and scientific and not nearly as daunting.

"But there's no teracene mass . . ." Emery mumbled. "So how does this thing work?"

"Maybe it doesn't," Owen suggested.

Cavalon nodded. A normal person would assume that this tiny, dark piece of Viator tech sitting out in the middle of the Drift Belt left undiscovered by humans for a thousand years would probably not function. But Owen had been off restarting millennia-old dark energy generators for months; she should know better by now.

Though he had to agree, the lack of a glowing green mass of teracene made him nervous. It looked as inactive and abandoned as the first dark energy generator had when they'd arrived.

He kneaded his knuckles into his cramping chest. He didn't think he had it in him to figure out how to fix another ancient Viator megastructure.

He took a few deep breaths. Logic would prevail. Why would the sovereign bother to tell them about these gates if they didn't work?

"But, okay, but . . ." Emery stuttered, "like, what are these gates? Do we really trust this?"

"We've made leaps of faith on Viator tech before," Rake said.

"Bigger leaps than this," Owen agreed.

The resulting conclusion went unsaid, though it hung depressingly in the cockpit like a big, wet, adventure-killing blanket. Because it didn't matter whether they believed it, or trusted it. To save the Sentinels in time, they had to try.

"How do we *use* it?" Owen asked.

"I'm bringing us in closer," Rake said. "Keep eyes on . . . everything."

Emery and Owen voiced their acknowledgment, then focused on their respective consoles. Cavalon leaned on Rake's headrest and kept a diligent eye on the gate as it grew larger on the viewscreen.

A few gruelingly quiet minutes later, the atlas lit. The grooves lining its bloodstained facets glowed with a soft, pulsing white.

Rake tensed as the holographic displays on the console slid away—all except her primary flight controls. The rest were replaced with a set of crisp white screens filled with Viator text.

"Uh, boss?" Emery squeaked.

Rake scanned the new menus. "It's the gate controls." She drew back her shoulders and began to tap through the menus, every press careful and calculated, like she was defusing a bomb.

Cavalon watched, ever grateful for Rake's composure under pressure. He didn't envy figuring out how to work a three-thousand-year-old relay gate, where a single incorrect command could just as easily drop them in a remote star system or fling them off to some far corner of the universe they could never return from.

Though, the more he thought about it, that actually didn't sound that bad. Exploring uncharted territories, finding new worlds, new species maybe. More importantly, they'd be as far from Augustus as physically possible. They could start over, create a new sect of humanity, one that sucked less.

He had to wonder what kind of society would spring forth from just the six of them. They had a nice spread—a Cautian, an Elyseian, two Viridians. He wasn't sure of Rake or Jackin's ancestries, but throwing a couple of wildcards in there could be good for diversity. At least 50 percent of their genetic material was snarky as fuck, so that could be fun. One hundred percent of them were criminals, so . . . there was that. Morally upstanding criminals, maybe, but still. Not that procreation was likely to be an option. The mutagen the Viators had dropped on them hundreds of years ago made the likelihood that any of them could generate offspring without intervention minimal. And besides, he'd never felt a particular need to procreate, purposefully or otherwise. Maybe it'd be better to just stay in civilized space and try to fix the humans they already had.

"Okay . . ." Rake let out a heavy sigh. "The route's been set. I'm sending the request. Cav, buckle up."

Cavalon slid into the empty port-side station, buckling the harness loose over his chest so he could stay twisted in the seat and watch the main console.

Rake tapped open ship comms. "Helm for Medbay."

"Aye, sir," Ford replied.

"We've arrived at the Arcullian Gate. We're ready to relay if you guys are."

"We're all situated down here, sir. Whenever you're ready."

"End point set," Rake said. "Systems check."

"Green across the board, boss," Emery replied. "Ready for, uh, relay, I guess?"

"Copy. Activating relay." Rake tapped to engage.

Cavalon licked his dry lips and stared at the viewscreen, unblinking. The three corners of the triangular framework sparked with static white light. Thin black tendrils wove out from each facet, forming a fibrous mesh over the opening. A soft glow lit behind the mesh—swaths of magenta, orange, and blue forming an impressive display of cosmic stained glass.

The console chimed. Rake tore her gaze from the viewscreen. "We're cleared to relay."

"We're supposed to fly into that?" Emery asked, voice creaking.

Rake's jaw muscles flexed. "Sure?"

Cavalon gulped. "Don't try sounding too confident or anything."

She shot him a flat look then turned back to the console. "Relay incoming." She engaged the ions and sped toward the triangular mesh. The cockpit grew brighter as the viewscreen filled with the shifting magenta, orange, and blue light.

Cavalon kept his eyes locked on the sparks of white static at the corners. High in his gut, a mass twisted, a roll of nausea wetting his mouth with bitter saliva. Pressure grew against his chest, and it became harder and harder to draw a full breath. The air in the cockpit felt thicker—denser somehow—and warmer.

Sweat pricked the back of his neck. He didn't know if it was an effect of the gate or his own nerves.

The ship groaned. Rake's hands remained steady at the controls.

In an instant, the blinding light disappeared. The console displays flickered out and back on.

The thickening sensation disappeared, and Cavalon's ears popped as the pressure of the room re-established itself. He blinked, eyes darting around the viewscreen.

The pattern of stars had changed. They'd relayed.

The look of unbridled shock on Rake's face sent Cavalon's heart kicking against his ribs. That'd been unnerving, sure, but it didn't even make his top ten list of unnerving things that'd happened since they started this journey.

"What's wrong?" he asked, but went unheard as the three women exchanged tense looks.

"Uh, sensors are clear," Emery announced, though her voice drifted off as her gaze focused on Rake. "Sir," she croaked, tone brimming with concern.

"Check coordinates," Rake said, clear effort behind the steadiness in her voice.

"Coordinates confirmed," Emery replied.

"Sir . . . ?" Owen said, throwing an arch-browed look over her shoulder.

"Yeah, I felt it too," Rake confirmed.

"Uh, guys," Cavalon stammered. "Care to loop me in?"

Owen met his eye. "That felt like getting on the Divide."

"*Just* like," Emery corrected. "Like, *exactly* like."

Owen's chin bobbed in agreement. Cavalon's eyes widened, mind spinning in its attempts to process what that could mean.

Emery licked her lips. "Maybe it uses—"

"No," Cavalon said, shaking his head firmly. "Stop what you're thinking right there."

"Why?" Emery whined.

"Because it's not possible."

Owen glowered back at him. "But it's just the play of dark energy against gravity, right?" she argued. "And technically there's plenty of both, now that we're inward."

"Yeah but not like—no, you can't just, like . . ." He held up a hand and made a pinching motion. "Move it around and do whatever you want with it. That's not how it works."

"You said yourself, we're rewriting the physics playbook," Rake said evenly, throwing a casual look over her shoulder at him.

Cavalon set his jaw, glaring at her. Owen's eyes went wide, and she pointed at Rake like her entire theory had just been proven.

"Though, maybe he's right," Emery said. "Because if it was that, shouldn't we have had to engage the effusion mode? Or we'd all be toast?"

Rake shook her head. "Maybe the gate accounts for that."

Owen's eyes brightened. "Right, yeah. Maybe it creates a torus bubble to fling us in." She spun to look at Cavalon. "It could? Right?"

"Fuck," he groaned, collapsing back in his seat. "I don't know anymore. Don't ask me. Divide shit is Mesa's wheelhouse."

"Well, Mesa is a hundred million light-years away," Owen said. "You're the best we've got."

"Gee, thanks."

"All right," Rake interjected, sucking in a deep breath. The floor rumbled as she engaged their ions. "Let's focus on saving Mesa's life, so we'll even have a chance to argue the physics with her later."

"Yes, sir," Cavalon and Owen mumbled.

"Set coordinates."

"Yessir," Emery piped, tapping at her screens. "Coordinates set."

"Engaging warp," Rake announced.

Cavalon's stomach dropped as the *Synthesis* accelerated to warp, speeding them ever closer to the Core.

CHAPTER EIGHTEEN

Seventeen years ago at Legion HQ, Oculus Adequin Rake reports to her first posting.

Shafts of sunlight cut through the high glass dome of the Citadel's grand solarium. Outside, glittering planetary rings carve out a striated sash of burgundy across an invariably flat blue sky. It's only rained twice since she arrived ten weeks ago, but every day, she acclimates. Her lips and skin and cuticles have gone from desiccated to merely parched, and her once-daily nose bleeds are now only weekly.

She follows her assigned senator across the vestibule. He is a young man elected mere weeks prior following the unexpected death of his predecessor. He is well-supported by his people on Artora but an unknown in the Quorum, and they treat him like a puppy needing to be housebroken.

His heeled boots clack against the expanse of white marble, emerald cloak flowing out behind him, his sage stole emblazoned with the Artoran seal. She subconsciously slips into step with his footfalls. If she's learned anything the last ten weeks, it's how to keep pace with the person beside her.

They reach the far side of the hall, and the senator pauses at the base of a towering glass staircase. His gaze drifts up, so her gaze follows.

On the landing stands a woman, queen consort of one of the five royal families comprising the Allied Monarchies. She is surrounded by a cadre of attentive escorts, both seasoned Legion officers and royal guards. The queen is engaged in conversation with a pair of senators. Her attentive eyes are the same vivid blue as the stretch of sky overhead. The circlet tucked in her gray hair is nestled so deep, it would be difficult to see if not for the small turquoise jewels catching the light along with each polite head nod.

The young Artoran senator leans in and mumbles the monarch's name. His tone is a mix of reverence and contempt.

She nods and stares at the woman. She has never seen a member of a royal family before. She would like to think it the same as seeing any other human, but it isn't. It also isn't like the imitations presented in serials. At least this one isn't.

This one's posture is relaxed, agreeable, patient. She interacts with the calculated patience of a tutor of the very young—effortlessly conveying simple concepts without contempt or arrogance. Her hair is drawn back into a simple chignon, her gray suit and necktie practical and unadorned. If you plucked the circlet from her hair, she could disappear into a mass of businesspeople hurrying down any city street.

The woman's poise is infectious.

Seventeen years later and ninety-three million light-years outward, that woman's grandson saves Adequin's life as she's falling, without harness or tether, into the Divide.

"You need to have a good hold on me," he insists. "All the strength your Imprints can muster."

He's right, but all she can think is how free she feels, weightless and unburdened, completely unable to affect the course of things. For the first time in decades, she is truly untethered.

"If we don't have a good hold on each other," he warns, "I might lose you."

She stares at him, his blue eyes earnest, fearful. Sweat beads on his forehead, pink blooms in his pale cheeks.

He's right to assume she doesn't want to hold on. But it's not for the reason he thinks—that together, their force might break the tether. That if she stays with him, it could kill them both.

The truth is something else entirely. She doesn't want to hold on, because letting go would be so much easier.

She's done enough. Lost enough. No matter what she does now, there's no possibility of saving Griffith. She chose the Divide over his life, and it's years and light-years too late to take it back, and she doesn't even know that she would if given the chance.

If she survives this, the war to come will consume her. No matter what she does, it won't be enough. They'll fail, and she'll be the one to lead them there.

But that's the life she chose. The life she begged for; the life Hudson risked everything to give her. The one Lugen spent half a decade grooming her for—the only life she's ever known. She has an obligation to carry on. To learn from her mistakes. Like watching playback from the helmets of dead comrades, over and over. It seems like callous punishment, but it's strategic—crucial, even. Study it, memorize it, figure out what you did wrong, what you could have done to fix it. Their loss gains you a new perspective, one you couldn't have seen before.

She already knows the answer. It doesn't matter what she wants. So she holds on.

Adequin woke to the soft pulse of her nexus alarm vibrating against her wrist. She silenced it and sat up, pressing her face into her hands, rolling her shoulders to sieve away the lingering tension.

At the sink, she stared into the grungy mirror and marveled at the rate her bruised arms had healed now that the infection had been eliminated. The creeping black veins had disappeared entirely. The bruises on her shoulders and upper arms were already fading, and the wounds on her forearms had started to scab over. A handful of her Imprints had traveled down to speed the healing process, no longer afraid of carrying the infection deeper into her system.

She ran her fingers over the silver and copper squares as they glided down her bicep. She wasn't sure it was sane to feel camaraderie with tiny squares of inanimate metal, but she couldn't help herself. They'd been fighting to save her life for weeks, and she'd had no idea.

Despite having talked things out with Cavalon, she was still having trouble parsing everything she'd learned on the *Presidian*. How understanding and thankful and cooperative Kaize had been. How they'd apologized for Jackin's injuries. How they'd saved Jackin's life.

And how earnest Kaize had sounded when they said the Viators weren't interested in more wars. As if the only thing that'd ever prevented peace had been humanity's warmongering.

From a certain perspective during the Resurgence War, that made a degree of sense. Humans had discovered the Viator fleet, instigated the fight, then focused solely on exterminating them for nine years without a moment's reprieve. But the war before that had to be taken into account.

Over a thousand years, the Viators had delivered every war crime imaginable and then some, not the least of which had been the deployment of the mutagen, targeted to ensure a slow but steady extinction, one that was still running its course. Humanity had almost been wiped from existence, and the Resurgence War ensured that wouldn't happen again.

Or that's what they'd been told. She'd argued with Griffith for years about how real their perception of Viators and the history of the Viator War was. How much had been truth and how much had been exaggerated or even outright fabricated for the sake of fueling civic unity.

Even if every terrible thing *were* true, that didn't make Kaize and their people responsible. Just like Adequin wouldn't want to be held accountable for the actions of Augustus Mercer and his manipulations of the SC to further his eugenic agenda.

Her nexus beeped, startlingly loud in the silence of her cabin. She swept it open. "Go for Rake," she croaked, voice still groggy with sleep.

"Sorry, EX." Emery's voice rang through. "Just wanted to give you that one-hour heads-up you asked for."

"Thanks, Circitor. Make a ship-wide announcement at ten and five."

It was time to see the man of the hour. She ran a comb through her hair and put on the outfit Owen had dropped off, some civilian clothing they'd scrounged up before they left the *Lodestar*. The narrow black pants were a little too short, but the shirt fit well, and she appreciated the oversized hooded jacket. Even though she'd healed enough not to require it, hiding the symptoms of her infection had become habit.

She made her way to the medbay, but found the exam table conspicuously empty. Ford stood spraying it clean with a disinfectant atomizer. "Sir," he said with a steady incline of his head, then explained, "he's tryin' his hand at a shower."

She lifted an eyebrow. "Is that a good idea?"

"He didn't really give me a choice."

"Stubborn," she sighed.

"Aye, not the best patient. Been less than twenty-four hours and he's already restless."

"Understandable, I suppose. Nothing like almost bleeding out, then being asked to negotiate with dangerous criminals a few hours later."

He let out a conferring sigh. "I'm runnin' somethin' through the synth for him, hopin' it'll keep him steady through it. Should be done in just a few."

She eyed the humming synthesizer on the counter. "What is it?"

"A cocktail we'd give field agents when we had to push 'em a few too many hours," Ford explained, setting the atomizer down on the counter. "Not exactly what the Legion would classify as 'sanctioned,' but it's safe."

She tilted her head. If he worked with field agents in intelligence, that meant he'd been part of Operations Intelligence. "You were OI?" she asked. "I had you pegged as cyber or signal."

He scoffed with feigned offense. "Those hacks? No, sir."

Her lips twitched in a smirk. "No offense meant."

"You're forgiven."

"Who were you with?"

He leaned against the counter behind him. "The Sixth, for a long while, until I was reassigned to the First."

She lifted a brow. OI in the First was an echelon of the Vanguard. Her gaze drifted to his collar, but she didn't see any indication of the *Volucris* tattoo like the one Griffith had.

Ford caught her eye, giving a slight grin. "I wasn't with them yet at the start of the war," he explained. "Came in a couple years later."

She crossed her arms and leaned a hip against the exam table. "I'm surprised we never met during the war—we were briefed by someone from OI practically every week."

"I only ever ran field support," he said. "First as a medic, then tactical and strategy ops. The suits you'd have had were mostly desk jockeys."

She nodded. "Is OI where you know Jackin from?"

Ford scratched the ashy stubble on his chin, tilting his head as if he had to consider it. "In a way, aye. When I was in the Sixth, we worked alongside his division pretty frequently—their counterintelligence echelon was attached to us from the late 190s up till the war. He wasn't OI himself though, if that's what you're thinkin'."

"But you knew him before the war?"

"Aye."

"Do you know what we're headed into with these routers?" she asked, pushing a few strands of hair out of her face. "How he knows them?"

Ford's jaw stiffened, but he kept his gaze level on her. "Aye, but . . . that's for him to tell."

"Yeah," she sighed. If only it were that easy.

"If it's an order, sir," he said, tone low and gravelly, "I'll tell you what I know of it."

She shook her head, gaze drifting down as she crossed her arms. "It's not an order."

Ford pushed off the counter, stepping to the other side of the exam table to lean next to her. "I'm guessin' intel on the routers isn't really the point?"

She licked her lips. "No. But it's just standard operating procedure with Jackin. I've been working with him over five years, and he still won't tell me a thing about his life before the Divide."

"It's 'for your safety'?" he surmised.

"Yeah. And for some reason I keep telling him it's okay, that I trust him, that he can tell me when he's ready. But if the worst had happened on the *Presidian* . . ." The plastic coating of the exam table squeaked as she gripped the edge of it. "I wouldn't even know who to send a notice to."

Ford's head bobbed in a slow, introspective nod. "Aye . . . I understand, sir. I've known him over twenty years, and I still don't feel like I really know him. And I even know where most of the wounds came from. Physical or otherwise."

Adequin rubbed the heels of her palms into her eyes and let out a heavy sigh, tension knotting in her chest.

"Just a thought here, sir," Ford went on, "but maybe he doesn't wanna tell you because he wants to start over with you. Leave all that stuff behind."

Adequin looked up to meet his steady gaze. She'd never thought about it like that.

"You see his past as a collection of the things that made him who he is," Ford continued, "so you think understanding that will help you understand him. But he doesn't see them as what's formed him, he sees them as the hurdles he's gotten past to end up here." He ran a hand through his thick hair and shook his head. "This cause—the Sentinels . . . he acts like it's a burden, but that's only 'cause he actually gives a shit." Ford let out a sigh and his low voice grew quieter. "I wouldn't wanna live in his past either."

Adequin stared for a few long moments, nodding slowly.

"It's you, by the way," Ford said.

She tried to meet his gaze, but he looked down at his boots, biceps twitching as he tightened his folded arms, the corners of his eyes creasing.

"What's me?" she asked.

"That he'd want notified," he explained, voice low and toneless. "Like you were sayin'. If the worst had happened."

A lump grew at the back of her throat.

Ford shook his head. "I've never seen him worry over somethin' like he did when you were late comin' back from the Divide. I thought he was gonna brood himself into an early grave."

"Worried?" she scoffed, her breath snagging. "Just seemed pissed from where I was standing."

The corner of his lips twitched up, though the amusement didn't reach the rest of his face. "Aye. But when he's mad . . . it's a good bet it's only 'cause he cares."

She kneaded the back of her neck. If frustration and anger were truly a gauge, then he cared a whole damn lot.

The synthesizer beeped. Ford pushed off the exam table to head for the machine, then slid the newly synthesized cartridge into a biotool. He returned, holding it out toward her, ashy white eyebrows high with expectation. "He should be in his cabin by now. Don't say I narced on him, 'kay?"

She gave an appreciative nod and took the biotool. "Thanks, Ford. I promise."

Adequin made her way to Jackin's room and rapped on the metal door, not bothering to use the control panel. They rarely worked properly. It'd just as likely shut off all the lights on the deck as crank the heat up, but it was not likely to emit a door chime.

A few moments later, the door slid open. "Hey, boss," Jackin said. He finished pulling on a black T-shirt over a pair of basic gray slacks—more pieces of the civilian clothing they'd brought from the *Lodestar*. His eyebrows rose as he looked her over. "Nice jacket. Ya know, I can't say I've ever seen you in anything that wasn't Legion-issue."

"Likewise. Speaking of definitely not Legion-issue . . ." She flashed the biotool at him. "This is a drug delivery."

"Mm. Whatcha got?" He scrubbed a damp towel through the wavy hair on top of his head.

"No idea," she admitted. "Ford synthesized it, said it should keep you upright and pain-free 'for a time.'"

"Sounds good," he said, letting out a heavy sigh. "But let's wait, make sure we get the most out of it." He discarded the towel over the back of a chair, then picked up a sealed compression wrap off the nightstand. Only a slight hitch faltered his steps as he paced to sit on the bed. "Though, I'm feeling okay, honestly . . . Do your Imprints give you energy boosts?"

"Yeah. Just be careful," she warned, following him in a few steps. "It's easy to wear yourself out before you get them trained. They only have you as a battery. If you're feeling energized, they're drawing from your body's chemicals to make that happen. Just like with the healing. They can elicit more from your glands, reallocate resources, but they're still limited by what your body can create in a given amount of time."

He quirked an eyebrow at her, lips tilted in a restrained smirk. "Okay, Animus Rake."

"What?" she scoffed. "They made us do weeks of training on them."

"Yeah, well, my Drudger friends didn't even give me a crash course." He tore open the compression wrap and started unrolling it.

"Once you're feeling better, I'll run you through it. I promised Cavalon the same thing months ago."

He smirked. "That'd be quite the class roster. How are your arms?"

"Better." She slid the baggy sleeve of her jacket above her elbow. The normal, untanned olive tone had begun to show through patches of thin bruising.

"Damn," he said. "That worked fast. So you really caught a Viator bug?"

"Apparently," she sighed.

"I guess we've learned our lesson about disinfecting ancient alien neural networks."

She rolled her eyes, then snatched the compression wrap from him as he finished unfurling it.

He frowned. "I can do it."

"I'm here. Let me help."

He relented, standing to hike up his shirt, elbows high. She began to apply the wrap, adjusting the first pass a few times to ensure it'd be tight enough to help, but not so tight he'd be uncomfortable.

She tried not to stare at the triangle of raw, red flesh on his upper abdomen, edged by black and purple bruises. His palms were mostly healed over with pink skin, though a few scabbed-over blisters remained. All because she'd asked him to check the atlas device.

Jackin cleared his throat. "Ford said to make sure it goes at least as high as the base of my sternum."

"Copy that." She refocused, stepping behind him to pull it around his ribs. The old scars on his back were shadowed in the low light of the dingy room—dozens of puckered striations stretching from just below his neck, disappearing under the waist of his pants.

Her hands pricked with sweat as she yearned to wring the neck of whoever had done that. But she'd have to wring that information out of Jackin first, and she wasn't holding her breath on that front.

She finished wrapping and secured the end in place, then stepped back to check her work. "Does it feel okay?" she asked.

He let his shirt drift down, rubbing his palms over his abdomen, twisting slightly in the new binding. "Yeah. It's perfect. Thanks."

She went to the wardrobe and pulled out the only item—a dark gray, diamond-quilted bomber jacket, then brought it over to him. He didn't take it from her, just stared at it, his dark brown eyes glossy.

"What's wrong?" she asked.

He blinked away some of his dazed look. "Just proud of you."

She let out a scoff. "Because I know how to apply a compression wrap?"

"Because we not only walked off that battlecruiser with our lives, but with our ship, intel for the mission, an upgraded atlas, and . . ." He glanced down at the lines of bright white Imprint squares on his right forearm. "An upgraded centurion."

She glanced down, gaze going unfocused as she ran her thumb over the soft fabric of the jacket.

"I get it now," he went on. "Why you've been struggling. You're good when the rules apply. Even when those rules mean figuring out diplomatic extraction from an enemy ship. But there aren't any rules for what we are now. We took structure away from you for the first time since you were . . . what, sixteen? You don't have a CO to follow. Anyone to report to."

She licked her dry lips and met his gaze.

He lifted a brow. "Bet you've been itchin' to send off an after-action report?"

She gave a relenting tilt of her head.

Jackin sat on the edge of the bed with a sigh. She sat beside him, kneading his jacket between her fingers as she folded it on her lap.

"You were trying to make me that CO," he said. "That higher authority to fall back on. You thought I'd be so established as the leader that when you came back, it'd be easier just to step in as second."

She let out a long, controlled sigh. He was right, as usual. But also as usual, she didn't have to like it. "Maybe," she admitted. "But only because I respect and trust you—and you're more than capable of it. You spend a lot of time trying to convince me of how good a leader I'd be, but you're the one that's been proving himself for the last six months."

"Maybe," he said, and she was surprised by the acquiescence in his tone. "We can both be good leaders, you know. It's not singular."

"I'll gladly cede the title."

"Not if I cede first."

She let out a tired chuckle and pressed her face into her hands.

Jackin rumbled a laugh and mussed the back of her hair. "What a pair we make, eh?"

She rubbed her warm cheeks and sighed out a breath.

"You need to take the helm," he said, at once emphatic and apologetic. "The *Presidian* only proved that. But we'll do it together, okay?"

She gave him an appreciative nod. He gripped her hand and warmth swelled in her chest. She didn't even care that he was trying to hoist leadership onto her again. She was just glad he was still alive to hand out judgments.

"You hanging in there?" he asked. "All things considered."

"More or less."

"It had to be hard, seeing the breeder again? Dredging up memories of Paxus, the end of the war, coming out to the Divide . . . Couldn't have been easy being faced with it all again."

She gave a shallow shake of her head. "I'm okay, really." Her fingers slid over the chain of her necklace. "Long time ago, now. Feels like a lifetime."

"Yeah," he rumbled, quiet tone reluctant. "You know, what you said at the dedication, about needing to grieve Griffith . . ."

She nodded.

"I know it's only been six weeks for you," he said. "But you're right. We have to move on to move forward."

"I know," she said, hating how anemic her voice sounded, even to her own ears. "But I don't know how. He was my best friend for ten years. And when he told me how he felt . . . I fell. Hard. Now I'm trying to crawl my way out of it, but without the person I'd normally turn to for help." She shook her head, exhaling a heavy breath. "I don't know if I can get over him without him. I know that makes no sense."

"It makes every kind of sense, Rake." His hand tightened around hers. "I may not have loved Bach like you did, but he was a good friend. And it's hard when friends leave, regardless of why. At least the Legion made it easy to know who to blame."

She gave a dry, joyless laugh. "True." She leaned her shoulder into his. "At least I had one steadfast thing through it all."

A smile played at his lips, but he hesitated, then his expression went flat, distant.

She recognized that look. It was the same harrowed recollection he'd had after he'd learned who Cavalon really was.

She wasn't the only one who wanted someone to answer for Griffith's death. For all the deaths. Jackin had a score to settle with the Legion long before that even; he'd made that much clear six months ago. While she'd risked her crews' lives, desperately clinging to her blind faith in the Legion, he'd fought to pull her into the light.

"Jack . . ." she began carefully, "I know you have more reason than most to hate the Legion, but I still don't know why. What happened?"

His brows knit. "It's all part of that same shit. Shit I can't tell you."

"Can't or won't?"

The rigidity in his expression softened and his eyes flitted down. He scratched his beard slowly, fingers drifting over the streak cut through by his scar. "I was with the CPD."

She blinked rapidly, unsure she'd heard him right. An offshoot of the military police, the Close Protection Division acted as bodyguards for Legion command and government personnel, generally while on special assignment or when traveling outside Core territories, when their usual details might not have the latitude to accommodate the safety requirements.

"Before I was CNO," Jackin explained. "Before the war. Just a CPD operative."

Adequin struggled to keep the incredulity off her face. She'd had over five years to accrue a list of possibilities: Maybe he'd been part of some dark branch of special forces, or deep-cover intel, or he'd been brought straight in as CNO from the private sector and they'd covered it up because of the scandal it'd cause to recruit a civilian directly into high command. But "bodyguard" had never made it onto the list.

She cleared her throat and struggled to keep her tone flat. "Really?"

"Underwhelming, I know."

"Not underwhelming, just . . . confusing. How did you go from CPD to high command that fast?"

He quirked a brow at her. "Look who's talking."

She gave him a flat look. "Titan to EX is hardly the same thing."

"It was a means to patch an . . . oversight," he said. "A complication from a mission—a VIP escort. One I shouldn't have even been involved in. The CNO thing worked for a while, but didn't hold up. After that, I had to come out to the Divide to sell the official story."

"Which was?"

"I died."

"You're dead?"

"Right."

"That's not going to work for me. I need my optio."

"*Centurion*," he corrected, and a fragment of a smile snuck through his stoic visage, fading moments later as if it'd never existed.

She held his eyes for a few long moments. His expression was rigid, shoulders tense, as if a burden had been hefted onto him. Even telling her that much had been difficult.

Ford had been right. More than she'd realized. Jackin survived the past by not living in it. She'd always feared if she forgot her past, she'd be doomed to make the same mistakes again and again. But if he *didn't* forget his, he might drown in it.

Clearing the hurdles and leaving them behind was the only way he could keep going. And it sounded like he had a much better track record getting over shit than she did. She'd been letting too many of hers fester for too many years. Maybe she needed to follow his lead.

"Thanks for telling me that, Jack."

He let out a stiff sigh. "I'm sorry I'm so cagey. It's my . . . Let's just say, instincts are hard to break."

"Tell me about it."

The ship intercom crackled to life. "Get your affairs in order, folks," Emery's voice piped through. "Deceleration from warp in ten."

Jackin blew out a long breath. "All right, doc." He offered up the inside of his elbow. "Hit me."

Adequin grabbed the biotool with Ford's concoction, sterilized the skin, then injected it into Jackin's arm.

His light brown cheeks flushed with red and mere moments later he stood straighter, moved more fluidly, eyes darting with increased alertness.

He pulled on a long-sleeved olive shirt, then she helped him into the jacket. It fit a little snug in his shoulders and chest, but they had a limited selection, so it'd have to do. He insisted he could get his boots on himself, but when she stepped aside to let him see how it'd go reaching his feet with the compression wrap on, he looked up from his slumped position and frowned. She tied his boots for him and tried not to give him *too* much shit.

"Decel in five," Emery announced.

Jackin let out a heavy sigh and zipped the front of the jacket. "Showtime."

CHAPTER NINETEEN

The *Synthesis* dropped from warp speed a hundred kilometers from the Corsairs' flagship. Adequin guided their approach on sublights. The vessel looked like a mobile way station, with a collection of exterior berths on the arching bow, opposite six large, round engine exhausts on the aft. Over a dozen freighters sat docked around the puck-shaped vessel. Strips of glowing blue outlined viewports, hull lights demarcated access to exterior fueling stations, and collision lights oscillated, guiding ships in and out of berths.

Adequin's pulse quickened, and it took her a second to realize why. Signs of life. A populated place in civilized space.

Jackin got on comms with the docking controller, performing a strangely stale exchange of what sounded like nothing but watchwords and secret phrases. Minutes later, they were sent clearance without further inquiry.

They docked at a set of berths encircling the top tier of the station, then she and Jackin disembarked. The station featured triple-redundant airlocks, but all three doors stood open as they passed down the long gangway and into a small, brightly lit entry vestibule.

Six guards in lightweight combat armor entered from the main station lock. They spread into an even formation on either side of the doorway.

A young woman no older than twenty strode in next, her steps light, skin almost as pale as her white suit, cheeks ruddy with a smattering of brown freckles. A loose, copper braid hung down her left shoulder, and her thin fingers adjusted the high collar of her tailored, knee-length white jacket. Adequin recognized the peculiar sheen of the slightly too-stiff fabric—likely threaded with an alloy of plastech, used to make high-grade armor. Not a cheap everyday outfit, to say the least.

The guards straightened as a man marched in last, well-built and wearing a mix of black and olive drab tactical gear. Scarred brown skin and the long cords of locked hair hanging down his back proved him at least fifteen years older than the young woman. His ream of locs was pulled back along the top of his head, shaved around the sides above his ears. He kept one fingerless-gloved hand resting against the grip of his holstered pistol as his eyes dubiously scoured first her, then Jackin.

Jackin gave a stiff nod at the dreadlocked man. "Gideon . . ." he grunted, the name more a growl of discontent than any kind of properly formed word. Jackin maintained a broad-shouldered, slightly menacing posture.

"*North*," Gideon replied, voice low and chalky. "You're lookin' old these days."

"Well, it's been, what, ten years?" Jackin said, his tone notably deeper than his normal voice. "Besides—I'm dead, remember?"

Gideon scoffed. "If only." He jutted his square chin to the young woman beside him. "This is Phaedra, Akemi's eldest."

"I remember," Jackin said, inclining his head to the woman.

"Welcome back, Mr. North," Phaedra said, tone pleasant.

"It's good to see you again," Jackin replied, a barely discernible waver in his low tone. "Though, I'm surprised you remember me. You couldn't have been older than seven or eight when I was here last."

"Nine," she corrected, smile broad. "And I do remember you, of course—you used to make my mother smile. As I'm sure you know, that is a rarity. In fact, I'm not sure she has done it since you left."

Adequin clamped her lips tight and tried to keep her expression even. Unsurprisingly, Jackin's history with the Corsairs had been more complicated than he'd let on.

Phaedra inclined her head toward Adequin. "And your crewmate?"

"My captain," Jackin answered, and left it at that, still fielding Gideon's uninterrupted glare.

"Good to meet you, Captain," Phaedra said politely, extending a hand. Adequin shook it. "Likewise."

Phaedra's gaze returned to Jackin. "You are here to see her?" she asked, tone expectant. At Jackin's nod, her smile broadened. "Then I am very glad to have you."

Gideon let out a low growl. "Phae, that's enough."

Phaedra's bright look snuffed out as she aimed a dark scowl at Gideon. "I'm just being nice, *Gideon*," she hissed. "It's not a crime—you should try it sometime." Her pleasant demeanor reappeared, smoothing the anger from her face as she lifted her chin back to Jackin. "This way, if you please . . ."

She swept her hand, and Jackin moved to walk beside her as they headed into the station. Adequin followed, keeping an eye on Gideon in her periphery as he and the guards trailed behind.

Her fingers twitched as they walked, anxiety amplifying the trickle of adrenaline accumulating in her veins. As a Titan, she'd had cause to work with the occasional router, but only the kind with nothing left to lose— someone who'd traded expulsion from the Core for "ongoing and indefinite cooperation with the System Collective Legion." That was, until they finally sold out the last of their contacts and had nothing left to leverage. She didn't want to think about what happened to them after that.

They wound through a few white-walled airlock corridors before exiting into a wide, brightly lit foyer. The Corsairs' emblem had been emblazoned on all four walls—a simple depiction of a hawk diving in profile, talons-first, its angular wings fanned out behind it like honed blades. Near the center of the room stood a short, stocky woman in her mid-forties, soft streaks of gray in her copper hair. From her cadre of attentive guards, she had to be the aforementioned Akemi. Overseer of the Corsairs.

Akemi watched them steadily, her wide-set eyes shadowed with silver and heavily outlined in black. The white fabric of her long-sleeved dress matched that of Phaedra's suit.

As they approached, Gideon passed Adequin, girding up next to Akemi while keeping his glower trained on Jackin. Phaedra popped up on the other side of Akemi, lips turning down as she tried to press the smile from her face. The likeness was clear from their freckled skin and round faces, though Phaedra stood almost a full head taller than her mother, and was slender with the lean muscles of youth.

"Welcome to the *Corinthian*," Akemi said. Her husky voice came edged with a slight Viridian lilt.

"Akemi," Jackin replied evenly, then tilted his chin toward Adequin. "This is the captain I mentioned in my message."

Akemi nodded in acknowledgment. "Welcome." Her gaze immediately returned to Jackin. "You do not look well, Tiercel."

Jackin gave a rigid incline of his head, not reacting to the apparent nickname. "I was injured recently. I'm still recovering."

"I see. That is a shame to hear." From her perfectly flat tone, Adequin had no idea whether there was any truth to the words. "I understand you're here to make a request of the Corsairs?" Akemi asked.

"Of *you*," Jackin corrected, the air of the vestibule stifled by the lingering silence.

Adequin chewed the inside of her lip. Jackin held Akemi's gaze, steel in his dark brown eyes, a corner of his mouth lifted in an almost-provoking sneer. He stood with his hands entwined behind his back, exuding an obstinate, yet patient purpose. His very presence had shifted into someone she was having trouble recognizing.

"Very well," Akemi replied finally. "We shall parley." She motioned at the cluster of guards that'd escorted them. "We will see your associate is made comfortable."

Adequin tensed. There was no way in hell she was letting Jackin out of her sight.

To her relief, Jackin interjected before she had to make her own appeal. "My captain will join us," he said, leaving no recourse in the statement.

Gideon's gaze turned onto Adequin. He blinked a few times, and his chiseled look softened, though marginally. He looked like he wanted to argue, but didn't speak up.

"Very well, Tiercel," Akemi said, tone resigned. She turned, her guards along with her. "Come."

Jackin moved to walk beside Akemi, leaving Gideon and his glower to follow shortly behind. Phaedra skipped ahead and Adequin trailed behind. A handful of the guards brought up the rear. Every few steps, Phaedra slid a glance back at Adequin.

They left the docking sector and headed into a lightly populated market quarter, a wide corridor hemmed by dozens of stalls—a place Corsairs could regroup and resupply between assignments. Eventually the corridor fanned out into an open atrium, where soft banks of synthetic sunlight lined the high ceilings. A new level of humidity pricked at her cheeks.

At the center stood a fenced patch of trees and cultivated flora, most of which she recognized as Viridian. Loose vendor stalls ringed the patio around the vegetation, and from the salty and savory scents in the air, it was clearly some kind of commissary.

Their procession earned hedged looks from passersby, and Adequin retreated deeper into her roomy jacket. She refocused on Jackin, who kept his chin up, holding himself with surprising poise. You'd never know he'd suffered massive internal bleeding and a deep flesh wound only a day ago. The Imprints, drugs, and compression wrap would help keep him functional, but only for so long.

The stalls eventually fell away as they passed into narrower, lightly populated corridors. Adequin wiped the sweat from her palms, not realizing how uncomfortable she'd been. It'd been a long time since she'd been surrounded by that many strangers.

Phaedra snuck another look over her shoulder, then ventured a couple of steps back to walk beside Adequin. She smoothed the front of her jacket. "Hello."

"Hi . . ."

"I'm sorry," Phaedra whispered, then leaned in close. "But, may I ask . . . are you Adequin Rake?"

Adequin licked her dry lips, unsure how to answer. But too quickly, her lack of response became response enough.

Phaedra let out a throttled creak from the back of her throat. "Oh my void," she whispered. She took a few deep breaths and tugged at the hem of her jacket. She straightened and held up an apologetic hand. "I am so sorry. I should not have cursed. Or asked that question. That was rude."

"It's fine."

"Wow. I wondered as soon as I saw you." Phaedra cleared her throat, notching her excited tone down a couple of decibels. "I've watched those vids a thousand times. The end of the war. All the fanfare and excitement. Oh my gosh. It's an honor, sir."

Adequin gave a cordial nod, not entirely sure how to react. She'd not stayed in the Core very long after the announcement, though she'd experienced a similar if not far more military-issue version of the same response from most of the new recruits that had arrived at the *Argus*. Phaedra might be the first civilian to recognize her. Besides Cavalon. Civilian or no, she'd never get used to people saddling her with that kind of reverence.

To her relief, any further inquiry was sidelined as they arrived at their destination. Akemi led them into a warmly lit meeting room, offering Adequin and Jackin seats on one side of a long, tapered conference table.

Akemi sat at one end of the table with Jackin on her left, and Gideon at her right. Phaedra sat beside Gideon, across the table from Adequin. The young woman twisted the small silver hawk pin on her collar, darting bright-eyed looks between her mother and Jackin.

Adequin narrowed her eyes. She was normally good at reading people, but she couldn't get a hold on what was going on. Phaedra seemed excited to see Jackin, even anticipatory, like she expected some grand reunion. But if there was some history between Jackin and Akemi, it was impossible to glean over their icy, stoic veneers.

"Should we engage the shield?" Jackin asked, though to Adequin's ear, it sounded much more like a demand. He sat in the same predatory manner as he'd stood, shoulders broad, pitched slightly forward like he might lunge at any moment.

Akemi regarded him, lips pressed thin, then waved a hand at Gideon.

Impressively, Gideon's scowl never left Jackin as he leaned into the center of the table and toggled a switch, then sat back. Adequin's ears popped and a shimmer of silver dappled the air before going translucent, engulfing the table in a very illegal transmission shield.

"Satisfied, Tiercel?" Akemi asked.

"Yes," Jackin replied. "Thank you."

Adequin raised a brow. "Okay, what's with the nickname?"

Akemi's eyes drifted to her, sparkling with amusement. "It is not a nickname. More of a . . . rank."

Adequin tilted her head. "What kind of rank?"

"You would have to ask him that."

Adequin grimaced. "Nonstarter, I'm afraid. Asking him about his past has never got me very far."

Jackin's gaze slid to her, mouth slack with disbelief.

A smile tugged at Akemi's lips. "You don't mean to say you've found Mr. North taciturn?"

"Jack? *Never.*"

Akemi laughed. Phaedra beamed a smile at her mother.

"I like this one, Tiercel," Akemi said.

Jackin crossed his arms. "Well, you can have her," he grumbled.

Adequin's smile turned wry as she recognized her own tactic—breaking tension with sarcastic banter. What had Cavalon done to her?

Gideon cleared his throat. "Can we get to the point, North?"

"Gladly." Jackin let out a heavy sigh. "We need ceronite. A lot of it."

Akemi licked her lips slowly, taking a beat before responding. "As you well know, our fleet does not feature jump drive technology. Plotting a jump in the Core is illegal, after all."

"We're shielded, Mi," Jackin said, "you don't have to spout platitudes. I'm not an SC inspector."

"You could be. How would I know?" A bit of her stoicism wavered with a thread of tension. "You've been a ghost for ten years."

"Don't make this harder than it has to be," he said. "We can be out of your hair as fast as you can load it into our cargo hold."

Akemi cast a bitterly amused smile, and her tone acidified. "I would love to know why you think I owe you a goddamn thing."

Jackin's already hard visage turned to flint.

A coy smirk played at Gideon's lips, and he took entirely too much pleasure in saying, "Yeah, how's life treating you, *North*? Is the Legion everything you'd dreamed it'd be and more?"

Adequin's mouth went dry at the potency of Jackin's looks-could-kill glower, and it wasn't even focused at her. Gideon took it in stride, entwining his hands over his stomach as he sat back in his chair.

Jackin's bruised knuckles went white as he gripped his armrests. Adequin shifted her weight, leaning forward to catch his eye. He reluctantly met her gaze, and she tilted her head slowly, a gentle nudge of caution, a suggestion to deescalate—versus lunging across the table to tackle Gideon, which seemed to be his current trajectory.

Jackin's jaw flexed, but the fire burned away from his look, and his anger softened, if fractionally. He drew in a sharp breath and returned a slightly less ready-to-explode expression to Akemi.

"Okay. Fine," Jackin said, voice cold. He cleared his throat, his anger rebuilding into obstinacy as he spoke. "You were right. Is that what you want to hear? They chewed me up and spat me out, just like you said they would, and it was shitty, and I never should have trusted them. Happy?"

"No," Akemi said, and Adequin could have sworn she caught a hint of remorse in the woman's husky tone.

Adequin looked between the two for a few drawn-out moments, unsure what to make of the look passing between them. She glanced at Gideon and Phaedra, who'd both averted their gazes.

From Jackin's withering expression, he'd understood perfectly, but he caught it within seconds, eyes narrowing to slits as he leaned his elbows on the table. He entwined his hands, a thumb working at the palm of the other, still bright pink with newly grafted skin.

When he finally spoke, his voice was a low rumble, gravelly on the edges. "Do I need to come back from the dead?"

Adequin's eyebrows raised, impressed by the threat he'd managed to weave into the simple question.

Akemi stiffened, almost imperceptibly, to her credit. An untrained eye would have missed it.

The table groaned as Jackin leaned in. "Don't think for a second I wouldn't do it."

Akemi's steel gaze flitted to Adequin, then back to Jackin. Her steepled fingers wove together, and she lowered her hands to the table. "It's that important?"

"Do I make idle threats, Mi?"

Her expression remained stony.

"You'll help us get what we need," Jackin went on, "then I'll leave you alone."

She exhaled a resounding sigh. "Fine."

"Akemi." Gideon chuffed out a hard breath. "You can't be serious."

Akemi turned to him, jaw tight. "It's that, or we toss him out the airlock. Do you have a preference?"

Adequin tensed, barely moving, though it drew Gideon's hardened brown eyes onto her.

"Mother!" Phaedra chided, showcasing the first semblance of a frown Adequin had yet to see cross the young woman's face.

Akemi let out another sigh. "Only a joke, Phaedra."

Adequin's attention darted to Jackin, then back to Gideon, who rolled his eyes and slumped back in his seat. Apparently it truly was a joke. She willed her pulse to return to normal.

Jackin wiped a hand down the side of his face. "So, do you have any ceronite or not?"

Akemi gave a grim shake of her head. "We shored up our stock years ago when we realized consolidation efforts were underway, but we're already running on fumes. Gideon?"

"Wait—" Gideon gripped the edge of the table, sliding his chair back as if about to stand. "I'm gonna get some lube if we're just gonna bend over and take it."

"Bloody void," Phaedra grumbled, shooting him a disgusted look.

"*Gideon,*" Akemi warned.

The muscles in Gideon's jaw worked as he held Akemi's gaze, struggling to shelve his contempt. "Fine," he grumbled, voice crackling. "I can check the manifests, but I'm sure most of what we have is already in our ships."

"Ceronite has become absurdly expensive," Akemi explained. "We are working on ways to manufacture it ourselves, but we're nowhere near ready for production. How much will you need?"

"Six kiloliters," Adequin answered.

Gideon laughed.

Akemi folded her hands atop the table. "Even if we siphoned it from every ship on our roster, we would not come up with half of that."

"Void," Gideon said, "what are you trying to move, a fleet?"

Adequin exchanged a wincing look with Jackin. Based on the size and shitty efficiency of the *Lodestar*, that metaphor might not be outlandish by modern standards.

Gideon crossed his arms and sat back. "You'd have to scour a hundred spacelane stopovers to get that much. The privately owned ones have all contracted mercs, and the government ones are crawling with Guardians. I'm guessing law enforcement types would be a problem," he said, then added with the verbal equivalent of an eye roll, "assuming you're still tryin' to be dead . . ."

Adequin's brow creased. "There are Guardians stationed at stopovers?"

"There are Guardians *everywhere*," Phaedra said.

"There really are," Gideon groused. "You'd think the fuckers could print them on demand. Bloody abominations."

Adequin bit the inside of her cheek. She'd assumed Cavalon's nuclear antics would have done more to set back the Guardians' progress. Though, Augustus would have had time to regroup, she supposed. She still had trouble remembering that her last five weeks had actually been six months. And Cavalon's trip to the Divide had taken three months, giving Augustus the better part of a year to rebuild.

Jackin slid Adequin a look of warning, masking the barest shake of his head as he bobbed his gaze back to Akemi. Adequin sat back, dialing down her curiosity. Right. No reason to advertise their interest in anything Mercer-related.

"We don't have time for a scavenger hunt," Jackin said. "But we're willing to work for it. We can take it straight from a factory, if needed."

Gideon's eyes glinted with amusement. "Well, then, that's easy. 'Cause there's exactly *one* of those."

Jackin raised an eyebrow. "One?"

Akemi's lips pressed into a grim line. "It's true, I'm afraid. The sole source for production and distribution."

"Where?" Jackin asked.

"It is part of a larger Larios Defense facility on Tethys."

Adequin's breath hitched. She swallowed over a few choice expletives. "As in, the satellite of Pherebos?" she asked. The fourth planet out from the Elyseian sun. Only two orbital rings from the Mercer homeworld.

"Correct," Akemi said.

Jackin ran his hands through his hair and sat back.

Adequin cleared her throat. "Raiding a shipment on its way outsystem would be safer than trying to infiltrate the factory itself. Could you get access to their delivery schedule?"

Gideon scoffed. "Can *Corsairs* hijack shipment schedules?"

"You're law-abiding haulers, not smugglers," Adequin said. Then lifted her eyebrows. "Right?"

"Right," Gideon agreed, a smile playing at his lips. "I'll look into it. Though to be honest, I can't see y'all lastin' very long in Elyseian space."

Adequin let out a heavy sigh. "You mean to say you don't think a thirty-year-old Drudger ship with a fabricated Legion transponder will make it through the most extensive security checkpoints in the Core?"

Gideon tempered a smirk, lifting one shoulder in a shrug. "Suppose you could try, if you're feelin' adventurous."

"Well," Jackin drawled, "then I guess we'll also be borrowing a ship. A very clean, very quiet ship."

Akemi exhaled sharply. "Gideon, what do we have in the hangar?"

Gideon didn't respond at first, rubbing a hand over his mouth. "Not much at the moment. There's a couple passenger ferries, and the freighters, of course."

"Oh!" Phaedra perked up, bright eyes darting between her mother and Gideon. "What if we gave them—"

"No," Gideon barked, though his ruthless stare seemed to stop her more than the harsh word.

Phaedra slouched, managing to frown with her whole body. "Why not? It's just sitting there."

Adequin narrowed her eyes at Gideon as he pressed his fingers into his temples.

"Spill it," Jackin demanded.

"It's not that we don't trust you," Akemi said, her tone that of mediation, "it's that it is a prototype."

"A *very fucking expensive* prototype," Gideon specified, his tone *not* that of mediation.

"It might not be safe," Akemi concluded. "We've not tested it yet."

Jackin sat back in his chair and crossed his arms. "I'm listening."

Akemi flicked her fingers at Gideon in a silent order. He grunted, then tapped the nexus band at his wrist and three white holographic displays projected over the center of the table. He spun the screens to face Adequin and Jackin.

"Bloody void," Jackin mumbled, his look softening as he slid forward in his seat.

Adequin leaned her elbows on the table, eyes scanning the specs. Bloody void indeed. Just from a cursory read-through she could tell this thing was stacked, with a reinforced, achromatic aerasteel hull and quad-sublight gliders—ultra-quiet, ultra-fast ion engines. The secondary systems listed a slew of defenses, including some kind of experimental warp dampener, a full ECM suite, and a cloaking generator unlike any she'd ever seen.

"Like we said . . ." Gideon rumbled, "a very fucking expensive prototype. I guarantee it has all the bells and whistles you'd ever want. Except the ability to pass SC inspections."

Adequin's brow furrowed. The whole point was a ship that could get through security checkpoints.

Gideon eyed her. "Don't worry," he said, "you won't need the ability to pass security checks, 'cause the nets won't even pick you up."

Nets were massive, expensive security grids used almost exclusively in Core systems. They collected transit fees and taxes, flagged expired registrations, and generally kept track of who and what was going where and when. Most nets were maintained by the Allied Monarchies, and thus grew increasingly frequent the nearer one got to a royal family's homeworld. Adequin had heard of—and utilized—plenty of methods of evading nets, ranging from brute force to simply finding a weak point. But she'd never heard of a ship that could ignore one entirely.

"It's that good?" Jackin asked.

"It's that good," Gideon assured him.

Jackin gave a grateful nod with little to no hesitation, seeming more than willing to take him at his word, and Adequin's confusion about their dynamic only grew.

"Do you have copies of the specs?" Jackin asked.

"Yeah," Gideon said. "I'll transfer what we have to your nexuses, but the manual is still a work in progress, so it's pretty sparse. I hope you've got a pilot who knows what the hell they're doing."

Jackin chuffed a laugh and threw an amused smirk at Adequin. She responded with a placating, thin-lipped smile. This definitely wouldn't be her first time working with a prototype—of either the flying or firing variety. When she'd first joined the Titans, she'd actually enjoyed the challenge of unpredictable tech. It'd helped hone her problem-solving skills. Now, she wouldn't say she relished the idea of a ship that might act erratically, but she wasn't dissuaded by it. Though getting herself up to speed while training Emery to act as her relief would be interesting. Emery had picked up the *Synthesis* quickly, but had no experience with any other kind of ship. Though, that could be a good thing. Habits could be hard to break.

"What's the armament?" Adequin asked.

"Couple laser cannons and turrets," Gideon replied, "and some weird mag-pulse style warhead launcher. There's a few automated point-defense brackets too. But you ain't gonna need any of it. You either stay quiet enough no one ever sees you, or you don't come back. You get caught in Elyseian space with this thing, you're toast."

Jackin sighed and sat back in his chair. "You clearly haven't seen her fly."

Gideon quirked a brow at Adequin, and Akemi's steady gaze narrowed slightly.

Phaedra gave a sly smile. "I think they will be just fine, Gideon."

"Well," Gideon let out a crackling sigh, "let's hope so, 'cause this ship's on loan. We need it returned in one piece." Gideon looked at Akemi. "Last I checked, our insurance doesn't cover illegal prototype tech. We'll be in a world of hurt if we have to pay out the lease on that thing."

"You'll get your ship back," Jackin said.

"Not much of an assurance," Gideon grumbled. "What's to stop you from taking off with it and disappearing for another decade?"

Jackin glared. "Can't say I'd mind getting that ugly mug of yours out of my face for another ten years."

"Boys," Akemi warned.

"Fine," Jackin relented. "If it's any consolation, I'm too injured to be much good. I'll stay and partake of the *Corinthian*'s medical facilities and act as collateral for the ship's return."

Adequin gripped the edge of her armrest, clenching her teeth as she cast a hard stare at the side of Jackin's face. He pretended not to notice.

That was not something they'd discussed. She glanced at Akemi and Gideon and their unreadable expressions. She couldn't say it was a bad idea for Jackin to stay put for a few days, but she didn't really want to leave him in this veritable viper's nest either.

"Speaking of staying behind," Gideon said, "how many are in your crew?"

"Six," Jackin answered.

"The *Wakeless*'s complement is two. I'd say four is doable with the atmo cycler, but I wouldn't push it past that. Can you leave another behind?"

"Our medic can stay as well," Adequin offered.

Jackin's jaw firmed, and he scratched at the scarred side of his beard, but didn't say anything. He knew as well as she did Ford was the best option. She'd need Emery to fly, Owen to hack, and Cavalon to science.

"We'll need ironclad credentials for the four of them," Jackin said.

Akemi dipped her chin. "That will be no trouble."

"Where the hell'd you guys get this thing?"

"Our Larios contact."

Jackin grimaced. "Still mired in royal affairs, eh?"

"The monarchies have their uses," Akemi replied.

Jackin gave a bitter grin. "I also need to see your materiels manifest. We'll need to borrow a few things."

"Very well," Akemi agreed. She and Jackin continued to negotiate specifics, and Adequin watched with increasing confusion. Because it wasn't much of a negotiation. It seemed expected that Akemi would grant Jackin anything he wished, and Gideon didn't even bother to continue challenging it. The threat of Jackin "coming back from the dead" clearly meant something serious to garner this kind of compliance.

When they were done, Gideon passed encrypted copies of the files to each of their nexuses. Jackin licked his lips, cheeks going paler by the second. His facade of pretending not to be half dead was starting to wear off.

"I'll put in your requests," Akemi said, giving Jackin a discerning once-over. "And prepare the ship for departure." She shifted her focus to Adequin. "We'll have our people gather a workup on the factory, and I'll schedule a meeting to review in the morning. We should have everything ready to go by 0900, if that is a sufficient rest cycle for your crew."

Adequin gave an appreciative nod. "It is."

Akemi turned back to Jackin. "You should get some sleep, Tiercel. You look like a walking carcass."

Jackin sighed and rubbed the back of his neck. "I will."

Akemi stood, inclined her head in farewell, and left. Phaedra gave Adequin a knowing wink as she bounded out after her mother.

CHAPTER TWENTY

✦

Adequin and Jackin exited the meeting room into the empty corridor. Gideon followed, dismissing the guards posted outside the door.

"I'll show you to your rooms," Gideon said, then headed down the hall.

"I know the way," Jackin groused, following behind.

"I'm aware."

Adequin took a few quick steps to catch up, narrowing her eyes at the tied locs hanging down Gideon's back as they swung along with his steps. Apparently she could take the Corsairs' illegal prototype ship for a joy ride into the heart of the Core, but they weren't trusted to walk to their rooms alone.

A few vigorously silent minutes later, they arrived at a hallway lined with wide double doors. Potted plants, unnecessary doormats, and ornamental hangings marked them as residences. Gideon guided them to an undecorated door at the end of the hall.

"Thanks for the pointless escort," Jackin said.

Dimples pitted Gideon's cheeks as he forced out a smile. It'd almost be charming if he didn't exist in a constant state of condescension. "You're very welcome, Mr. North." Gideon turned his full focus onto Adequin, locking her with uncompromising eye contact. "We weren't introduced." He extended his hand. "Gideon Burr."

She slid a glance at Jackin, unsure if she should give her name; he'd never called her anything but his captain. At Jackin's dismissive eye roll, she replied, "Adequin Rake," and accepted the handshake.

One corner of Gideon's mouth lifted. "I thought so. Looks like Jack is keeping good company these days."

She hesitated at the shift in formality. He was all North and glares moments earlier, now it was just Jack and compliments.

"We could do without any rumors," she said. "I'd appreciate it if you kept our arrival quiet."

"That goes unsaid," he replied.

She licked her lips slowly as she took in his earnest expression. She really did not understand what was happening between all these people. It was the most confusing loyalty dynamic she'd ever witnessed.

"I'll send someone to escort your crew." Gideon started back down the hall, then cast a glance over his shoulder, a glint in his eye. "It was good to meet you, Adequin. Let me know if you want to get a drink later."

Adequin blinked, too stunned to form a coherent response.

Jackin stood stock-still, lower jaw forward, his hard gaze staring after Gideon as he rounded the corner and disappeared.

"Hey, Jack . . ."

His eyelashes twitched.

"Jackin."

He finally blinked, tearing his eyes from the end of the hall to look at her. "Yeah. Sorry."

"I'm not gonna take him up on it, if that's what's got that scowl on your face."

"No. It's fine."

"What's wrong?"

He scratched his beard, frowning. "Why'd you agree to leave Ford?"

She sighed. "Even if we could take five people, there's no way in hell I'm leaving you here alone."

"I can handle myself."

"You almost died yesterday, Jack."

His lips pressed thin, and he didn't seem keen to respond as he tapped at the room's control pad.

The doors slid open, revealing a living suite many degrees nicer than she'd expected. Plush carpets dotted dark laminate floors, and textured, burnt-orange wallpaper covered the walls. Warm light shone from wall sconces and shaded fixtures. A platter of fresh food had been laid out on the kitchen island, and the aromas mixed with a diffused scent of rainfall lingering in the temperate air.

These weren't everyday visitor accommodations. She'd expected a threadbare serviceperson quarters with communal lavatories, or maybe a section of whatever shared living space they'd rent out to subcontractors to rest between assignments. This residence had a full kitchen, a large living area, and a hallway that led to at least three additional rooms. This was a setup for people of distinction.

Jackin beelined to a sunken sitting area on the left. He slumped into one of the modular sofas, grimacing as he slouched, pressing a hand against his upper abdomen, his well-held facade melting away.

Adequin pulled off her baggy jacket and laid it over the back of the couch. She grabbed a few of the plusher-looking pillows from the other sofa and stacked them against the armrest beside Jackin.

"I'm fi—"

"Shut up and lie down."

His shoulders sunk, and he turned to lie on the pillows. A breathy groan accompanied each attempt to raise his legs onto the couch. He got one up, then Adequin lifted the other. Sweat pilled on his forehead as he straightened out with an effort.

She went to the kitchen and found an entire shelf of the well-stocked fridge lined with water bottles. She took one refillable glass bottle, then found another plastic one with a gaudy label touting it to have the "highest legal concentration of epithesium on the market!" She brought the dosed one over to Jackin, and he accepted it with only a slight pout.

She sat in the armchair at his feet, resting her elbows on her knees. "You pushed yourself too hard," she admonished.

He rubbed the heels of his palms into his eyes. "I couldn't let them see me weak. I have appearances to uphold."

"I noticed. You were like a different person. One I'm not sure I recognize."

He dropped his hands, and though pain tightened his features, his eyes rounded with reassurance. "Don't worry," he said, tone soft, the constant edge of threat gone from his voice. "The Jackin you know is the real one. They've not seen that side of me. Most people haven't."

She licked her lips, picking at the label on the water bottle. "How do you know these people, Jack?"

He ran a hand over his beard, a furrow tightening between his eyebrows. He gave a slow shake of his head.

She knew it'd been pointless to ask, but she had to try. She opened her water bottle, suddenly wishing she'd hunted for something stronger.

"I was raised by Akemi's father," Jackin said suddenly.

Adequin quickly swallowed a few times, trying not to choke on the gulp of water she'd just taken.

"Abraham Kashmir," Jackin went on. "He adopted me when I was seven."

She blinked at him, lowering the water bottle slowly. "Well . . . shit. I read that super wrong."

He quirked a brow. "What?"

"I thought you and Akemi might have history."

He winced through a smirk. "We certainly have history, but definitely not that kind."

"So you're basically siblings?"

"Basically."

That was why the dynamic had felt so complicated. And so foreign. They were family.

"Phaedra didn't really treat you like an uncle," she said.

Jackin sighed, twisting open the cap of his water bottle. "That's because Akemi never let me be one to her. Phae doesn't know. Mi didn't want her to have a legionnaire for an uncle. To them, I defected. I'm a traitor, especially in Gideon's eyes."

"How's he fit into all this?"

"He grew up on the *Corinthian* too. He's the son of Abraham's former right hand. And now he's Akemi's."

Jackin craned his neck, trying to take a drink without spilling. She stood and helped him lean forward, then slid another couple of pillows behind the rest, propping him up higher.

"Thanks," he sighed, then took a much safer sip.

She sat back down. "If they think you're a traitor, why are they willing to help now?"

"Well . . ." he began slowly, eyes focused on the glittering blue and pink label of his water bottle. "They can't really say no to me, 'cause it's technically all mine."

She let out a throttled scoff. "What?"

"Growing up, Abraham groomed me as overseer," he explained. "He expected me to take over when he retired. He favored me, and Akemi's always resented me for it. For that, and the fact that he left it all to me."

"But you're dead," she said slowly.

He nodded, taking another sip. "Yeah, but she knows if I wanted to, I could contest my death certificate and take it all back from her. Not that I ever would. But she doesn't know that. So she lets me have my way."

Adequin slouched into the cushioned back of her chair and sighed. "I'm guessing regardless of Abraham's wishes, you didn't really want to take over?"

"Not in the least. Akemi knew I didn't want it, which made her even angrier."

"Hence the palpable animosity."

"That's part of it, yeah," he admitted.

"What's the other part?"

He recapped the water bottle, then set it aside. "Abraham got sick shortly after I enlisted. Akemi's the superstitious type, so when he died, she was convinced it was my fault. That my 'betrayal' broke his heart, weakened him." He licked his lips and blew out a soft, wavering breath. "Hell, maybe she's right. They all took it pretty hard, but he took it the worst."

"When you enlisted?" she asked.

"Yeah. To them, it felt like a double betrayal. I not only rejected the role they wanted for me, but I basically joined the bad guys."

"Why *did* you enlist?"

His gaze grew distant, and she could see the wheels churning in his head, picking over what was safe to divulge and what needed to stay close to the chest. "That's . . . complicated."

Adequin nodded, stomach knotting with equal parts chagrin and guilt as she thought about how *everything* with him was labeled as "complicated." Though to be fair, everything she'd learned so far held up to the designation.

"My family had mutagen defects," he said.

Adequin froze in her seat, afraid if she breathed too hard or shifted too much, it might break whatever trance he was in that was causing him to tell her all this. Maybe it was the drugs Ford had given him.

He stared past his feet and didn't look at her as he continued. "My parents, me, and my older sister. We lived on Myrdin when the second round of the Heritage Edict went through."

"Shit," she sighed. Spearheaded by Augustus Mercer forty years ago and sanctioned by an already-corrupt Quorum, the Heritage Edict was one of the first carefully planned moves in his eugenics war, disguised as an attempt to correct the plummeting fertility rates caused by the Viator mutagen.

"My parents had enough saved to get mine corrected," Jackin explained, "but it cleaned them out. When the edict went through and they were forced to relocate, they had to go to a work camp in the Outer Core to earn their correction vouchers."

"Void," she breathed, slumping back in her chair.

"Abraham was an old friend of my dad's," he went on, "and they had him legally adopt me so I could stay in the SC and keep my citizenship." He let out a heavy sigh. "So, yeah. I enlisted because . . . I guess I wanted to do what I could to make it right. To make things better." He scoffed. "I didn't know at the time it would be so impossible to make a dent in it."

Adequin's brows pinched, the cool glass of her water bottle squeaking as she twisted it between both hands. "I'm sorry, Jack. That had to be hard."

"Over thirty years ago. Old wounds at this point."

"Still . . ."

By the glossy, distant look in his eye, thirty years may have deadened it, but not erased it.

Adequin glanced up as the door swooshed open and a cacophony of boot scuffs and voices crashed into the quiet calm of the room.

"He'd mobilized half the Mercer Guard before they realized it was just a paper bag," Owen said, and Emery snorted a laugh.

"In my defense, I was wasted," Cavalon retorted as he followed them in.

Owen scoffed. "That's your excuse for everything, dude."

Cavalon grunted as he adjusted the weight of the three rucks crossed over his back. He wore an oversized jacket with the hood drawn up. His beard and longer hair helped hide his classic Mercer looks, but he'd still be pretty recognizable to anyone who kept tabs on the Allied Monarchies. And routers stayed well-informed.

Ford walked in last, tall frame laden with duffle bags and medical supplies. His long-suffering eyes homed in on Jackin, then sharpened onto Adequin. "He okay?"

"Fine," Jackin assured him, craning his neck to look back at them.

Adequin and Ford barked in unison, "Lie down!"

Jackin frowned and slumped into the pillows.

"Damn, nice digs, boss," Emery piped, wide green eyes drifting across the room. She ran her fingers over the narrow, granite-topped kitchen island. "How many organs did we have to sell to afford this?"

Ford began unloading his bags beside the door. In the middle of the entryway, Cavalon leaned forward and dropped the rucks off his shoulders with a huff. He flung his hood off as he stood back up, throwing his overgrown blond hair into a staticky, rumpled mess.

"Come sit," Adequin said, in lieu of "*Welcome to Jackin's criminal empire.*" "We need to update you guys on the new plan. Owen, you have that bug scanner?"

Owen dropped her ruck to her feet and dug inside, producing a bite-sized piece of black and gold hardware from her bag. "Got it, sir."

"Go ahead." Though positive their pathetic circumstances and obvious desperation would make anyone eavesdropping disappointed they'd gone to the effort, it couldn't hurt.

Owen hooked the device to her nexus, then activated a scanner screen. She stepped around the room, swiping her wrist in swaths over every wall, piece of furniture, and decoration. Ford took over to help sweep it high over the walls and across the ceiling fixtures.

In the end, they found two well-hidden bugs, though Owen claimed they were inactive. To make sure, Emery inactivated them further by crushing them under the heel of her boot, then tossing the tiny bits out the door and into the hall.

Adequin summoned them to the sitting area, where they unapologetically partook of the platter of meat, cheese, and fruit while she stepped them through what they'd learned, and what the plan would be moving forward. When she announced the location of the factory, Cavalon stopped chewing, his look growing haunted and withdrawn. He dropped the rest of his hunk of cheese, then crossed his arms and sat back with a frown.

Though no one liked leaving Jackin and Ford behind, the idea of getting to work with secret tech enthused both Emery and Owen. Ford suggested he use his free time aboard the *Corinthian* to poke around on the galactic network and reach out to contacts to see what intel he could dredge up for future Sentinel use, including some star charts of the outer sectors. Though their upgraded atlas told them a great deal, it'd be good to know if the SC had any colonization efforts underway in the more remote systems of the Drift Belt, Perimeter Veil, or Lateral Reach, where they'd go hunting for their base of operations. If they made it back with the ceronite.

When they were done, Adequin tried to convince Jackin to move into one of the bedrooms, but he insisted he preferred the firmer couch to the softness of a mattress. Though Ford was a good half meter too tall for it, he offered to take the other couch and stay on Jackin watch. Owen and Emery skipped off to one of the two bedrooms before Adequin could suggest otherwise, but she didn't actually care. They already shared a room aboard the *Synthesis* anyway, and Adequin had bigger things to worry about than fraternization.

Her and Cavalon's room had two beds and an ensuite larger than her entire room aboard the *Synthesis*. By the time she showered and got into bed, Cavalon had stopped twisting and turning in his sheets, his breathing slow. She figured he was asleep, so his voice startled her in the quiet calm of the tepid room. "All okay, sir?"

She summoned her most assured tone to quietly murmur, "All okay."

Because all *was* okay. They couldn't get the ceronite directly from the Corsairs, but they'd be getting everything else they needed—a location, an intel workup, supplies, and a stealth ship unlike any she'd ever seen before. She should be pleased. She'd even gained a few long-overdue answers about Jackin's past. Though she'd been left with even more questions than before.

She forced her eyes closed and inhaled deeply. She had to focus on the mission. That was what it was all about, after all. They were working toward the future young Jackin had hoped for, the reason he'd enlisted. To make sure what happened to him and his family never happened again. They had a greater purpose, and she couldn't lose sight of it.

"Rake," Cavalon said, then waited for her to look over. Though shadowed in the dim light, his eyes were open, clear, unblinking. "We'll get it done," he said, in *his* most assured tone.

Adequin swallowed. Shrouded in dark in the warm safety of the room, it was easy to believe him. "We will," she agreed.

Cavalon let out a wistful sigh and turned over, shrugging the sheets up to his chin. "Good night, Rake."

"Night, Cav."

CHAPTER TWENTY-ONE

The following morning, Cavalon kept his hood drawn and his eyes down as he lugged a rifle case across the deck of the *Corinthian*'s main hangar. The adults had been in an intelligence briefing with the overseer all morning, leaving him, Emery, and Owen to pack a plethora of new supplies and weapons from the Corsairs, including a crate of high-end security tech Owen had practically started drooling over.

Cavalon was intensely curious to learn how Jackin had swung this deal, which not only had the Corsairs falling over themselves to give them whatever they wanted, but had granted them access to an incredibly fancy ship. The *Wakeless*. He'd never seen a ship so nice in his life, and that was saying something.

It was about as large as a standard yacht, with the sleek body styling of a showy starfighter. The way the matte black coating on the hull absorbed light had a strange way of making it hard to look at. From most angles, the entire thing looked two-dimensional. Though, light-absorbing paint wasn't likely the reason the ship had been classified as a prototype . . . or why it was highly illegal.

Sweat beaded his forehead as he struggled with the large weapons case. He'd kept his Imprints inactive to ensure none of the routers noticed him exhibiting superhuman strength. He also hoped the pain of overworked joints and muscles would distract him, because his damn brain kept repeating the same shit on a loop and wouldn't shut up about it: They were headed into Elyseian space. Toward his homeworld. Toward his grandfather. Every instinct he possessed wanted him to hijack the nearest ship, fly in the opposite direction, and never look back.

But it was fine. It *would* be fine. Rake was in charge, and there was no one he trusted more to keep them safe.

Cavalon dropped the rifle case off in the *Wakeless*'s compact cargo hold, then trudged back down the short ramp as Emery and Owen passed, carrying one of the empty ceronite canisters.

He paused at the foot of the ramp to let his burning arms and shoulders rest. Until he'd started hauling shit around without his Imprints, he'd almost forgotten that he'd been accidentally starving himself for weeks with overdoses of epithesium. After a week of full rations, he was already rebuilding strength, but he'd lost a lot of stamina. He needed to get back on track once they'd returned to the *Lodestar*. Once they survived this.

Phaedra stood nearby directing subordinates; she'd been overseeing their supply requisition all morning. She signed off on something on a tablet, then passed it to an old, gruff-looking router who lurched away, scowling at Cavalon as he passed.

Cavalon slouched deeper into his monstrous hood. Though he knew he was well-hidden, he couldn't help but think that every skeptical glance meant they knew exactly who he was.

Emery scampered down the ramp and up to Phaedra. "Hey there, question . . ."

"What can I help you with?" Phaedra asked pleasantly.

Emery lowered her voice. "Do you guys have gum?"

Phaedra cocked her head. "Hm. Yeah, probably."

"Like the real stuff," Emery added. "Not the synth crap."

"Oh, of course not," Phaedra replied, deadly serious. "I will see to it." She opened a comms screen on her nexus. "Ivan, please add a few packs of gum—"

Emery pointed upward, urgent.

Phaedra's eyebrows climbed. "—make that a few *dozen boxes* of gum."

"Uh . . . okay," the man replied.

Phaedra mouthed, "*What flavor?*"

"Grape," Emery whispered.

"Grape," Phaedra spoke into the comm. "A *pallet* of grape gum."

"I'll . . . see what I can find," the man replied, then clicked off.

Emery smiled and gripped Phaedra's shoulder. "Phaedra . . . you've made a true ally today."

Phaedra's pale cheeks reddened as she grinned ear to ear. "Pleased to help, Miss Flos."

Cavalon watched in open amusement. If Phaedra was the intended heir to this situation, he really wanted to be around to see that transfer of power. He'd never met such a pleasant criminal before.

"Hey, buddy." Owen gripped his shoulders from behind and jostled him as she descended the ramp. Cavalon glanced back as she came around to face him. "Care to put those fancy Imprints of yours to work?" she asked.

"Wanna say that a little louder?" he hissed.

"Man," she breathed out in exasperation, "no one cares. You really think anyone's going to assume some scruffy-ass-looking dude in a ragged coat is an exiled crown prince just because he can carry a crate a little better than most?"

"Maybe," he grumbled.

"Much more likely they'd assume you have a blackmarket set that somehow hasn't killed you yet."

Emery trotted up to join them. "We should get a move-on," she said, then shifted into her slightly more serious I'm-a-circitor-now tone. "Bosses'll be here any minute."

Cavalon gave a mock salute and headed back to the *Synthesis*'s cargo hold. Tangy copper flooded his saliva as he summoned his Imprints, then grabbed both the remaining ceronite vessels, one under each arm.

"Happy?" he asked Owen as they crossed paths on the ramp.

She rolled her eyes. "Show-off."

A few trips later they'd finished packing—including Emery's grape gum—right as Rake, Jackin, and Ford approached from the main corridor.

Rake wore a set of streamlined combat armor that fit her well enough, it could have been tailor-made. It was still weird to see her in anything other than a Legion uniform, or some battle-damaged version of one. Three similar sets of armor awaited him, Emery, and Owen aboard the *Wakeless*—more spoils of Jackin's negotiating skills.

Jackin had dark bags under his eyes and a slight hitch to his step, clutching the atlas pyramid under one arm. Ford hung back a few paces, expression tight with concern, as if he expected Jackin might faint any moment and need catching.

"Sirs," Emery said, giving a soft salute as they approached. "How'd it go?"

"We'll cover specifics on the flight," Rake said. "But we'll be moving ahead with plan B."

"Shit," Emery grumbled. "They couldn't find the delivery schedule?"

"No, they found it," Rake said. "There's just no deliveries scheduled. And none have left for the last five weeks."

"What?" Owen asked. "Why? Some kind of strike?"

Rake shook her head. "We don't know."

Cavalon frowned. "Does that mean what I think it means?"

"If you think it means we'll have to infiltrate the factory warehouse, then yes."

Cavalon bared his teeth in a forced smile. "Great." Exactly how he wanted to spend the day. No problem. It'd be fine. They'd be fine.

Rake passed small plastic cards to Emery and Owen, then to Cavalon. "Let's not need these," she said, almost wistfully, as if putting the words out in the universe would make them come true.

Cavalon turned the metal-edged, hard plastic card over in his hand.

A silver holographic image of the System Collective flag lifted off the front corner as it caught the light. Impressive fakes. As good as the ones he used to procure in order to pass as a civilian for . . . reasons.

He was "Raul Sullivan" from Myrdin. Various barcodes lined the front, over a faded background of the System Collective's federal building on Myrdin, with his portrait at the center. The begrudgingly accommodating Gideon had dropped by to take the photos just this morning, uncaring of Cavalon's protests about having not showered. And shit if he didn't look just like his dad in that damn picture. He really needed to shave.

"I'm Alexa Basham from Cautis Prime," Emery snickered.

Owen laughed. "Yeah, you sound *real* Cautian. I'm Liliana Miles."

"Liliana," Emery purred. "I like that. Kinda spicy."

Owen gave her wolfish smirk.

Emery returned focus to Rake. "We're all loaded up, sirs. I double-checked the manifest myself."

"Thanks, Circitor," Rake said. "We'll start preflights in five. I'll have you shadow me as I boot up."

"Copy that, sir." Emery nodded to Jackin and Ford. "Centurion, Circitor. Keep a light on for us."

"Stay safe," Jackin said, then passed the atlas to Emery.

She tucked it in her ruck, then slung the bag and climbed the short personnel access ladder into the *Wakeless*. Owen followed. Cavalon started to go after them, but hesitated as he realized Rake wasn't following.

Her chin lifted as she looked over the ship, chest swelling with a deep breath, expression unreadable. Jackin took her elbow and turned her to face him. "Remember what we talked about," he said, voice low.

"I know."

"*Adequin*," he said, his tone a firm appeal. Rake froze. "Be careful," he implored. "Please."

Rake gave the barest of nods. "We will, Jack." She looked at Ford. "Keep him locked in the medbay? I need him at full strength ASAP."

"I'll do my best, sir," Ford said with a depressed sigh. He clearly wasn't holding out much hope. "Good luck."

Rake exchanged handshakes with Ford and Jackin, and though as formal and proper as always, they had an air of awkwardness Cavalon couldn't quite put his finger on. Hopefully not because they thought they might be saying goodbye forever.

Rake climbed the ladder and disappeared into the *Wakeless*. Cavalon started after her, but a grip on his arm stopped him partway. Jackin looked up at him, brow creased with that same perpetual worry he'd worn for six straight months.

"Sir?" Cavalon asked.

Jackin cleared his throat. "You know better than most how dangerous it is to go where you're going right now."

Cavalon's breath came up short, but he managed to croak out, "Yeah. I know."

"And you know I don't trust the Quorum, or the Allied Monarchies, especially your family."

A knot constricted in Cavalon's chest. "Yeah . . ."

"But I *do* trust you."

Cavalon's ability to respond vanished along with every word he'd ever learned to say out loud.

"I can see the effect you have on Rake," Jackin went on. "She'll listen to you. Don't let her do anything stupid. If things go lateral at the factory, just get out. Make it back here in one piece. We'll rework it from another angle. We need you. Both of you."

Cavalon nodded. He knew what Jackin meant. Rake was the most courageous and determined person he'd ever known. That combination could easily get her killed. "I'll do my best, sir."

"Promise me."

"I promise," he said, surprised by his own steadfast reply. It'd been automatic. He couldn't say no. The way Jackin looked up at him, cracked lips parting, helpless. Unlike how he'd meticulously orchestrated the Sentinels' progress over the last six months, Jackin had zero control over what was about to happen. If the only play he had left was to enlist Cavalon's aid, he was really scraping the barrel.

Jackin gripped Cavalon's elbow, firm but gentle. "Thank you," he said, and the faith in his bloodshot eyes sent a strange warmth twisting in Cavalon's chest.

He managed a nod, then climbed aboard the *Wakeless*.

Three hours later, Cavalon sat strapped in a crash seat, wringing his sweaty hands. Rake and Emery occupied the two crew seats, quietly hunched in conversation as Rake guided Emery through the ins and outs of the ship.

Cavalon picked at his cuticles. The meter on the *Wakeless*'s sleek black-glass dash ticked down to fifteen minutes. His eyes had gone dry from staring at the countdown the entire trip. The strength of his whole "it'll be fine" mantra had depleted with each passing light-year.

Owen sat in the crash seat beside him, leg bouncing with what one might assume was nerves, but it was Owen, which meant it was actually anticipation. Maybe even excitement. After they'd accelerated to warp,

Owen had time to review the *Wakeless*'s systems, which sent her into a Mesa-style rant about the tech and how much of it she'd thought had only been theoretical. She was clearly impressed—encouraged, even, that they might truly be able to sneak up on Tethys and the Larios Defense Technologies fortress with no one noticing. Cavalon once again found himself envious of her confidence. She didn't seem at all bothered that they were heading to the most dangerous system in the galaxy. If anything, she was looking forward to it.

Cavalon's capacity of *not* looking forward to it could not be overstated. His throat burned and his stomach seethed with bile. He was pretty sure his ulcers had ulcers.

He'd been to Tethys plenty of times, for plenty of reasons. It was home to a multitude of industrial properties held by various royal families. The trade-off was clear: "tax-free research zone to promote industrial development" meant "bribe disguised as legalized tax evasion so Augustus Mercer can keep tabs on your research."

Cavalon had personally overseen the commissioning of the very Larios Defense Technologies facility they were about to infiltrate. His memories of that day were hazy, however, so he hadn't been able to provide much insight on the intel front. He'd been mid-bender at the time, and though the stimulant cocktail Augustus's cronies had forced into his arm had gotten him through the ceremony, he'd crashed hard afterward. The only account he knew had been the grim secondhand retelling Owen had heard from a cousin. Not one of his proudest moments. Only after he'd gotten sober had he started feeling embarrassed by his drunken antics.

He closed his eyes and let out a deep breath, pulling his mind from the past to focus on the future. Which wasn't hard to do sitting in a bleeding-edge prototype ship. He'd grown so used to the Sentinels' outdated technology, he'd half-forgotten what a modern ship looked like. Though, the *Wakeless* was a few steps beyond modern. He at once feared and appreciated how illegal essentially every piece of tech surrounding him was.

The clean interior design of mostly dark gray with black accents reminded him of the Saxton family's line of luxury yachts. Even the layout was similar—not that there were all that many ways to configure a ship this small. A short hallway at the back contained four doors leading to the airlock, a small bunk room, a lavatory, and the ladder chute down to the cargo hold.

A soft chime signaled the forthcoming dulcet tones of the *Wakeless*'s AI. Cavalon startled at the sudden noise, heat flooding his face.

"Dude," Owen muttered under her breath, "you gotta chill out."

He wiped his sweaty palms down the front of his pants. "I'm very chill, thank you."

The AI's creepy holographic human face materialized above the dash. Rake glowered.

"Warp deceleration in ten minutes," the AI intoned, its digitized lips trailing just behind its words.

"Thanks, hon," Emery piped from the copilot's chair. She chomped happily on her newly acquired grape gum.

"You're welcome," the AI replied.

Emery's eyes rounded as she looked to Rake. "Can we name her?"

Rake slid her a flat look. "No." She turned her attention to the disembodied face. "Computer, dismissed," she grumbled, and the AI disappeared. Rake muttered a couple of expletives under her breath, then spun her seat around to face Cavalon and Owen.

Emery frowned, and she craned her neck as she hunted for her own seat control.

"On the front right," Rake said patiently.

"Ah!" Emery clicked the control, and she held her chin high as the seat spun.

"We'll do a flyover and reassessment on arrival," Rake said, "but we're going to have a preliminary briefing so we're all on the same page to start." Rake expanded a holographic globe of Tethys over half the dash. "These scans are from two days ago."

Emery's eyebrows climbed. "Nice. How the heck did we get these?"

"Ford helped their techs pull them from Legion satellite data," Rake answered.

"Dude's not just a medic, is he?" Owen surmised.

Rake shook her head, but didn't elaborate. She slid her fingers to zoom into a quadrant in the northern hemisphere. The globe morphed into a topographic map. "The factory itself isn't part of the main campus," she explained. "It's twelve klicks south, here . . ." She scaled in even more, and the colorless topography morphed into detailed satellite imagery. "Just south of the river. We'll make our approach here, south-southwest. Here's the LZ Ford recommended. We'll have to hoof it on foot, about two klicks."

"How're we gonna cover that approach?" Emery asked.

"The Corsairs gave us a couple armored drones," Rake said, then pointed out two spots on the map. "We'll post them as lookouts here and here. If it's as desolate as the heat map says it is, that should be plenty."

"Did they happen to provide any concealment for us?" Owen asked.

"Yeah," Emery replied. "Emitter cloaks."

Cavalon quirked a brow. "What're those?"

"Personal cloaking generators," Rake answered. "They'll help keep us off satellites and most sensor arrays. We only have three, but someone needs to stay with the ship and run support anyway. Emery, I think it's best if that's you in case we need a quick exfil. You comfortable with that?"

"Absolutely, sir."

"We'll cover more details once we get fresh eyes on the target. Any quest—"

The AI's chime sounded. Rake bristled.

The computer's face materialized. "Warp deceleration in five minutes."

"Computer," Emery said, tone as pleasant as Phaedra's, "can we deactivate the incoming verbal notification chime?"

"Of course."

"And the creepy face thing too?"

"Certainly." The creepy face disappeared.

Emery batted her lashes at the dash. "Thanks, doll."

Rake's jaw skimmed, then she mumbled to Emery, "Thank you."

"I gotchu, boss."

"Unsecured personnel detected," the AI said. "Please secure all crew in preparation for deceleration."

Rake, Emery, and Owen started buckling their harnesses. Cavalon checked his, still secured from the acceleration, shirt doused with sweat under the straps.

Rake tapped open a few screens. "Computer, prep for a cloaked deceleration."

"Acknowledged."

"Acknowledged, *sir*," Emery corrected.

"Apologies," the AI replied. "Acknowledged, sir."

Emery flashed a satisfied smirk while Rake rubbed her temples.

"Sir," the AI began, "may I make a suggestion?"

Rake sighed. "Sure."

"You may render the vessel essentially invisible by modern standards by activating the *Wakeless*'s proprietary Phantom protocols copyright Larios Defense Technologies 225 AV. The mode was designed for this express purpose."

Rake stared at the dash. "You said invisible?"

Emery rubbed her hands together excitedly.

"I said invisible," the AI replied, and Cavalon could have sworn he heard a hint of snark in the placid tone.

"All right," Rake agreed. "Why the hell not."

"Apologies, sir," the AI said, "but 'why the hell not' is not listed on the approved—"

"Computer," Rake growled, "engage Phantom protocols on deceleration."

"Acknowledged, sir. Deceleration in thirty seconds."

Cavalon kneaded his hands and waited for the telltale floor rumble and the drop in the pit of his stomach. Emery's gum smacked in the dead silence of the cockpit.

Then, with absolutely no preamble whatsoever, an array of new screens populated the dash.

"Deceleration complete," the AI announced. "Phantom protocols engaged. Running security checks."

Cavalon's eyes sharpened. The display confirmed a successful warp deceleration, yet he'd not felt even the mildest discomfort.

Flying in this thing felt like a simulation. He half-expected they'd deplane only to find themselves still in the hangar of the *Corinthian*, with Gideon and all his guard pals standing around laughing at them.

"Phew," Emery whistled. "Rough landing."

Owen snickered. "No kidding."

A yellow holographic screen materialized in front of Emery. "If you have detected an issue with warp deceleration," the AI intoned, "please log the experience for review by our technicians as per article 19A of your lease agreement."

Emery's eyes rounded with amusement. "Uh, sorry, hon. I was just kidding. Decel was perfect."

After a beat, the AI chirped, "Understood."

"Opticals on-screen," Rake ordered.

A wide, narrow strip of viewscreen materialized high over the rest of the controls. Cavalon gulped.

The curved rim of the massive gas giant Pherebos dominated the left side of the frame. To the right, growing larger every second, the dull green orb of its moon, Tethys, covered with patches of white clouds.

Cavalon's breaths grew thick, and he was suddenly glad he wasn't wearing one of those damn space suits that liked to yell at him about how "dangerous" his heart rate was becoming.

"Security checks clear," the AI announced. "For optimized concealment, a two-hundred-second interlude is recommended to allow warp engine stabilization before initiating sublight gliders."

Cavalon coughed as he almost choked on his own saliva.

"Understood," Rake said. "When ready, take us into geostationary orbit over the coordinates."

"Acknowledged, sir."

"Uh," Cavalon sputtered, "this thing has sublight gliders?"

Emery lifted a shoulder, clearly not understanding why that was newsworthy. Rake still glowered at the dash, too worried about keeping an eye on all the things the AI was already monitoring to pay him any heed.

He was a fucking astromechanic, why hadn't he looked at the specs of this thing? Sublight gliders meant much faster acceleration and deceleration than standard ion engines, as well as a faster maximum velocity. It'd been proprietary Saxton tech last he knew. It was looking more and more like someone in the Saxton family was in league with Larios Defense Technologies. Or maybe LDT had upped their game on corporate espionage.

There'd been so much focus on the support systems, he hadn't thought to marvel at what might be under the hood. Or maybe he'd been too distracted by the fact that they were dropping into his grandfather's backyard.

"Geostationary orbit achieved," the AI announced.

Cavalon spun to find the horizon of Tethys dominating the bottom half of the viewscreen. The ship had accelerated, decelerated, and banked into orbit without him even noticing. He had half a mind to ask Rake to ask Emery to ask the AI to tell the maneuvering dampeners to relax a little bit. It was damn unnerving. Maybe he was just used to getting thrown around by the *Synthesis* and its shitty systems.

"Initiate preset scanner package alpha," Rake ordered.

"Acknowledged, sir."

Rake glanced over her shoulder. "Owen, you ready back there?"

"Yes, sir," Owen piped. "Request sent."

"Computer," Rake said, "connect to ancillary device. Grant full systems access."

"Acknowledged, sir. Flight control access cannot be granted and will be withheld."

"Understood," Rake said.

A yellow-green bloom of light drew Cavalon's attention to Owen. A square tablet sat in her lap, projecting a three-paneled holographic screen into a trapezoid in front of her.

"Where the hell did you get that?" Cavalon asked.

"That scowly Gideon guy."

"No, I mean just now."

Owen quirked a brow. "Are you kidding? I've been sitting here setting it up the entire warp. Man, you're really out of it—you need to relax."

Cavalon leaned back in his seat and blew out a hard breath. "You know, what really helps is telling me to relax all the time."

"Well, if you'd just do it already, then I wouldn't have—" Owen's terminal beeped and she tapped open a connection screen. "I'm in, sir," she announced.

"In what?" Cavalon asked.

"Shh," she said, leaning into the screens. "I need to focus."

"Sorry," he whispered, and slunk deeper into his seat.

He closed his eyes and let out a long sigh, trying to exhale the tension from his rib cage. He did have a purpose, and not an unimportant one at that: to get the ceronite. To make sure it was fresh, uncontaminated, and the right composition and concentration. Too dense and it could clog the system, probably cause a few more fiery explosions. Too watered-down and it could simply not work. He also fully intended to pack up at least twice as much as they needed, if possible. He knew exactly what he'd done wrong to cause the fault, and Mesa would already be well underway with the fix. But after all this, he'd feel a thousand times better if they had some extra in reserve.

"Huh," Emery said, tilting her head at her screen. "Factory radio signals are weirdly quiet."

"How quiet?" Rake asked.

"Like, zero transmissions quiet."

"Yeah, and I think I know why," Owen said warily, still tapping around in her three-paneled display. "Looks like they're on production hold until next quarter. Whole place is shut down."

Rake rubbed the back of her neck. "That explains why there were no shipments scheduled."

Emery frowned. "Are they gonna have what we need?"

"According to the System Collective charter," Rake said, "it has sole production *and* distribution. There must be a storage facility. Computer, display thermal scans of the target area."

"Acknowledged, sir."

"Cav?" Rake threw a look over her shoulder. "Can you take a look at these overlays?"

Oh, right. Time for him to actually do something.

He unbuckled from the sweaty harness and paced the few steps to stand between Rake and Emery. Rake tapped to overlay the topographic and satellite imagery with the thermal scan. His eyes scoured the map, hunting for any signs of ceronite—the spectral signature would be an obvious one, if the scanners on this thing were that detailed, though the shape of the canisters alone might make it distinct enough.

"Analysis complete," the AI said. The scans flashed and narrowed in on a location west of the main factory. Holographic markers and floating pods of information sprung to life, detailing the AI's findings. "Radiative signatures, heat concentrations, and physical configuration suggest 99.8 percent match for target location."

Cavalon frowned at the dash. "Hey, that's my line."

Rake's head tilted in consolation. "Thanks, Cav."

He sighed and returned to his seat.

"Sir, do you concur?" the AI asked.

Cavalon glared at the black glass of the dash. If he didn't know better, he'd almost think it wanted praise.

Rake gave an absent nod, increasing the opacity of the satellite overlay. "There's only two bay doors on the west side, and I don't see any haulers. But this access road leads directly to the spaceport. It has to be the right place. Mark as target location."

"Acknowledged, sir."

Rake looked over her shoulder. "Owen, how's it looking back there?"

Owen sat hunched amongst her yellow-green displays. "Uh, yeah," she mumbled, tone wary.

"What's wrong?" Rake asked.

"Sorry, sir," Owen said, then straightened up, still staring at her screens. "Something a little strange is going on."

"Strange how?"

Owen frowned, shifting in her seat. "I was able to get into the primary sec-system with the Larios backdoor, but it's showing as view-only. I can see the firewalls, camera systems, sensors, everything. But I can't make any changes. There's a secondary authorization requirement to unlock full admin permissions—part of the lockdown."

"What's the secondary auth?" Rake asked.

"Biometric," Owen answered.

Rake sat back in her seat, running stiff hands down her face.

"Direct-intact biometric, to be exact," Owen went on.

Cavalon gave an absent nod. Now they were getting to words he recognized.

Owen's forehead creased as she reviewed her screens. "Pretty impressive setup, actually. I've not seen one like this before."

Emery quirked a brow. "What's direct-intact biometric mean?"

"It means it requires a genomic DNA sample," Cavalon answered.

Though security wasn't their speciality, Mercer Biotech had had a corporate security division for over fifty years. *Officially*, Larios Defense Technologies produced the industry-standard for biometric identification and authorization, but that was only because Augustus hadn't gone public with what was going on on the 129th floor of the Mercer Biotech headquarters.

Owen's lips pinched into a tight frown. "With this setup, said person has to be alive and conscious. No way to spoof it. That I know of." She chewed her lip. "Must be because they're out of production. There're no workers trying to go in and out, so they don't need standard security protocols. They just power up a couple drones and lock the whole place down."

"Are you able to access the authorized clearance list?" Rake asked.

"Yes, sir." Owen hunched over her screen and started tapping.

Cavalon eyed Rake, her posture straight, eyes clear with determination. He could see it now—she'd figure out who was on that list, hunt them down, shoot them with a stun charge, and haul them to the factory. Nothing but a minor inconvenience.

No one was worried about any of this but him. It was really hard to say if he was overreacting or if they were underreacting. Though to be fair, they were trained to keep their cool in stressful situations.

He glowered at Owen. *She* wasn't. But that didn't surprise him in the slightest; she'd always been recklessly cool under pressure.

Owen sat up straight. "Got it." She threw a file from her tablet onto the main dash. Rake tapped to open it.

Cavalon's heart stalled out as he stared at the single name on the list: Augustus Cornelius Mercer.

"Bloody . . ." Rake trailed off into a string of mumbled expletives. Emery pressed her face into both hands, and Owen's wide eyes stared at the "list," unblinking.

Cavalon wanted to be surprised right along with them, but he just wasn't. It was par for the fucking course of his entire twenty-eight years of life. Augustus was everywhere, all the time. At every university he'd enrolled in just to have a way to avoid him for ten years, in the tragic pasts of the disgruntled soldiers that'd tried to beat him to death at Kharon Gate, at the factory Cavalon needed to access in order to save four thousand starving soldiers—the fucker was probably on this damn ship right now; it wouldn't even surprise him.

"I hate to say it, sir," Owen said warily, "but if Larios engineers worked with Mercer Biotech to code these entry points, it's probably worse than we thought."

Rake ran a hand over her forehead and nodded. "Yeah."

252 ◂ J. S. DEWES

"Worse how?" Cavalon asked.

"It means it's not only about getting a door open," Owen said. "The whole facility is on biometric lockdown. Until your gramps arrives to clear it, any perimeter breach or attempt at accessing the systems would set off an alarm. There's no sneaking past this."

"Well," Emery said, pitching her voice up with forced cheer, "at least the factory's definitely empty, right?"

"Sure . . ." Owen gave a relenting tilt of her head. "But it being empty inside doesn't help us if there's no way to get inside in the first place."

"So, uh, what?" Emery began, smacking hard on her gum. "We have to lure him to the facility somehow? Trick him into unlocking it?"

Cavalon shook his head at Emery and her attempt at optimism faded. There was no "tricking" Augustus into anything.

Rake exhaled a long breath, the tendons in her neck flexing as she chewed over the problem.

Owen gripped Cavalon's knee and leaned in, brow furrowed, expression dire. "Have you considered just asking real nice?"

He let out a throttled chuckle and met her gaze, trying to soak up the playful glint in her eye to extinguish the stab of pain in his chest. "Ya know, I haven't," he consented. "Maybe I should give it a go."

Then a wave of hot nausea sliced through him as a solution careened its way forward from a part of his mind that clearly hated him. It stalled out his thoughts for the better part of a minute before he could regroup.

He dismissed it, reconsidered it, and dismissed it again.

After a dozen or so times of that loop, it started settling in as a viable option. A dangerous option, but a viable one. Maybe the only one.

He looked at Rake, who still sat staring into the middle distance, gaze flicking as she worked the problem over. Coming up empty, over and over again.

"Any ideas, sir?" Emery asked, voice thin.

Rake's jaw flexed. "No."

Cavalon gave a dry swallow. He had to step up, had to shove his fears back into his past where they belonged. Time to emulate all the fearless people he'd surrounded himself with. He was one of them now, after all. That's what he'd worked so hard to become the last six months.

Besides, what was the alternative? They return to the Corsairs, talk out more options, realize they don't have any. They become intergalactic highwaymen, setting traps to net ships with jump drives. Pirate their way from spacelane stopover to spacelane stopover, stealing piddly reserves of ceronite until they finally collect enough to fuel the *Lodestar*. It could take years.

Cavalon inhaled, hating how much his breath wavered as he blew it back out. "Um . . ." he stammered, proud of how he was already plowing forth with brazen confidence.

In unnerving unison, Rake, Emery, and Owen turned to stare expectantly at him.

He cleared his throat. "I have an idea."

"Are you fucking insane?" Owen asked, hazel eyes wide.

Emery sat frozen in her seat, pale skin blanched, her wad of purple gum threatening to fall from her gaping mouth. "Yeah, uh, what she said," she croaked out.

"I agree," Cavalon said, striving to keep his voice even, "it's a last-resort kind of a thing, but even our Titan is coming up short on solutions. If I'm reading the room right, last resort is where we're at right now."

Rake hadn't responded yet. She sat still in her seat, elbows on her armrests, fingers tented over her lap. Strands of her tied-up hair fell around her face. "Tell me about this device," she said quietly.

Cavalon's chin bobbed. "Well, Augustus is primarily two things—paranoid and diabolical. This hits on both those characteristics pretty strongly. It's a . . . I guess what you'd call a bioterrorism safeguard. In the event he's affected by some kind of genetic weapon that would alter his genome."

Owen scoffed. "Because anyone but him is likely to unleash a bioterrorist attack?"

Cavalon lifted a shoulder in a weak shrug. "It isn't like he's without vengeful enemies. And like I said—paranoid."

Emery shook her head. "I don't get it—what the hell's it for?"

"It stores a clean, unalterable copy of his genetic code," Cavalon answered. "Ostensibly, it exists to pass down to the heir in the event of his untimely death. In actuality, it's because he's paranoid as fuck. A living failsafe, he calls it."

"What does that even mean?" Emery asked.

"It means if he could get it to a lab, it'd let him repair his own genome. In the meantime, it'd act like a . . . mini-him. It would allow him access to anything coded to his DNA, including any Mercer Biotech sec-system."

Owen scowled. "Since when do you guys have your own security tech?"

Cavalon gave her a flat look. Her lips twisted with a slight pout, and she sat back in her seat.

Rake shifted in her seat. "And we're sure this is a Mercer Biotech system?"

"Well, it's first and foremost an LDT system," Owen answered, "but with a Mercer Biotech shell. We'll have to get through both layers. The Larios one's the easy part."

Rake let out a hard breath, refocusing on Cavalon. "Why would your grandfather make something like that? It's such a massive security risk."

"I know," Cavalon said, licking his dry lips. "But to him, the idea of losing that level of control is inconceivable. The reassurance of having a solution in his back pocket outweighs the risks. And to be fair, passing something like that off to the heir on your deathbed is safer than having any kind of admin hand over code sitting on a mainframe, waiting to be released on his death."

"Because then anyone with access to the mainframe would have the power to initiate the handover," Rake surmised.

Cavalon nodded. "Which they could then implement at any time. This way, no one can take control, no one can instigate a coup, his security team can't turn on him, his heir can't expedite succession. He has full control until the secret device no one knows about is passed off. And trust me when I say this is top-secret shit. It's part of passing the mantle, though I never got that far. He doesn't know I know about it."

"Then how *do* you?" Owen asked.

"My father told me. Before he died he started getting . . . paranoid, himself." The words caught, and he quickly cleared his throat to mask it. "Rightfully so, it turns out. He knew Augustus would never tell me himself, he never trusted me like he did my father. Dad thought I should know. That someone else should know."

"And you know where it's located?" Rake asked.

"I do."

"Where?"

"Um," he began, taking in their expectant stares. "His bedroom."

Emery blinked. "Excuse me?"

"At home," he said.

Owen barked a laugh.

"*Home?*" Emery croaked. "Like, 'Mercer Manor' home?"

Owen leaned her elbows on her knees, rubbing her face briskly with both hands.

Rake stared at him, expression blank, maintaining her impressive calm with apparent ease. "Are you sure about this?" she asked.

A nervous half-laugh, half-cough bubbled up. He collected himself and rasped out, "*No.*"

She crossed her arms and sat back, considering it. Considering him.

He kept his eyes glued to hers and shook his head slowly, pushing every worry and confidence and lament he had into the look passing between them. Because at this point, they didn't need to talk it out. They'd come this far. If this was the answer, the thing that could save them, how could they say no?

It'd be him and her. He didn't need another mission briefing to know that. She wouldn't want to risk anyone else. She'd need him to get them inside, to guide them into the bowels of the southern wing, to his grandfather's residence. Into places Cavalon had never even been himself. And he'd need her to be a Titan. To be Rake. They could do it, but only together.

Rake nodded. Cavalon's pulse raced.

She turned around to face the dash. "Emery . . ."

Emery spun as well, keeping a nervous eye on Rake in her periphery. "Yessir."

"Plot a course to Elyseia."

CHAPTER TWENTY-TWO

The *Wakeless* broke atmosphere over Elyseia and descended into a mass of thick, gray clouds. Adequin inhaled to a count of four, then blew her breath out even slower. She'd taken part in some shockingly dangerous missions in her day, yet the prospect of pulling this off rivaled them all. One did not simply walk into a royal residence, take what one wanted, and walk out.

She'd intended to arrive, gather intel, then find somewhere to lie low for a day or two and work through scenarios. But mere minutes after they dropped from warp speed, Owen had caught a story on the media feeds: the king of Elyseia had traveled to Viridis to attend an Allied Monarchies state dinner, the heir presumptive at his side—Cavalon's "shithead" second cousin. Would His Majesty use the opportunity to declare his heir publicly? Would the Cautian princess finally announce her scandalous rumored engagement? What fashion atrocity would the Viridian prince commit this time? Intrigue, scandal, etcetera.

What the vapid reports meant that actually mattered to them was that Augustus and the heir were off-world. Which meant their respective retinues of Mercer Guard were off-world. It could mean fewer patrols, and Adequin knew from experience—inattentive guards. It was a chance to relax when the boss was away. It could be an opportunity that might not come again for weeks. Which meant they had to take it.

They had exactly two advantages—though Adequin was reticent to call them that, more like the only things that made it even remotely possible to consider. For one, they had access to Cavalon's secret entrance—an old relief bunker from which he'd come and gone from the manor for most of his adult life, where he'd built the nuclear missiles. And two, Owen's history as a cog in the Larios Defense Technologies corporate wheel gave her a thorough familiarity of the types of military-grade security systems used in royal residences.

Along with lax guards, the entry would be the easy part. Getting out would still be a nightmare if things went wrong. A fact which escalated Adequin's already-soaring anxiety. This kind of operation required weeks of preparation—it needed a half-dozen backup plans, each with its own set of backup plans. Not thirty minutes of her skimming over limited data sets and confering with the ship's docile AI just so she could pretend like she had anything even remotely resembling a mission workup.

Not that she planned to tell the others that. The more brazen confidence she could exude, the better off everyone would be.

Emery had warily proposed sending Jackin an update, seemingly as a suggestion of proper protocol, considering mission parameters had radically changed, but Adequin suspected she simply wanted someone to know where to find their bodies. But, cutting-edge stealth ship or no, sending a message, even encrypted, was a risk. Not only for them, but for Jackin and Ford—and all the Corsairs—on the receiving end. And Jackin was supposed to be dead, so drawing attention to his whereabouts with cryptic messages was a nonstarter. They had a quiet ship and a quiet way down, and they needed to keep it that way. Jackin could yell at her later.

Adequin wiped her sweating palms and focused on the *Wakeless*'s dash. The alert displays remained quiet. Gideon had assured her the ship's atmospheric stealth capabilities were as robust as the stellar ones. That was a pretty high bar, considering they'd gone completely unharried scouting Tethys, then silently dropped from warp speed and flown into Elyseian protected space as if the security net weren't even there.

The console let out a soft beep as they descended from cloud cover, revealing an impressive stretch of skyline on the viewscreen. At the center, the seat of the System Collective—the Meridian—a curved blade of silver-blue glass, its tapered peak piercing the mottled gray clouds. Rows of mirrored skyscrapers encircled it, descending in height in every direction until the density dispersed into wide, tree-lined boulevards, biodomes, and sprawling urban manors.

Multilayered tracks wound from the maze of spires into the outer city—paths for electric trams, buses, and monorails. A half kilometer up, private transports sped along skylanes demarcated with strips of blue light—heavily tolled to ensure the routes remained only lightly trafficked, and thus reserved for the upper echelon.

If she'd been uneasy in the *Corinthian*'s lightly populated station, she was about to be really fucking uncomfortable on the streets of the most populous city in the Core. The planet of Elyseia and the city shared a name, and were generally considered one and the same, though the city itself didn't take up more than seven or eight hundred square kilometers. A massive, shallow ocean covered half the planet, and any landmass outside the confines of the city was protected conservancy.

"Target location on-screen," the AI announced.

The viewscreen dimmed the surrounding areas, highlighting a quadrant of the outer city known as the Royal Quarter. The district was home to dozens of private residences, each the size of a city block, along with their much larger target: Mercer Manor.

It felt a little strange to think of Cavalon's home—or former home—as a target. He hadn't seemed bothered by it; in fact, he hadn't seemed much of anything since they'd decided on this course of action, sitting mute in his crash seat, blue eyes unblinking in a thousand-kilometer stare. She couldn't really argue with the strategy of emotionally distancing himself. It might be the only way to get through it. Either way, she really hoped he'd pull through. She needed him as functional as possible.

As they drew closer, the viewscreen focused on a square swath of land confined by massive security walls at least ten meters high and three meters deep. Within sat a sprawling three-story estate. Its facades formed the outline of a square with a central courtyard, brimming with colorful foliage. The manor's impressive outer facades displayed extravagant masonry laden with colonnades, massive arched windows, and balconies with intricately carved balustrades. Along the northern and western facades, a tiered, slate patio extended out into the lush, trimmed lawn. Hedged gardens sat to the north, opposite a massive private spaceport on the south lawn.

Emery's gum chomps slowed. "Void," she breathed. "Y'all seriously call that thing a *manor*? That's at the very least a castle. If not a palace." She peered over her shoulder at Cavalon. "That's where you grew up?"

He growled out a light scoff of affirmation.

Emery let out a low whistle. "That explains a lot . . ."

The AI helped Adequin find a viable landing zone in an expansive conservancy a couple of kilometers south of the Royal Quarter. "Phantom protocols" or no, they couldn't exactly land in the middle of a busy city street unnoticed.

A few minutes later, the *Wakeless* set down beside a copse of bushy conifers on a grassy hill within the conservancy. The entire northern half was closed to the public, with a single dirt access road for park rangers that looked like it hadn't been used in months.

They remained in the *Wakeless* for twenty minutes to ensure their landing had gone undetected, giving Adequin and Cavalon more than enough time to suit up and prepare their loadouts. Their light combat armor was thin enough to be worn under the fashionably baggy black-and-silver-threaded tunics and hooded jackets the Corsairs had provided. They equipped the emitter cloaks they'd planned to use on Tethys, as well as two personal shield generators—mid-grade models with wide reach, but low absorption capacity.

Adequin took as many weapons as she could realistically conceal without weighing her down—a large combat knife, a plasma pistol, and a few disk grenades of various function. And the main attraction: a collapsible, rapid-priming gauss rifle Gideon offered up at the last minute. Regardless of his invariably surly attitude, by the end of the intel briefing, he'd appeared to have warmed to their plight, and even seemed invested in their success. Though maybe he just really wanted his ship back.

She preloaded a magazine, then secured the collapsible rifle in a holster on her low back. She encouraged Cavalon to take a pistol and a knife at the very least.

Owen updated their nexus software with an add-on from the Corsairs' crate of security tech, then patched them into her command terminal so she'd be able to run support remotely if needed. She gave Adequin a quick primer on the codebreaker attachment for her nexus, though it mostly served as a refresher—she'd used similar tech hundreds of times as a Titan. They synced a remote comms system to their nexuses, adhering a tiny node behind the ear at the top of their jawbones that allowed for aural and speech conduction, permitting quiet remote communication without obstructing the ear canal.

When they were sure their landing had gone undetected, Adequin passed a reluctant Emery the atlas medallion off her dog tags, then exited out the personnel hatch.

Her feet dropped onto a patch of soft, dry dirt. Stalks of shoulder-high, tasseled grass shifted around her as a light wind drifted in, bringing a waft of pine from the conifers. She drew in an invigorating breath of unmanufactured air: temperate, thick with the scent of soil and grass and moisture. From deep within the tree line, birds chirped out a high-pitched, staccato song.

Her eardrums pulsed, full and painful as if she'd just dove into deep water. She stretched her jaw to pop them, and her ears buzzed. She thought it was feedback from her jaw mic for a few seconds before remembering the sensation from years ago.

When returning groundside after a few weeks or months in space, her ears would spend a few minutes ringing with a resonant inverse of the drone of background noise her brain expected to hear, but was no longer there—the round-the-clock hum of HVAC and ship systems. The crisp, clear quality of the noises around her seemed starker in its absence. It almost reminded her of the tranquility of a spacewalk.

She stepped forward, hesitating as a roll of vertigo gripped her. Though the gravity on Elyseia matched the standard used in most ships, the distribution of it somehow seemed more . . . concentrated. The ground tugged more thoroughly on the soles of her boots, compelling her down toward the core. Thankfully, the dense perimeter of trees surrounding the landing zone helped lessen the nausea stirred by the abruptly flat, open horizon.

When her dizziness abated, she took a few slow steps away from the ship, the tassels of grass brushing her shoulders. Her gaze drifted to the marbled clouds roiling overhead, then to the gently swaying tree branches. A tan, hawkish bird keened as it caught on the breeze, drifting northeast against the headwind.

Cavalon stepped up beside her. "Everything okay?" Even at a whisper, his voice thrummed, vivid and sharp, stinging against her eardrums.

"Yeah," she said, blinking a few times to pull her gaze from the scenery. "Just been a while since I was groundside."

"Oh, right . . ." He rubbed a knuckle into one ear, stretching his jaw. "Over five years. How's it feel?"

Her hand shifted to her gun as some manner of tiny creature scuttled through the brush nearby. She scratched her chin, then met Cavalon's eye. "Might take a little getting used to."

Static crackled in her surveillance. "Sigma Three for Sigma One," Emery said, her voice muted and bassy through the jaw conduction.

"Go for Sigma One," Adequin replied.

"Engaging optical concealment," Emery announced.

"Copy that, Sigma Three."

Adequin glanced back at the *Wakeless*, or where the *Wakeless* had been. Now nothing but a swath of flattened grass remained.

Cavalon let out a soft whistle. "Damn."

"Can confirm," Adequin said. "No visual."

"Copy no visual," Emery replied. "We're all set, boss."

"I'll be ready on comms if you need an assist," Owen said. "But your codebreaker's all set."

"Thanks," Adequin replied. "We're going dark for now. No transmissions unless it's an emergency."

"Copy that," Emery said. "Good luck, you two. Stay safe."

Adequin closed the line, then led Cavalon north through the tree line. At the perimeter of the conservancy, an easy hack administered by the codebreaker allowed them to interrupt the signal and climb the security fence unnoticed. They waited for a lull, then melded seamlessly into the light foot traffic. Adequin thanked the void for the threatening gray of the clouds and spurts of light rainfall, making her and Cavalon's raised hoods unremarkable.

The impeccably clean concrete sidewalks were narrow, built for pedestrians only, with no visible cracks or weathering. Eventually the pedway widened into a busier thoroughfare lined with small shops, residence accesses, and patches of curated greenery. Turnstiles every few blocks allowed lift access to underground public transit levels.

Advertisements played on any available vertical surface—both holographic projections and built-in viewscreens. Adequin knew if they'd connected to the global network feed, they'd be assaulted audibly as well as visually. She'd forgotten what it was like to be bombarded by ads every second of every day. She hadn't missed that part of civilized space.

Cavalon led the way, maintaining a steady pace a step in front of her, hood drawn, shoulders back, radiating stoic silence. He kept a paranoid scowl focused on the pavement a few meters ahead, as if at any moment, one of the oncoming pedestrians might leap out to identify him.

It may have been his idea, but it was still a lot to ask of him. Probably too much.

She took a few quick steps to catch up, then took his hand. His pace slowed a fraction, palms clammy but fingers warm as they entwined hers. He didn't miss a step as he edged a look at her from under his hood. He gave an appreciative nod.

She'd learned long ago, it helped to lean into the guise. They were just two people taking an afternoon stroll through the streets of Elyseia. Not two traitors breaking into a royal residence, the home of a tyrant, a murderer. With that murderer's grandson at her side, it was much more difficult than she'd expected to keep her unease in check. There was so much more to lose than just one failed mission.

She tried to exhale through the cramping ache in her ribs. She knew what she needed to do: compartmentalize. She was a soldier, not a friend. She had an objective to accomplish, nothing more. Only the procedure mattered—clean entry, clean retrieval, clean extraction.

Cavalon slid her another glance, this one discerning and a bit worried. His grip on her hand tightened, loosening the ache in her chest.

He led them past a large stand of public transit lifts and into a congested neighborhood with even more advertisements. She kept her chin down, though she couldn't keep her eyes off the passersby with their trendy layered attire and smart businesswear, gazes inward as they watched feeds or carried on remote conversations via cerebral nexuses. It was jarring to see so many civilians going about their lives as if everything were completely normal.

When they got to within a couple of blocks of the manor, Cavalon moved off the main street and down a service road behind a row of shops. They turned into a narrow alley, where Cavalon slowed his purposeful walk. He cast a furtive look both ways, though they hadn't seen a soul since they left the main street.

His eyes scoured the alley wall, lips pinching in calculation. He stopped short and took a few steps back, then forward again, then reached out and touched two fingers to a seemingly inconsequential area of the smooth metal. A portion of the wall jittered with static light, then seemed to dematerialize, revealing a narrow door frame and control pad.

Cavalon entered a short access code, prompting a soft *shink* of metal on metal. He pushed the hinged door open, and Adequin followed.

A staircase descended before them, the landing barely wide enough to stand side by side. The blue-tinged overcast daylight disappeared as Cavalon sealed the door.

Adequin's eyes were still adjusting to the pitch-dark when she sensed Cavalon passing her, boots scraping against the concrete stairs. With her armored combat boots, Adequin had to turn her feet sideways to fit on the narrow steps.

At the foot of the stairs, a single hallway stretched out, dotted with open door frames, spilling green-tinged light into the inky shadows of the corridor.

Adequin glanced into the first open door they passed, a temporary storefront offering an assortment of firearm modifications lined up behind bulletproof glass. In the next room, a grizzled proprietor and a clean-cut woman in a suit haggled over the price of something in an unmarked black case. In the next, a harrowing card game, serious enough to require a glowering bodyguard for every one of the inscrutable players.

Cavalon marched on, not giving a second look into any of the dozen rooms they passed, each filled with similar goings-on. Adequin chewed the inside of her lip, marveling at the dark maze of back rooms tucked into the folds of an otherwise chic, prosperous city.

"I gotta say," she said softly, just loud enough for her mic to pick up, "I didn't expect to find a black market this deep into the Royal Quarter."

Cavalon's equally quiet response crackled through. "Every city has its seedy underground—usually literal. Even self-proclaimed utopias."

"Sure, but so close to the royal manor?"

Cavalon let out a soft hum, then glanced over his shoulder at her. A bare fixture cast a sliver of light across his pale skin. "Yeah . . . I may have had something to do with the location of this particular seedy underground. And its prosperity."

"Ah." That made a lot more sense.

"Don't tell Gramps."

"Wouldn't think of it."

For the next few minutes, they wound their way through ever-darkening hallways. Finally, Cavalon took a left into a concrete-walled passage narrow enough he had to walk with his shoulders turned. Adequin slipped the small headlamp node from her pocket and adhered it to her right temple. She clicked it on to the lowest setting, casting a soft beam of light into the dank hallway. Cavalon did the same.

They came to a dead end capped with a square, hatch-like door. A panel beside it indicated controlled-access. Adequin expanded the codebreaker on her nexus, but Cavalon held up a hand. "No need. This one's mine."

He flipped open the panel cover. It scanned his hand, then his retina, then he typed in a passcode so impossibly long, she stopped trying to memorize after the twentieth digit.

Finally, the door slid open, revealing a narrow chute lined with ladder rungs. Cavalon slid down, landing with a soft splash of water.

She climbed down, a thin, tangy scent pricking her nostrils as she stepped into a couple of centimeters of standing water. Overhead, the hatch hissed shut. Her headlamp revealed a wide passage with slightly bowed walls in either direction. Faint waterlines were visible, but it was so clean, it took her a moment to realize where they were. Even Elyseia's sewers were nicer than the streets she'd grown up on.

"This way," Cavalon said. "There're a few more coded passages."

There were indeed a *few* more, seven to be exact, each with a code as long as—and different than—the first. It might have been a *secret* way in, but it was not a fast one.

After a few more minutes, they came to an old brick foundation wall. The reinforced steel door set into it was different than the rest—older, wider, the dark metal discolored by streaks of rust. Cavalon opened an access panel over the controls and started his unlocking procedure.

A minute later the old door let out a yawning creak, and the seal cracked. Cavalon pulled it open. A stale, dusty scent lingered on the air, clashing with the dankness of the sewers.

Shoulders stiff, Cavalon stepped inside and paced straight to the exit on the opposite wall. Adequin pulled the heavy steel door shut behind her, tugging until the locks thudded into place.

Turning, she swept the beam of her headlamp across a dust-coated workstation, covered with various tools, wiring, and circuitry. An empty missile cradle sat to one side.

She glanced at Cavalon.

"Is this . . ."

"Yes," he croaked, but didn't turn.

She stepped to the workbench. A row of hand-drawn schematics lined the far wall, the edges of the thin paper worn and curled up over the tacks holding them in place. Alongside were printed diagrams of missile components, covered with scrawled annotations. Pages and pages of scribbled notes littered the worktop, written in a style of shorthand Adequin had learned years ago, but forgotten.

Her eyes drifted down. A concerning number of empty biotool cartridges littered the dusty floor around a circular waste bin. She didn't need to see the labels to know what they'd contained.

She'd known this had been a dark time in his life, but seeing tangible evidence of it was more disheartening than she'd expected.

"Cav?"

He didn't turn around.

She approached, gripping his elbow to turn him to face her. His eyes didn't meet hers, blinking rapidly as he licked his lips, jaw skimming.

"You okay?" she asked.

"No." His voice wavered.

She gave his arm a reassuring squeeze.

"This place is just . . ." He let out a long sigh. "Full of bad memories."

"I know."

"I wasn't in a very good place when . . ." He gestured vaguely behind her. "All that happened."

"But it brought you to us," she said. To her, is what she meant. But she didn't say that, and she didn't know why. Maybe it felt too selfish. He'd done far too much for too many people for his worth to be distilled down to one individual's needs.

Cavalon's gaze settled on her, blue eyes glassy.

"And we'd all be dead, many times over, without you," she added.

He shook his head. "The path you take isn't justified by the end result."

"Maybe not always," she assented. "But if we can't count on redemption . . . the Sentinels don't stand a chance."

He gave an ambling nod, brows knit.

"You don't have to be proud of your past, Cav," she said. "But you *should* be proud of your present."

He scrubbed a hand over his beard a few times, letting out a long, crackling breath. Then he stepped forward, wrapped his arms around her, pulled her close. The abrupt warmth of his proximity felt stark in the damp cold of the bunker. With her cheek against the side of his neck, she could feel his pulse hammering, the quiver of his breath as he tried to force calm.

She tightened her arms around him. Despite the stale, musty haze lingering on the air, she drew in a long, invigorating breath, exhaling as evenly as she could manage. He would stay strong if she did.

After a few moments, he let out a sharp sigh, then took a step back, pushing his hair off his forehead. "Sorry, sir. I know I'm not supposed to . . . hug my superior officers."

"I think we're past that."

He offered a weak, stilted smile. "Let's get this over with."

She tapped her nexus open and brought up the overhead Cavalon had sketched out. "Where will we be coming out?" she asked.

"Here," he said. "There're two coded passages between here and his residence, then the entry to the residence itself will be locked as well." He indicated three highlighted thresholds along the path. "We'll need the codebreaker for each. Once we're in his residence, we should be in the clear. He doesn't even let his personal guard in there."

"Okay," she said, reorienting their position in her mind's eye. "I'll follow your lead. You ready for this?"

"No."

"I'd be worried if you were."

Blowing out a sigh, Cavalon spun toward the door. He punched in one more thousand-digit code. The door opened, and he swept a hand forward, inviting her into Mercer Manor.

CHAPTER TWENTY-THREE

Cavalon peered through the carved ornamental screens as he lingered in the shadows of the long gallery. Beyond, the colors of his childhood assaulted his eyes. Everywhere he looked: maroon and gold. Over the polished, bone-white marble floor lay an impressive stretch of maroon carpeting, embroidered with intricate patterns of gold. Above the gilded throne hung a tapestry of maroon emblazoned with the Mercer seal: a stylized tree of life, flourishing roots forming the base, with a thin trunk elevating branches that curved upward, each capped with a flowering bloom.

Heart thrumming relentlessly, Cavalon suddenly wished for a dose of the composure that kept Rake so unnaturally calm under pressure. Three steps into the manor, and he already regretted ever opening his stupid mouth. This had been a fucking *terrible* idea.

"We'll just pop on over to Elyseia," he'd said. *"Drop by the house and grab a thing real quick. No big deal."*

Bloody void. Someone should have stopped him.

Rake edged a shoulder into him.

Right. No need to loiter. The sooner they started this, the sooner it'd be over.

He crept down the dim gallery toward the pair of ornately engraved, six-meter-tall doors at the far end. As he moved, his eyes scanned the room as it flickered by through the grated openings. As with most of the eastern wing, the throne room was a primarily ornamental leftover from the days before the System Collective formed, when there'd been no communal seat of power like the modern-day Meridian at which to congregate. Now, at least in the case of the Mercers, the decadent room served as a site for only the most stuffy of formal affairs.

Which meant no one should be hanging around in the eastern wing, and they should be able to move somewhat freely, since paranoid Augustus didn't believe in interior security cameras—a prudent choice for the morally bankrupt.

That meant all he and Rake needed to worry about was tripping a door alarm or physically stumbling into the manor staff or the Mercer Guard. Thanks to Owen's preloaded security measures, they wouldn't show on proximity scanners either. Their nexuses had been set to create a signal barrier, which not only blocked them on scanners, but grabbed an aggregate of the surrounding background noise and created a patch in its place. A complete absence of signal would look just as suspicious as an anomaly.

So they only needed to keep their own scanner active, and their eyes and ears open. *"Easy,"* Rake had claimed. Cavalon's unbridled defeatism didn't agree that was exactly the right word.

He reached the gallery's egress and stepped out, making a point of keeping his back to the throne. He didn't need a fresh mental image to replace the barely faded one that already tormented him: his grandfather on that throne, his father on that throne, him on that throne. He didn't give a shit about any "two-thousand-year-old familial legacy." He'd rather see it all burn.

They approached the exit, and Cavalon's Imprints buzzed onto the backs of his arms. He pressed open one of the heavy doors just far enough for them to slip into the hall, then shouldered it closed behind them.

In the entry hall, a surprise: more maroon.

The wide hallway stretched out, the design motif of opulent and stuffy persisting with plush carpets over needlessly expensive imported stone.

Cavalon forced one foot in front of the other.

Rake followed off his right shoulder, her eyes scanning the coffered ceilings and gold-framed artwork lining the walls, the shittiest of which could have fed an Outer Core planet for a year.

Cavalon's heart rate plagued him as he led Rake into the receiving hall where he'd started the first of many fistfights with Shithead Second Cousin, only a few days after Cavalon's father died. Shithead had the balls to demand Cavalon abdicate. Birthright or no, Shithead had proclaimed, a lazy, selfish, disgraced addict was unfit to take the mantle. Cavalon had already done enough to besmirch the majestic legacy of the Mercer name. He'd tank two thousand years of tradition and honor and dignity and prestige, etcetera, etcetera. He couldn't even be bothered to clean up his act in time to speak at his own father's funeral, so how could he possibly be expected to helm the Mercer Legacy?

Shithead had deserved worse than the broken nose Cavalon had given him.

A minute later, they arrived at the egress from the eastern wing—their first sealed passage.

"This's it," Cavalon whispered.

Rake opened the security interface on her nexus. "Watch our six," she instructed, and stepped to the control panel.

Cavalon complied, staring back down the hall. A moment later, a click sent panic-spiked relief through him. The door slid open, the soft whoosh deadened by all the plush maroon.

Rake had drawn her gun at some point, and now held it at the ready while she cleared their entry into the next hall. She signaled him to follow, and he let the door lock behind them. One down, two to go.

Though devoid of real humans, the reception gallery was full of artistic depictions of them. A transition between the throne hall and the manor proper, the gallery was meant to intimidate visitors with expensive artistic proof of the Mercer legacy. Including centuries-old depictions of armor-clad ancestors during the Viator War, all the way up to present day, with a half dozen of himself at various stages of development. It truly surprised him Augustus hadn't pulled them all down and burned them in some kind of ritual disowning ceremony.

Cavalon led the way again, gaze low as every one of his ancestors seemed to give him disapproving side-eye. Farther down, Rake hesitated, pausing at the foot of a three-meter-tall painting. She stared up at the larger-than-life-size depiction of a woman in a fitted suit, narrow shoulders draped in a silken mantle, lips pressed into a thin, imperious line. A soft aura of golden light haloed the Mercer nuptial crown nestled in her dark blond hair. The day the most promising geneticist since the Viator War became a queen.

"Corinne?" Rake asked.

Cavalon blinked, surprised at first that she knew her name. Then he remembered—six months ago, Rake had mentioned they'd met once at Legion HQ, sometime during her first posting. That'd been the first time he'd spoken about his grandmother in years.

His eyes drifted across the overly extravagant depiction. If the artist had known his grandmother at all, they would have never painted her that way. Despite her unnervingly high IQ and everything her marriage had afforded her, she'd remained one of the most down-to-earth people Cavalon had ever known.

He cleared his throat. "Yeah. A much younger Corinne than you met."

Rake nodded, still staring up at the image, her expression unreadable.

Personally, Cavalon had always wondered what the hell that younger Corinne had been thinking. From Augustus's angle, it made sense, as far as strategic marriages went. Find the most talented prodigy in genetics, coerce them into marrying into the Mercer legacy, proceed to mine their extensive intellect for your maniacal needs.

Though Cavalon supposed that worked both ways. No matter how many grants or fellowships or corporate sponsorships Corinne might have procured, no one could have offered more resources for genetic research than the Mercer family.

"Sorry," Rake mumbled. "Let's keep going."

Cavalon led her onward, down the hallway where he'd thrown up in at least seven of the twelve ornamental vases, a left past the room where his father's wake had taken place, then a right into the narrow attendant's passage where the Guard had caught up with him the day Augustus arrested him.

At the end of the passage they paused to check Rake's scanner, then snuck across a corridor toward a wide door framed by massive gilded columns.

Rake gripped his arm to tug him to a stop beside the doorway. She held up her nexus screen. It showed a single contact in the room beyond.

After waiting for the lone attendant to depart, they cut through what was surely the new first most-expensive room Rake had ever been in: the grand ballroom. Sweat beaded on the back of Cavalon's neck as they crossed the vast expanse of Viridian hardwood, inlaid with Cautian metal designs and accented with Artoran gemstones, a glittering display of extravagant chandeliers overhead.

On the opposite side, they waited inside the door while two Mercer Guards passed. The two men chortled under their breaths with aimless, nonsensical mirth. Cavalon exchanged a nervously amused look with Rake. She'd been right about the guards taking a break when the boss was away. Evidently, that extended to getting high while on patrol. He couldn't blame them. He'd gone to far worse lengths in an attempt to drown out his affiliation with this family.

When the guards had disappeared around the far corner, Cavalon led Rake out of the ballroom and up a long flight of bifurcated marble stairs to the second floor. At the landing, he took a right down a long, curving corridor, doorless other than their destination—the second locked threshold. He kept an eye both ways down the arcing hall as Rake opened her codebreaker menu and got to work.

After a very long few minutes, she let out a soft hiss. "Shit," she whispered. "The primary encryption keys didn't work. It's running new sets. Gonna take a minute."

He nodded, waiting, still scanning the hallway. Staying static for so long grated on his nerves. It gave him too much time to conjure up more worst-case scenarios.

He wrung his hands to stop his foot from tapping out his nerves. "How's it—"

But the words dropped from his throat as Rake pressed fingers to his lips and her gaze shot up.

Then he heard it—voices, down the hall. Too low to make out words, but too close to retreat down the opposite length of doorless corridor.

He shot her a panicked look.

She glanced at her nexus, the numbers oscillating as the codebreaker worked through encryption sets. She flicked open a second screen. The scanner showed the two contacts on a steadfast intercept to their location.

Rake's jaw firmed. She met his eye as she softly drew her pistol from its holster.

Cavalon felt the blood drain from his face. "No . . ."

"Yes. Gun out."

He shook his head. He was not ready for this to go lateral—not yet, at least. "Wait, let me try—"

A quiet peal of laughter rang out. Rake took aim down the hall while Cavalon faced the control panel. Hand shaking, he pressed his palm to the screen.

The control panel flashed green. The door slid open.

Cavalon blinked, stunned.

Rake slipped inside before it'd even finished opening. She reached back and yanked him through by his hooded jacket. The door hissed shut right as the conversation rounded the corner.

Cavalon pressed his back to the cool metal door, panting out sharp exhales between barely controlled inhales.

Pistol raised, Rake paced the area, sweeping her aim as she checked a few long angles before returning to him. "How the hell did you get it open?" she whispered.

He tried to lick his cracked lips, but his mouth had gone completely dry. "I can't believe he never had me removed from the system."

Rake holstered her pistol. "He probably thinks you're dead."

"Still. Ultra paranoid, remember?"

"Maybe the guards were hoping you'd come home someday."

He chuckled.

She stared at him.

He wiped the mirth from his face. "Oh, you were serious?"

"You said you were amicable with some—like the one that taught you how to cook poorly? It's possible, right?"

He sighed. "I think the time for them to care about me ever coming home again would have been when they were dragging me off to certain death in the first place. But sure, maybe."

Rake gave a relenting tilt of her head, then checked the scanner again. "Looks like we're clear for now." Her gaze slid across the overlarge room, to a seating area on the left. Staged in front of a large marble fireplace sat a plush rug surrounded by white leather sofas and armchairs. More concerned with function and comfort, and somewhat less opulent. Somewhat.

"What is this place?" Rake asked.

"The residence hub."

She quirked a brow.

He cleared his throat. "A family that actually liked—or at least could tolerate—one another would use it. Sort of a central meeting place." Unsurprisingly, the modern-day Mercer family didn't spend a whole lot of time hanging out together and bonding. Presently, the area served merely as access for the individual residences, most of which had sat unoccupied for decades as the ruling Mercer family's numbers dwindled. Maybe if Augustus hadn't been such an invariable dickhead, Cavalon's father might have considered having more children.

Unsurprisingly, with the only two occupants off-world, the hub was empty as Cavalon led Rake to the entrance to Augustus's residence. The codebreaker ran through eleven sets of keys over ten minutes. Though the air control was temperate as always, sweat ran down Cavalon's spine, sticking his shirt to his back as he waited.

"We're in," Rake said finally. Her nexus beeped, and the door clicked, then slid open. Cavalon gulped.

They stepped inside, then let the door seal behind them.

Cavalon's stomach turned.

Tobacco, vanilla, citrus, sage. The sickly sweet scents burned his nostrils, bringing heat to his cheeks and water to his eyes.

It smelled like his grandfather. And it took every shred of will he had not to turn and run.

Dim wall sconces lined the entry corridor, the undecorated walls covered in navy wallpaper. A muted blue-gray carpet ran the length of the hall over thick boards of sable hardwood. After staring at so much warm maroon and gold tones, the new color scheme felt bleak.

"Where to?" Rake whispered.

"I don't know," he croaked out. "I've never been in here."

"Ever?"

He wet his lips. "Ever. If the layout is the same as mine and my father's, then the bedroom will be the farthest room on the left."

"Okay," she said. "Keep on my six."

She watched him steadily for a few seconds, and he found the will to nod mutely, though he knew the nod to be a lie. A huge, fucking lie.

He wasn't sure why he found this part in particular so massively intimidating. They'd just snuck through half the length of his childhood home. Inside this residence was the safest they'd been since they arrived.

His pulse should have slowed, not sped. The sweat slicking his back should have dried, not spread to his palms and armpits and knees and elbows and every other part of him.

"You okay?" Rake whispered. She stood a few paces ahead, staring back at him, the dim sconces casting a glint in her amber eyes. Ready to plow brazenly into the unknown.

This was just another infiltration to her. One of dozens, maybe hundreds. This likely didn't even make it onto the top ten list of most intimidating things she'd ever had to pull off.

He had to focus. Think like Rake. This was simply a part of the job, the first of many objectively hard steps. Get the failsafe device, sneak back out the way they came, then to the *Wakeless*, steal the ceronite from the factory, return to the *Corinthian*, pickup Jackin and Ford, take a quick Arcullian Gate shortcut to Poine Gate, then back out to the Divide, install the ceronite, quadruple-check everything was in working order, jump the *Typhos*—*Lodestar*—to Poine, jump away into the Drift, then to whatever lush, food-and-water-filled planet Ford had picked out for them while they were gone. No big deal.

He sucked in a breath and nodded at Rake. "Sorry. I'm ready."

Rake gave a firm nod, then started down the hall, pistol raised. Cavalon followed.

Ten meters down, the corridor expanded into a circular antechamber, and Cavalon could tell the layout wasn't going to be the same as his own residence had been. Augustus's was far, far larger, for one, with a half-dozen doorways lining the curved outer wall. At the center was a small sitting area arranged around a smooth, puck-shaped platform that would project a holographic fire pit.

Rake moved to the first door on the left. She activated the controls and it slid open—no codebreaker required. She cleared the small guest lavatory with a quick sweep of her pistol, then moved on to the next door.

She tapped the controls and her codebreaker activated. Twenty seconds later, the door slid open.

A yawning expanse of navy carpet stretched out over more dark wood flooring. On the far wall hung three sets of long, thick drapes, drawn closed over the windows, not a shred of daylight visible around the edges. Along the side wall, a large mattress sat before a headboard of inlaid wood. Augustus's bedroom.

Cavalon rubbed at his nostrils with his knuckles. The scent of him was even stronger in here.

Rake moved inside, sweeping her aim to each corner, behind a thick armoire, then a set of tall bookshelves. She disappeared into the ensuite, then reappeared moments later. "Clear."

She holstered her pistol and stepped toward one of the nightstands. Cavalon headed for the other. He slid open the drawer, pushing aside a small book and a remote intercom. He knelt to shine his headlamp into it, reached in and felt around the edges, checking for hidden compartments or trap doors. Nothing.

"Not here," Rake said.

Cavalon's stomach twisted. "Not here either." He met Rake's furrowed brow over the mound of decorative pillows. "You check the desk."

She nodded, and he moved to the armoire, tugging open the heavy, carved doors. Inside hung a dozen suits, pressed and smelling of a clean ocean breeze. He pushed past them to the back, then checked around the bottom and both sides. Though it wasn't likely—Augustus wouldn't keep it on him, since that would defeat the purpose—Cavalon dug through the pockets of each garment. Again, nothing.

He crossed the room to where Rake was picking through the cabinets beside the desk. He knelt at the drawers on the opposite side. "Have you checked—"

The words dropped from his throat as Rake's nexus vibrated, the sound like a drill in the deadened silence of the fabric-filled room.

Rake froze as she tapped open a screen on her nexus. "Shit," she hissed, "we've got contacts in the entry."

Cavalon spun to the door, and sure enough—shuffling footfalls and muffled voices. Growing steadily louder.

He started to choke out a response, but his breath caught as Rake began to move. She threw up an arm and caught him across the chest, driving him backward. He stumbled along with her as she retreated behind one of the sets of drawn window curtains.

Darkness shrouded them, and Cavalon's pulse thundered in his ears. Rake's arm remained steady across his chest, and he clung to it like a lifeline.

Muffled voices, soft laughter. Between the familiar chortling and lighthearted tone of the conversation, he got the feeling it was the two drugged-up guards. From their complete lack of subtlety, he didn't think they'd come looking for intruders, at least. They'd simply decided to give themselves a self-guided tour of the off-limits areas of the manor.

His fingers shook, adrenaline pumping through his trembling limbs. His eyes darted, and he identified the source of his confusion. The alcove was not home to a window as the curtains had suggested, only a dark niche barely large enough to conceal both of them.

All thoughts of questionable architectural design vanished as a muffled hiss sounded through the over-thick drapes. Rake's arm tensed, pressing against his chest, edging him farther back into the windowless alcove and up against the wall.

Cavalon swallowed down a gasp of shock as his head spun in the dark. His stomach turned, and it took him a long moment to realize why.

They were moving. Revolving.

A soft whirr sounded, a quiet thunk, then nothing. Darkness still shrouded them, and they'd stopped moving. But they were no longer in the alcove.

The cool, crisp air now smelled of disinfectant and cleaning solution—a familiar, sterile odor that sent an icy chill down his spine. He blinked into the darkness.

One by one, narrow banks of lights switched on, each sharp click causing a nervous spike in his heartrate.

The lights revealed a square, windowless room of white walls and gleaming white tile floors. Against the left wall sat metal supply shelves, a steel fridge, and a cabinet full of small tanks of murky liquid and tubes of fluid. A square of recessed glass dominated the wall to the right. It almost looked like a viewscreen, though it was covered with a frosted, white film.

At the center of the room sat a long, narrow workstation, the polished black countertop neatly lined with scopes, diagnostic machines, flasks, beakers, test tubes.

Rake's lips parted. She lowered her arm from his chest as her gaze drifted over the room. Over the *laboratory*.

A sudden puff of smoke engulfed them. Cavalon hunched on instinct, arms crossing tight over his face as the smoke hissed out around them. He waited for his eyes to burn, his breath to constrict, his skin to boil. But nothing happened.

Rake hacked out a few dry breaths and Cavalon coughed, more from the surprise than the smoke itself, which was odorless and seemingly harmless.

Finally, the smoke dissipated.

"Decontamination complete," a computerized voice intoned, sending Cavalon's pulse thundering into his throat.

Rake grabbed the front of Cavalon's jacket and dragged him forward a few steps. She glared back at the revolving hatch they'd come through and the decontamination system that'd just assaulted them. "Where are we?" she asked, tone clipped.

Cavalon wiped his hair from his forehead as he shook his head, staring out across the clean room.

"Cavalon," Rake said, tone firm, "are we safe here?"

"I have no idea," he breathed. "I don't know what this is."

This facility hadn't been on any schematic he'd ever seen of the manor.

Rake let out a soft growl, closing her nexus screens with a flick of her wrist. "We'll have to wait out that patrol," she said, voice low. "But my scanners aren't working in this room. We won't know with any certainty whether they've left."

Cavalon nodded mutely, taking a few cautious steps toward the central workstation. Beside an inlaid terminal rested a matte-black cytoscope headset and gold-laced interface gloves—a model that'd still been a prototype, last he knew. A leaden weight grew in his chest as he took in the rest of the diagnostic machines and instruments around the room. He didn't like what his subconcious was trying to tell him.

"What is all this?" Rake asked.

He took a dry gulp. "Well. These are tools used for genetic engineering." He focused on a small, square device beside the cytoscope.

Rake looked between him and the device a few times, then said, "What's that?"

"A thermal cycler," he said, voice frayed. "Used for sequencing . . . genotyping." And cloning. For some reason he didn't understand, his mouth chose not to say that part.

Rake stared at him for what seemed like a long time before she said, "An at-home lab's not that out of the ordinary, right? Convenience?"

"Maybe . . ." He cleared his throat. "But there are things here you wouldn't need if you were only doing research." They were the kinds of things Cavalon had only seen one place before: inside the Guardian cloning facility, just before he'd destroyed it.

Rake, never a step behind, gave a slow nod. "You think he's cloning Guardians at home."

Cavalon tilted his head, stretching out his neck. "It's pretty small, but maybe he's only doing one at a time."

"Why would he bother, when he has whole facilities dedicated to it?"

He shook his head. "Other than being a workaholic, I don't know. I guess it'd be a good way to keep some clones off the SC's radar. A few for his own private army, maybe."

Which he shouldn't need, so long as his Guardian military and law-enforcement takeover plan came to fruition. But this was Augustus Mercer. His contingencies had contingencies.

Cavalon rubbed his fingers over his lips. What this lab more than likely meant was that his grandfather was attempting newer, even more prodigious levels of illegality. Augustus had been able to find a work-around for cloning sentients by spending decades pumping out propaganda, framing the Drudgers as mindless heathens, as Viator-adjacent plagues to mankind. But there were still System Collective laws restricting what horrors could be wrought on a genome, flora or fauna, sentient or otherwise.

Rake looked to the right side of the room, where a second terminal was affixed to the wall beside the frosted glass pane. "There could be valuable intel here," she said. "Do you think it's safe to access these terminals? Extract the data?"

"I can check," he said, nodding his agreement. "Owen gave me a probe for that exact purpose. Even at our Mercer Biotech facilities, the research labs are air-gapped. It's a fair bet this one is too. That should make it simpler."

It was at least worth a few minutes to check, because she was right—there could be a trove of tide-turning data on these terminals. Even if relegated to the Guardian project, having any data on how they were engineered could allow Cavalon to find a weakness they could exploit in the future.

He expanded his nexus, accessed the program Owen installed, then tapped to run it. His screen flashed green as it forced a remote connection with the computer, then the probe gave him the go-ahead. He initiated a data clone—no pun intended—and the transfer began.

A minute later, his nexus beeped its completion. Owen's probe cleaned up its tracks, then severed the connection. Cavalon stepped toward the wall terminal next, drifting to a stop as the holographic displays sprung to life on his approach. It flashed a "sign-in complete" notification, then a welcome screen appeared, fanning out a collection of frequently accessed menus.

His eyes narrowed. "Rake," he said, voice thin, "why's the computer acting like . . ."

The remainder of his sentence drifted from his mind as the fog covering the square of glass cleared. He looked through the window. Blinked. Wiped his eyes, then blinked again.

Beyond the glass, a small room—a short bed, narrow desk, sky-blue walls, well-stocked bookshelves. Clean, sparse, and well-kept, like a life-size dollhouse room on display.

Then his mind faltered, stuttering out for a few long moments. He scrubbed a hand over his eyes and willed his thoughts to reset.

Because on the bed sat . . . a child. A boy. Reading a book.

He was no older than six or seven, with the bright, clean blond hair of only the very young. He wore a hooded sweatshirt and brown khakis, his legs tucked underneath him. He leaned to one side, slouched into an oversized pillow as he read.

It had to be a viewscreen.

But as Cavalon walked closer, the perspective of the room shifted. It was truly a window. Or more likely, a one-way mirror. Because as he stepped face-to-face with the glass, mere meters away, the boy didn't look up, didn't stir in the slightest. He merely bounced his head softly as he flipped to the next page of his book.

Rake stepped up beside Cavalon, the olive skin of her cheeks gone pale. "What the hell is this?"

Cavalon tried to open his mouth to respond but didn't know what to say. He needed more data.

He stepped to the unlocked wall terminal. Panic swelled in his chest and he had to force his eyes and mind to focus on the displays.

He accessed a recent files list, then opened the first item. Some kind of log. Each entry was timestamped, one every few days. He scrolled through, eyes steady on the dates, stretching back decades. He stopped scrolling and started tapping open entry after entry.

"Attempted new calibration method using a sampling of 01's nucleotide arrays; results proved untenable. Additional genotyping required. Develop subsequent bioassays based on chart 32–11b."

"Experienced a third failure when attempting to alter 02's post-translation modifications. C's methylation theory may prove correct after all. Reversal to transcription stage may be required."

"The subsumption of additional protein-coding genes into the sequence has proven more challenging than expected. With C's recent . . . departure, the plan to develop both aims concurrently is no longer viable. A target reassessment may be required in order to ensure proper allocation of resources, as this project must remain the priority."

Cavalon flipped through a dozen more, unconsciously hunting for keywords he didn't want to see.

He looked at the boy. This wasn't a Guardian cloning facility. This was a *person* cloning facility.

And this poor kid was one of them . . . But there'd been at least two subjects mentioned in the reports—01 and 02.

Oh, holy shit.

A dense heat pressed against his eardrums, and Cavalon grew vaguely aware of Rake speaking to him, tugging at his sleeve, gripping his arm. He ignored her. He had to.

He still needed more data. He had to be sure.

Fingers trembling, he tapped open a starred log from years ago:

"Therapeutic and transgenic treatments have not had the desired effect. A blunter approach may be required, however trials based on former standard operating procedures may prove too time intensive for current constraints.

"Additionally, environmental factors seem to have played a much larger role than originally expected, with algorithm adjustments producing diminishing returns. Where 01 has fallen well within acceptable parameters, 02 regresses with every day. A ground-up redesign of outset parameters may be in order, and devising a proper containment method will be critical.

"It appears in vivo testing will be the only sufficient method moving forward. Thusly, development of project track 03 will commence immediately following—"

Fuck.

Heart racing, Cavalon backed out of the logs, opened another menu, hunted down another file. With both hands, he expanded the digitized genetic code across the entire width of the screen. His eyes scanned the lines of sequencing.

"No . . ." The feeble attempt at speech cracked from the back of his throat. "No, no."

"Cav, please talk to me," Rake said, and the pleading edge to her tone yanked him from his fixation.

He met her eyes.

"What's going on?" she demanded.

"This sequencing . . ."

"That kid's? What about it?"

"I recognize it."

"What? Why?"

"Because it's mine."

The muscles in Rake's face twitched almost imperceptibly.

But before she could generate any true reaction, a few things happened at once: the terminal screen closed in favor of a yellow "access revoked" warning; Rake's nexus buzzed out a signal burst alert that came far, far too late; and the ulcer plaguing Cavalon's ulcer considered if maybe it too deserved an ulcer of its very own, as a chalky voice came through the speakers of the terminal and spoke a single word, "Grandson."

CHAPTER TWENTY-FOUR

Cavalon took an instinctive step back. His vision tunneled as he stared at the terminal, at the source of the voice.

Rake had pivoted away and drawn up against the wall beside the the window, hiding from sight of the terminal screen. She drew her pistol, sharp gaze surveying the room behind him.

"Cavalon." The chalky voice spoke again. Augustus's voice. His tone came flat, if not a bit weary around the edges. "Do you care to explain what you are doing in my home?"

A sudden rash of heat flared in Cavalon's chest. "Do *you* care to explain who the fuck that child is?"

"I know you viewed the genome," Augustus said, his tone infuriatingly patient. "That's what triggered the silent alarm. You already know what he is."

"So, what?" Cavalon snarled, cheeks burning. "You don't like how I turn out, so you clone me? Try again? That's some shitty planning. I loathe you, remember? I thought I made that pretty damn clear with all the screaming matches and hydrogen bombs. If he's me, he'll hate you just as much."

Augustus let out a stilted scoff, part laugh, part genuine pity. "Dear boy," he breathed. "Clone *you*? Don't be so naive."

Cavalon glared at the screen, mind spinning.

What was he talking about? The code on file for the boy matched his own—he knew it, had no question about it.

Then a realization bubbled to the surface, and his menagerie of ulcers burned. He swallowed back a swell of vomit.

No. Just. No.

"I reviewed the security logs," Augustus said. "Why do you think you were able to gain access to the hub with your own clearance?"

Cavalon looked down at the backs of his hands. Turned them over, stared at the lines creasing his palms.

"Or why the lab granted you access?" Augustus went on. "Or why this terminal automatically logged you in? And surely you must be seeing it by now. Have you not looked in the mirror lately?"

Cavalon pressed the heels of his palms deep into his eyes. He looked like his father. Yes. And his father looked like Augustus. But everyone looked like their parents. That was how it worked.

And his . . . mother. Cavalon had known her, she'd been real. He'd been young, when she died, very young, almost too young to remember things. But even now, almost thirty years later, she was still burned into his memories, clear as day. Holding him, playing with him, loving him. That had been real, he knew it.

His lips parted with a few false starts. He grounded his thoughts long enough to croak out, "I had a mother."

"No. You had a womb who knew too much."

Cavalon's pulse thundered in his ears, breath stifled in his throat. In his periphery, Rake shifted, but he couldn't bring himself to look at her.

"With my third attempt," Augustus went on, disregarding the magnitude of what he'd just unearthed, "I took a more mechanical approach than I had with you and your 'father.' One mired by fewer . . . loose ends. As for the current state of the child, well, I do apologize if it offends your sensibilities. However the seclusion is necessary. I allowed you too much freedom. It was shortsighted of me, in retrospect. A controlled environment was clearly the only way to get the desired results."

Cavalon's fists tightened. "Void, he's not a fucking experiment—he's a human being!"

"Is he?" Augustus asked, tone infuriatingly calm. "According to SC law, he's not."

Cavalon stared, sweat dripping from his temples. The lingering implication went unsaid, but hung heavily in the resulting silence: "And neither are you."

A high-pitched tone rang in his ears. His voice and mouth and lips conspired against him, working without his consent. "So what's the plan?" he croaked out. "Just keep cloning yourself until one doesn't hate you? Third time's a charm?"

"As much as you would like to deny it, your father did not hate me. He may not have agreed with all of my policies, but he at least respected me—something you have never deigned to attempt."

"Give me a fucking reason to!"

"Think of it this way—it's your own fault this one exists. If you'd cooperated, I would have never needed to try again. But you were faulty, just like the last one."

"By faulty you mean we had *free will*?" he snapped.

"No," Augustus scoffed. "Will is permissible. Will can be broken, redirected, reconditioned. You had stubborn qualities that made doing so a difficult task. Defensiveness, capriciousness, apathy, dishonesty, disloyalty. And such wanton selfishness. Not to mention a complete inability to function under pressure. All surmountable, or at least they should have been. But what I engineered for you in resilience, ingenuity, and intelligence, you negated with your brazen indolence."

Cavalon let out a low growl. "You have no idea what I'm capable of."

"What you're *capable* of," Augustus snarled, any lingering patience in his tone vanished, "was irrevocably squandered long ago."

Cavalon flinched at the familiar chastising tone, dread seeping into every bone in his body. Teeth clenched, he managed to mutter out, "You've always underestimated me—"

"You *are* me," Augustus said, "so I know exactly what you *should* be capable of. When I was your age, I had already been king for over ten years. I ascended alone, without my father, without my mother, without guidance, and single-handedly rebuilt the Mercer legacy from the worn, effete ashes it'd become after the Viator War. Before I ascended, the System Collective languished in stagnancy—mute with grief, unable to devise a future after so many centuries at war. And now every single day, my legislation works to restore humanity. So yes. By all rights, you *should* be capable of so much more. But you squandered it. Where I thrived, you floundered."

Cavalon's chest heaved. He waited for hope to rise, for a swell of fortitude to straighten his posture, for determination to harden his visage, for any sign of the fearless soldier he'd been trying to become. But as the moments dragged on, it never came . . . and he knew why.

He'd come from the very pinnacle of privilege. Been given every chance and then some to become an effective, productive, contributing member of society. Instead, he'd spent his formative years aggravating tutors, exploiting friends, and disappointing family. He'd insisted on studying astromech so he'd have an excuse to work with his hands instead of his brain, and when that didn't work, he attempted to silence his nagging, overactive mind by dousing it with illegal chemicals. And when he returned home to a dead father and decided he didn't care for the political landscape, he'd started building bombs, when he could have been using that brainpower to *help*. To negotiate, to collaborate, to invent, to build, to elevate mankind. Not to destroy.

So he couldn't muster some eloquent, emphatic rebuttal. Because Augustus was right.

"I know you think me to be cruel," Augustus said, the ire gone from his tone. "But I am a reasonable man, Cavalon. That silent alarm was exactly that—silent. You are free to leave. Right now, unharried. Leave Elyseia, and never return to the Core. We can both forget this entire incident."

Cavalon blew out a long sigh through his hands. He dropped his arms to his sides and his gaze went straight to Rake. He didn't know why. Maybe he wanted her approval to take Augustus's offer, or maybe it was just morbid curiosity, so he could see how disappointed or horrified or sickened by him she looked.

He realized his mistake far too late.

Augustus pushed a hard breath through the comms. "Void, Cavalon. What have you done?"

Cavalon tried to control his reaction, to stop his cheeks from reddening, to keep his gaze from flitting helplessly around the room, while simultaneously doing all of those things.

Of *course* the single camera Augustus would risk in the entire compound would be on the access terminal for the dungeon where he kept his illegal clone inside his shadowy villain's lair of a laboratory no one even knew existed. Contingencies within contingencies.

"What?" Cavalon grated out, pouring his effort into sounding honestly confused.

"Who is with you?"

"What? No one."

"I should have known you'd never have the spine to return on your own."

Cavalon's head spun and the room tilted, the air stifled from his lungs.

"If you tell me who it is," Augustus said, "the damage can be mitigated."

He sucked in a quick breath. "Who *who* is?" He tripped over his own words. He didn't know why he was even bothering.

"This changes things, I'm afraid." Augustus sighed. "I am sorry, dear boy, truly. You should have stayed dead."

With that, a piercing siren. The shrill noise cut through Cavalon's eardrums and the shock released the panic attack's hold on his breath, air rushing back into his lungs in a dizzying burst.

Rake lunged forward. She shoved him aside as she unclipped the rifle from her back, unfolding it in two swift motions. She fired. The terminal glass shattered, the sharp sound cutting through the relentless sirens. Exposed wires sparked and circuitry caught flame.

Rake said something his brain chose not to hear as he darted to the other terminal recessed in the counter. He tapped frantically but the screen lockdown continuously flashed: "Access denied."

"What the hell are you doing?" Rake snapped. She seized his shoulder and tried to spin him, but he held firm.

"There has to be a way to get to him," he muttered, tapping the screen in vain.

"Oh . . . shit, Cav, we can't—"

With a frustrated growl he pushed away from the counter and marched up to the square window. A dry, burnt copper taste permeated his mouth as he summoned the full strength of his Imprints to pound against the glass. It didn't even shudder a millimeter. The child didn't look up.

Boots squeaked behind him. "Cav, we have to leave. Now."

"No, Rake," he begged, fingers working the edges of the inset frame, as if he could dig through the seam somehow.

"We don't have the right tools," Rake replied, "and even if we did, we don't have enough time."

"I can't leave him," he croaked, his hands drifting to a stop on the cold glass, eyes falling on the boy's ruddy, round cheeks. Slightly disheveled blond hair. The cowlick he wouldn't grow out of until he was fourteen.

"Shit . . ." Rake breathed. She tugged on Cavalon's shoulder again, this time gentler. "Back up."

He looked at her as she unclipped something from her waist.

"Step back," she insisted, yanking the grenade fully off her belt.

"Void, Rake!" Cavalon threw out a hand to stop her. "He's way too close to the glass!"

"You want him out of there or not?" she growled. Her jaw flexed and her ire softened. "This is a directed percussive charge. It'll fracture glass, but won't breach walls. He'll be fine."

Cavalon lowered his hand, and a wash of resignation weakened his muscles. The thought of accidentally blowing the kid up almost pushed his lingering nausea into an actual fit of vomiting, but he ignored it and reminded himself how much he trusted Rake's judgment. He gave a stiff nod and backpedaled.

Rake set the charge, then jogged back, pulling him to kneel behind the counter. She covered her ears, and he covered his own just as the explosion cracked through the air. Test tubes rolled off the vibrating counter and shattered against the floor.

Cavalon rushed toward the window, but stopped short as the thin haze began to clear.

The wall remained intact, as Rake had promised. But the glass also appeared completely untouched. Within, the boy's gaze had drifted up and he stared at the ceiling. He scratched the back of his neck before returning to his book.

Cavalon stared, mouth agape.

"I'm sorry. We tried." Rake's tone rang in his ears, threaded with regret.

Cavalon ran to the window, pounding his fists against it, but nothing happened.

She seized a fistful of his jacket. "We have to go!"

"Rake!" He tried to shove her off.

She didn't let go. Roughly, she spun him to face her, gripping the side of his neck with one hand. "Listen." She locked eyes with him. "We'll come back. When the time is right, when we're ready. When we can actually help him. I promise."

He blinked, mouth gone dry.

"But right now," she continued, "we have to *leave*."

Heat rose to his face, and he shook his head. "What about the failsafe device?" he croaked out, desperation clawing at the edge of his tone. "We still need a way to get the ceronite, or this was all for nothing."

Rake's eyes glassed over and her brows knit. "We won't need the device . . ." She hesitated for a fraction of a second before her jaw firmed. "We have you."

His breath drained from his lungs and numbness spread out, limbs growing heavy, cumbersome. His vision tunneled as his mind emptied itself and walls went up.

Rake gripped him by the collar and hauled him onward.

CHAPTER TWENTY-FIVE

Cavalon's feet dragged as Rake towed him to the revolving doorway. His head churned and his sight dropped to blackness.

Curtains swayed, followed by successive, lilting pops like far-off gunfire. Rake shoved him and his knees hit carpet.

Some primal instinct brought his arms up and his head down, stowing himself low and close to the side of the bed. Pillows erupted in bursts of feathery plumes.

Silence throttled the air. A hand gripped his collar, hauled him to his feet. Rake again. She pulled him on. Past one, two, three dead guards.

No. Not guards.

Guardians.

Three dead Drudger Guardians with their chalky white carapaces, clad in molded plastech—high-grade ablative armor. The same kind he'd seen mass produced and delivered to the facility he'd destroyed with the bombs he'd built only two wings away from where Augustus kept a clone boy they'd just left behind.

A *third* attempt.

Because Cavalon's father had been the first attempt and Cavalon had been—*was*—the second attempt.

When he'd destroyed that cloning facility, he thought he'd had the upper hand for once, but he'd been so, so wrong. He couldn't win a battle against Augustus when he wasn't even fighting the same war.

His chestplate cut into his neck as Rake dragged him through a hazy sea of blue carpet. She marched in front of him, posture straight, rifle tucked into her shoulder, amber eyes focused with unrelenting mettle.

He realized then a strange oddity: The universe had not come crumbling down around her. She was not devastated beyond repair. She was capable of continuing on as if all of existence hadn't changed, irrevocably. As if she weren't hauling a carbon copy of a brutal autocrat behind her.

Cavalon trudged on, because she continued to drag him, and fighting seemed both futile and taxing. But he honestly didn't know why she bothered.

They stopped short.

"Cavalon?" A familiar voice amongst new commotion.

He focused on the tone—on the breathy, resonant quality. A strange, twisting bitterness tugged in his chest, because that voice reminded him of a younger version of himself, one who'd not been much older than the third attempt, who was still back there, trapped in Augustus's lab.

He had to go back. He turned, but a firm grip on his arm stopped him. A thin, shrill tone escalated. Rake's rifle priming.

Cavalon became vaguely aware of mounting interpersonal tension. Humans threatening humans with deadly weapons.

A bizarre instinct to mediate kicked in. With an effort, he lifted his eyes from the floor to the source of that resonant voice: a woman, mid-forties, short black hair, clad in the tailored, high-collared maroon regalia of a Mercer Guard captain. And not just any Mercer Guard.

"Deveraux?" his throat croaked out.

The ringing in his ears ebbed, and the world snapped into focus. Six Mercer Guards flanked the woman, rifles raised.

"Cursed pearl of the void . . ." Deveraux's eyes rounded. "Junior? I thought I'd seen a ghost . . ."

His ears heard the rest of her words, but his brain rejected most of them. He already knew what she was going to say, it was everyone's new favorite thing to say these days: how much he'd grown to look like the first attempt.

Rake shifted, still gripping his arm, rifle at the ready. It would look like she'd taken him hostage, except Rake had foolishly put herself between them.

Why was she protecting him? She'd been there; she knew what he was.

Rake's eyes darted between him and Deveraux, unsure, tentative. Her finger slid fractionally against the trigger guard.

"It's okay," his voice said.

Rake's grip loosened. Her rifle stayed raised.

"Void in the light," Deveraux said, staring at him past Rake. "What in the hell are you doing here? We thought you were dead."

He swallowed over many words before some fell out. "I should be."

Deveraux watched him carefully for an impossibly long moment, during which Cavalon could see the fine lines creasing her eyes and the few strands of gray hair at her brow, though he refused to meet her gaze.

She lowered her voice. "Cavalon? Are you okay?"

"He's in shock," Rake explained, then continued speaking, asking questions, fielding answers, working on their extraction like a good human who wasn't losing their grip on reality.

A question bloomed in his mind, and such a stupid one at that: Why station Guardians at the manor? Why would Augustus replace highly skilled, loyal security guards who'd served for decades—some of whose families had served for generations—with Drudgers?

The answer helpfully played itself out around him.

Because Guardians couldn't tell their people to stand down, to continue their patrol, to never tell a soul what they'd seen. Because Guardians couldn't make the decision to guide the Titan and her mute clone tagalong onward while warning them of the batteries on the roof and explaining their only chance at a safe pickup was at the northern wall beyond the gardens.

Because Guardians couldn't betray him.

"Take care of him. Good luck."

And Deveraux was gone as quickly as she'd arrived.

Something like regret soured the back of Cavalon's throat. He was starting to feel again, and he wanted nothing to do with it. He withdrew.

"Cav, please." Rake's voice, soft and encouraging, but with a dire edge. "I know it's hard, but I need you *here*. Just for a few minutes."

He blinked away the visual haze. Before him, a paned window looked out onto the lawn. Below, a terraced patio sloped away into the well-kept, lush green grass. Farther off lay a large manicured garden, walled by tall, trimmed hedges, interspersed with twisting vines and smooth, white-barked trees.

"Cav, can you hear me?"

"Yes."

"Deveraux said there're guns on the roof—anti-aircraft, so the *Wakeless* can't come in close. And turrets in the lawn. We need to get through those gardens to the north wall for extraction. She said it's a maze, but you'd know the way. Can you get us through?"

The words made sense, but something struck him as odd. "We're leaving?" he asked.

"Yes."

His throat let out a bitter chuff. "We can't run from him, Rake."

"We can. We *are*."

He could tell she'd really tried to mean it, but her voice came weak, dry, constrained with the full knowledge of what he'd really meant: They could physically run, but that would never be the same as being free of him. Now that they knew what they knew, it'd be so, so much worse than before.

"We can make it," she went on, the strength building in her tone. "Deveraux's going to misdirect them to give us a head start. But I need your help."

He wiped his sweaty palms on the front of his jacket, chin oscillating somewhere between a shake and a nod. As a kid, he'd spent countless hours in those cultivated mazes, hiding from the wrath of Augustus. It made an ironic kind of sense that all that time spent running away would help him run again now.

"Cav. Say you're with me." Her tone was both invitation and command, a mixture only Adequin Rake was capable of.

If he wanted the chance to have a full, proper existential breakdown, he would have to sideline it, separate it out.

He pushed his defeatism down and drew forward his brazen, irrational, headlong-into-the-shit optimism.

"I'm with you."

CHAPTER TWENTY-SIX

Relief coursed through Adequin as she watched Cavalon's haunted look recede, his jaw stiffen, his shoulders draw back. That was the Cavalon she'd been waiting for. The one she'd seen slip away with every insidious word Augustus had uttered. The one she needed to get them out alive.

She opened a line to the *Wakeless*. "Sigma One for Sigma Three."

"Si—r—" Emery's voice crackled, then fizzled away.

"Sorry, sir," Owen chimed in. "Trying to keep our signal scrambled. Go ahead now."

"Change of plans. New pickup is at the edge of the lawn, due north of the gardens, you'll see it on approach. Stay at the wall, don't come any closer. They've got AA batteries on the roof."

"Copy that, boss," Emery said. "On our way."

Adequin unbuttoned her jacket and dropped it to the floor. Cavalon yanked his off awkwardly over his head, further disheveling his sweat-drenched hair. She tugged him away from the window, primed her rifle, and fired.

The stock kicked hard into the Imprints coating her shoulder. The window shattered, tempered glass fracturing into granular pieces as it fell away in banded chunks. She collapsed her rifle, holstered it, grabbed Cavalon's arm, and hauled him forward.

"On my back," she instructed, and he locked his arms around her shoulders as she spiked the winch attachment from her belt onto the window-pane. Her boots crunched broken glass as she stepped onto the ledge.

Cavalon's grip tightened as she turned, bent her knees, and pushed off, rappelling two stories to the ground.

Gunfire spattered the hewn slate patio before her feet even landed. She severed the winch from her belt and grabbed Cavalon's shoulder, roughly pulling him behind the low wall rimming the patio. Shards of stone and slate rained down as more fire peppered the wall. The turret was in the lawn, maybe ten meters out.

Adequin crawled along the inside of the railing, keeping low. Cavalon followed.

At a break in the wall, she peered around the corner. A set of deep, languid stairs stretched out into the lawn. A narrow, arched entrance to the gardens lay about a hundred meters from the foot of the steps.

Even with their shield generators, considering the short cooldown cycle of that turret, they wouldn't stand a chance at making it that far.

"That archway's where we need to go?" Adequin confirmed.

"Yeah," Cavalon said. "It's the only way in on this side."

They hunched as another burst of turret fire cracked out, fracturing more shards of slate and sending small plumes of dust into the air.

"Sigma Four," Adequin said.

"Go for Four," Owen replied.

"Any chance of an assist with this turret?"

"On it, sir. Tracker variety?"

"Yeah, Mk-IV I think—heat sink cooldown has been about six seconds between triple bursts."

"Understood. I'll send out a signal burst to interrupt its power cycle. It should disorient its targeting for five, maybe ten seconds."

Adequin bared her teeth. "Five or ten?"

Owen hesitated. "Hard to say, sir—if it's a newer model, and they've kept the firmware up to date, probably only five."

Adequin blew out a sigh, edging a look back to the shattered window they'd come through. They were too short on time to keep talking about it. The Guardians would find them sooner than later. Whether it was five or ten, they'd have to make it work.

"Okay," she said. "Give us a two-second lead on that burst, and we'll make a run for it."

"Understood, sir."

"Cav, we're going to sprint, as hard as you can."

He wiped sweat from his forehead. "Yeah. Okay."

"You'll take point. Move your Imprints to your left side, mostly your flank—concentrate them heaviest where your armor doesn't cover."

He nodded his agreement while she followed her own advice, copper tinging her saliva as she rearranged her Imprints to her left side.

She pulled Cavalon's shield generator off his belt and tapped a few settings to activate it. It gave off a short, high-pitched squeal as it primed. She adhered it to the back of his belt then activated her own.

Staying low, they carefully swapped spots, and Cavalon crawled to the corner of the stairs. Adequin rested her hands on his back, ready to follow off his flank. Hopefully she could gauge the correct angle to stay between him and the turret, and soak up any shots once their shields dispersed. She had more Imprints than he did, and hers had far more experience deflecting and absorbing gunfire. Even if it'd been almost six years.

"If the turret resumes before we've made it halfway," she said, "we'll need to strafe. Veer right first, and I'll guide you verbally after that. If we're over halfway, though, just go for it. Speed is crucial here. Put everything you've got into it, okay?"

His head bobbed in an ongoing nod. "Yeah. Okay."

"Sigma One and Two are ready when you are, Four."

"Understood," Owen said. "Here we go. Five, four, three, mark."

Cavalon took off down the steps. Adequin rushed after him, briefly stunned at how fast he moved until a spike of adrenaline honed her focus.

The turret reared, then coughed out a few dry fires. It buzzed with a string of warning tones as its barrels reset.

Adequin's legs burned, footfalls hitting hard in the lush grass. She kept the jammed turret in her periphery as they sped past it.

Around the halfway mark, Cavalon stumbled over a low point in the lawn, and Adequin almost ran into his back. She caught his shoulders and kept going, spurring him onward. Regained his footing, his legs pumped hard until he was a few steps ahead of her again.

With a dread-inducing whirr of reanimated hydraulics, the turret took aim. Their five-to-ten seconds were up.

Still close on Cavalon's heels, Adequin shifted left. The first spray pelted her upper back, sending feedback from her shield sparking out in white waves of static. Another round peppered the ground to their left, throwing bursts of grass and dirt into the air. The third round hit her back again. The force sent her stumbling, but she kept her footing.

"Rake!" Cavalon shouted, throwing a frantic look over his shoulder.

"I'm fine! Keep going!"

They were only ten meters away.

The cooldown was up and the turret fired again, this time catching the back of her leg. Her shield choked and fizzled out, and the final bullet tore through her armor, grazing the outside of her calf. Her left leg gave out, knees hitting hard against an inlaid stone path that led to the garden's entrance.

Cavalon skidded to a stop.

"Don't—!" She wanted to tell him not to stop, not to be an idiot, to keep going, but he'd already started back toward her. His shield sparked around him as it soaked up a full round of turret fire. He gripped her arm and pulled her to her feet. They kept running.

Her injured leg throbbed and she limped, but kept pace, iron flooding her saliva as she forced herself to continue. She angled to his left again, anticipating another round of turret fire within seconds. But it never came.

There was only one reason the turret would cease fire. She didn't even have to look back to know what was coming, but she did anyway.

Ten armed and armored Guardians ran across the lawn toward them.

Faster than she'd ever seen Drudgers move. Their rifles raised to aim at them in unnerving unison.

A spray of gunfire scorched the gnarled hedges to their left as they sprinted under the arch and inside.

Within the concealed gardens, massive, ancient tree boughs formed a thick canopy overhead. Hazy shafts of light trickled between the leaves. Adequin darted after Cavalon as they cut through a small paved entrance, then into a maze of hedgerows of varying heights, dotted with flowering fruit trees and multicolored shrubs. An invigorating blend of sweet and earthy scents filled the air, each lungful powering her aching muscles. Her wounded leg burned, and she keenly felt the existence of every remaining bruise on her arms.

Cavalon's pace slowed fractionally as he wove between the flora, ducking under thick branches and into narrow, hidden openings between groomed rows. Hot electric needles stung her left calf with each stride. Blood soaked her pant leg, chafing and itching as it collected under the cracked armor.

With the turret out of the picture, she re-tasked a few of her Imprints to staunch the worst of the bleeding, but she needed most of them to continue fueling her stamina.

"Sigma Three for Sigma One." Emery, staticky over comms.

"Here," Adequin panted out.

"The AI says our shields can take three, maybe four rounds from one of those batteries. That means ninety seconds, give or take."

"Copy," Adequin huffed. "Stay back until we've reached the wall, then drop in and grab us."

"Sounds like it's gonna be a hot pickup, sir?"

Adequin grimaced, sweat stinging her eyes. "Yeah. Possibly very hot."

"We'll be ready," Emery said, tone firm.

Adequin flinched, ducking left as a sharp crack of plasma fire singed the white bark of the trees to her right. Gunfire pelted the canopy, raining down pink and white blossoms. Greenery flamed before fizzling out, leaving charred limbs blackened with smoke and ash.

As they rounded a corner, Cavalon spun and grabbed her wrist. He took a hard left, tugging her into the shrubs, through another invisible break in the rows. They came out the other side into a neatly trimmed path of towering hedges. Cavalon headed right and she followed, their footfalls on the gravel throwing up clouds of dry dust.

They tore around another corner, and suddenly, they were out.

Adequin's pace slowed as she got her bearings. They'd exited at the far north side of the gardens, into a small open lawn crossed with gravel paths and dotted with fountains, topiaries, and massive, abstract sculptures of sandy stone that reached up into the mottled gray sky.

About a hundred meters away at the farthest edge of the sculpture garden sat a wall, ten meters high, covered with vines of flowering red and green ivy. The north wall.

Cavalon stuttered to a stop, sucking in breaths, hands on knees.

"No," she panted, gripping his shoulder, "we have to keep going." He nodded, inhaled deeply, and took off again.

Boots crunched behind them as the Guardians began pouring out of the hedged garden.

"Right!" she shouted, and thankfully Cavalon listened, dashing right as they opened fire. Adequin strafed right, then left, each bolt a near-miss, cracking into the sculptures and topiaries around them.

Up ahead, beyond the wall, trees swayed with a gust of wind. Leaves and blossoms tore free of the ivy as the *Wakeless* appeared over the edge of the wall, its visual stealth melting away. Two turrets ascended from the top of the ship, then discharged a rapid cycle of rounds.

Cavalon ducked as the laser bolts flew over their heads. When the fire ceased and the cacophony quieted, Adequin looked back at the smoky destruction behind them. The northern entrance to the gardens had caught fire, leaving charred branches and smoldering leaves, with at least a half-dozen Guardian corpses.

Adequin heaved out a few short breaths. Even if that'd killed them all, more would be coming. They kept running.

"Guys!" Emery shouted over comms. "On your ten!"

Adequin threw a look to her left. At least fifteen more Guardians advanced across the lawn, already nearing the western edge of the sculpture garden.

Four accelerated from formation, overtaking the pack. They gripped black hilts on their belts, then unsheathed long, silver blades with deep inset tracts. With a flick of their taloned fingers, white light engulfed the blades in a coating of plasma.

Their rifle-toting counterparts behind them opened fire. Adequin followed Cavalon as he dove behind a low fountain to escape the barrage.

She pressed her back against the ridge, breath labored. She unfolded her gauss rifle, tapping the side to modify the fire pattern to spray, sparing the briefest moment to be thankful she'd brought a ballistics rifle. Their plasma pistols wouldn't work nearly as well against this plastech armor.

"Shit." Emery's voice crackled over comms. "I'd really like to help you out again, boss, but I'm afraid I'm gonna catch you guys too. These guns aren't made for groundside ops."

Adequin's instincts told her to retreat, to draw back. They could never make it to the wall before those Guardians cut them off. And getting through their line would be impossible. They should disappear into the gardens, try to fall off their radar, maybe find a way back inside the manor, sneak out the way they came.

In the direction of the manor, a distant groan of metal on metal rang out.

She snuck a look over the edge of the fountain. On the roof, the barrel of a large anti-aircraft battery pulsed out three successive bolts of thick plasmic energy, so large they seemed to move in slow motion as they arced over the length of the massive lawn. Each pelted the side of the *Wakeless*, melting into the shields. The ship listed with each hit.

"Em!" Adequin shouted. "You're too close!"

"I know! One sec, boss!"

The *Wakeless* dipped over the inside of the wall, lowering toward the ground. The personnel hatch slid open, and a figure hovered in the frame. Adequin was too far to tell for sure, but it had to be Owen. She'd donned a set of heavy black combat armor and toted a heavy rail repeater, well over half as long as she was tall. She secured her helmet, then dropped the two meters out of the hatch, landing on the ground in a plume of gravel dust as the *Wakeless* rose back up.

"Covering fire comin' at ya," Owen called out. She took a knee behind a planter and steadied the bulky rifle on the ledge, then opened fire.

The volley of plasma bolts sprayed the line of Guardians. Two immediately fell, while the others scrambled to more defensible positions in the garden. With their attention split, Adequin grabbed Cavalon's arm and they ran. Pain fired up her injured leg and her lungs burned. Her Imprints rushed to aid her speed, but they were already overworked, sluggish after spending so many weeks keeping that infection at bay.

Her breath caught as a familiar whistle soared in from the left.

"Incoming!" she shouted.

A large stone planter exploded. She dove left into cover behind a sculpture. A shard sliced her cheek as she tucked into herself, fragments of concrete and stone and packed dirt raining down.

More explosions rang out across the garden, throwing up a thick haze of dust and debris. Through the smoke around her, she reached out for Cavalon.

Panic flooded her chest with a spike of ice-cold adrenaline.

She'd gone left. Cavalon had gone *right*.

They'd separated. She'd let go of him. How could she let that happen?

Pushing to her feet, she shouldered her rifle. Cleared the guilt from her mind. She started toward him, or where she thought he'd gone, the air still clouded. She coughed, squinting through the haze, hunting for any sign of him.

From the smoke, a sharp crack.

A hard pressure kicked against her chestplate and the air vacated her lungs as she hit the ground. Blackness tugged at the edges of her sight, but she fought to hold onto consciousness. As she strove for air, she shifted, sensing a commotion nearby.

Through the thinning haze cut the flash of a plasmic blade. Two figures tumbled into view a few meters away—one of the blade-wielding Guardians pinned Cavalon to the ground. Cavalon bared his teeth and struck the Guardian in the side of the head hard enough its helmet flew off, skidding across the gravel.

Snarling, the Guardian brought his blade down just as Cavalon lifted his arm up. The blade sliced through his wrist. Cavalon screamed.

Rage surged through her. She reached out, grabbed her rifle, tried to aim it, but her hand went limp as her head swam with the lack of air.

Cavalon's cries were drowned out by more grenade blasts, kicking up a cloud of dust between them.

She tried to shout to Owen, but her voice stalled out with no air to feed it. She willed her lungs to respond, a dense pain crushing her sternum. Something was wrong.

Right. She'd been shot. In the chest.

She tore at her chest plate. Unhooked the fasteners.

The pressure abated, air sliding into her lungs. Her vision spun. She coughed, hacking up bile onto the ground. She tossed the ruined chest plate aside.

Taloned hands reached out of the haze and grabbed her. Hoisted her up, over its shoulder. Her rifle's strap had caught on the edge of her vambrace. Growling, she hoisted the gun into her hands, then shot the Guardian in the back of the knee.

It crumpled and she fell along with it. She rolled over and fired again, hitting it in the neck. It fell back, twitching, dark red blood staining its pierced armor. She lurched to her knees and fired a third time. It stilled.

She adjusted her nexus. "Sigma Four? Can you hear me?" She tapped the node on her jaw. Only static.

Thick dust still clouded the air. She could hear but not see the *Wakeless* lay down another round of fire, right as the manor's batteries discharged again.

Wiping the sweat from her eyes, she drew in a deep breath and got to her feet, then shouldered her rifle.

A Guardian marched out of the haze. She shot it point-blank in the chest. It flew back, its ribs crumpling.

She paced through the smoke, hunting for cover, hunting for Cavalon. Her comms crackled.

"Four?" she panted.

"Here, sir!" Owen replied. "Getting hard to see what the hell's going on down here."

"Find Cavalon. He's injured. Get him out of here."

"Sir, where are you?"

"Don't worry about me. He's priority. I'll get to you."

Two Guardians appeared in the thinning haze. She lunged toward them before they could react.

She shot the left one in the neck while she hooked a leg around the other to knock it prone. She swiped the plasma blade from the belt of the dead one, while the living one turned over and threw out a fist. It struck the bridge of her nose and sparks fired in her vision.

Blood seeped down her face, pain shrouding her senses. She fell to her knees, but still managed to activate the blade. She stabbed the prone Guardian through the neck. It sputtered and hacked before falling still.

Adequin panted as she crawled up to the base of a small fountain. She wiped the blood from her face, trying to stop it running into her eyes. She snuck a look over the fountain. The dust had cleared enough she could start to see where she was.

Somehow, she'd ended up at the western side, near the lawn. Most of the Guardians were now between her and the *Wakeless*.

Her comms clicked.

"Oh, shit, buddy," Owen said, her voice weak.

Adequin's jaw tightened. "You got him?"

"I got him, sir . . . Fuck . . ."

"Is he okay?"

"He's alive, yeah. In route to the ship now."

Relief coursed through her—dizzying, exhausting relief. She wiped more blood from her brow.

"Sigma Three," she said, "if you can give them some covering fire, do it. Don't worry about hitting me, I'm clear of it."

"Uh, copy that, sir," Emery replied warily.

Adequin leaned out to look across the destroyed, smoking garden. The *Wakeless* rose over the wall again, descending to just above the ground. It opened fire. Guardians dove for cover. The cargo ramp lowered.

The batteries on the manor clanked to life. Plasmic bolts rang out. The *Wakeless* stuttered as the shields absorbed the impacts.

Adequin squinted, watching as Owen hauled a half-conscious Cavalon up the ramp.

"I got them," Emery barked. "Sir, where are you?"

Adequin wiped the blood from her nose, looked down at her torn, throbbing calf, at the dried blood staining the cracked armor, feeling the sluggish, desperate clawing of her Imprints along her skin. She sucked in a lungful of air and blew it out slowly.

She tapped her nexus to open a comm line direct to Emery.

"Em. Listen."

"Listening, sir."

"You need to engage Phantom protocols, get spaceside, and get out of here."

"Sir—"

"They'll muster reinforcements, and increase system-wide patrols. You need to find somewhere to lay low for a while till things calm down. Got it?"

"Sir, where are you? You can tell me all this from the damn ship—why are you telling me now?"

Adequin licked her bloodied lips and clamped her eyes shut. "You know why."

Emery didn't respond immediately. "Sir, respectfully, yeah right. There's no way in hell I'm leaving without you."

"Yes, you are."

"Rake—"

Another round of plasma bolts pelted the *Wakeless*. The shields sparked and wavered.

"Take off. Now," Adequin growled. "Don't make me repeat myself."

Emery's voice came faltering and soft. "Sir, I . . . No—I can't leave someone behind. Especially not you."

"I'm pinned down," Adequin insisted, striving to keep her voice even. "I can't get to you, and you can't get to me. If you don't leave right now, those batteries are going to overwhelm your shields and shoot you down. Then we'll *all* be dead, and so will every Sentinel."

A wavering breath, then silence.

Adequin ground her teeth. "You leave right fucking now, Circitor. That's a direct order from your excubitor. Do you understand?"

Adequin tensed as three Guardians rounded the fountain toward her. They slowed, fanning out in a wide arc.

"I understand," Emery croaked, then her tone softened. "Aevitas fortis, sir."

Heat seared her cheeks. "Aevitas fortis, Em."

She severed the comm link and eyed the Guardians stalking closer. Bitter regret tugged at her stomach as she thought about how useful that damn Viator summoner technology would be about now.

Turned out, she'd been right to be anxious about this op. She could try to say it'd gone bad because she was rusty, or they hadn't had enough time to prepare, or enough experienced personnel, or a thousand other excuses. But in the end, none of that would have made a difference. The failure had been in the choice. To go toe-to-toe with the most dangerous man in the galaxy. To threaten him. To underestimate him.

But Cavalon was safe, and beyond that, she didn't care about winning or losing.

She did care, however, about breaking her promise to Jackin. To stay safe. To not do anything objectively stupid. To come back alive.

He'd acted like he wanted that assurance for the sake of the mission, for the sake of the Sentinels. But she knew he'd really meant her. Because that was what he'd promised Griffith. To save her from herself.

Now there were no more choices left to make, good or bad. All she had left to do was what she'd done her whole life: fight.

Rifle in one hand, sword in the other, she pushed to her feet. She thumbed the button on the hilt and the long silver blade caught with jittering plasmic fire.

The Guardians closed in.

CHAPTER TWENTY-SEVEN

Cavalon struggled to catch hold of it, but consciousness eluded him.

After what felt like a very long time, he cracked open his crusted-over eyes. Dark gray smears with black accents surrounded him. The *Wakeless*'s crew quarters.

A blur of wavy brown hair and worry paced over him. His eyes drifted closed again.

"What are we gonna do? We need a medic—what if we're making it worse?"

"We're not making it worse," another voice replied, tone infused with forced calm. It took him a moment to register it as Owen. "The medbot did everything it could. The AI said he'll be fine."

"Fine? You call that fine?" That was Emery.

"Babe, he's alive, isn't he?" Owen replied. "You saw that shitshow. That alone is a miracle."

Cavalon tried to sit up, but his shoulders and neck cramped. Every muscle in his body burned. He opened his mouth to speak, but only a soft groan came out.

"Shit. He's awake."

He forced his eyes open again. A hazy Emery and Owen stood over him.

"How do you feel?" Owen asked.

"Very shitty," he croaked. He slid his elbows back, and Owen put an arm around his shoulders to help him sit up.

He went to rub the sleep from his eyes, but hesitated. Something wasn't right.

He stared down at his left hand. At least, where his brain felt like his left hand was. But his eyes saw something different than what his body felt.

A gauze wrapping coated his forearm . . . or, most of his forearm. What he expected to see at the end of his wrist was conspicuously missing.

"Patient vitals elevated," the AI intoned.

He clamped his eyes shut.

The fight came back to him—the Guardian racing out of the dust, so fast, too fast. He'd had a gun, he'd had a knife. There was nothing he could do against a fucking *plasma sword*.

In retrospect, trying to parry it with his arm might not have been the best choice.

A surge of vomit rose and he barely fought it back down.

Owen rubbed his shoulder. She said some words he was sure were meant to be consoling, but he couldn't pretend to be consoled at the moment, so he ignored her.

He cleared his throat. "Where are we?"

"I took us out to a cave on one of the asteroid moons around Attica," Emery said.

He nodded mutely. A gas giant three rings out.

"The AI said its magnetosphere makes it the safest place to lay low," she explained.

The AI was right. It was the best place in-system to keep a low profile. The network of subterranean crevices made it a favorite of routers and vagabonds of all flavors. He knew this, of course, because of what a shitty person he was.

When he was at university, he'd been conscripted by an up-and-coming cartel. Spaceport security had increased and they needed help finding ways to smuggle the drugs planetside. Cavalon's solution had been simple: The system's primary veterans' service center, Ivory Hall, was close to campus. Veterans arrived via the Legion spaceports, which had security checks, of course, but the guards were known to be lenient when searching personal baggage for their trustworthy comrades-in-arms.

It hadn't mattered that these men and women were often already users, and that he was exploiting their addictions for personal gain—personal gain he didn't even need. He was wealthy beyond reason, and enabling them and subsequently ruining their lives accomplished nothing more than giving himself easy access to apex and the rush of putting something over on Augustus.

He bit the inside of his cheek, huffing out a short breath. It was ridiculous to think anything he did now could make up for what a terrible fucking person he used to be. Or what a terrible fucking person he literally was, down to every strand of his cloned DNA.

"Cav?" Owen knelt beside him, round hazel eyes unblinking. Emery stood over her shoulder, arms crossed tight.

He realized then: They didn't know what he really was.

And they didn't have to know. What good would it do to tell them?

Though, maybe it'd be for the best. Then they could eject him out the airlock and be done with it already.

"We're trying to figure out next steps," Owen said. It was a question, a request. They wanted his input.

"Next steps . . ." he muttered. "Well, what's Rake think?"

They stared at him.

He stared back. Warmth crept up the back of his neck.

Emery's pale cheeks ignited with a rash of red, and she paced away. Owen hung her head, a few wavy curls falling from her braid. She kept a hand on his knee.

"O . . ." His voice wavered. "What's Rake think?"

Owen cleared her throat. "She told us to take you and leave—"

"*What?*" he growled. He used his right arm to push to standing, blood running hot. His vision spun, but he stayed upright. His left arm and nonexistent hand pulsed with pain as adrenaline shot through him.

Emery returned from the other side of the room, eyes watery. "She gave me a direct order to—"

"Fuck orders!" he shouted. "You don't leave people behind!"

Owen let out a steadying breath. "We had no choice, Cav. She was cut off and surrounded, and our shields were almost depleted."

"How can you be so calm about this?" he snapped.

Owen's jaw flexed. "Because it's over. I can't go back and save her, but I can make her sacrifice worth it. We owe it to Rake to keep going. To save the *Lodestar.*"

Cavalon stared, chest heaving, fascinated by her composure, wishing he could leach some of that self-control for himself, but his rising fury wouldn't let him.

Before he could start needlessly screaming again, a realization settled in. They didn't leave her. *He* left her.

He'd gone right and she'd gone left, and instead of trying to find her, he'd cowered behind cover, frozen in fear, unable to function without her there to drag him forward.

He buried his face in his hands—in his right hand. His left arm dropped to his side, and a frustrated growl escaped the back of his throat.

"I'm sorry, okay?" Emery croaked out. "It's not like I wanted to leave her."

"We have to go back." With every syllable, he strove to keep his voice calm. "We cannot leave her at the mercy of that monster."

Owen cleared her throat. "That's both a suicide mission, and . . . potentially in vain. They had her surrounded, and more were incoming . . ."

Cavalon set his jaw. "You can't really think she's dead."

She gave a stiff shrug. "Man, I have no idea—but you were on that battlefield. They were shooting to kill."

"So we just *leave* her?" he shouted, anger rising again. "We just assume she's dead?"

Owen looked to Emery. "You're the captain now, Em. What do we do?"

Emery's eyes went wide, and she shook her head, then pointed at Cavalon. "No, no. He's an animus—he's the ranking officer."

"He's a fucking scientist," Owen growled. "And presently in shock. This is on you, babe."

"No way. I'm not equipped for this." Emery ran her hands through her hair. "I'm just a pilot—and barely even that."

Cavalon nodded. She was right. They needed an adult.

He cleared his throat. "We have to call Jackin."

With the nets on high-alert and all the signal trackers flying around from system patrols, the AI claimed its out-system comms security to be less than 15 percent.

Cavalon quieted his reeling mind long enough to remember seeing a comms menu on the newly "liberated" atlas device. After a decent amount of trial and error, and some real hasty translating, they figured out how to use it to send a message to the *Corinthian* over an encrypted, apparently secret, Viator frequency. Or maybe it was just more teleportation magic, who knew.

It'd worked, as a flustered Jackin arrived hours later, ferried by a Corsair ship piloted by Gideon.

Jackin boarded the *Wakeless* alone, and the personnel airlock hissed shut behind him. He dropped his suit helmet off, staring at each of them in turn. His bloodshot gaze landed on Cavalon, then lowered to his left arm, which Cavalon held awkwardly bent at his side. He'd discovered a need to keep it tucked up against his ribs as though in a sling, as if it were merely broken and would mend itself over time.

Jackin scratched his forehead. "Void, kid . . ."

Cavalon rubbed his handless arm and frowned.

"Where's Rake?" Jackin asked. "What the hell was that message about?"

"Sorry, sir," Emery said. "We left it vague on purpose . . ." She exchanged a wary look with Owen. "We wanted to be careful."

Emery collected herself with an effort, then launched into a straightforward account of the events since they'd left the *Corinthian*. Cavalon was glad she was the one giving the summary and not him, because if he had to admit what'd really happened at the manor out loud, he might descend into a fugue state. And he didn't have time for that until *after* they saved Rake.

Jackin visibly flinched when Emery said *"forced to leave without her."* He didn't look exactly surprised, more like his worst fears had been confirmed.

The muscles of Jackin's jaw worked as he stared Emery down. Then his glower turned onto Cavalon. "How the hell could you let that happen?"

Heat clawed at Cavalon's cheeks. "Why are you mad at *me*?" he snapped. "Emery's the one who flew away!"

"Sir," Emery squeaked, "she ordered me—"

"Because *you* were with her!" Jackin shouted at Cavalon, ignoring Emery. "You swore to me you'd stop her, you were responsible—"

"Oh come on," Cavalon growled out a harsh scoff. "No one is *responsible* for Rake."

"That's the whole damn point! We all need her, all the time, we rely on her, we take from her, we put it all on her shoulders until she's got nothing left—and then we fucking *leave her behind*?"

A hard, unrelenting silence permeated the cabin. Cavalon exchanged a round of cowed looks with Emery and Owen.

Jackin shook his head slowly, still scowling at Cavalon. "I trusted you."

Heat spiked in Cavalon's chest, but his rage petered out as it was overtaken by a surge of bitter guilt.

He'd failed Jackin nearly as much as he'd failed Rake. Just when he was beginning to gain ground. He'd promised not to let Rake do anything rash, and he'd not only let it happen, but had suggested the idea himself. He'd personally led her to her demise.

"Fine," he said, voice wavering. "I fucked up, okay? What do you want me to say? I'm acutely aware of what a terrible human I am right now, but I can't change what happened, and I can't fix it alone. We don't know what to do. We need you." He exhaled, steadying his breath with an effort. "Sir."

Jackin's glare softened, mouth turning down, brow wrinkling. After a long few moments, he wiped at his eyes, then drew in a breath and stood up straight. "What do we still need in order to get the ceronite?"

Cavalon's lips slackened. "What about Rake?"

"We'll take care of it," Jackin replied calmly, too calmly. "First we get the ceronite, then we deal with Rake."

"It could be too late for her by then."

Jackin's shoulders swelled. "It could be too late for her already!" he shouted, his resonant tone reverberating in the small cockpit. "Maybe you shouldn't have left her behind if you're so worried about it."

Prickling heat stung Cavalon's chest.

"Sir, no," Emery said, stepping toward them, "Cavalon's right. That was my fault. Rake ordered me to, and I thought I had to listen, but I shouldn't have."

Jackin tamped down his fury with a clear effort, then looked at Emery. "No. You were right to follow orders. It's not your fault." He scratched at the collar of his space suit. "Mercer won't kill her. He's too smart not to realize her value. Rake got us off that Viator ship in one piece, she can keep herself alive in Mercer's dungeon for a couple hours."

Cavalon licked his dry lips, wondering why the hell Jackin thought he knew anything about what Augustus would or wouldn't do, but he couldn't say the assessment was wrong.

"This ceronite has thousands of lives riding on it," Jackin continued. "We secure it first."

"Sir?" Owen asked warily.

"Go ahead."

She cleared her throat. "Unfortunately, we have no way into the facility. They weren't able to secure the device we needed from the manor."

Jackin let out a heavy sigh and scratched at his beard.

Owen continued. "The AI's doing a cursory analysis of some data Cav downloaded from one of Augustus's terminals. But there's no sign of anything resembling genetic code yet. And even if we had that, without the device itself, it wouldn't work as a living sample . . ."

Owen went on as Cavalon's attention listed.

Maybe there'd never been any "device." Maybe it'd always just been that fucking . . . *child*. Augustus wouldn't need a failsafe to enable his heir to succeed when he was printing his own clones to take over for him. No wonder he never named Shithead Second Cousin as heir. He planned to name that poor child clone.

That could be why his father had told him about the "device" in the first place . . . He'd known about the boy, and the guilt had overwhelmed him, and he'd had to warn someone. But then why claim it to be a device, and not just say "*your grandfather's holding children hostage*"?

Maybe by that point, he was afraid for their lives, and worried Cavalon would react badly if he found out the truth. Rightfully so.

"Stop," Cavalon said, his own voice shockingly loud in his ears.

Jackin, Emery, and Owen all ceased their discussion to look at him with blank shock as if he were a potted plant that'd decided to speak.

He summoned what few dregs of courage he had remaining. "We don't need the device."

Jackin left to return to Gideon's ship briefly while Emery helped Owen and Cavalon pull their loadouts. Cavalon shoved down his anger and grief and depression and focused efforts on compartmentalizing.

He went through the motions as Owen helped him suit up, as he cross-checked systems, as Emery flew them to Tethys, as he, Jackin, and Owen deployed the armored drones, activated their emitter cloaks, then cut through the two klicks of dormant woods and up to the staff access door on the southern face of the looming, black, windowless ceronite factory.

"Are you sure about this?" Owen asked as they stepped up to the security terminal. Her lips twitched as she tried to fight an expression off her face. Disgust, presumably. Cavalon couldn't blame her.

"I'm sure."

Jackin remained a silent prodigy of stoicism as Owen helped Cavalon tug the glove off his right hand, then removed his visor for him.

Cavalon slicked his hair off his forehead, then pressed his right palm against the terminal. The screen flashed green.

In his periphery, Jackin shifted.

The retinal scan activated next. A small needle pricked the skin of his middle finger, drawing tissue and blood samples. A dial on the terminal screen spun for a few long moments. It let out a small, affirmative tone.

"Identity confirmed," the computer chirped.

"Lockout's been cleared." Owen's voice wavered as she stared down at her nexus screen. "We have full access."

A wave of welled-up, ice-cold, stingingly bitter relief flooded Cavalon's veins.

That was it, then. The proof he needed. He'd been hanging on to a thread of residual hope, that it'd all been orchestrated, some elaborate lie to fuck with his head.

At least he no longer had to wonder.

Cavalon pulled open the door and walked inside.

CHAPTER TWENTY-EIGHT

Adequin woke to fifty thousand volts firing into her back.

"Up."

The jolt ceased, leaving a sharp iron taste in her mouth, her skin tingling, and her Imprints furious. They tore along her skin, unsure where to land. They wanted to help her rise, to strike out, to take the fucker's weapon and turn it against them. But she lay facedown on the floor with her wrists bound behind her. She tried to shift her weight, and her limbs felt like barely molten metal—heavy, sluggish, and searing with pain.

Taloned, bone-white hands gripped her arms and hauled her up. Her vision swam. She forced her knees to straighten, putting her effort into staying upright as the Guardian dragged her forward.

She looked down at her aching feet, oddly snug in a pair of slip-on house shoes. The rest of her armor was gone as well, and she wore a set of gray, short-sleeved, baggy medical scrubs. Her hair had been combed and tied back, her wounds cleaned and dressed, and she no longer smelled of blood, dirt, and smoke, but rather . . . citrus and sage.

While she was unconscious, they'd bathed and dressed her?

The familiar cool metal chain grazed the back of her neck, along with the tug of the weight of two sets of dog tags. That set her mildly at ease. Mildly.

She blinked the haze from her eyes and forced herself to focus. The Guardian led her down a long, windowless corridor. Well-armed Drudgers and humans alike stood post every few meters along both sides of the hall. She was a little flattered they took her capacity to escape so seriously.

The end of the hall culminated in a set of wide doors. A human attendant stepped forth, a thin balding man with ruddy white skin. He lifted his pointed chin, staring down his long nose at her. "The protocol is as follows: Upon His Majesty's entry, bow from the waist once. For your first address, use 'Your Majesty.' After that, 'sir.' Do not speak until His Majesty has, and do not sit unless His Majesty does."

Adequin's temples throbbed as she squinted at the man. This guy could not be serious.

He eyed her bound hands, wrinkled lips pressing thin. "No physical contact of any kind is permitted. Speak only when spoken to, and do not query His Majesty unless invited to do so. When your visit has concluded, bow from the waist again and await His Majesty's departure before rising. Do you have any questions?"

A dry scoff escaped her throat. "No."

His contempt was palpable as he stepped to the door and pulled it open. The Guardian dragged her through, and the door clicked shut behind them.

Inside, Adequin's gaze immediately drifted to the coffered ceilings high overhead—a grid of massive wood beams inlaid with embossed copper panels. Along the back wall over a bank of built-in bookshelves, tinted daylight cast through strips of blue and maroon stained glass. Massive portraits of bygone Mercers lined the walls, each regal pose as intimidating as the next. A soft, unsettling scent of sage hung in the air.

The Guardian shoved her forward, and she almost tripped on the edge of a woven carpet. The Drudger yanked her to a stop a few meters in front of a massive wooden desk.

"On your knees," it ordered—its voice notably discernable, with vocal cords capable of clear human speech. Genetically altered.

She readily knelt. Standing had become a burden she held no interest in continuing to endure.

Minute after long minute passed. She surveyed the room, filled with exotic trinkets, gilded relics, and real, bound books. Her vision coasted side to side, ambling lazily even as she struggled to focus. And nothing hurt quite as much as it should. The effects of painkillers.

A faint click sounded on the far side of the room. A door slid open, and Augustus Mercer walked in.

Adequin strove to keep her pulse steady, chin raised, jaw firm.

He stopped beside the desk, gaze drifting over her, expression unreadable. His brilliant blue eyes were too much like Cavalon's.

He must have been seventy or so, without the slightest stoop or hitched joint to betray his age. Over a black suit, he wore a knee-length tailored jacket of thick, dark gray wool, the cuffs and wide lapels embroidered with golden fleurs-de-lis. His once-blond hair was now a stark white with accents of steel gray, lightly bound by an understated circlet: an arc of thin, twisting silver branches reminiscent of the Mercer seal. He looked so frustratingly regal in the damn thing. Though no one had ever said he didn't look the part.

He activated a terminal over the ornate desk, expanding a small holographic screen. His eyes gave it a cursory scan before returning to her.

The Guardian nudged her with the end of its shock baton.

Oh, right. *"Bow from the waist once."*

She did nothing.

An electric trill sounded as the Guardian activated its baton.

Augustus's chin lifted, and he held up a placating hand.

The Guardian's posture stiffened. The line of dull gray Imprint tattoos on its neck clicked softly, and a glint flickered over each square. The Guardian's focus drew inward, its deep brown, humanlike eyes fogging over. It turned off the baton and took three rigid steps back, retreating to stand a few meters to Adequin's right.

Augustus exhaled a soft sigh. "Miss Adequin Rake," he said languidly, in a way that made each word sound like he'd spent hours hand-selecting it for an artisanal cheese board. "Or should I say, Idra Le Calvez."

She started, unable to keep the shock from her face. Her heart strained against her ribs, the rush of adrenaline setting her on edge. Blinking rapidly, she did her best to breathe through it.

He tilted his head. "I imagine you haven't been called that in quite some time."

She held his gaze, expression steady.

"It may not be common knowledge," he went on, "however, it is part of your service record. The sealed section, of course. But it's there."

Her eyes twitched, and she found herself striving to keep her composure. She was pretty sure she failed.

There was no way that was in her service record. If it was, then someone had known—someone other than Hudson—and she'd have never passed the background checks required for her clearance level, or her rank.

Augustus quirked a white eyebrow. "Did you honestly think Reneth would let any old orphan with forged papers into the Titans without a thorough background check? He must have wanted you very badly to overlook that not-so-little transgression."

She gritted her teeth at the blatant familiarity with which he used Praetor Lugen's first name. His intent, no doubt. But that meant . . .

Her gaze flitted down. Lugen had known. All that time, he'd known about her past. Known that she'd lied about who she was.

No. Void. She clamped her eyes shut, pressing the insidious thoughts from her mind.

This was a tactic. Augustus was trying to whittle away at her, find her weak spots and exploit them, just as he had with Cavalon. She had to fight it.

Every word he said could be a fabrication. He could simply be glancing at a blank screen, making shit up in that twisted mind of his. There were other ways he could have found out about her birth name.

"May I ask the reason for your visit?" he said, tone steady and casual, as if commenting on the weather. "I never got around to finding out from my grandson. He was being rather combative, as usual, and didn't seem of the mindset to be forthright, regardless."

Adequin shifted against her metal cuffs, ignoring the growing itch of sweat beading on the back of her neck.

Augustus lifted a knee to sit on the edge of the desk. "You seem to be on edge, Miss Le Calvez. Please know, I'm not going to hurt you. You don't need to think of me as the bad guy."

She blew out a sharp breath through her nose, and failed horribly at maintaining her silence. "I'm pretty sure locking children in your bedroom makes you a '*bad guy.*'"

"Well." He folded his hands in his lap. "She speaks at last."

"Why torture an innocent boy?" she growled, throat scratchy. "Why not just clone one to adulthood like you did with the Guardians?"

"Can't, I'm afraid. Generating adult humans has not . . ." He exhaled a long sigh. "They never turn out quite right."

Fucking void . . . What the hell had he been up to in that lab?

Her inconsiderate brain chose then to remind her of the look on Cavalon's face when he realized they were going to leave the boy behind. Maybe Cavalon had been right. Maybe she should have tried harder to get him free.

"What do you even want with him?" she asked, tone hard.

Augustus's mouth pressed into a thin line. "I believe you to be far more intelligent than that question indicates, Miss Le Calvez."

She gritted her teeth. "How are you going to explain an heir suddenly appearing out of thin air? Your son is dead and you banished your grandson."

"Oh," he said, tone light, "he'll be Cavalon's bastard."

Her cracked lips parted.

"Illegitimate, sure." He gave an acquiescent tilt of his head. "But I'll find some hapless woman willing to claim he slept with her. See, with Cavalon's . . . *issues*, she was too afraid to come forth earlier. I'll be the magnanimous king taking in the poor street urchin Cavalon so callously abandoned. He'll have the blood of a royal with the upbringing of a commoner. Beloved by all."

Adequin clenched her jaw. As a child, tired and naive and desperate, she would have eaten that up. To see someone like herself end up in a position like that . . . It was a brilliant move, and she hated it.

Augustus gave a meager smile that didn't reach his eyes. "But we're not here to talk about my great-grandson, are we? Let's discuss how you tried to get yourself killed saving Cavalon. How well is he paying you?"

She glowered.

"Interesting." His eyes narrowed slightly. "I did not think him capable of inspiring loyalty in another person."

"How's it feel to be wrong?"

He scoffed a laugh. "I'm wrong more frequently than you might imagine, Miss Le Calvez. It's how we learn from our mistakes that define who we are. Something Cavalon has never been capable of."

"Have you considered your DNA as the root of the problem?"

He laughed again, heartily this time, in a way that did not sound feigned or forced. "I can see why my grandson has taken a liking to you. You're quite similar, in a sort of . . . violent-opposites way."

"Yeah, well. Looks like when you sent him off to die with the Legion . . . you might have picked the wrong ship."

Augustus's eyelashes twitched as he struggled to maintain his disaffected amusement. She held his gaze, unblinking until her eyes burned. Because she wanted him to believe it, if nothing else, so when the Sentinels finally dethroned this entitled asshole, he'd know that in delivering Cavalon directly to her, he'd set it all into motion himself.

"Believe it or not," Augustus said, tone low and measured, "I didn't send him to the Sentinels to die. I'd hoped the opportunity would help straighten him out."

"Bullshit," she growled.

The Guardian started toward her with its baton, but Augustus held up a hand to halt it.

"You just wanted him to suffer," she continued. "Death would have been too easy a punishment for what he did."

Augustus watched her with a curious glint in his eye. "I'd like us to consider the circumstances, for a moment, Miss Le Calvez. For Cavalon to arrange something that meticulous, to somehow conceal it, even from me—that takes a great deal of diligent forethought." He folded his hands over his raised knee. "Yet . . . he had no plan for what came after. No way to escape. It was *days* before I was able to discern the truth, to discover the perpetrator. He stayed. He lived in the manor that entire time. Waiting for me to figure it out. He'd arranged for his own death and was trying to get me to do it for him. But I wouldn't. In sending the boy away, I saved him from himself."

A hard nodule twisted in Adequin's stomach. She gave a firm shake of her head. "I don't believe you."

He let out a long sigh. "That is your prerogative. What is your take on the matter, may I ask?"

"That you couldn't stomach the thought of killing another clone of yourself. After you'd murdered Cavalon's father."

The first sign of a truly uncontrolled emotion flashed across his visage—nostrils flaring along with a succession of rapid blinks. Anger tinged with regret or grief, gone in half a blink.

"Is that what he told you?" Augustus asked, the words slow with forced evenness. "That I murdered his father?"

"He said he has proof."

Augustus scratched the white stubble on his chin. "Mm, yes, well. Historically, what Junior perceives as truth has not tended to prove wholly accurate. He believes a great many things that support the narrative he has constructed for himself. But I assure you, Cavalon is fully aware of the true circumstances behind his father's death. After all, he is the one who found him."

A chill tore down her spine, and she struggled to keep the confusion from her face.

"It's true, I'm afraid," Augustus went on, voice thick with genuine grief. "Cavalon Sr. ended his own life." His gaze withdrew, eyebrows tight, lips parting along with a sharp inhale. Adequin analyzed the expression, searching for a tell that wasn't there.

A dense weight saddled her shoulders.

Regardless of her awareness of the depths of his deceptions, Augustus had a way about him that made every word he uttered seem like fact. So even though he offered no evidence, her inclination was to believe him.

He'd been right about one thing. Cavalon's nuclear plan to provoke Augustus, paired with no exit strategy whatsoever, looked very much like a death wish. And Augustus's quickly masked reaction spoke to a hint of remorse. If Cavalon's father really had taken his own life, and Augustus regretted it . . . maybe he really had been afraid Cavalon might be suicidal. Maybe Augustus really did send him away to try and save him from himself.

She ground her teeth. No. Fucking hell.

She had to get her head on straight. She somehow kept forgetting who she was talking to. She was trying to apply empathy, reason, and logic to an immoral, manipulative asshole's mindset. She had to stop letting him get in her head.

Though, it didn't matter if it was the truth or just more lies. If she got out of this alive, she could never ask Cavalon. He wouldn't intentionally lie to her, so if it was the truth, and he'd buried it that deep, that's where it belonged.

Augustus tilted his head. "Even now, I can see it."

Her brow lowered. "What?"

"You, shoring up a defense for him." He crossed his arms lightly over his chest. "You know, I watched playback from my Guardians' optical transmitters. You two make quite the team. Though, from what I saw, you were doing the heavy lifting. I do know how that feels." He let out a soft tsk and shook his head. "Just like my grandson to take and take from those around him until there's nothing left to give."

"You don't know him," she growled.

"Maybe not. But you know what he really is. Our paths may have diverged at a point, but fundamentally, he and I are the same. I understand the complexities of that boy's mind better than anyone. And you don't have the first clue what you're dealing with."

A sudden suspicion gripped her at the oddly urgent, beseeching shift in his tone. She held his hard gaze, watching the subtle, admonitory tilt of his head, the way his blue eyes creased with pity, all working to plant a seed of doubt, a single question. Of whether Cavalon would turn as vile and dangerous as Augustus.

She pressed her lips together hard, drawing her focus inward. He was adept at turning shit around on her, she'd give him that. But two could play at that game.

"If you know him so well," she began, "then surely you could have predicted this outcome. Or noticed how troubled he was, at the very least. Sensed his breaking point and stopped it before it all went so wrong."

Augustus's crossed arms shifted, fingers drumming lightly against the thick fabric of his jacket sleeve. "It's not that it went unnoticed," he said, tone chalky, placid. "I did try to get the boy help. I don't know if it was too late, inadequate, or simply beyond my reach. But as I said before, I make mistakes. Cavalon was one of them."

"Might genetic cleansing also be?"

He let out a sigh, heavy with disappointment. "After seeing your service record, I'd hoped for a more strategic understanding from you, Miss Le Calvez. Though, I suppose languishing at the Divide for so many years hasn't given you much perspective. I shouldn't be surprised you don't understand the scope of it."

She raised an eyebrow. "Scope of what?"

"Of what was lost during the Viator War." He stood up off the desk, shoulders drawn back, hands smoothing down the long front of his jacket. "Of what humanity was before the shambles it's become due to the mutagen. And what it will take to get it back." He gave each of his embroidered cuffs a meticulous tug. "The work may be difficult, but it will be worth it, in the end. Short-term pain for long-term gain."

"By short-term pain," she growled, "do you mean legalizing the segregation, enslavement, and murder of millions?"

His expression flattened, and his tone took on a fervent edge. "This isn't about wanton killing; this is about restoring the balance the mutagen took from us. If the survival of our species isn't enough to persuade you, then what of the morality? Of the ongoing grief humanity endures due to the mutagen's effects? Of those losing loved ones daily? We can put a stop to that pain."

"That's a nicely practiced defense you have on standby."

"Not a defense. Rationale based on firsthand experience." He rubbed his hands together slowly as he shifted to sit against the front of the desk. "Did you know, Miss Le Calvez, that my parents died due to their mutagen defects?"

Tensing her jaw, she tried to hold steady through her surprise, though she was pretty sure he noticed. She'd assumed the Mercer line had avoided the worst of it, considering they'd been the ones to devise the corrective treatments. Far more surprising was Augustus admitting something that personal.

"They were hardly over forty when they died," he went on, a flinty edge to his tone. "If they and their forebears had dedicated more time to *properly* eradicating the mutagen, we would not be in this position now. But as with most things, I'm left to clean up the mistakes of others." He ran a thumb along his jaw, gaze narrowing slightly. "Though, to each their own. While I wished my parents had lived despite their mutations, I'm willing to bet you wish yours had died even earlier because of them."

"My parents didn't die of mutations," she said evenly.

"No, but they did die *with* mutations. Remarkably, those mutations didn't transfer to you."

Adequin blinked a hard, slow blink, forcibly biting back a groan. She didn't want to know how he knew that.

"Rare, but not unheard of, certainly," he added. "I myself am in that same select category." His gaze brightened as he scanned her, looking almost intrigued. "You know, you could apply for permanent Core citizenship with a genome like yours, Miss Le Calvez."

"Fantastic. Can I put you down as a reference?"

"You would no longer need to rely on the Legion in order to renew your documentation. You could retire from service. Maybe move into the private sector."

She withheld a scoff. Was he trying to bribe her? He'd vouch for the quality of her genome and give her a lifelong pass to Core citizenship if she . . . what? Joined the Mercer Guard?

Yet, a nodule of hope stirred in her chest. If he thought she still needed a reason to retire, that meant he didn't yet anticipate what they really were. Or rather, what they were becoming. He probably thought Cavalon had simply persuaded his new Titan friend to help him steal the data they'd downloaded from the lab, as a continuation of his crusade against the Guardians.

She cleared her throat. "Not everyone enlists just to gain citizenship," she countered.

"Of course, my mistake. What was it then, the promise of adventure? Honor and duty? The 'call to serve'?"

"More like forced circumstance," she conceded, voice dry.

Augustus gave a soft, knowing smile that sent a shiver down her spine. He twisted to reach over the desk, palming the holographic screen and guiding it toward the front edge to rest beside him. "I had time to do a little digging on my flight back from Viridis. It appears the circumstances around your parents' deaths were rather nebulous." His gaze skimmed over the screen. "Some shoddy investigative work, I'd say, though to a more discerning eye than the Saxton Guard—which to be fair, does not take much—one might also see it as a . . . rather impressively shrewd exploitation of the system."

She set her jaw, focusing all her efforts on not reacting. On most counts, he was right. Except it hadn't been *shoddy* investigative work, it'd been *no* investigative work. The sheriff had claimed it was the Saxton Guard's jurisdiction and vice versa, and it was in that nebulous gray area of the laziest lawmen in the Outer Core that the truth behind her parents' deaths would forever lie.

Though Augustus's ice-blue eyes remained static, the wrinkles at the corner of his mouth twitched upward. He ran two fingers over his chin. "I'll be honest," he began slowly, and the tone of his voice rang so low and mellow, so devoid of pretense, it caused her adrenaline to spike. "At the time of reading, I'd assumed you wouldn't be capable of it. But . . ." His look drifted over her slowly, one white eyebrow twitching upward.

She held his gaze, unblinking. If Augustus wanted to think her capable of parricide at barely fourteen years old, who was she to dissuade him.

"Your Majesty, I apologize . . ."

Adequin's gaze flicked past Augustus to the back wall. The ruddy-faced attendant stood in the far doorway.

"Sir, you have an urgent off-world call." The man's look fell on Adequin, lips pursing. "Regarding . . . present matters."

"In my study," Augustus instructed, and the attendant nodded and left. Augustus inclined his head to Adequin. "If you'll excuse me a moment, Miss Le Calvez."

He left out the back door, and Adequin blew out a heavy, resounding breath.

She became acutely aware of the massive weight of tension knotting her shoulders. Sitting back on her feet, she slouched, her wrists chafing against the metal bindings. She rolled her neck and slid a look toward the Guardian on her right.

The line of square Imprint tattoos running up its chalky white neck was a dull matte gray, not the gold and bronze given from the Mercer family's Imprint machine. The Guardians' Imprints were in all likelihood human-engineered, which meant they were either highly volatile and unpredictable like the blackmarket kind, or they had been designed for a different purpose, like the punitive Imprints the Legion had created for the Sentinels. Maybe they were what Augustus had devised as a governor mechanism—"mind control" via their Imprint interfaces.

What she really cared about at the moment was whether they enhanced its strength. The more the drug-induced haze bled from her system, the more confident she felt that she could take this one. Though if she couldn't get her bindings off, fighting her way through that hallway would prove impossible.

She eyed the Drudger's Imprints again. Augustus had said they had optical feeds, and the way they'd worked in tandem in the garden without ever speaking a word to one another . . . As soon as she engaged this one, the others would be alerted.

As if privy to her thoughts, the Guardian snarled at her, its talons clacking at the hilt of its shock baton. She smiled coldly.

Minutes later, Augustus marched back in, pace elevated, movements skittish. He'd removed his embroidered jacket and the sleeves of his dress shirt were rolled, revealing tidy lines of stationary gold and bronze Imprint squares along his right arm, just like Cavalon's. He yanked to loosen his tie, then unfastened the top buttons of his collar.

Adequin's eyebrows twitched. Their conversation had proved how adept he was at suppressing his emotion. If he was this openly agitated, something was up.

He stopped beside the desk. "I'd say I'm sorry to see you go," he said, and her heart skipped a beat, "but no matter how prodigious an asset you may be, your loss will be worth it, in the end."

Her pulse picked up speed. Did "loss" mean execution or release?

"I know how wars are truly won, Miss Le Calvez," he went on. "And it's not with ships and guns and grandiose military strategies. Or exceptional leaders, even those as distinguished as yourself." His brow pinched, and his eyes creased with a tinge of pity. "I hope you understand the magnitude of what you've sacrificed today. I cannot imagine it will be worth it, in the end."

Her brows knit. She didn't know what that meant, but her instincts kicked in a warning to ignore it, it was just another manipulation. He was trying to get in her head, cultivate uncertainty.

"I'm sorry our time was cut so short," Augustus continued. "I did hope to hear more about how my wayward grandson earned the respect of someone such as yourself. We'll have a chance to catch up another time, I'm sure."

With a nod from Augustus, the Guardian sheathed its shock baton. It pulled a biotool from its belt and marched toward Adequin.

She flinched and twisted aside, too late. It injected the cartridge into the side of her neck. With a wash of warmth, her muscles went slack. Darkness descended before she even hit the floor.

CHAPTER TWENTY-NINE

Ten years ago at Legion HQ, Dextera Adequin Rake sits across from the commander of the First, Praetor Reneth Lugen.

It's past midnight. Crisp moonlight cuts through slatted window shades, casting a cold glint across the dark office.

"I want you to serve as liaison," he says from behind his broad desk, from behind his guarded veneer she can never quite see past. "You'll report to me and only me."

"Our ranks are lateral," she says—she *accuses*. That's how it's always been. It's what makes the Titans different. What makes them what they are.

He steeples his fingers. Tells her why it's different. It's not a rank; it's a role. His explanation is convincing, but he's also hiding something, and she cannot determine what. He plays his cards close. Always willing to offer just enough to keep her at hand, yet withholding so much. She can't help but feel there's a dam welling, waiting to break.

It's a skill he tries to teach her over the years, to think beyond the mission, beyond the campaign, set up a longer strategy. Sequester information, parcel it out shrewdly, and let people die if it means that knowledge is protected until the time has come to deliver it.

She tries to take it to heart, tries so hard, because she wants to make him proud.

"Why me?" she asks, though she already knows the answer.

He needs her to follow her instincts, to trust that intangible insight of hers that tells her what the right path is. He speaks of this with reverence, as if it's a supernatural sixth sense, a singular ability only she possesses, and it will help him win the war if only he can harness it. She's a WMD, to be positioned and activated at his discretion.

The trouble is, she doesn't care. He's more a parent to her than anyone else ever claimed to be. He trusts her, he believes in her, and that's all she's ever wanted. So she agrees.

But as the years pass and the war wanes, he grows more distant, more guarded. As if the ongoing conflict provides him a shield that cracks with every step they take toward victory.

One day as they strategize together over star charts and takeout, she looks up to catch him staring at the maps with glassy-eyed reverence. He stares at the end of a war, an end they built together.

With that one look, she knows a truth he would never admit: He is afraid of what remains when the war is won.

Six years later she gathers a small crew, boards the *Synthesis*, leaves the Divide, and arrives at the Core.

The *Corinthian* sits vacant. Gates are abandoned. Hails go unanswered.

Farther inward, cracked battlecruisers drift amongst spans of debris. Mute wastelands linger between systems. The Core worlds burn in perpetual silence. Scorched earth, salted fields.

It's another future. Not hers, but someone's.

Here, the Sentinels are all that remain of the human race.

Seeing this, she can feel it again, tugging at her core, racing toward her, ever faster, insatiable: the devouring edge of the universe.

For the first time, she wonders if it's aggregate. If the futures they see at the Divide aren't time-fractured ripples of their own possibilities, but instead glimpses of entire other universes. If it's not just the balance of their own mass against their own dark energy, but if by stopping their own collapse, they've put infinite other cosmos and infinite other lives at risk.

She knows one unequivocal truth: The Divide will find a balance, one way or the other. It will get its pound of flesh. It will pit species against species and universe against universe until nothing but stardust remains.

Adequin woke covered in cold sweat.

Her eyes flew open. She pushed to sitting as her hand went to her hip—where her holster should be. But it was still gone.

Her gaze darted, surveying her surroundings. She sat on a cot against the wall of a small ship hold, empty except for a few mismatched crates opposite the sealed cargo hatch.

Her head pounded. She swallowed a flinty, metallic taste and looked down at her knees, pushing aside the olive-drab blanket draped over her legs. She still wore the baggy, gray medical scrubs. At least her bindings were gone.

She rubbed the heels of her palms into her eyes.

A whir sounded, followed by the clang of footsteps on metal. She looked up to find Gideon approaching from the cockpit access hatch. He wore no armor, only a plain T-shirt and cargo pants, his long locs hanging loose over one shoulder as he stopped beside her cot.

"Void, you were really out," he said. "What they hell'd they give you?" He passed her a water bottle. The plastic crinkled in her fingers as she took it.

She shook her head, then took a few gulps of water, the cool liquid smooth against her raw throat. "Where am I?"

"My ship. The *Crucius*."

"And where's the *Crucius*?"

"En route to the *Corinthian*. We should be there any minute."

Her pulse spiked. "What? You need to scan me for trackers, they would have had multiple opportunities to—"

"Hey, I checked," he said, holding up a hand. "Don't worry. You're clear."

She nodded mutely and the surge of adrenaline abated, leaving her already-weary muscles even more taxed. She took another long drink, then looked up at him. "Jack sent you to get me?"

"He did."

She rubbed her dry lips. Gideon's tone thus far had been . . . not scathing. Something was up.

Augustus had said a sacrifice had been made. And the only "sacrifice" she could conceive of her crew attempting would be Cavalon offering himself up in her stead. Which sure as hell better not be the case.

"Where's my crew?" she asked.

"The *Wakeless* already returned safely to the *Corinthian*. They brought back the ceronite, got it loaded up on that mobile garbage heap of yours and everything."

She stretched her jaw while she waited to see if he was done beating around the bush. "Where's *Cavalon*?"

"North will explain everything when we get back."

She held his gaze for a few long moments. He did a decent job of affecting his usual sardonic nonchalance. But he blinked too rapidly, too many times.

Shit.

Fury welled within her. She tossed the water bottle on the cot, then pushed to standing. Gideon caught the blanket as it spilled off her lap, his brow wrinkling.

"Did Cavalon go back to Elyseia?" she demanded. "Tell me."

"You need to rest," Gideon said. He tried to drape the blanket around her shoulders. "You're in shock."

She tugged the blanket off. "I'm not in shock. I was trained for—"

"That doesn't mean you're not in shock," he insisted. A hint of a scowl leaked into his expression. She found it oddly comforting.

The ventilation system kicked on and a cold breeze pricked her skin. Her willingness to argue dwindled as another wave of fatigue hit her limbs.

Gideon picked up the blanket and held it out toward her. "I need to head back to the helm; we'll be decelerating from warp soon. You okay for a few?"

She took the blanket, then sat on the cot. "Yes."

He gave a reluctant nod, then disappeared back into the hatch.

She pulled the blanket around her shoulders and leaned against the cool wall of the hold. She breathed deeply, in through the nose, out through the mouth.

It didn't make sense.

When they were in the lab, Augustus had been more than willing to let Cavalon go. He hadn't wanted him dead, or even captured—he only wanted him gone. So why trade for him?

Maybe he realized Cavalon posed a greater threat than he was willing to admit. Or maybe Cavalon had offered to return the data they'd stolen. She had a hard time seeing that as a meaningful sacrifice, but then again, she didn't know what information had been on there. And she knew now better than ever what Augustus Mercer was capable of. If he'd been that visibly worked up about getting data back, then she didn't even want to know.

Gideon set down in one of the *Corinthian*'s private hangars on the top tier of the vessel. When the cargo ramp lowered, Emery and Owen were already walking through the bay door.

Emery jogged to meet her. Her fierce hug robbed Adequin of breath and didn't let up. With her arms clamped to her sides, Adequin lifted a hand to wave at Owen.

"Hey, sir," Owen said, pressing out a thin smile, eyes round with relief. "Glad to see you safe."

"Rake," Emery breathed, her hold tightening. "I'm so sorry. I can't believe I left you."

"Em—" Adequin choked out. "I can't breathe."

"Shit." Emery let go and took a step back, wiping a knuckle under her eye. "Sorry, sir. Uh, for the hug . . . and leaving you to certain death."

Adequin gripped her shoulder. "Hey, not dead. See?"

Emery pinched her lips, head bobbing.

"And don't apologize," Adequin added. "You followed orders."

"I didn't want to, though."

"Yeah. But sometimes, that's what being a good soldier means." She let out a heavy sigh. Or maybe most of the time.

The bay door slid open, and her eyes drifted past Emery. And onto Cavalon.

Emery stepped aside as Adequin moved toward him, and they closed the meters between them in a few strides.

She locked her arms around him. Dizzying relief washed the fatigue from her limbs. His left arm hung loose, but his right hand clasped the back of her neck, clutching her into his shoulder.

"Thank the void," he mumbled into her hair.

She let go to look him over—his hair was as rumpled as always, but clean and damp, his loose linen shirt freshly laundered. He had a few deep scrapes on his cheek, and a thick wrapping of gauze covered his left wrist . . .

Her face flooded with heat. His hand.

The memory came back to her—the Guardian tackling him out of the dust, the white-hot blade slicing clean through his wrist.

A fresh wave of vindictive fury rolled through her. As if she needed more reasons to want to kill Augustus Mercer. "Shit," she breathed. "I'm so sorry. I got separated—"

"It's not your fault," he said. "We got separated. Let's maybe just . . . not do that anymore." His right hand tightened around hers.

"The ceronite?" she asked.

He gave a shallow nod. "Yeah. Jackin met up with us. We just . . . we needed help."

"But you got it?"

"Yeah. Twice what we need, just in case."

"Good," she said, letting herself enjoy the warm relief loosening her strained shoulders. "Good." She cleared her throat. "Cav, how am I here right now?"

He hesitated, pale cheeks blanching.

"Augustus acted like we took a hit for this," she said. "What happened? I thought maybe you'd try to trade yourself for . . ."

She trailed off along with his forlorn head shake. His bloodshot eyes rounded. "If I thought trading myself would've worked, I'd have done it. In a heartbeat."

An uncomfortable, clawing heat scratched at the base of her neck.

She glanced back at Emery and Owen, who stood at the foot of the *Crucius*'s ramp beside Gideon. All three had averted their gazes.

She looked back at Cavalon. Her heart sped. "Cav . . ." She pushed out a stiff breath. "Where's Jackin?"

His lips parted, impotent, apprehensive.

Gideon's stocky frame appeared in her periphery, but she didn't take her eyes from Cavalon.

"*Cav?*"

Gideon's fingers grazed the back of her arm. "Come with me."

Cavalon's mouth opened wordlessly, his eyes apologetic.

She tore her look away, then followed Gideon out of the hangar.

Numbness descended as Adequin trailed Gideon through the *Corinthian*. They left the public passageways into a secure-access control facility near the center of the ship.

As they walked, Adequin's calf began to burn, sharp pricks of pain clawing into her foot. Her Imprints buzzed sluggishly, too depleted to offer much beyond deadening the spikes of pain. She'd managed to completely forget about getting shot. Augustus must have given her a healthy dose of painkillers.

Finally, Gideon turned down a long corridor lined with inactive ancillary systems consoles. At the end of the hall, he opened a door into a small communications suite. He queued something up on the terminal, then activated a transmission shield.

He made to leave, but paused in the doorway, brow tight while he fished something out of his pocket. A chain with two glass and metal pendants. They clinked together as he passed them to her, then left without a word, door sealing shut behind him.

Adequin's fingers tightened around the dog tags. Her injured leg shook as she lowered herself onto the stool facing the terminal screen. A single file had been queued up. A video recording.

She tapped it open. The recording expanded.

Jackin sat in a pilot's chair, the view of a camera on a ship's console. The filename stamped it as the *Crucius*—Gideon's ship. Only a few hours ago.

Jackin's voice crackled over the speakers. "Hey, boss."

Adequin's ears pulsed in the heavy silence, a soft hissing static lingering during his long pause.

His gaze fell as he scratched his beard before looking back up. "One last sitrep, I guess."

Adequin tried to inhale, but she could only take a shallow, stifled gulp.

Jackin shook his head slowly. "I'd promised myself I'd stop sacrificing for people, but . . . that's not how it works, is it? When you love someone, it's not sacrifice, it's just the thing you're going to do."

A dull warmth swelled in her cheeks. She looked down and forced her hand open. The chain laced between her fingers, the red indendations from the hard edges of the tags dented into the skin of her palm.

"I have a lot to cover . . ." he said. "And not much time. But I want to start with an apology."

She looked back up. Focused on the screen. Drew in a long, deliberate breath to suppress the acidic swell rising in her chest.

"I know we've spent a lot of time arguing since you got back," he went on. "Maybe I've been too hard on you. I don't know. You wanted to lean on me, but I was just as scared of not knowing the right answers as you were." He gave a sluggish shake of his head. "And now I'm just . . . mad at myself. I was trying so hard to be a good second, I forgot to be your friend. I'm sorry for that."

His visage flattened and he rolled his shoulders, drawing his spine straighter.

"I imagine you're wondering how we got here. Why Augustus was willing to trade a former Close Protection operative for a venerated war hero. Well," he croaked, then cleared his throat. "That VIP escort I told you about . . . the reason I'm 'dead.' You were just in her former home."

Adequin froze, mind racing, but he continued before she could fully process it.

"That mission was to escort Corinne Mercer out of the Core, to a secure blacksite." He shook his head, expression slack. "She'd asked for asylum from the Legion, said she'd become a political target, feared for her life. I only found out after we left that it was Augustus she'd run from. She'd discovered something in her research, something dangerous. Something she didn't want him to know about."

He leaned back in the pilot's seat, exhaling a heavy sigh.

"When my CO offered me the mission, I readily accepted. Didn't even blink an eye when there was no risk primer, no training, no backup. I was just so hungry for purpose. I had renounced my life as a Corsair for a job that amounted to an underpaid bodyguard. Taking on a mission of that caliber . . . I felt like I was finally doing something meaningful, for once. Helping affect the change I'd wanted. Or at least, that's how my ego framed it."

He scratched the scarred side of his beard absently, gaze drifting off past the dash.

"When I got back, it didn't take Augustus long to figure out I was connected to her disappearance and track me down. And the Legion didn't do a damn thing to stop it. I didn't have any of the post-op protections slated for a mission like that—nothing more than a twenty-minute debrief and a lie detector test. It's like they wanted me to take the fall. And . . . maybe they did."

He scrubbed his knuckles over his chin, then let out a resounding sigh.

"So, yeah. You've seen the scars. Suffice to say, I doubled down. I actually managed to convince myself it was a test. That if I held out, I'd finally prove my allegiance. I still, somehow, held a torch for the Legion and what I thought it represented. What I thought the SC could be. That resolve fueled me, and I got damn good at keeping it from him. Regardless of how good he was at keeping me alive through it. But he wasn't as methodical then as he is now. He was acting out of emotion, and being sloppy, and it cost him. Eventually, Lugen extracted me."

Adequin twitched, her trance interrupted at the mention of her former CO. She bit the inside of her lip, iron hitting her tongue as she fixated on the screen.

Jackin stared right at the camera, right at her, one eyebrow lifted. "Yeah," he sighed, tone resigned. "That was the first I'd learned of his involvement in any of this too." He licked his dry lips, giving a grim shake of his head. "Apparently, he was the one Corinne had made her plea to. He'd done what he could to facilitate, then handed down the actualization orders to the CPD. At that point, they'd screwed it up enough, he had to step back in to clean it up. I still don't know how he got me out of there without Augustus knowing the Legion was involved.

"That's when I got a new identity and he placed me as CNO—to keep me out of the Core and on a capital ship. One of the safest places in the galaxy . . . except the Divide. Which is where I ended up mid-war after Augustus found me again."

He sat stock-still, eyebrows pinched, downcast. He almost looked ashamed.

"That's a long story," he went on, tone flat, diluted. "Let's just say, I . . . escaped before they got me very far.

"After that, Lugen admitted how hard it'd be to continue keeping me safe. So he staged my death, sent me out to the Divide, said things would calm down after the war, maybe Augustus would finally let it go, but . . ." He ground his teeth, a bitter, dark look gleaming in his eyes as his voice hardened again. "I know Lugen risked a lot . . . but that was only to cover his own tracks. He knew if I ever broke, Corinne's trail would lead back to him. At best, high command turns a blind eye to everything Augustus does—at worst, they fucking cover it up *for* him. They're the reason he has so much unchecked power.

"Regardless of what they'd like everyone to believe, the Legion isn't some neutral bystander in the bureaucratic pissing match that is the

System Collective. They're just as corrupt as the Quorum or the Allied Monarchies, and you should never forget that. After the *Argus*, you weren't ready to accept that. You still held a candle for them, just like I did, for far too long. But at least you know better now; you still have a chance to escape the Legion's clutches. And hopefully the SC's."

The tendons in his neck flexed as he leaned against the pilot's chair.

"So, that's it, Rake. That's why I've been such a cagey jerk all these years. I never thought I'd care about someone enough for any of this to matter again . . ." He let out a long sigh, tone growing heavy. "But now we're all in the thick of it. I can't keep you from it anymore. I'd assumed the Resurgence would be the war that'd define our generation. But that war's still on its way. And I want you to be ready."

He inhaled deeply, shoulders drawing back.

"Before I left, I had Abraham's attorneys draft conveyance paperwork and start the process of contesting my death certificate. When it clears, the Corsairs' assets will transfer to you."

Adequin's lips parted, and she stared unblinking at the screen.

"The Sentinels are going to need allies," Jackin explained. "It's the only thing I have to give, and I hope it helps. Gideon will help you manage Akemi if you get on his good side. Which I know you will." He tilted his head and winced slightly, tone softening. "Maybe just not . . . *too* good. He and I haven't always seen eye-to-eye on things, but you can trust him, if you can tolerate him. He's a good man."

He glanced down, scratching at his wrist as a stark white slash of Imprints cut across his light brown skin.

"I never got that crash course you promised. But I'll figure it out. Maybe they'll help me this time around." He looked back up. "I'll hold out as long as I can. I don't have the vindictive resolve of my youth anymore, but I know what's at stake. And I'm willing to die protecting it."

He rubbed his lips, squeezing his eyes shut for a few long seconds before refocusing on the camera.

"But he won't kill me. Not till he gets what he needs from me—Corinne. And I can't give him that. I can only hope you'll . . ." His gaze drifted to something high on the dash. He looked back at the camera. "Our new centurion will have something for you when you get back."

Adequin's brow creased, caught off guard by the change in tone. He'd meant Puck, but what the hell was he talking about?

"Someone needed to know in case we didn't come back," he explained. "In case *I* didn't come back. Rake, use it, and use it fast. Then the Sentinels . . ." He shook his head slowly, and a bitter smile tugged at one corner of his mouth. "I'd planned to show you myself. I wanted to see the look on your face. And see you in the light of a real sun for the first time . . ."

He wiped his forehead and let out a hard breath.

"I wanted to be with you for this, Rake, I really did. Both to relish the wins, and to help shoulder the losses. But I know you're ready, or you will be." His tone wavered, taking on an earnest edge. "You have to take the time. After everyone's safe, stop being a soldier for like, a minute. Maybe two. Let yourself be sad, be lonely. *Miss* him . . . *Then* be furious. Get fuckin' angry. Go do what I never could, and raze the whole broken system in your wake."

He ran his thumb over the scar on his cheek, down his neck to his collar. He licked his lips slowly, and his gaze hardened.

"I'm going to make you promise me something, since you're not here to refuse . . ." He paused, eyes lingering on the camera, as if waiting for her to listen. "Don't come after me."

She stared, her heartbeat growing suddenly sluggish, heavy. Her fist clenched, the hard edges of his tags cutting into her palm.

"Do your job," he went on. "Get the Sentinels to safety. For the love of the void, do not attempt a rescue. Augustus *wants* you to rally the troops and come after me. He wants an excuse to enact martial law—don't do it."

A dense heat pressed against her temples. She took in a thin breath, struggling to regain control through the knifelike stab of pain beneath her sternum.

"Earlier," Jackin continued, voice low and scratchy, "when I said you'd been leaning on me so much . . . honestly, I relished it. That you felt like I could offer you even a shred of advice. That's the kind of difference I'd always wanted to make." He frowned, shaking his head. "But that was just arrogance. Feeling wanted, needed. That's never gotten me anything but pain. And I don't want you to carry that same burden. So I have to ask this . . . and I need you to take it to heart, please, Rake." He wiped a hand across his glistening eyes. "I need you to not need me."

He leaned forward and the video cut off.

CHAPTER THIRTY

Adequin didn't bother wiping the tears from her cheeks as she stepped out of the comms suite. Gideon waited, leaning against one of the consoles lining the hall. His eyebrows climbed slowly, and he stood as she walked toward him. Fingers shaking, she fastened Jackin's dog tags around her neck along with hers and Griffith's.

"So," she said, voice hoarse, "that's what you meant by 'North will explain everything when we get back,' huh?"

He wavered his head back and forth in a noncommittal shrug. "It wasn't a *lie*."

"Did you watch it?"

"No."

A hard breath escaped her lips as that damn razor-sharp pain drilled into her chest again. She closed her eyes, plying her knuckles into her sternum. She inhaled a slow, controlled breath, took hold of the rising tide, and dragged it back down.

Then she turned toward the wall, leaned over, and threw up on the floor beside the console. Cold sweat pricked her forehead and her throat burned.

Gideon patted her back tentatively. She wiped the corners of her mouth, an acrid warmth rolling through her, threatening to tighten around her stomach again. She took a few long breaths until the nausea settled.

"Okay," she croaked, forcing her spine straight, then facing Gideon. "*Now* I might be in shock."

He gave a sympathetic grimace.

"Why didn't you tell me?" she accused.

"He made me promise to get you back here first."

She ground her teeth. Of *course* he did. "I'm surprised you'd be willing to keep promises to him," she said. "You act like you hate him."

He let out a crackling sigh. "There's some tension, yes . . . but it's more a brotherly thing."

"You weren't overly brotherly when we first came asking for help."

"No. But if I had known you guys were going up against the Mercers . . . Well. It would have changed things."

She sighed. "Yeah, well. That wasn't part of the original plan."

"Yeah . . ." He rubbed his chin, looking her over. "You know, I might consider mounting a brotherly rescue if I had a Titan by my side."

She met his dark brown eyes. There was a hint of challenge there.

But also . . . determination. He was serious.

She bit the inside of her lip. The Corsairs had serious resources at their disposal. Though not enough to consider any kind of direct assault against the manor, or wherever they were holding him. Finding out where he was would be a massive undertaking all on its own. It'd take weeks of digging up leads, of reconnecting with old contacts, establishing a network of trustworthy sources. Then planning the extraction, executing it, and of course, accounting for the aftermath. They couldn't simply snatch Jackin and run away. Augustus would hunt down every Corsair in the galaxy and start executing them until they came forward. His reach was too wide. For it to ever truly be over, they would have to capture him, or kill him. That would have to be part of the plan going in.

It'd make them terrorists instead of liberators . . . but it *could* work. The Corsairs could be the weapon she wielded to end it.

But at what cost?

She met Gideon's flinty gaze. "It's him, or four thousand of my soldiers."

Gideon cocked his head, jaw skimming back and forth a few times. "Simple math on paper, yeah, but . . ."

Adequin's Imprints energized along with a swell of bitter fury. Her hands tightened to fists.

Adequin steeled her composure and followed Gideon through the maze of inner hallways to Jackin's apartment. She thanked him, and he left.

She stood outside the door to collect herself, then tapped the controls and stepped in.

Cavalon, Emery, Owen, and Ford sat in silence in the sunken sitting area. They stood as she entered, their expressions blanched with confusion and worry. Except Ford's. His was nothing but furious.

She stepped down to join them. Emery held a glass of amber liquid out toward her. She took it, threw it back in one gulp, and dropped the glass back into Emery's hand. She looked down, putting her hands on her hips as the warm whiskey settled in her stomach.

"What's the plan, boss?" Emery asked warily.

Adequin drew in a steadying breath. They stared at her, awaiting her decision.

Gideon's mention of math had awoken something in her: a nodule of hard logic buried deep in her chest. One she'd resisted for so long, but had been cultivating beneath the surface over the years. Lugen had stoked it in her a decade ago, and Jackin had been struggling to pull it forth ever since they fled the *Argus*.

Jackin was right. Going after him would not only be selfish, it'd be immoral. For what would likely be a vain recovery attempt, thousands would die—along with the end of what might be the only chance the SC had at standing against Augustus Mercer and his eugenics war. There was so much more at stake than the Sentinels.

She had always let her heart guide her. But that wasn't always the right thing to do.

The guilt of leaving him behind should consume her. Maybe it would, someday. For now, she had to do what was right for her soldiers. The Sentinels needed her. And she had to not need him anymore.

"No change," she said, tone steady. "We take the ceronite back to the Divide."

Ford's shoulders swelled. "Sir—respectfully—the hell we are."

"It's what North would have wanted," Owen said.

"Fuck all to what he wants!" Ford roared. "We can't leave him there!"

Emery gnashed her gum with a folded brow. "Sir, I gotta agree. How can we leave one of our own behind?"

Cavalon let out a bitter scoff. "You already know exactly how—you just did it a few hours ago."

Emery's chin dropped.

"*Dude*," Owen admonished.

Cavalon glowered. "We wouldn't even be having this discussion in the first place if you'd waited for Rake—"

"There was no waiting!" Emery retorted, her pale cheeks ablaze. "We were gonna get shot down—"

"You're a Titan," Ford accused, ignoring the others and facing Adequin squarely. "This is your job."

Adequin shook her head. "An extraction of that magnitude takes resources and intelligence and *time*. None of which we have at the moment."

"So, what?" Ford scoffed, furious. "We go back for him later? No fucking way."

"The longer we leave him there, the worse off he'll be," Cavalon agreed. She met his haunted gaze. "He'll break him. You know he will."

Adequin gave a firm shake of her head. "That's a risk we have to take. He didn't give himself up so we could all get ourselves killed trying to save him."

Ford growled. "He's already gone through this once; how the hell can you stand by and let it happen again?"

"That's *enough*, Circitor." Her hard tone silenced their bickering, ringing loud in the sudden quiet. She glowered at each of them in turn, jaw set. "Everyone seems to be under the impression that this is up for discussion. It's fucking not. The decision's been made. We take the ceronite back to the *Lodestar*. We save four thousand Sentinels. That's what Jackin wants, and that's what we're doing. End of discussion."

Emery chewed on her fingernails with a knit brow, Owen gave an apologetic frown, and Cavalon stood slouched, drained, wearing his fatigue like a mantle. Ford's anger was still palpable, but he didn't look like he intended to push the issue.

"Listen," Adequin said evenly. "You know I want him back. But sometimes the decision you *want* to make, isn't the one you *can*."

She stepped up out of the sitting area and headed for the exit.

"Flight checks in twenty."

CHAPTER THIRTY-ONE

There was a long, rhythmic pulse conveyed by the *Synthesis*'s chassis-mounted warp dampener coils, which only someone lying facedown on the floor for hours would notice.

Cavalon was in the unique position to appreciate the steady vibration frequency of his cabin's decking, interrupted every thirteen minutes by the atmospheric cycler, and every twenty-nine minutes when the energy converter apportioned power. All like clockwork, except the HVAC, which had kicked on randomly at least fourteen times. Which, all things considered in their little closed system, should *not* be in a state of ongoing adjustment. An occasional correction here or there, sure. But it shouldn't need to remedy itself seven times an hour. Which meant something, somewhere in the ship was either generating too much heat, or not enough.

He'd nearly summoned the will to get up and hunt down the thermal leech and vanquish it, before he remembered one small detail: He didn't have a fucking left hand anymore. That'd complicate attempts at drowning his misery with mechanical engineering.

His pulse threatened to elevate again, so he refocused on the vibrations and cyclic pulsing. On the banal, yet infuriating inefficiency of the climate system. On how around every corner in this ship, there lurked a new take on latent Drudger BO.

At least the *Synthesis* felt like a real, lived-in ship. It'd earned its idiosyncrasies tenfold. Unlike that damn prototype they'd been on. The one that'd made such irresponsibly short work of getting them to Elyseia. The one that'd allowed them to delude themselves into thinking it was safe and sane to walk into Mercer Manor. The one that'd left Rake behind. And the one that'd taken Cavalon back to safety while Jackin flew to his death.

Cavalon hated that ship.

"Cav . . . ?" Owen's voice.

His jaw loosened, releasing the clamp his teeth had on his inner cheek. "Hey," he mumbled into the floor, not looking up. He'd feel worse about not being a gracious host, but yeah. Fuck that.

Clothes rustled, and he could sense Owen sit on the floor beside him. "You weren't responding on comms," she said.

"Sorry. Nexus is kinda . . ." He lifted his left arm in a limp flop. He hadn't had the mental energy to figure out how he was going to keep his nexus band on his forearm without a hand to stop it from falling off. The only reason it hadn't in the first place was because the band had been partly seared to his cauterized flesh from the heat of the plasma blade.

Owen audibly swallowed. "Wanna tell me what the hell's going on?"

"Just waiting here on the floor until my shift starts."

"I mean, should we talk about how you got us into that ceronite factory?"

"I think you already know how."

She let out a grating breath. "Void. That fucker is such a damn nightmare excuse for a human." She rubbed a reassuring hand over his back. Or rather, an attempt at reassurance. "I'm sorry, CJ."

"I think my father knew."

Her hand stopped. "About himself? Or you?"

"Both."

"Really?"

"I don't think there's any way he couldn't have."

"Do you think that's why he . . ." Fabric rustled, and her nails clicked as if she'd started picking at her cuticles. "Sorry. Never mind."

He squeezed his eyes tighter, tasting salt as a series of tears failed to escape the lines of his face and pooled between his lips. "He lied to me my whole life."

"Because he loved you," she countered. "He wanted you to have a happy childhood—or at least, not a *worse* one. And the only way to do that would have been to keep it from you."

Cavalon pressed his forehead hard into the metal floor. "You had something?"

"What?"

"You said you tried to call me on comms."

"Oh. Right."

A small metallic object clicked against the floor beside his right ear.

"The files you downloaded from the manor finished decrypting," she explained. "I figured you might want to see it before we get back to the *Lodestar* and have to pass it off to Intel."

He tried to nod, but just ended up squishing his nose into the floor a few times.

"You gonna be okay, bud?"

"Yeah. I'll be fine. Just not feeling super sociable at the moment."

"I get it." She rubbed his shoulder again. "Try to get some sleep, okay?"

"Okay."

She stood, hesitated at the door for a long while, then left.

Owen was right. He should sleep. But he didn't value common sense very much.

His right hand closed around the data chip.

He pushed to standing, then almost fell over as blood rushed to his head, and he barely caught himself on the edge of the small sofa. After his vision righted, he shuffled to his bed.

He pinned his ruck awkwardly with his left elbow, yanking a few times before getting it unzipped. He pulled his partially melted nexus band from the pocket of the dust-laden cargo pants he'd worn on Elyseia, unable to think of a single reason past Cavalon had decided to keep the stupid things. Probably so he could be reminded of the worst day of his life every time he opened his ruck.

He dropped his nexus on the table in front of the sofa and sat, exhaling a creaking groan as he leaned forward and affixed the chip to the band. He activated the holographic interface, opened the archive, and began surveying the files.

It took less than ten minutes for him to wholeheartedly regret his decision.

He closed the display with an exhausted swipe of two fingers.

Fucking hell. Cloning humans and raising children in hidden labs wasn't enough. It always had to be one more thing. Shitbaggery begets shitbaggery.

He leaned forward, elbows on knees, pressing his hand against his face. The political threat Augustus posed did *not* need to be bolstered by a physical one. He wasn't equipped to deal with it. None of them were.

Why did everything always have to get worse? He was truly sick of it. He'd already had to leave an innocent kid behind, then Rake, then Jackin. And who knew what kind of dystopic shitshow they'd find upon returning to the *Lodestar*. Enough was enough.

Fucking Owen. He'd done a masterful job of repressing everything until she'd shown up.

A small voice in the back of his head slapped him, saying, "No, *stop that you idiot, that's the old you talking, the one that blamed everyone else for everything and pushed everyone away and achieved staggering levels of self-destructive narcissism.*"

Thankfully, he had a decade of experience ignoring that voice. It was quite possibly his most proficient skill.

What was the point? They could fly back to the *Lodestar*, pose as the "victors" of some grand expedition, install the ceronite and jump everyone to void-knows-where, plant some crops and commandeer some ships and ransack some abandoned supply depots. That'd be just fine. Not starving to death would be great, in fact.

But that timeline had gone from nebulous to completely unrealistic. Augustus was many, many things, but not stupid.

The moment Jackin had called, Augustus would have started to put the pieces together of what it all meant—of Cavalon showing up with an exiled war hero, of a former CNO trading his life for hers. It'd only be a matter of time before he addressed it, decisively.

Cavalon closed his eyes and let out a slow breath.

Fate of the galaxy be damned, his mind would not stop going back to that damn kid. His skin crawled. He'd never not felt trapped in Mercer Manor, but he'd almost never *literally* been trapped there. That kid not only had no choice, but likely had no idea he was even being held against his will.

Then there was the time they'd left Rake at Augustus's mercy. If Cavalon hadn't been so insistent on trying to get the kid out, those few minutes might have made the difference between them both being able to escape. Then Jackin wouldn't have had to make a deal, and instead of being tortured by Augustus for the rest of his life, he could be with them now, inflicting Cavalon with that disappointed scowl for having attempted something so blatantly dangerous mere hours after promising he'd pull the plug if things went lateral.

Then again, maybe Jackin had been expecting too much from someone who amounted to a failed science experiment—a defective copy of a genocidal maniac.

Bloody void . . . He was a clone of Augustus.

The bare thought hit him so unexpectedly, he flinched. He scrubbed his right hand through his hair and down his face, scratching hard at his beard.

Snyder and all his OCR cronies had been right. Cavalon really had been the bad guy all along. More literally than any of them ever imagined.

The nodule of pressure building in his chest matured into a festering tumor—a lump with all the acidity of bile and the simmering pus of an infection, wrapped in an all-too-familiar casing of rampant self-hatred. He'd had plenty of reasons to despise himself over the years, but now he had *the* reason.

For hours, he'd been able to hold back the tide. Ignore it. Pretend he was okay by suppressing it like a reasonable, adjusted, competent adult human. But he wasn't actually any one of those things. Not nearly.

He needed . . . something.

The medbay was quiet, dimly lit and a bit eerie, still strewn with evidence of Jackin's prior occupancy—unopened gauze packs, clotting and tissue-knitting cartridges, and a transfusion kit hanging on the wall.

Cavalon ignored it all as he dug through cabinet after cabinet, crate after crate, shoving aside saline cartridges and bandages and extra biotools. He wiped sweat from his brow with the inside of his elbow. His left-handlessness made ransacking really, really difficult, and he didn't fucking appreciate it.

They'd stocked this medbay to the gills before they left the *Lodestar* and supplemented their stores before leaving the *Corinthian*. It had to be somewhere.

"Hey, lad . . ."

Cavalon glanced over his shoulder to find Ford looking ominous and unreasonably tall in the dim light of the door frame.

"Everything okay?" Ford asked.

"Yeah no. I need some apex." He pressed on a frown and rubbed his left forearm, then mumbled, "It's not even there anymore, and it still hurts."

Void, what a devious fucking thing to say.

Knowing he was being a lying jerk didn't stop him from grimacing as if racked with pain.

Ford stepped inside, moving to the far right of the room in a strange, languid arc. He stopped on the opposite side of the exam table. "Not sure apexidone is the best choice for that kinda pain," he said.

"No, I . . ." Cavalon's pulse beat hot in his throat. "It's right. It needs to be apex."

"Does it?" Ford asked, tone even.

"Yeah. I mean, I know what works for me, is all."

"I'm not sure ya do."

Cavalon stared at him, at the tense way he held his shoulders, at his arms crossed tight over his chest. Then he realized the reason for Ford's meandering entrance path: He'd put himself between Cavalon and the far cabinets. One of the only places he hadn't looked.

Cavalon skirted the exam table.

"Now, lad . . ." Ford said, a hint of hard warning in his tone. He took a large step back, then gripped Cavalon's arm as he tried to pass, pulling him back toward the table.

Copper tinged Cavalon's saliva as his Imprints surged into his right shoulder and he drove his fist forward.

Ford started to step back, but took the hit square on the chin. He cringed and retreated, his long legs taking him well out of Cavalon's reach.

Cavalon stalked after him.

"EX to medbay, stat," Ford growled into his nexus just before crossing his arms to block Cavalon's wildly telegraphed right hook. All he fucking had now was a right hook.

Ford took another large step back, arms raised to defend, but hands loose and open in a pacifistic manner that only worked to stoke Cavalon's fury. He feinted left and as Ford moved to block, Cavalon drew a low cross under the man's elbows and hit him in the stomach. Ford grunted out a hard breath.

Cavalon's face burned, raw adrenaline fueling his weary muscles. He kept pressing, and Ford kept up his cowardly retreat, blocking, dodging, and rolling away, taking them on a long, curving arc around the perimeter of the medbay.

Until suddenly, from over Cavalon's shoulder came a narrow, scarred, olive-skinned arm covered with shifting silver and copper Imprint squares. Fucking Rake.

She crushed her forearm against his throat. He tore at it but couldn't get free of the hold. He struggled for breath until blurred vision and hot tears converged into blackness.

CHAPTER THIRTY-TWO

Adequin sat on the floor beside Cavalon's bunk, trying not to be pissed at herself. She should have seen this coming.

After the manor, Cavalon had pushed forward. Continued on and gotten the job done despite everything he'd learned. But now they'd entered a lull. She knew from experience what that really meant: time to process—a far more intimidating proposition than to keep fighting.

She ran stiff hands down her face and exhaled a long breath. He would have to deal with what he'd learned. But he couldn't relapse. He couldn't fall apart, not now, not ever.

Augustus had been right about one thing—the way to win this wouldn't be through military strength alone. The Sentinels could turn every legionnaire outside the Core, but if Augustus had the hearts and minds of the people and government—and control of the media—then they'd be framed as nothing more than terrorists, inciting wanton destruction. They would have to fight on two fronts. And they'd need Cavalon—alive and sober—for both.

Cavalon let out a soft grumble. He shifted, grimacing, and his eyes opened to slits, shaded in the dim light of the bunk's alcove. He blinked at her for a few seconds, then his fingers drifted to his throat. "You . . . knocked me out?" he rasped.

"I did."

His brow furrowed. "Why am I not in the brig?"

"Should you be?"

"You're right. Airlock's safer."

"I'm not spacing you."

"I'm the literal enemy. You need to get rid of me."

"I'm not getting rid of you."

"I could be a sleeper agent."

"You're not a sleeper agent."

"How do you know?" he shot back, petulant challenge in his tone. "He can control the Drudger clones. Why not his human ones as well?"

"You think if he could control you, he'd have let you do anything you've done the last six months? Or twenty-eight years?"

He let out a barely audible grunt.

She watched him stare at the ceiling. "Were you really looking for apex?" she asked.

He didn't respond, face slack with apathy.

She twisted toward the bed to face him, drawing in a long breath, taking her time as she searched for the right words. "There's something you said to me," she began, voice soft, "back when we restarted that first dark energy generator. After my harness ripped, and I fell, and you came after me. You said that if we didn't have a good hold on each other, you might lose me."

His lashes fluttered, but his expression remained unchanged.

"After what happened with Griffith, it stuck with me," she went on. "With every generator I restarted, I couldn't stop thinking about it . . . how easy it is to get complacent. To let go of people and not realize you've even lost your grip." She chewed the inside of her lip, grazing her thumb over the cluster of tags underneath her shirt. "I think I did that with Jackin. I never meant to. I was so focused on what I needed from him, I lost sight of what he needed from me. I feel like I let go."

Cavalon's gaze flicked down, the corners of his eyes glistening.

"I don't intend to make that mistake again," she said, tone wavering. "I won't let you go."

His brows knit and his eyes closed, pressing a few tears into trails down his cheeks.

"It doesn't matter where you came from," she said. "How you were brought into this universe. All I know is the man I see here now. And he's not in any way the man I met back there—imperious, self-righteous, manipulative . . . wielding information like a weapon, holding it to your neck like a blade." She cleared the thickness from her throat. "When we met, you told me you weren't your grandfather, and I asked you to prove it. And you did, in spades. Never forget that."

His eyes remained closed, and more tears chased the first. He didn't respond for a long while.

Finally, his right hand drifted across the surface of the bed toward her. She took it.

He tried to wipe at his face with his gauze-covered left arm, then frowned. "This is not the battle-damaged version I had in mind for myself."

She lifted a brow. "The battle . . . what?"

He sighed. "I was thinking a menacing eyebrow scar or something."

She reached over and wiped his cheeks for him. He cast a weary smile.

"You know, you have options." She sat back on her feet.

"Regrowth?" He grimaced out the word like it was a contagious disease. "I've heard that's, uh . . . traumatic."

"Yeah," she consented, "but I've known plenty of people who've done it. It's painful, and takes a long time, but it turns out good as new."

"Yeah," he sighed heavily. "I think I'd rather have a prosthesis. The less of me that's . . . well, *him*, the better I'll feel."

"Understandable. Good cybernetics aren't cheap, but it sounds like you have the cash to cover it."

"Not if I'm gonna give all my money to the Sentinels."

She scoffed. "What?"

"We're gonna need cash." He turned on his side to face her, brow quirked. "How else do you plan to keep feeding all those starving Sentinels we're trying so damn hard to save?"

"Well, yeah, but—"

"I'm giving you all my money, okay? I don't wanna hear another word about it."

"Well . . . okay. In that case, I think we can find room in the budget for your hand."

He gave a weak grin. "Thanks, but I'd rather just continue suffering if it's all the same to you."

"Yep. There's the defeatism. Things were getting too optimistic for my liking."

He smiled, but the amusement slid from his expression seconds later, and he stared past her silently for a long while. When he spoke again, his voice came low and hoarse. "Was it worth it, Rake?"

She drew in a deep breath. "We got what we needed to get everyone back to the galaxy. That's all that matters."

"But at what cost?" He returned his bloodshot eyes to her. "What did you have to sacrifice for that?"

"What *we* sacrificed," she corrected, tamping down on her quickening pulse. "The Sentinels lost a great leader. Probably their best one."

"Sure," he said, tone dismissive, "but *you* cared about him. Personally. How many people are you gonna let the universe take from you?"

She held his gaze for a few long heartbeats, unable to look away, wishing she had a better answer. But that was just what the universe did. It took. That was its prerogative.

"We can't give up," she said, tone firm. She focused on that thread of strength she could call on even when she wasn't sure of her own words. "We're too deep in this. Just like when we were caught in that dark energy wave, there's nothing we can do but go along for the ride. Try to save the ones we can, and . . . let go of the ones we can't."

Cavalon rubbed his eyes, then rolled onto his back and let out a particularly resounding sigh. "Speaking of 'the ride' . . . Owen gave me the decrypted archive from Augustus's lab terminal."

A spear of dread nagged at her barely gathered resolve. Shit.

"I was looking it over," he continued, "before I, uh . . . found the need to plunder the medbay."

"Do I even want to know?" she asked.

"Probably not."

"Tell me anyway."

"Well, I only looked through maybe ten percent of it. I wouldn't call it evidence, but . . . I'm pretty sure I can infer the meaning. He's designing a genetic weapon."

She blinked, lips suddenly very dry. "For . . . Wait, a what?"

"It looks like it auto-targets mutated nucleotides," he answered, like that explained something. "Or at least, that's what it's meant to do. There was data missing, there must be a component he's still working on, or he's keeping phases segregated on other terminals."

"Wait, back up," she said. "'Auto-targeting mutated whatever' means what?"

"Well, uh . . . basically, it means it'd terminate hosts with mutagen defects. Though, not only those caused by the Viator mutagen. I think it'd trigger for all 'defects'—natural or otherwise, good or bad, active or dormant. Anything that doesn't meet the 'standard' coded into the weapon."

She pinched the bridge of her nose. What the *hell*, Augustus? "Bloody void," she breathed. "And it's a weapon? Like a bomb?"

"No. At least, I don't think so. Like I said, it's missing some pieces, the research seems fragmented. My guess is, it'd be a virus. Something that could be easily disseminated—and difficult to trace. Then when they send him samples to 'see what happened,' he can be all, '*Oh no, such a tragedy. Their genomes were weak and inferior to begin with, though, so something like this was bound to happen.*' I mean, honestly . . ." He exhaled another sigh. "It makes perfect sense. It's the ultimate eugenic solution—no need to keep finding creative ways to subjugate the people you find objectionable if you just outright kill them." He scrubbed his right hand through his hair. "Though the even scarier thing is how easily it could get out of hand."

"How so?" she asked, not sure she wanted the answer.

"That's the thing with the bio part of biotech. You think you're making this very tailored, designer weapon, but then—*oh shit*—it mutates, and it thinks *everyone's* DNA has 'defects' and then, well. Then *everyone's* dead."

Her brow knit. "Surely he knows that, though?"

"Oh, he knows," Cavalon assured. "He just doesn't care. To him, it's an acceptable risk."

Adequin pressed her face into her hands. "Why is he like this . . ." she mumbled, scrubbing her palms against her cheeks.

"Do you really want to know?" he asked, the strained levity falling from his tone.

She dropped her hands, lifting a brow. "It was rhetorical, but, yeah, I do. He said his parents died of mutagen defects, but is that really what this is all about?"

Cavalon's brow creased. "He told you that?"

She nodded.

"Damn." He rubbed his fingers over his lips, then added almost under his breath, "You musta really gotten under his skin."

"Why? Not common knowledge?"

"No. It's kind of a . . . family secret. The official story is a skylane accident. Faulty route sensors or something. He didn't want the truth getting out, besmirching the Mercer name. So he covered it up."

She leaned an elbow on the top of the mattress, resting her head in her hand. "Even back then, he was scheming."

"Yeah," he agreed with a sigh.

"Do you know what actually happened?" she asked.

Cavalon licked his lips slowly. "I only know what my grandmother told my father, who told me, but, I guess they were both sick for a long time. For years, Augustus worked night and day on cures. They suffered along the way—both from their illnesses, and from his attempted treatments." He shifted onto his shoulder, then met her eye, tone cautionary. "He kept them alive longer than . . . well, than he should have. To buy himself more time."

"Like, cryogenics?"

Cavalon's dry lips parted with a hitched breath as he shook his head mutely. "No."

She stared, head buzzing. She found it strange now, seeing the honest and sober fear in his brilliant blue eyes, that she ever thought they resembled Augustus's.

He cleared his throat, sweeping his hair away from his forehead. "So, when they died regardless of his efforts, he held himself responsible. He was supposed to be the foremost authority in genetic engineering, so in his mind, if even *he* couldn't save them, then humanity had a big problem. One he intends to fix, no matter the cost."

Adequin chewed on the inside of her cheek, worry nagging at the back of her mind. Worry, because she at once felt sympathetic, mad at herself for feeling sympathetic, and afraid . . . because really, it was empathy, not sympathy. She understood Augustus's reaction all too well, because she'd felt it herself. He wanted vengeance. Reparations for his parents' deaths . . . But it'd been directed at something that was impossible to change. Something that'd become an intrinsic part of the human race—the Viator mutagen. Now he was trying to rewrite centuries of history, and he didn't care who suffered or died in the process. He truly thought his genetic cleansing was a service to humanity.

"To be honest," Cavalon scoffed, hard and bitter, "I get it. Most of the Mercer legacy is built on our efforts during the Viator War—both reverse-engineering the mutagen to create a version we could unleash on the Viators, and slowing the cascade of mutations in humans. We were supposed to save humanity. But the longer this goes unresolved, the longer it seems like . . . maybe it was nothing but a shitty patch job. Maybe we did screw it up. Maybe it's too late."

"No." She gave a firm shake of her head. "There's got to be some way to fix it outside of just . . . *executing* everyone with mutagen defects."

"There is—kind of. The correction treatments. You know," he snorted, tone resentful, "the ones people are pressed into lifelong indentured servitude to pay off, if they even *can* in their lifetime. Then their kids are too poor and have to work their own corrections off, then *their* kids are too poor—and so on and so forth, the systemic wheel turns."

She rubbed the back of her neck. "Don't suppose Mercer Biotech wants to hand out the treatments to everyone free of charge?"

He sighed. "Well, no. But even if they did, it's not that simple. A lot of the mutagen's behaviors still elude us, and not every mutation can even be treated to start with. And those with corrected mutations can still pass defects on to their offspring, and those might not surface for generations, so they end up silent carriers. That's part of what's made it so elusive. The Viators made it . . . really fucking well. We act like the Mercers of old were all prodigies of genetic engineering, but the Viators in their heyday were so *massively* beyond better than us, that even almost five hundred years later, we're still trying to figure it out."

"So . . ." she said, voice haggard, "are you saying he's right?"

"No. Yes. I don't know." He scrubbed a hand over his eyes, huffing out a hard breath. "Either way, it doesn't make what he's doing any less monstrous."

She laid her forehead on the edge of the bed. Clamping her eyes shut, she drew in a slow breath, warm against the wrinkled sheets.

"Sorry," Cavalon said. "I don't mean to put this on you. I probably shouldn't have even brought it up."

She looked back up. "No, you were right to tell me. Besides, he's our lodestar, remember?" A glint of bitter amusement lit in his eye. "We've always got to be looking that direction," she went on. "We'll handle it. Somehow."

He nodded and laid his head back against the pillow. "I'm sorry I punched Ford."

She coughed a dry laugh. "It's okay, but you should probably tell *Ford* that."

"I will." Cavalon's gaze went distant, the blond and gray of his beard looking dark against the washed-out paleness of his cheeks.

"You know, my room stinks like a Drudger's armpit," she said.

He blinked once, and his gaze drifted onto her. "That sucks."

"Care if I bunk on your couch till we get back?"

He didn't respond at first, and she could practically see his wheels turning. He wanted to be tough about it, to convince himself he wouldn't relapse, that he didn't need her to babysit him. After all this time, he still wasn't used to people trying to keep him healthy and alive. And ideally *happy*, though that was a big ask at the moment.

But she didn't have to encourage him, or think up another excuse, because he replied with a quiet, "Yeah. Okay." A little color returned to his cheeks. "If you need to."

"Thanks."

CHAPTER THIRTY-THREE

Five days later, Adequin guided the *Synthesis* into one of the *Lodestar*'s hangar bays.

She put the ship in standby, grabbed the atlas pyramid, and met the others at the personnel hatch. Emery and Owen offered heartening smiles and Cavalon gripped her shoulder. Ford stood facing the hatch and didn't look over. Other than calling her to the medbay to subdue Cavalon, he hadn't spoken to her the entire trip.

The ramp lowered, and she was reminded of when she'd first returned to the *Lodestar* over two weeks ago. Though their circumstances were even worse now, the dread of forthcoming responsibility didn't settle on her in quite the same way. It was there, certainly, lingering beneath the surface. But there was no one to fall back on now. With Jackin gone, she would have to take the reins, and take them firmly. Or the mutiny he'd feared could easily become reality.

The ramp clanked to a stop. At the bottom, Puck and Mesa stood waiting, expressions a mixture of worry and hope.

As Adequin descended toward them, Puck snapped a salute, fist to chest. "Excubitor, welcome back. Good to see you safe." Dark bags hung under his eyes and his bronze skin had a sickly yellow undertone. He'd always been thin, but he seemed even lankier, the fabric of his uniform loose around his arms and torso.

Mesa didn't appear to have fared much better, though her naturally small frame within the boxy Legion uniform made it more difficult to see the effects. The Savant's overlarge eyes rounded as she noticed Cavalon's left arm. His cheeks reddened as he cradled the elbow closer.

"Er, *mostly* safe," Puck corrected himself with a frown. His eyes darted between the five of them. "Where's North?"

Ford tensed.

"I'll explain later," Adequin replied. "Ford?"

"Sir."

"Take Owen and summon a team of oculi, then coordinate getting our cargo offloaded and to the right people. The ceronite needs to go down to the engine deck first, then those food processor parts should go straight to the mess in the hands of the mechanics who can install them."

"Aye, sir."

Ford and Owen headed toward the cargo ramp.

Cavalon chewed his bottom lip as he leaned toward Mesa. "Everything go okay with the neutrino capacitor?"

"Yes," she said, voice thin and edged with worry. "It has been fabricated, installed, and tested. The team is ready to proceed when we are."

"I'm ready," Cavalon said, then glanced at Adequin.

"We'll be ready when you are," she assured him.

"Then let's go, Mes," he said with a sigh. "The sooner we get this over with, the sooner . . . it'll be over."

Mesa gave a rueful nod and tapped her nexus. "Very well. I will summon the team to the engine deck at once." She headed toward the exit and Cavalon followed. "I do have one question about resetting the reserve calculations . . ."

They fell out of earshot and Adequin looked back at Puck. "Let's go over the rest in my office."

"Sir," Emery asked, eyebrow arched. "Should I help Cav, or . . . ?"

"No, you're with us," Adequin instructed, tilting her head to indicate she should follow as they started toward the exit. "It's time you start sitting in on some of the day-to-day. If you intend to be an officer, that is."

Emery's cheeks paled. "Oh, uh. Yes. Sir." Her lips pinched with a restrained smile, and she held her hands behind her back as she followed.

Adequin, Puck, and Emery made their way through the quiet ship to Adequin's office. While they waited for Beckar, she busied herself making inroads on emptying the whiskey decanter.

He arrived a few short minutes later, looking more or less his strapping self, though he kept tugging up the waist of his pants, and looked a bit like a new recruit who'd been issued the wrong size uniform but was too afraid of the quartermaster to ask for a new one. It was alarming the difference noticeable after only two weeks.

Beckar pulled up another chair and sat beside Emery and Puck in front of the desk. Stomach warm with whiskey, Adequin returned to the glacial desk and sat in the high-backed chair.

Beckar gave a rundown of the ship's system statuses, and thankfully there were no pressing concerns that needed addressing before travel could be considered. He'd scrambled teams to double down on the combat systems projects Jackin had started, meaning they'd have a semblance of workable defenses and a quarter semblance of workable ordnance.

Unfortunately, the crew had been faring somewhat less well than the ship itself. The good news was that their single jump toward Kharon Gate had brought them to within a safe, reasonable distance of the Divide, eliminating the time ripple phenomena and causing the anxiety-inducing side effects to plummet. However, for every soldier who'd recovered from the Divide's effects, two or more had been hospitalized due to diminishing rations.

As Beckar finished explaining the details of their rationing strategy, Adequin's eyes drifted over his square chin, hanging wide over a too-narrow neck.

"And are you eating enough, Optio?" she asked.

"Yes, sir."

"It doesn't look like it."

"Well, sir, rations have been lowered by another sixteen percent since you—"

"Aren't you eating more than the standard ration?"

"Well, no, sir," he stammered.

"You need to be."

He blinked. "But, sir . . ."

She glanced at Puck. "You, too. We all need to be." She looked back at Beckar. "You eat, your officers eat. The animuses and CIC techs eat. Starting immediately. We can't afford mistakes. We need to stay sharp if we're going to get everyone safe. That means keeping our leaders functional. The MREs and processor parts we brought back should be enough to make up the difference, at least in the short-term. Understood?"

Beckar's chin bobbed in a single nod. "Yes, sir. Understood."

"Speaking of somewhere safe," Adequin said, "we need to do our best to be ready as soon as the jump drive's fixed. Who's our best navigator?"

Emery, Puck, and Beckar all dropped their gazes as the word "*Jackin*" hung awkwardly in the air between them.

Finally, Beckar cleared his throat. "She's not a nav by trade," he said warily, "but Legator Ashwell has the most experience on a bridge, of all the officers. That I know of. I've heard her claim to know her way around jump routines."

Adequin nodded. "Very well. Put her on the call list for tomorrow. 0600."

Beckar nodded, tapping into his nexus. "The drive will be done tomorrow already?"

"Cavalon said it'd only take a few hours, so it should be ready tonight. But everyone needs a good night's sleep."

"Understood, sir. I'll prep my techs. Other than Ashwell, are we keeping the original plan?"

"I don't see any reason to change it," she agreed, then looked to Emery. "Emery, we'll need you and Eura flying the *Synthesis* and the *Courier* for the tug tomorrow. Then you'll each be responsible for picking up one of the crews at the two gates before we jump."

"Copy that, sir," Emery replied. "Tug sounds fun—what's that?"

"With no sublights, we need another way to guide the *Lodestar* into the relay mass."

"Oh, right," Emery said, gnashing her gum. "I guess that's a thing, huh? So we're really able to pull this beast with only our two little ships?"

"Not really," Puck said with a heavy sigh. "The mass ratio is abysmal, but the thrusters will help, and we'll have to fire off what little large-mass ordnance we have to give us a boost. All together, it'll work, but it's going to take a while. North already did the calculations when we prepped for the jump last time."

"We're looking at about three hours," Beckar said, "depending on how close we actually land to the gate."

Emery's cheeks paled. "Dang. Okay."

"Let's make sure Ashwell knows how important it is to fine-tune that jump," Adequin said, and Beckar nodded. "Also make sure Eura and the folks at Kharon and Poine know the pickup plan."

"Understood, sir," Beckar said.

"Emery, I want you to shadow Beckar this afternoon while he coordinates this."

Emery slid Beckar a grin. "Sounds fun, sir."

"We'll meet again in a couple hours to coordinate with Ashwell. You're both dismissed."

"On it, sir," Beckar said. They saluted, then left.

Puck watched them go, shifting his weight, brow creased deep as he turned to her. "What happened to Cavalon?"

She shook her head. "We had a close encounter with some Guardians."

Puck's brows rose. "Guardians, capital G? As in the mind-controlled Drudgers being cloned to replace every legionnaire?"

"Yeah. Those."

"Damn. And, uh . . ." He wrung his hands, frowning. "What about North?"

Heat scratched at her collar, but she ignored it. "He's alive," she forced out, cementing her tone with as much certainty as she could reasonably fake. She tried not to think about how that might actually be worse. "It's because of him we were able to make it back here at all. For now, that's all that matters. We need to get our plan in order to ensure this exodus goes smoothly."

"Understood, sir. Before he left, Jackin gave me a, uh . . ." Puck's gaze drifted down as he rubbed the back of his neck.

"Yeah," she sighed. "He mentioned you'd have something for me."

"Yeah." Puck's throat bobbed. "Sir, it's . . . *coordinates?*"

She gave a tentative nod, unsurprised. There wasn't much else it could be.

"And not only coordinates," Puck went on, "but the whole list of jump paths to get there." He leaned toward the edge of the desk and lowered his voice as if they might be overheard. "He said it's a viable refuge, access to food and water. Not listed on modern star charts. I have no idea where he got it."

"Lugen," she muttered, sitting back in her chair.

"Sir?" Puck said, eyebrows high. "Did you say *Lugen?*"

She blew out a breath. It had to be. Apparently, her former commanding officer had a history of producing safe havens out of thin air. Jackin must have learned about this one back when they were still in contact during the war. It'd probably only have a few airdrops of old MREs, but she'd take it. Cavalon may have offered up a fortune and then some, but that money wouldn't do them much good until they could establish—and defend—supply lines. Anything this "refuge" could offer in the meantime would mean fewer lives lost.

"It doesn't matter where he got it," Adequin said. "I trust it. What are the coordinates?"

Puck unfastened the top strap of his vest, then dug inside his shirt and produced a small data chip. He passed it across the massive desk to her. She clipped it to the side of her nexus and opened the file, then reached for the atlas—trying to ignore the traces of Jackin's dried blood still lining the grooves. She took off her dog tags and swept the triangle medallion over the peak.

The screens opened to their last settings: the communications interface that Cavalon, Emery, and Owen had used to send their encrypted message to Jackin. She backed out to the main menu, input a query, then opened the map. The large office flooded with holographic light as a wide expanse of the Drift Belt spread out around them.

"Void . . ." Puck muttered, wide-eyed gaze drifting over the hundreds of points of light. "It wasn't always like this?" he asked, voice squeaking.

"No."

Gesturing to open an inset query menu, she ran a search for the coordinates. The map rotated and zoomed in, the space between dots of light expanding as it narrowed in on a far upward section of the Drift, almost into the Perimeter Veil.

She stared at the small, innocent orb of light hovering at the center, marked with the query results symbol and a designation in the Viators' galactic archive: 51683–4. Or possibly one of its moons. The planet itself had gone largely ignored by even the Viators' record keeping, lacking details of its atmospheric composition and geography.

"Okay," she said with a sigh. "I guess this is where we're headed. We should keep the specifics of where we got it quiet, though."

"Of course, sir."

"You trust Ashwell?"

"I do, actually," he said, no hint of wariness in his tone. "She really stepped up helping Warner and his team manage the, uh . . . I don't want call them 'riots,' but . . ."

She glared at him. "*Riots?*"

"Let's call it 'large groups of people in one place voicing concern about the lack of food,'" he suggested. "It was only for a few days, right after you guys left, when everyone realized we were going to be sitting here for another couple weeks. It's died down since. Everyone's too tired to complain."

She sighed.

"I don't know anything about her navigation skills," Puck went on, "but if Beckar thinks she's capable, I believe him."

"How's Beckar been doing?" she asked, a thread of skepticism in her tone.

"Don't let that symmetrical mug fool ya, sir," Puck said, a smile stretching his lean face. "There's brains to go with that beauty. He's solid."

She pressed out a long breath. "Okay. Let's coordinate with Ashwell as soon as possible. Jackin saved us time by providing the jump list, but we should input them into the system ahead of time, so there's no waiting on nav. I want us to be ready as soon as the animuses are."

"Copy that, sir." Puck opened his nexus. "I'll schedule a meeting with Ashwell ASAP."

"While we're at it, we should check our stopovers against the atlas to ensure they're not dropping us too close to a nebula or ion storm. When Jackin made that list, he didn't have access to this set of maps."

Puck glanced up at the dots of starlight filling the office. "Copy that. We might need your help working with this, uh . . . new system."

"That's fine, I'll be there, whenever it is. Just let me know."

He looked up from his nexus with narrowed eyes. "But you'll remember to take your own advice, sir?"

"What?"

"To eat? Maybe sleep?"

"Yes," she sighed. "I will."

"Okay, good. Sorry, sir. It just seems like the 'keep the EX alive' niche might need filling now that North is . . ." His gaze lowered, the corners of his lips tugging down. "Sorry, sir."

She gave a firm shake of her head. "It's fine, Puck. You're dismissed."

He retreated to the exit, mumbling more apologies. The door sealed, and Adequin headed back to the decanter.

CHAPTER THIRTY-FOUR

At 0600 the following morning, Adequin stepped into the CIC.

Puck, Beckar, and Ashwell stood at the far end of the large, square command table. Six technicians stood behind the chairs of their stations, including Galen, the drive technician who'd helped with their last jump.

"Excubitor on deck," Beckar announced.

Everyone's posture went straight as they saluted, then stood with hands clasped behind their backs, expressions a mix of apprehension and sheer exhaustion.

Adequin stepped in far enough to let the door seal behind her, tugging the hem of her new uniform jacket. The impressive noiselessness of the room's acoustics weighed on her eardrums.

"Good morning." Her gaze drifted across each of them as she stepped into the blue glow of the war table. "Everyone ready to get the fuck out of here?"

Tentative smiles stretched faces along with less tentative nods. Puck chuffed a laugh.

"Me too," she sighed. She set the atlas pyramid on the war table. "Legator Ashwell, thank you for filling in for us on short notice."

Ashwell inclined her head. "Glad to help, sir." The angular blond haircut that'd once hidden half of her seemingly permanent scowl had been shaved clean, the shorn hair patchy and uneven, simply not growing back in some spots. Adequin had heard rumors of Ashwell's ship having food processor issues before any of this even started. She and her crew were probably worse off than most.

"This is going to be a long couple of days," Adequin said, addressing the entire room again. "But if we play our cards right, we can be groundside the day after tomorrow. And step one is getting to Kharon Gate. Stations, please."

The technicians sat, and Beckar went to stand behind them. At the table facet to Adequin's left, Ashwell expanded an array of preset navigation screens while Puck stepped to Adequin's right.

She opened a comm line to the engine deck. "*Lodestar* Actual for engine deck."

"E-deck here, sir," Cavalon responded.

"CIC is ready. How's it looking down there?"

"Double-checked it all again this morning, sir. We're good to go."

"That's what I like to hear, e-deck. Stand by for jump."

"Standing by," Cavalon confirmed.

Adequin minimized the comms screen, then looked to Beckar. "Optio, begin jump prep."

"Copy, jump prep," Beckar responded. "Galen, bring the drive on-line."

"Initiating," Galen answered.

"Set and lock coordinates," Adequin said.

"Setting coordinates," Ashwell replied, then a moment later, "and locked."

"Drive is live, sir," Galen said. "While you were gone, we got the spool time down to twelve minutes."

"Understood. Optio, cross-check systems while we wait."

"Aye, sir." For the next several minutes, Beckar paced behind his technicians, handing out orders to double-check the primary systems, then the secondary, and so on.

"Spool's complete," Galen said finally. "Panel is green, sir. Jump is a go."

"Stand by for jump," Beckar said. He turned an expectant look onto Adequin.

She drew in a steadying breath. "Execute jump."

"Executing . . ."

Adequin blinked heavily as her head spun, vision edged with white. A fog settled within her, obscuring her instinctive sense of direction. Silence hung in the air until cut through by an affirmative ding. The screens over the war table flickered and reset.

"Jump complete," Beckar said.

"Confirm arrival coordinates."

"Checking coordinates," Ashwell replied, then moments later, "coordinates confirmed. Successful jump."

A fatigued but genuine wave of relief and exultation rippled through the CIC. Puck threw Adequin a grin, straight white teeth gleaming.

"Tell me we're nice and close," Adequin said.

"We're *real* nice and close," Ashwell assured her, seeming genuinely pleased. "Almost spot-on with what Centurion North had estimated."

"All right," Adequin said. "All's a go on the tug; send the orders."

"Copy, mobilizing tug," Beckar replied, then he and Puck started relaying orders over comms.

Adequin reopened her line to the engine deck. "*Lodestar* Actual for e-deck."

"Go for e-deck," Cavalon replied.

"We have a successful jump."

He breathed out a crackling sigh. "That's great to hear, sir. We're not on fire this time, so we're feeling pretty good ourselves."

A grin tugged at her lips. "Relay next. Going to be a while on this tug, though."

"Copy that, sir. We're standing by. You know, I think I can get our respool down by another minute or two if you want me to look into it while we wait."

Adequin's jaw flexed, then she shook our head. "Good to know, but let's not press our luck. I'm just glad it's working at all."

"Agreed, Excubitor," Mesa's voice joined in. "It is not worth the risk of—"

"Okay, okay," Cavalon grumbled, "no need to gang up on me. It was only an idea."

Adequin smirked as she dismissed the connection.

Beckar approached. "We're all set on the tug, sir. Both ships have tethered up and ordnance has been fired. We're looking at just shy of three hours."

"Thanks, Optio."

She steadied her breath as she leaned both hands against the top of the war table. Now, her favorite part: more waiting.

Adequin sat in one of the surprisingly comfortable, padded crash seats against the back wall of the CIC. She'd just started to nod off when Beckar walked up, eyebrows high.

"We're on approach, sir," he said. "Five minutes."

"Thanks." She pushed up out of the chair, then paced to the war table. She steeled her resolve and opened a ship-wide comms line.

"Sentinels, this is your excubitor," she began, hating the echo of her own voice in the overhead speakers. The soft lull in the CIC quieted as chairs squeaked and every pair of eyes turned toward her. "In a few minutes, the *Lodestar* will be relaying through Kharon Gate, to the Drift Belt. Today, the Sentinels return to the galaxy."

The techs applauded, a few hugged. Puck grinned, stretching to give her shoulder a firm grip.

"We've been waiting for this day for a long time," she continued. "I want us to take a moment to say a proper farewell to the Divide. Out here, we've lost comrades, we've lost friends . . . and for a long time, we'd lost hope. But we've also learned a lot. I know I have.

"I learned that when decent, capable people work together, they can accomplish great things. I learned how profoundly smart and resourceful and fearless you all are. I learned what resilience really looks like. We are unique, in that. The Divide has made us stronger, and we'll carry that as an asset into the next phase of this journey.

"Today, we leave behind the shackles the Legion saddled us with. We're no longer exiled—we're liberated. We're no longer degenerates—we're *liberators*. Because one thing we will always be is Sentinels. We're still protectors, still defenders, and we'll return to the galaxy to show our people that—though they may have forgotten us—we have not forgotten them, and we intend to carry out the oath we took to protect mankind from 'threats unknown.' That unknown has become increasingly evident, and it's our duty to bring it to light and put a stop to it before it's too late.

"That journey begins now, as we leave the Divide. So join me in saying goodbye, in saying thank you, in saying fuck off—and I pray to the void we're never forced to return to this pitiless abyss again."

The techs cheered, and Beckar beamed at her from across the war table. A glint of respect shone in Ashwell's bloodshot eyes.

Adequin closed the comms menu.

Puck jostled her shoulders, grin wide. "Did you just come up with that on the fly, boss?"

She tilted her head. "Pretty much, yeah."

"Damn," Puck said. His eyes glistened, and he lowered his voice. "North would be proud."

Heat burned her cheeks, and all she could manage was a tight-lipped nod.

A voice crackled over comms. "Kharon Gate Command for *Lodestar*."

"Go for *Lodestar*," Beckar replied.

"Gate is ready, sir," the operator said. "Relay course: one node—Poine Gate, Soteria Cluster, Drift Belt. Nav, please confirm."

"Confirmed," Ashwell replied.

"Relay set," the operator said. "Cleared for departure, *Lodestar*."

"Thank you, Gate Command," Beckar said. "*Lodestar* is on approach. The *Synthesis* will be around to pick you up shortly. *Lodestar* Actual for *Synthesis* and *Courier*—drop your tethers and break away, I repeat, drop your tethers and break away."

Emery and Eura voiced their acknowledgment.

"Prepare for relay," Adequin ordered.

Beckar passed out commands, then nodded at her. "Ready for relay," he said. "Incoming in forty-three seconds."

Less than a minute later, Adequin's muscles tensed as her sense of time distorted, as if a fraction of a second had been sliced clean from her existence. Screens all around the CIC flickered and reset.

"Relay complete," Beckar announced. "Report."

The technicians voiced rounds of affirmative system checks.

"Reorient."

"Orienting," Ashwell said, tapping through menus.

A few quiet minutes passed with only the beeps of consoles and soft breaths as the technicians and Ashwell focused on recalibrating their systems.

"We're oriented," Ashwell said. "Queueing up jump coordinates."

"*Courier* is on approach with the Poine security team," the comms technician announced, then lowered their voice. "*Courier*, you're cleared for docking, hangar bay A5. Confirm."

Klaxons cut through the silence, shattering the momentary calm. Dread clenched Adequin's chest.

The crown of soft blue light ringing the room shifted to crimson, and the dark gray walls fell to a deep, wine-red.

Adequin hung her head. No. It was too soon.

The air clogged with new tension, and Ashwell's voice rang thin in her ears, edged with trepidation, "Multiple contacts off the starboard quarter, bearing . . ."

Adequin's knuckles went white as she gripped the edge of the war table. But she didn't have time for rage or embitterment. "*Do your job*," he'd said. "*Get the Sentinels to safety.*"

She inhaled deeply. The room snapped into focus. "Optio, set condition alpha."

"Copy alpha. Doyle, shields," Beckar ordered, then threw open the ship-wide intercom. "Alert all stations: We are condition alpha, I repeat, condition alpha. All hands to combat-ready."

"Shields at one hundred," Doyle, the defense technician, responded.

"Somebody tell me what we're looking at," Adequin said.

Ashwell expanded a three-dimensional map over the war table— jittering, incomplete outlines demarcating Poine Gate and a handful of indistinct vessels, with the *Lodestar* at the center.

"Seven contacts," Beckar announced. He stared at the display, eyes wide. "Scanners are still working on it—looks like a primary ship with at least six dispatches."

"Transponders?"

"Not sure yet, sir, they're throwing out jammers."

"Puck—"

"On it." Puck jogged to slide into one of the unused technician stations.

"We have a hit on the starboard quarter," Doyle announced. "Impact nominal. Hull integrity unchanged. Shields barely felt it, sir."

Something akin to relief loosened her tense muscles for a fraction of a second. They might not have guns or engines, but at least they could take a beating.

Adequin looked to Beckar. "Optio, we need to pull someone for tactical—you can't do both."

Beckar nodded, but before he could offer a solution, Ashwell said, "Sir, I can cover it. I'm no use until we jump again anyway."

Adequin inclined her head. Ashwell stepped around to the side opposite Adequin and began opening new screens.

"*Courier's* secured," the comms tech announced.

"Where's the *Synthesis*?" Adequin asked.

"They haven't relayed through yet," Ashwell replied.

Adequin ground her teeth, praying to the void that whoever was attacking them didn't try to destroy Poine Gate before the *Synthesis* made it through.

"Begin jump prep," Adequin ordered. "We need to be ready the second the *Synthesis* is aboard."

"Understood, sir," Beckar said. "We'll be ready."

"Another hit, sir, starboard quarter," Doyle said. "Impact nominal. Shields ninety-nine percent and recharging."

Adequin scrubbed a hand over her jaw. "I'm correct in thinking we fired off most of our ordnance as thrust earlier?"

"Correct, sir." Beckar frowned. "And they're out of range of our plasma cannons. Obviously, we can't move closer."

"What about the laser batteries?"

He grimaced. "They pull too much. We've been trying to figure out a work-around, but we're not there yet. Even with power from unused decks, we don't have enough energy to spin them up."

"We have a damn star on board, and we don't have enough power?"

"The reactor was never patched into the main power grid, sir—our capacitors couldn't handle the load."

"Can confirm," Puck said, throwing a look over his shoulder. "Mesa said it'd cause a cascading failure that would 'catastrophically melt down every transformer on the ship.' Direct quote."

Adequin blew out a hard breath. Of course it would.

"Additional contact off the starboard quarter." Ashwell palmed through screens. "It's the *Synthesis*, sir. They're through."

"Give me a direct line," Adequin ordered, and Ashwell passed her a comms screen. "*Lodestar* Actual for *Syn*."

"Here, sir," Emery replied.

"Full burn and get your rear shields up, you have contacts on your five."

"I, uh—oh shit, copy," Emery, said tone frail, wavering. "Maxing out, and Ford's on top of shields. Shit—"

"Em? You there?"

"Yes, sir, we're under fire. Damn, these guys are fast."

"Can you tell what they are?"

"Look like Evorsors," Ford's low voice answered.

Adequin gritted her teeth. Starfighters—and nice ones. Dangerous ones. "Em, combat landing authorized—sending a crash team to meet you."

Adequin caught Beckar's eyes, but he was already working on it. "Prep a crash team to A4, stat," he called out.

"Understood, EX," Emery replied, her high-pitched voice wavering. "Never done one'a those before . . ."

"Em."

"Sir?"

"You got this."

"Yeah," Emery said, some strength returning to her tone. "I got this."

"Ford, the *Syn*'s got a healthy armament, can you hop on guns?"

"Aye, sir," he replied, tone assured. "I got'er covered."

"Stay safe. Command, out." Adequin closed the line. "Beck, prep the starboard flaks to cover their approach."

"Copy flaks," he said, then turned to reissue the order.

"I'd *really* appreciate knowing what we're up against," she called out. "Anyone?"

"Almost got it!" Puck replied. "I patched into the *Syn* to steal their outboard sensors."

"Good idea." Ironically, most of the systems on the Drudger's old, shitty ship were still better than their *really* old, shitty ship.

"Got it!" Puck called. "Partial transponder packet coming your way, sir—for the primary vessel."

A small screen materialized and she expanded it, eyes scanning the results. "Puck, is this . . ."

"Yeah," he said, throwing a tight-lipped grimace back at her. "Looks like a Proteus."

Adequin tensed her jaw. Medium-sized, medium-speed vessels, Proteuses were overall incredibly "medium" on paper. But in actuality, they were some of the most advanced gunships on the market. Out of the box, they barely met the SC's codes for a civilian ship, and thus were available to anyone with the cash to cover the exorbitant price tag. The factory model included fast but efficient engines and an absurdly overdone defensive suite, with essentially no armaments. However, common practice involved registering your very medium legal ship, then adding on a few dozen undeclared after-market upgrades.

The price tag narrowed down the list of potential adversaries to only the wealthiest of the wealthy, which in their case, narrowed it to a list of one: Augustus Mercer. He'd sent his fucking Guardians after them.

Even if the Legion had somehow caught on to their intended mutiny, they wouldn't have brought a Proteus, for starters, but they'd also have protocols they'd at least have to *pretend* to follow: a transmission log proving they'd issued warnings or ordered them to stand down, proof of armament discharge and defense maneuvering. Some kind of figurative paper trail. They wouldn't risk coming in guns blazing, fighters away.

She had no idea how Augustus had caught up with them so damn fast, considering they'd taken an Arcullian Gate shortcut that'd shaved weeks off their return journey from the Core. Then again, the Corsairs had mentioned the substantial increase in Guardian presence. Maybe Augustus had stashed a Proteus full of Guardians in every sector, just waiting to carry out his evil bidding.

Jaw flexing, she dismissed the line of thought with an effort. It didn't matter how—they were here, and they needed to be dealt with, and she didn't have the first clue how to do that.

She *wanted* to deploy fighters to counter their Evorsors, throw out an army of scanner drones to give them an actual, useful, not static-ridden lay of the battlefield, or just launch a dozen nukes at them and call it a day. But they didn't have any of those things. They didn't even have engines with which to attempt any kind of maneuvering. All they could do was jump.

Part of her wanted to stay. To make a stand. The Sentinels versus Guardians, facing off at the Divide. To prove there and then to Augustus they weren't going to take his shit.

She could practically hear Jackin scoff in the back of her mind—that they'd never outlast them. They'd sit and eat through each other's defenses for hours, and when the Proteus's gave way, they could outmaneuver, repair, reset, return, and hit them again, and when the *Lodestar's* shields finally died, they could do nothing. They'd probably run out of power before they'd even run out of parts, not to mention how quickly they'd run through what few malnourished shield mechanics they had.

The best thing she could do for the Sentinels was run.

"Sir," Ashwell said, looking up from her screens, breathless. *"Synthesis* is secured. Hangar sealed."

"Execute jump."

CHAPTER THIRTY-FIVE

"Coordinates confirmed," Ashwell said. "Successful jump."

"Sensors are clear," Beckar announced.

"Maintain condition," Adequin said. She kneaded her knuckles into the knot of tension at the back of her neck.

Ashwell looked over, hollow cheeks flushed red. "Can they follow?"

"Yes," Adequin replied. The concept of an "untraceable jump" had come about less than fifty years ago, but even that was a misnomer that meant "took too long relative to respool times." Every jump was still traceable, on some level. And the *Lodestar*'s ancient drive technology would leave a blazingly obvious trail in its wake. It would only be a matter of time before the Proteus pursued.

"Galen," she said, "keep both eyes on that drive respool. Let us know the second it's ready."

"Aye, sir."

Adequin swiped open a line to the engine deck. "Cav, you there?"

"Here."

"Remember that idea I told you was too dangerous and totally shot down?"

"Yeah, I'm on it."

"Thank you."

Beckar leaned in, lips pinched, voice low. "Sir, a faster respool will help, but it won't solve it."

Puck approached, and Ashwell rounded the table to join them.

Adequin pushed out a hard breath, glancing at the three of them. "They'll run out of charge before we do, surely? We have the damn power source sitting in our hangar."

Puck sighed. "Technically, yes, they'd deplete before we would and need a recharge cycle. But we're comparing a top of the line modern drive, to . . . well, probably the shittiest one in existence. No matter what the animuses do down there, there's no way our respool timer will ever match theirs."

"We're not even really fighting their respool," Ashwell pointed out. "It's their tracer we're up against. As long as they can trace our jump faster than our respool, we'll never outrun them."

Adequin flexed her jaw. "And I'm guessing they'll break our defenses before we'd ever be able to outlast their jump charge?"

"More than likely, sir," Beckar confirmed. "It'll depend on their respool time, which I'm guessing we'll find out shortly."

"Yeah," Puck agreed. "The *Lodestar*'s a brute, certainly, but considering the state of the hull, once our shields are down, a few well-placed nukes is all it'd take."

"Assuming they have nukes on board," Adequin said.

"Assuming," he assented.

"And that our AMS fails to pick them off on approach."

Beckar gave a hissing grimace.

Adequin dragged a hand through her hair. "Seriously? We don't have an anti-missile system?"

"We don't have a *functioning* anti-missile system," he corrected.

"Interceptor missiles?"

He shook his head. "Best we have are a few dozen chaff decoys . . ."

"Void." She let out a crackling sigh. She was trying to be optimistic, but they weren't making it easy on her. "Okay. So, what you're saying is defensive plays will only drag out our eventual demise?"

Beckar frowned. "I mean, I wasn't going to put it exactly like that, but . . ."

She pressed her fingers into her temple, head pulsing with a dull headache. "Any idea how long we have till they trace us?"

Beckar looked to Puck, who looked to Ashwell. Beckar sighed. "I'm not sure, sir. Without knowing more about their tech, we can only estimate how long the initial trace will take. They probably realize by now we don't have engines, so they'll adjust coordinates and recalculate the path so they don't coalesce with us. That'll delay them somewhat."

Adequin nodded, frowning. Coalesce—the oversimplified, less traumatic way of saying "jump directly into the mass of another ship."

"Contact!" Doyle sounded.

Puck, Beckar, and Ashwell rushed to their respective stations. Adequin faced the war table squarely. "Optio, mark that time."

"Copy," Beckar replied. "That was four minutes, ten seconds."

Adequin let out a low growl. Four minutes of downtime during a twelve-minute jump cycle meant *eight* minutes of salvo.

"Shit," Ashwell grunted. "Looks like they're a lot closer than before."

"Doyle," Beckar began, "prepare to slide shield concentrations on our marks. Sanchez, what're our vectors?"

"Nothing yet, sir," the scanner tech replied. "We're gettin' jammed even worse this time."

Adequin bit back a curse. "Puck—I'll approve that thinly veiled request to bunk with Mesa that's been sitting in my inbox if you do something about those signal jammers."

Puck let out a breathy whistle. "Damn, sir. Not that I really needed more motivation than not dying, but copy that!"

"We have a hit, port quarter," Doyle called out. "Shield patches are holding, but our sensor array's not liking all the sudden activity—I'm losing my read on hull integrity."

"Get a team on it," Adequin ordered.

Beckar nodded. "E-deck's scrambling a crew."

"Multiple hits, starboard quarter," Doyle called out. "Impacts nominal."

Ashwell grimaced. "Sir, that sounds like they've brought their starfighters around to try and split our shield concentrations."

Adequin ground her teeth. And they couldn't roll or maneuver to counter it.

She had half a mind to check if Emery had *actually* crashed the *Synthesis* on landing, and if not, take it out herself to clean up those Evorsors. But by the time she got out there and picked a fight, she'd have to turn around to dock for the jump. And opening a hangar bay with enemies so close would be a huge risk. The safest place for them and all their ships was inside this one.

The floor rumbled and Adequin's gaze shot up. "What the hell is that?"

"We have a direct hit," Doyle said, "port bow, panel 816—DC away."

"Port bow shields were interrupted, sir," Beckar explained, brow low as he met her gaze over the war table. "They're recycling now. Array is still on the fritz; we need outboard sensors clear to give us a read on our vectors."

"*Puck*," Adequin growled, dragging out the syllable into a warning.

"Sorry, boss! Just got it!" he shouted, then started handing out orders to the other technicians on how to circumvent the jammers.

A minute later, Ashwell's fists unclenched, and she slapped the top of the table. "Fucking beautiful," she said, then shouted to Puck, "It's working!" She scaled the tactical map over the war table, centering in on the *Lodestar*. The holographic lines of the ships sharpened, and a grid overlaid along with a cascading list of vectors and coordinates.

Ashwell handed out approach vectors to Beckar and Doyle, who worked to ensure their shields held up under the Guardians' flanking tactic.

Adequin chewed on the inside of her cheek, racking her brain for what little knowledge of this kind of combat she had stored away from the war. She slid through the *Lodestar*'s system menus, hunting for some tactic or maneuver they could exploit. Eventually, she paused on the mostly grayed-out list of anti-missile systems.

"Beck?" she said, looking up to meet his gaze. "Those chaff decoys you mentioned?"

"Aye, sir?"

"Could we deflagrate them?"

He lifted an eyebrow. "I don't know what you mean, sir."

"Pull a team," she ordered. "Anyone flagged under ordnance, plus a chemist, if we have one. If we grind down the iron in the missile, it'll be combustible—I've seen techs do it with artillery chaff. The starter should act as ignition, and if the missiles use a CO_2 ejection system . . ."

Beckar coughed out a nervous laugh. "Shit. Yeah, we can try, sir. We won't have time before we jump, though."

"That's fine," she said. "We have more rounds coming, don't worry. Tell them to be fucking careful, though."

"Aye, sir." Beckar got on comms to prep a team.

If she could take out *one* of those bloody Evorsars, she'd be happy.

The floor rumbled again, shifting hard enough Adequin's Imprints activated, ensuring she kept her balance. Ashwell and Beckar gripped the edge of the war table to stay upright.

"Multiple direct hits," Doyle said, "starboard quarter, panels 137, 145, 192—DCs away."

"They're damn good with those starfighters," Ashwell growled. "It's like they know where our patches are pulling from." Ashwell's scowl sharpened. "Shit—Beckar? Do they *know where our patches are pulling from*?"

Beckar's white cheeks paled. "Uh—Centurion?"

Puck hissed. "Well, our three-hundred-year-old ECM suite is, uh, well, three hundred years old. And half of it's offline, so . . ."

"Anything we can do to make it harder on them?" Adequin asked.

"Uhh . . ." Puck's face slowly contorted to a grimace as he drew out the syllable. "Shoot them down?"

She glowered, then turned to Beckar. "I don't suppose our flaks are on individual turrets?"

"They are actually, but there's only one control terminal for each battery."

"Puck? You hearing this?"

"Yessir, I'll get Owen on it!"

Beckar's brow creased. "Sorry, sir, but . . . what?"

"We're going to hack the control grid to give access on"—she glanced over her shoulder—"nexuses, Puck?"

"Nexuses, sir," he confirmed.

"Oh." Beckar rubbed his jaw. "Do we have enough gunners, sir?"

"We have four thousand soldiers, Optio, most of whom should be capable of shooting a damn gun."

He frowned. "Of course, sir."

She lowered her voice. "Hey—you're used to doing things by the book, I get it." She glanced at Puck. "It's probably good we have some balance, honestly. Don't ever be afraid to rein us in if you think we need it."

He nodded. "Understood, sir."

"Now start pulling some people to fill those gunner slots."

"Aye, sir."

"Respool complete," Galen shouted. "Jump ready!"

"Execute." Adequin closed her eyes as the room seemed to shift around her. When she opened them again, the flurry of activity over the war table had vanished, leaving an empty grid.

"Jump complete," Beckar said. "Confirm arrival coordinates."

"Coordinates confirmed," Ashwell replied. "Successful jump."

"Sensors are clear," Beckar confirmed.

"Maintain condition," Adequin said. She was already getting real sick of that string of call/reports. "Puck, work with Doyle's team and do what you can to mitigate those reads on our patch pulls."

"Yessir."

"Hey, Command," Cavalon's voice rang over comms, clear and airy. "Got somethin' for ya."

Adequin tapped open the line. "Tell me it's a puppy."

He laughed. "Sorry, no. But how about twenty-five percent less respool time? Eh?"

"That'll do. Nice work, e-deck."

"That'll be just shy of nine minutes," Beckar said. "Still a four-minute arrival, but only a five-minute salvo."

She let out a sigh. "I'll take it. Someone key in that math for me—I want to know how many jumps we have in us. Assume a similar amount of damage as we just took."

"On it, sir," Beckar replied, then a minute later, "that gets us to around forty-two jumps."

Adequin paced to the crash seat where she'd left the atlas pyramid, then brought it to the war table and activated it. The crew startled briefly from the influx of light, and she quickly scaled it down using one of her presets: the standard two-meter-wide globe they'd used before it'd been "liberated."

She narrowed the map to their location, hunting for the closest Arcullian Gate. Though it'd probably take them way off track of where they wanted to go, it might be the only reasonable way to lose the Guardians.

Of course, the closest was the one they'd taken to the Core—deep into the Drift Belt, over five days away at warp speed.

"Ashwell, plot a rough course for me, just need an estimate of how many jumps it'd take."

Ashwell brought up a new menu. "Ready, sir."

Adequin read off the coordinates while Ashwell input them. A few seconds later, Ashwell looked up, expression tight. "Estimate is sixty-seven jumps, sir."

"Damn. Okay, thanks." She closed the atlas, then made a gathering motion with one hand. "Officers."

Puck, Beckar, and Ashwell converged on her again.

"We're going to have to think outside the box," she said. "What can we do to shake them?"

Puck rubbed a hand over his shaved head and Beckar blew out a long sigh.

"What if we jumped into the Veil?" Ashwell suggested.

Adequin chewed her lip, considering it. There were enough stellar nebulae in the Perimeter Veil to give it its well-deserved name, and of all the places in the galaxy to give them a chance at masking their jump trail, that would be it. But they couldn't even make it to the Arcullian Gate in the Drift in the amount of jumps they had left, let alone all the way to the Veil.

"It's too far," Adequin said. "It needs to be something we can accomplish in fewer than forty-two jumps."

Puck rubbed a hand over his shaved head. "Nothing is within forty-two jumps. Just the empty Drift in every direction. We either need to figure out a way to maintain our shields so we can jump farther—a lot farther—and take more damage, or come up with a way to mask our trail."

Ashwell shook her head. "Even if we can keep the shields going, that only helps if we have some way to stop them—or lose them. Otherwise we'll just be leading them right to the refuge."

Adequin gritted her teeth. They were right. They didn't have the fire-power to destroy the Proteus, and they could only defend against them for so long. They had to find a way to get them off their trail. But she had no idea how.

She did have a couple geniuses downstairs, however.

"Cav?"

"Here, sir."

"I don't suppose there's anything we can do about masking our jump path?"

He gave a nervous laugh. "Oh, hell no, sir. This monster leaves a real damn obvious path of neutron radiation in its wake."

"In the Viator War," Mesa's voice joined in, "ships such as this had a follow-ship whose sole purpose was to mask a jump signature by accelerating the rate of decay—"

"That's great," Cavalon interrupted, "but we don't have a fancy scrubber ship, now do we?"

"No," Mesa bristled, "but that does not change the relevance of the fact."

"We're looking for short-term ways to *not die*, Mes, so yeah, it kinda does."

Adequin sighed. "M'kay, guys—muting you again," she said, sliding the controls.

So much for her geniuses.

"Contacts!" Doyle shouted.

Adequin dragged a hand through her hair and braced herself for another round.

"Confirm coordinates," Adequin sighed.

"Confirmed, sir," Ashwell said, tone weary. "Successful jump."

Beckar tapped his screens, and the countdown timer appeared over the war table.

Adequin rubbed the tension from her neck with a heavy sigh. "Maintain condition." She left it at that, the others starting the procedure for the same nine-minute cycle they'd been on for the last five jumps. By now, they knew the drill.

At least this last time, the Proteus had jumped in a great deal farther away. By the time they'd made their approach and started their flanking barrage, the missile team downstairs had readied their first prototype deflagrated chaff missile. It narrowly missed its target, but still exploded and sent the Evorsor careening into its neighbor, which proceeded to lose control long enough that *it* drifted through a spray of flak fire that'd been aimed at the formation of Evorsors following up.

It might have been an accidental takedown, but it was still a takedown, and that was good enough for her. They couldn't afford to be snobbish about their wins.

Three jumps ago, Puck had figured out what the Guardians had been exploiting to trace their shield patches and blocked it, so now Adequin could safely say the *Lodestar*'s old-school shield patch system was proving its worth. But it would still only last them so long. And like Puck had said, what this old behemoth could take once the shields were down would be minimal at best.

"Contact!" Doyle shouted.

Adequin's adrenaline spiked, blood rushing into her ears. It'd only been a few seconds. It was *way* too soon.

"What the hell?" Ashwell voiced Adequin's indignance. "They couldn't have traced . . ." Ashwell hunched over her screens. Her brow furrowed. "No jammers, sir. Single contact. At nine thousand klicks and holding."

"Huh . . ." Puck mumbled. "Transponder signal's unmasked. Stripped of details, but broadcasting clean. The *Callisto*?"

"They didn't jump in, sirs," the scanner technician clarified. "They were here when we arrived."

Adequin scoffed. "What?"

"Excubitor, we have, uh," the comms technician sputtered, then looked over his shoulder at Adequin. "Excubitor, we're being hailed."

She stared at him, and all she could think to say was another, "What?"

"Shit." Ashwell let out a low growl. "I'm locked out of nav."

"Engines too," Galen called.

Adequin threw a hard look Puck's direction. "Puck?"

"Uh . . . oh, shit," he replied, voice tense. "Yeah, looks like they way-laid us. Musta slid in and grabbed our transit systems before ECM reset. Post-jump reboot on this old boat is slow as an ice-cold bureaucrat. Same reason we didn't catch them on scanners straight away."

"Can you force them out?" Adequin asked.

Puck grimaced. "With this ancient ECM suite . . . ? Maybe. If given enough time, but . . ." He glanced at the looming countdown Beckar had started. Three minutes until the Guardians arrived.

Adequin ground her teeth. "Get that ship on comms. Now."

"Hail accepted," the comms tech replied. "Patching it in."

A video interface materialized in front of Adequin, the edges jittering like a fractured time ripple before settling into a clean image.

A woman stood in frame, with dark brown skin and thinly braided black hair woven with colored threads—an old Cautian tradition. She wore a pair of dusty black spaulders over a burgundy flight suit that had no discernible badges. The woman acknowledged the connection with an affable tilt of her head.

"Hel—"

"Why the hell did you waylay my ship?" Adequin growled.

The woman's congenial visage faded slowly into confusion. "Uh, yeah. Hello to you too," she said, her husky voice relaying cleanly through the war table's speakers. "Levi Kaplan here, captain of the *Callisto*. Great to meet you . . . ?"

Adequin ignored the prompt. "Release my ship," she demanded.

"I'd be happy to do that," Kaplan replied, "but first I need to speak with your progenitor."

"Excuse me?" Adequin snapped.

"Your progenitor," she repeated plainly, as if that somehow added value to the conversation.

"Listen," Adequin said, tone gruff, "I have no idea what you're talking about. Who the hell are you? There's no transit authority in the Drift."

"We're not transit authority . . ." Kaplan's eyes narrowed. "Where'd you get these coordinates?"

"Where'd *you* get these coordinates?" Adequin countered, aware her petulancy wasn't helping, but her patience had worn thin six jump cycles ago. "It's a free galaxy, last I checked. Now release my ship."

Kaplan's brows pinched. "Apologies, but I'm not authorized to do that."

"*Authorized?*" Adequin growled, then reined in her rising anger with an effort. She forced out a steadying breath, grinding her knuckles into the war table. "Listen. We have hostiles incoming. You wanna keep talking, you dock and do it in person. Otherwise your little scout ship is gonna get rolled over by a decked-out Proteus and a fleet of Evorsors in about . . ." She glanced at the countdown timer. "Fifty-seven seconds."

Kaplan's brows rose. "Wow, that's . . . specific. But not much of a threat. We could just jump away, you know."

"Please do. That'll release the lock you have on my fucking engines, and we can all move on with our lives."

Kaplan's voice grew hard, any residual wry wit evaporating. "You cannot continue on this course without—"

"Forty-six seconds," Adequin said. "Either dock, jump, or take your chances with the Proteus. This conversation's over." She severed the link, and Kaplan and her slack-faced indignation disappeared along with the comms menu. She didn't have time for random bullshit. If they wanted to play a game of chicken with a capital ship, they could get in line.

Silence permeated the CIC. Beckar stood across from her, expression slack while he stared at the now-empty space over the war table. Adequin drummed her fingers hard against the glass top. The countdown ticked to thirty seconds.

Over her shoulder, a terminal beeped. "Sir," a technician said, "we have a docking request from the *Callisto*."

"Approved. Bay D9."

"Copy D9," the tech replied.

Ashwell let out a sigh of relief. "Nav's back, sir."

"And engines," Beckar confirmed.

Adequin tapped her nexus, opening a line to Warner. "Rake for Warner."

"Here, sir."

"Bring as many as you can muster, armed. Meet me at D9."

"Copy D9, sir."

She made for the exit. "Ashwell, jump the millisecond we've re-spooled. Beckar, you have command."

Beckar stared after her, mouth gaping.

"It's cool," Puck sighed. "She does this sometimes."

The door slid shut behind her.

CHAPTER THIRTY-SIX

The main hangar door stood open when Adequin arrived. She headed left.

A small civilian scout vessel had landed in bay D9—the *Callisto*. The ship's olive-gray, armored hull was devoid of any branding or call sign. Warner stood at the center of two dozen MPs, all fanned in a staggered arc with their rifles trained at the stern of the vessel.

As Adequin crossed the threshold into the smaller bay, her head swam with vertigo.

"Successful jump, sir," Beckar called over her nexus. "That's four minutes till salvo."

"Copy that." She sealed and locked the bay door behind her. "Bay D9 is secure."

"Understood, sir."

Adequin marched toward the *Callisto*. The MPs parted as she cut through them, and Warner passed her a rifle. She shouldered it, flicking off the safety. Boots shuffled as Warner's team tightened in behind her.

In the hatch at the top of the extended cargo ramp stood three figures—Kaplan alongside a woman and man wearing tactical armor the same shade of faded burgundy as Kaplan's uniform. All three prudently kept their guns holstered.

The two guards waited at the hatch as Kaplan stepped down the ramp. Her gaze drifted to the aerasteel beams overhead. "Where the hell did you get this ship?" she muttered. She wiped the awed look from her face with an obvious effort, eying Adequin's rifle steadily. "Listen. Even though it blatantly defies protocol, I released the waylay as a show of—"

"You think I give a shit about your protocols?" Adequin barked. "Who the hell are you?"

"See," Kaplan sighed, "this's why I need to speak with your progenitor—"

"I think I've made it pretty damn clear I don't know what that means."

Kaplan held up a placating hand. "It's just part of the process. Someone triggers the alert buoys, we waylay them, confirm identity of their progenitor, verify the manifest, provide escort the rest of the way. Simple checklist . . . usually."

Adequin pinched the bridge of her nose as she struggled to make sense of it. Letting go, her fingers fell to her collar, to the cluster of tags underneath her jacket—hers, Griffith's . . . Jackin's. Her mind cleared as the pieces shifted into place, generating at once relief and overwhelming anxiety.

Jackin hadn't given them coordinates to some random backwater planet to hide away on. He'd given them *the* coordinates. The ones he was trying to take with him to his grave, for the second time. Of fucking course he had.

Adequin lowered the aim of her rifle. "This 'progenitor' you're supposed to speak with . . . is it Jackin North?"

Kaplan's brow unfurled, chin dipping in a reluctant nod. "Can we speak with him?"

She shook her head. "Afraid not."

Kaplan's expression cycled from confusion to fear before her gaze drifted over Adequin's shoulder to the MPs. She licked her lips slowly. "But you do know him?" she asked, tone guarded.

"Yes. He gave us these coordinates," Adequin explained. "*Willingly.* He was my second. My optio."

Kaplan's tense posture softened, though only a fraction. She lifted a brow. "*Was?*"

"He's alive, but . . ." Adequin shook her head. "Not here."

Kaplan's gaze narrowed—the same look of throttled confusion she'd had when they first called. "You know . . ." She eyed the badges of rank on Adequin's shoulders. "You kinda skipped your part of the introductions earlier."

From her measured look, she was asking a question she already knew the answer to. Adequin didn't have the time or willpower to be circumspect, anyway. "Excubitor Adequin Rake," she replied.

"Shit," Kaplan breathed, drawing out the word as her face lit up. She threw a look to one of the guards. "I fucking *told* you." She returned a wide smile to Adequin. "Boss man's gonna be so happy. I'm gonna get my centurion bars for this."

Adequin's brow creased. "Wait, what?"

"For saving you."

Heat built in her chest, and her grip on her rifle tightened. She took two long steps forward. Kaplan retreated until her feet clipped the end of the ramp. She caught herself and her spine straightened, shoulders drawing back with instinctual rigidity. Adequin stopped when they were toe-to-toe, glaring straight into Kaplan's rounded, dark gray eyes.

"Listen," Adequin growled. "You're not 'saving me' right now; all you're doing is wasting my time when I should be in the CIC captaining my damn ship while Drudgers try to kill us all. I suggest you start giving me some answers very, very quickly, as it's been a *very* long two weeks since I last threw someone out an airlock. But please, keep trying my patience."

"Sorry, sir, I—" Kaplan stammered. "I didn't—I'm sorry, sir."

Adequin licked her lips slowly. "You Legion?" she asked.

Kaplan's shoulders loosened slightly. "Not anymore," she said, a thread of bitterness evident in her tone. "You?"

"Not anymore."

A wary grin tugged at Kaplan's lips. "That's good. I'd hate to have to shoot you."

Warner stiffened, but Adequin lifted a hand to stand him down as she clicked on her rifle's safety. "Maybe you're no longer Legion," she said, "but you clearly answer to someone. Who's this boss you're talking about?"

Kaplan let out a heavy sigh, then lowered her voice considerably. "Same taciturn motherfucker you answered to for years. He told us to keep an eye out for you guys months ago, but we didn't even know if you'd made it to the Drift. He's gonna be damn happy we found you."

Adequin ground her teeth. She'd assumed as much. Fucking Lugen.

During their call at Kharon Gate six months ago, he'd been as oblique as ever. He hadn't refused them aid, but he hadn't offered any either. Apparently, he'd had a blacksite stashed away, but either wouldn't or couldn't tell them over that comm line. More likely couldn't. Because he'd had something more important to keep safe. Corinne Mercer.

The decking shifted, and Adequin softened her knees as her Imprints slid to help her keep her footing.

Kaplan stumbled, but remained upright. "Shit . . ." Her eyes darted around the hangar. "Can I ask who's after you, sir? Legion?"

Adequin grimaced. "Would you believe me if I said Augustus Mercer's clone Drudger army?"

Kaplan's lips twisted with chagrin. "Unfortunately, yes."

The floor shook again. The aerasteel beams overhead groaned in protest.

Kaplan's gaze drifted up. "Listen," she said, a sudden eagerness in her tone. "There's a *much* faster jump route we can give you."

"What? How?"

"You're pathing around the Rotellan Traverse?"

"Well, yeah—"

"You don't have to. There's a way through it. We didn't discover it till well after North got his list. But we have to shake this tail of yours first. We can't risk leading them even remotely close to where we're going—especially if they're cronies of Mercer."

Adequin let out a hard sigh. "Yeah, I understand. I just don't know how. We have no engines on this thing, only a jump drive that takes nine damn minutes to respool. They'll breach our shields in less than forty jumps—barely six hours."

"*Forty* jumps?" Kaplan said, voice pitching up with disbelief. "A ship this old must need a recharge before then."

"It doesn't—we have a star on board, so it just keeps charging it all the time."

Kaplan's furrowed brow flattened, and she scoffed out, "You have a *what*?"

"Wait," Adequin mumbled, gaze drifting over her shoulder.

They had a star on board.

She met Kaplan's wide, expectant eyes. "I have an idea."

CHAPTER THIRTY-SEVEN

Thick sweat clung to every centimeter of Cavalon's skin. The sweltering heat of the engine room stifled his thoughts, wearing on his already-thin patience.

He chewed over a few choice expletives while he acted as a human doorstop, holding up a maliciously designed *horizontal* access panel for one of the engine's primary manifolds. He knew there was a valid reason—should the lock not be engaged, the ship's gravity would keep it in the closed position. He still felt the best course of action was to mentally smite the engine's designers and all their descendants.

Owen had shimmied inside to help him do something he'd have been perfectly capable of had he two sets of metacarpals. Though at the moment, her "help" felt more like "frustrating the shit out of him with her inability to understand a perfectly simple manual firmware update procedure."

"No—not there," he grumbled, gesturing vaguely with his handless left arm. "The other—there—no, down—"

Owen's brown cheeks burned red. "Bloody void, bud, I'm really trying to help; you just have to use your goddamn *words*."

Cavalon clenched his teeth, exhaling a loud breath out his nose. "I'm. *Trying*."

The jump engine whined, building to an onerous crescendo, and Cavalon's pulse along with it. His stomach turned and he closed his eyes as his sense of direction blurred, like he'd passed out drunk and woken up somewhere familiar, yet completely unexpected.

"Jump complete," Beckar's voice crackled over ship comms, echoing out from the console platform along the back wall.

Mesa tapped the jump drive control screen, and the neutrino capacitors roared as the photovoltaics bridge activated, beginning its slow, *gentle* feed of ceronite into the fuel cells.

Every single time it went off, Cavalon felt as though his heart were going to burst out his throat and the whole engine would rupture into magenta fire.

He glanced at the giant "thirty-five" hovering over the terminal glass beside Mesa: a looming holographic reminder of how fucked they'd soon be.

"*Animus Mercer*," Owen growled from inside the manifold. "It's hot as a Drudger's crotch in here, but you know, take your time or whatever."

"Shit, sorry." He refocused. "Okay. The port is a half meter up from the floor, to the left of that little forked hourglass thing."

"Ah, I see it." Owen slid the sync module into the access port. The activation light cycled to green, then beeped happily.

She removed the card and shimmied out of the manifold. Cavalon dropped the heavy door behind her.

Owen stood, wiping the sheen of sweat from her brow. "Goddamn, that was way harder than it should have been."

"Agreed," he sighed.

Her scowl melted and she stuck out her bottom lip, then gripped his left arm at the elbow. "Sorry, bud. I know this is harder on you than it is on me."

Across the room, the main door slid open and Emery marched in, grease staining her cheeks and arms. "Hey, friends, need any help?"

"Babe," Owen said, breathless. She marched to meet Emery, planting a frantic kiss on her lips before engulfing her in a hug. "Thank the void. Where have you been? I heard the EX suggest a combat landing?"

Emery's neck drew up straight, a smug grin twisting her mouth. "Combat landing indeed, but I did *not* destroy the ship, so you're all welcome. Banged it up a bit, had a couple things to fix, but we got it back in working order."

"What the hell's going on?" Owen asked. "We haven't gotten any details from Command."

Emery shook her head. "Someone's in pursuit, a flagship and a couple squads of starfighters giving us hell. Ford said the main ship's a Proteus—he thinks it's gotta be Guardians."

Cavalon blew out a hard sigh. "Yeah, he'd be right." The Mercer Guard had a whole fleet of modded-out Proteuses for various nefarious purposes. Surely Augustus would have redeployed them with Guardian complements instead. Slowly replacing the Guard just like he was slowly replacing the Legion.

"On our way in," Emery went on, "Ford shot down *four* of those damn Evorsors. That guy's good, let me tell ya."

"EX on deck!" a mechanic's voice echoed across the sweltering chamber.

Everyone but Cavalon's training kicked in as they all paused their work to snap salutes.

"As you were," Rake said before they'd even all finished trying to stand up straight. She met Cavalon's eyes and tilted her head toward the console platform.

He nodded. "O, take Em and do that same patch for the other five manifolds, please. Mesa can show you where."

"Yessir."

Mesa joined Emery and Owen, and they headed down the decking deeper into the engine.

Cavalon stepped onto the console platform just as Rake arrived. Her face was scrunched with a not unfamiliar look, a hunting, curious, ready-to-try-something-dangerous glint in her eye which he simultaneously respected and despised. He really hoped she hadn't come expecting some kind of solution to this endless chase.

He cleared his throat. "I'm having them try to sync the duty cycles of the six intake manifolds, but honestly I don't think it's gonna do much, if anything. There's a hard limit on these old drives because of the—"

"Hey, hey—" Rake put a hand on his shoulder, shaking her head. He choked off the remainder of his lengthy explanation. "I understand," she assured him. "I have a question."

She slid a furtive glance toward the soldiers working around them, and his gaze drifted to follow, then rebounded onto her. "Um. Okay?"

Her amber eyes locked back onto him. "When we turned on the reactor, you said you were worried about its stability."

"I worried about a lot of things, but yeah, I remember."

"Specifically," she said slowly, suspiciously slowly, "you worried it might supernova if you had to pull the plug mid-activation. Were you serious?"

"Uh, yeah, but I mean, you don't have to worry. It's stable."

"Okay, but what if we . . . didn't want it to be?"

He blinked at her. "Didn't want it to be stable?"

"Right."

Oh void. He liked this even less than he'd first thought.

He ground his teeth for a few seconds, flexing his jaw. "I *just* made this for you," he growled, "and now you want me to *blow it up*?"

Her gaze shot toward the others, and she gripped the side of his arm, drawing him closer to the console. She lowered her voice. "It's the only way I can see to get out of this. We have fewer than thirty-five jumps till they KO our shields, and the report from defense so far confirms it. Our power reserves will be too depleted at that point to recharge without a break. We can't outlast them, and we don't have the firepower to take them out."

Cavalon pinched the bridge of his nose and decided to just play the fuck along because he didn't know what else to do. "Void, Rake. I'm not saying I'm not a fan of using our ship as a bomb, but we're *on* the goddamn ship."

"Help's on the way," she said, glancing back at the door.

He stared at her. She looked back at him.

"What?" she asked.

"Your mouth just said 'help is on the way.'"

She gave him a flat look.

He narrowed his eyes at her. "Why are you acting like *I'm* the one who's not making sense?"

"Arks are incoming," she said, "I'll explain the details later, okay? We can get everyone off the *Lodestar* before we, ya know . . ."

He pushed a hand through his sweat-soaked hair. "If the Guardians see us taking arks away . . ."

She shook her head. "We're only going to send ships during the four minutes before they can follow us through the jump. They won't even know we're abandoning ship."

"Then why do we even need to blow it up?"

"If we leave the ship behind, as soon as we don't jump after those five minutes, they'll realize something's up. Then it'd be easy to back-track and trace one of the ark trails. We can't risk them following in any capacity—we have to destroy them. It's the only way to keep us, and the place we're headed, safe. Remember, it might feel like we're dealing with Drudgers, but we're really dealing with Augustus. Let's not underestimate him again already."

Cavalon scrubbed his hand over his face. "*Fuuuck*," he groaned.

"I'm sorry," she sighed. "But can you do it?"

He dropped his hand and met her gaze, her eyes filled with a calculated hope that said, "*no worries, only everything is riding on this*," which he'd seen far, far too many times for his liking in their short time together. He blew out a hard breath. "I'll confer with Mesa on the specifics, but . . . yeah."

She gripped his shoulder, brow softening, eyes rounding. "Thank you, Animus."

Cavalon left Emery and Owen in charge of their engine team, then went with Mesa to the reactor bay.

A wall of stifling air hit him in the face as they stepped inside. He paused to look over the twenty-meter orb: the rings of scaffolding, fronted by the cluster of workbenches he'd left in total disarray. He really hadn't missed this place. It felt like returning to a house you'd built that'd tried to kill you—you were proud of the house you'd built, but it'd fucking tried to kill you.

"Void, it's hot," he groused.

"Well," Mesa said, stepping up beside him. "There is a star in here."

"Did you try rerouting the launch tube cooling vents like I suggested?"

"We did, but the effect has been nominal. As I said, we have a *star*—"

"Yeah, yeah, I know." Not for long.

Mesa unstrapped her duty vest and Cavalon shrugged off his own, tossing it on one of the stools as they approached the main workbench. He shoved aside a few tablets and water bottles, then brought up the status screens. Everything nominal. He couldn't help but be a little impressed with himself. And Mesa, obviously.

"My first thought is the cryostat," he said, peering at her across the workbench, through the glowing holographic screens. "We could simply . . . turn it off."

Her lips pressed thin. "We could. But I am afraid that would not have the desired effect. It may simply melt, resulting in a large hole in the ship. Which is not what the excubitor wants, if I am understanding correctly."

He sighed. She was right. The chance of that working was too slim. They needed a sure thing. Or a surer thing, at least. Because once again, they were just making shit up as they went along.

He pushed aside a few screens, leaning his right fist on the workbench. "While building it, this whole thing felt like a house of cards. There must be some way to trigger it."

Mesa shook her head as she glowered down at the terminal.

"What's wrong?" he asked.

"Well. My concern is that, technically, the mass is not large enough to do what we want it to."

"Sure, but technically the mass isn't large enough to create fusion either, and it does. The dark energy generators had those outlet cowls for a reason—so the mass could be forcibly expelled. That indicates some kind of thermal runaway."

"True, but it does not *prove* thermal runaway. There were many aspects of the original design we did not duplicate because we could not discern their function. As I mentioned in our original design discussion, I believe one of those very well may have been a protocol which would have ejected the mass *prior* to destabilization, as to avoid damage to the structure. But as noted, I believe that would result in . . ."

He sighed. "Right. Melting through the floor." He crossed his arms. She was right. As always. No surprise.

He checked the time on his nexus. They needed to come up with something. Fast. They had less than five hours until Rake needed this done, and they'd need time to actually implement the solution as well.

He scratched at his beard harshly, blowing out a long breath. Augustus had engineered him this neurotic, obsessive, capable brain. Now was the time to use it. He just had to think like a homicidal dictator who actually *wanted* to destroy the thing he'd spent six months building and almost died for multiple times and that Rake had risked her life for and that Jackin had *given* his life for . . .

Oh, yeah. There was that.

"Okay . . ." he began carefully. "Hear me out."

Mesa inclined her head. "I am listening."

"If the problem is that we don't have enough mass . . ."

Her pinched brow softened as her overlarge Savant eyes rounded with realization.

He smiled. "Then we'll just have to make more."

CHAPTER THIRTY-EIGHT

Twenty-six jumps and four hours later, Adequin, Puck, Beckar, and Ashwell were all that remained of the CIC crew. The vacated technician seats made the acoustic silence feel even heavier. Rarely was a command deck so empty mere minutes from battle, with its shields at less than 9 percent.

Kaplan's husky voice crackled through comms. "Ark seventeen is away. Ark eighteen just finished queueing, but we should be able to get them underway before the cut-off."

"Copy that," Adequin said. "Don't cut it too close—hold them back till next round if needed."

"Will do." Kaplan clicked off.

"Okay," Adequin sighed, leaning both hands on the war table. "We're getting down to it. Beckar?"

"Sir."

"Me, you, Cavalon, and Kaplan will be the final ship out."

"But, sir, you agreed to come—" Puck tried to protest, but she held up a hand and he stopped short, lips pinching tight.

"*Puck*," she continued, "you and Ashwell will be responsible for attending the penultimate wave of arks. It'll be most of the mechanics, the damage control teams, final security squads, Ford, whoever he kept back from medical, and Mesa. They should be starting to queue up now. Kaplan has the complete list. I'll stay with Cavalon in case he needs any last-minute help. He wants to keep eyes on it right up until our last jump."

Puck frowned. "Because we're . . ."

Adequin nodded. "Blowing up the ship."

"With a . . . supernova?" Ashwell asked, one eyebrow arched.

"Essentially, yes."

Ashwell and Beckar exchanged a daunted look.

In the heavy silence of waiting, Adequin did her best not to think about how if any one person's math had been slightly off, this whole balancing act could come crumbling down.

After four minutes, the cycle began again: proximity alarms, contacts off the port quarter, Evorsors deployed, incoming approach vectors. Each side of the war table brimmed with holographic light, each of them responsible for twice as many screens as they should be. Then, finally: jump ready.

"Execute."

"Jump confirmed," Ashwell said.

Adequin gave a firm nod. "Puck, Ashwell, you're dismissed."

"Sir," Puck said, "let me—"

"*Amaeus*," she cut him off, tone hard. He froze, stunned at hearing his first name. She lowered her voice. "Go get Mesa, and get the hell off my ship. That's an order."

He gave a shallow nod. "Sir," he said quietly, then left with Ashwell.

"Beckar, you good?" Adequin asked.

"Yes, sir," Beckar replied. To his credit, he only seemed marginally flustered at being left alone in the CIC of a three-hundred-year-old ship about to lose its shields while being rigged to go supernova.

"I'm going to check on the remaining arks," she said, "then head to the reactor bay. We'll meet you in hangar D before the final jump."

"Understood, sir."

Adequin grabbed the atlas off the war table and left the CIC.

CHAPTER THIRTY-NINE

Cavalon stood before a slew of holographic screens at the main workbench, T-shirt soaked with sweat, a paragon of one-handed code editing.

Though code editing really meant code deleting. Just straight up erasing huge swaths of it. Safety protocols, removed. Performance test codes, gone. Hazardous indicator failsafes, goodbye forever.

Across the workbench, Mesa stood engrossed in her own task of tricking the system into thinking the containment chamber was larger—infinitely larger, like the size of all outer space larger. Her black hair hung disheveled from its braid, strands clinging to her warm beige skin, at once flushed and tepid with exhaustion and stress. Thankfully, she hadn't caught on to his wholesale, burn-it-all-down approach. If she did, she'd put the pieces together, and he'd have to fight her about it, and probably drag her off kicking and screaming, and it'd just be a whole damn mess he didn't want to deal with.

When he finished eradicating safety measures, he ran a quick correction routine to ensure none of the changes could be reverted, then returned to the compression system code he'd been pretending to work on prior.

Pretending, because he'd already done everything he could. The reactor was designed to restrict expansion outside the containment chamber—that was the whole point. A contained reaction. A little star hanging out in its safe little bubble of hyper-compressed gravity. Now they wanted to let it loose, to make it grow—but the fact didn't change that they'd created a system incapable of it.

In not wanting to kill themsleves and everyone else, they'd done their jobs well. Shut down the divertor, the cryostat picks up the heat load until the solenoids demagnetize and the fusion fails, then the remaining superheated mass falls out the bottom of the ship. Shut down the cryostat, the structure melts—including the solenoids—and the whole thing liquifies before falling out the bottom of the ship.

Even if he knew how to circumvent that endless cascade, he didn't have time to enlist Puck or Owen to write new code—it could take days if not weeks to figure out, and at this point, they had minutes. There was only one way to get past it. In the end, the solution would not be brains, but brawn. Or fortitude, really.

He looked up to find Mesa staring at him, her overlarge Savant eyes unblinking through the haze of holographic interfaces.

"Cavalon," she said, tone flat.

He swallowed. "Mesa. All done?"

"I am finished. And you?"

"Almost," he said, trying hard not to glance nervously at the jump countdown. "Just a couple things I need to tweak."

She stood with her hands folded atop the workbench, lips pressed thin.

He awkwardly wiped a bead of sweat from the bridge of his nose with the gauze wrapping on the end of his left arm.

Yes, he could tell her, but he didn't see the point. Her Savant constitution would never allow for standing inside an active fusion reactor, even if the inner casing would provide some manner of protection. That'd only give her a couple extra minutes before bursting into flame.

She continued staring at him.

"So . . ." He cleared his throat. "I heard your work influenced the xenotech curriculum at Altum Institute. That's pretty cool."

She blinked once.

"Owen told me," he explained. "Sorry I never asked about it before. I've never been great at the whole friend thing."

"I appreciate the sentiment," she said slowly. "However, I feel as though you are . . . burying the lede, as they say."

He quirked a brow. "Who's this 'they' you reference every time you use an idiom? You're saying it. You are they. You can just say it."

Something like irritation tightened her visage. "Stop avoiding the question."

"You didn't ask one."

She stared at him, waiting.

"It's fine," he said, injecting as much strength into the statement as he could muster. Time to sandwich his lies with truths. "Yes, it's a problem. Yes, I considered triggering it remotely, and yes, I know we don't have the time or equipment. But I *can* trigger it on a delay."

There was the lie bit. That was not something that could happen. It had to be done physically, by hand. Singular hand, in his case. Luckily, repatching the hydrogen duplication module so it'd be wired directly into the photovoltaics bridge would only require *one*. It might be a little awkward, but he could do it.

"The delay is what I'm working on right now," he explained. A bit of a soggy final bun on the truth-lie-truth sandwich, but it was good enough. He gestured to the open screen in front of him, then held up his left arm. "The coding is somewhat complex, and I'm a little slower than normal at the moment."

She frowned. "Then let me help you with the input."

He shook his head. "It's a one-person job; you know how hard it is to dictate code—you refuse to do it yourself."

"This is different—"

"Why, because suddenly I'm a cripple and I need help?"

"Do not condescend to me."

"Really it's *me* I'm condescending to."

"*Cavalon.*" The way she growled out the name made his heart catch. She blinked at him, eyes glistening. "Do not push me away."

They stared at each other, unmoving. The heat of tears swarmed behind his eyes, but he blinked them away, forced them back down.

Fucking Mesa. With her brilliant brain, brilliant all of its own merit, not because it was some engineered clone of an evil genius's brain. She'd sought knowledge, strived for perfection, challenged herself, learned everything she could—all while surviving a nine-year war.

He couldn't break, or couldn't let her see him break, at least. She had to believe he didn't need her. Because the Sentinels needed that brilliant brain of hers to be on that last ark.

"I can't *speak* Viator, remember?" he said, striving to keep his voice even. "By the time I translate it and retranslate it to you, I could just input it myself."

Her lips pressed into an impervious line.

The hangar door slid open. Puck walked in, pace brisk, two rucks strapped either way over his back.

He approached the workbench. "Nice work, you two." He inclined his head at Cavalon. "Hey, man. Thanks for this." He glanced down at his nexus. "Mes, you ready?"

Mesa's eyes stayed locked on Cavalon.

Puck scratched the back of his neck. "EX ordered me to get you, then 'get the hell off her ship.' So . . ." He rocked back on his heels, rubbing his hands up the sides of his pants. Finally, he let out a long sigh. "Okay, guys. This is getting kinda weird."

Cavalon sighed. "Just trust me, okay? Please, Mes." He rounded the table and gripped one of her thin shoulders with his right hand. "I've got this. But to ensure the timing's right, I have to be here till the last jump to input the final equations into the delay."

Puck took Mesa's hand, and her gaze finally broke as she looked up at Puck with a thin smile. "Ready."

Puck turned and they walked to the exit.

"See you soon, Cav," Puck called over his shoulder. Mesa said nothing. Cavalon kept up his ruse of gibberish code input even after they'd gone. There was nothing left to do. He'd already linked his nexus to the CIC's nav computer, so he could tell when the fuckers jumped in and started firing on them, and he could wipe them—and anything within a few dozen light-years—out of existence.

Two jumps later, he startled as the hangar door slid open. Rake walked in.

Shit.

Her gaze slid over the reactor orb as she approached the workbenches. "Almost ready?" she asked.

"Yeah, uh, one sec," he said, voice cracking. He had no idea what to do. This wasn't part of the plan. She was supposed to have left on the same ark as Puck and Mesa.

"Need anything?" she asked, stepping up beside him, leaning one hip on the workbench.

"Um, what's the countdown, exactly?" he asked pointlessly.

"Twenty-two minutes till the last ship leaves."

He tapped aimlessly at the holographic menus.

"How do you plan to pull this off, anyway?" Rake asked.

"Well . . ." he began, then made a production out of clearing his throat. He had to get rid of her. He had to be boring enough that she'd walk away and go back to her ark and leave with the other officers like she was supposed to. "We're using the photovoltaics bridge to tie the reactor's hydrogen duplication system into the solar energy conversion array, then we'll use the ceronite as a starter to kick off a feedback loop that will rapidly generate mass within the shell, while simultaneously taking the core compression system offline."

She nodded slowly.

"The expanding mass alone will incinerate the *Lodestar*," he explained, "and the Guardian ship, in all likelihood. But for good measure, it'll have grown way too fast, and burn itself out of fuel within seconds. As it cools, it'll collapse, and voila—one supernova. Just like you asked."

"I see," she said, decidedly underwhelmed.

He opened a few other unrelated menus, giving her a curious look. "You know, I can catch up, in a minute, if you wanna go, or whatever."

"I can wait."

"I thought you were going with Mesa?" He tried to appear disinterested as he tapped at the screens, but it was no use.

Her amber eyes locked on to him, the color gone from her cheeks.

"What's wrong?" he asked.

Her jaw skimmed side to side. "Mesa told me you lied."

His heart slammed against his ribs. He regained control of his reaction, doing his best to seem confused. "What?"

"You gonna lie to *me* too?" she accused.

"Lie about what?"

"You can't trigger it remotely."

He bit down hard on the inside of his cheek. She was right; he couldn't lie to her. "Fine." He huffed out a hard breath. "We're out of time, and I don't have the tools either way."

"You intend to stay behind," she said, tone unnervingly flat.

"This is my star," he growled. "So, yes. I'm going to be the one to do it."

"Mesa felt the same way." Rake's glassy eyes searched him. "She wanted to stay. To be the one to do it. Do you know why instead, she let you lie to her face, then told me?"

His pulse beat hard in his throat, and he could only shake his head once.

"Because she was afraid she couldn't overpower you."

He stared, his short breaths loud in his ears. A palpable pressure strained the air around them.

Between blinks, Rake made her move. A metallic bitterness tinged his saliva as his Imprints flew into motion.

Her right hand darted to his left. He tried to knock it aside with his elbow, but he was too slow—she already knew the gaping weakness that was now his left side, she'd had time to plan it all, figure out the single most efficient thing she could do to take him down. Fuck her and her goddamn prowess.

Her fingers dug hard into his shoulder. She slammed her forearm against his chest, using the momentum to throw him to his back. His breath fled his lungs as he slammed into the decking. Pain whited the edges of his vision.

Her knee dug into his hip bone. Before he could regain his senses, she'd locked one side of a pair of mag-cuffs onto his left bicep, just above the elbow, the metal cold against his bare skin. She reached for his right elbow, and as he realized what she was trying to do, a surge of strength rushed into him.

He shoved her, but she barely swiveled away, her full complement of silver and copper Imprints coating her bare, scarred forearms and the sides of her neck. She forced his right arm over his chest, and the second mag-cuff closed around his bicep, locking his arms in an awkward X in front of him.

He growled, Imprints cutting into his chest muscles as he flexed impossibly against the restraints and shouted, "Rake, stop!"

She gripped his collar and yanked him to his feet. His vision swam with the sudden motion, adrenaline surging, scalding his cheeks. She hauled him toward the door.

"You don't even know what to do!" he protested.

"A connection must be made between the hydrogen duplication system and the photovoltaics bridge," she recited, gaze straight ahead, an icy bastion of composure. "By design they're separately derived systems, so they must be manually coupled. This can be achieved by accessing panel 18C within the posterior access tunnel."

He bared his teeth. Fucking Mesa—what the hell?

"She's wrong," he lied, grimacing as sweat stung his eyes. "The compression won't—"

"The compression system won't allow an influx of mass. She told me you'd try that. That's why the compression system must be taken offline within twelve seconds after activating the feedback loop."

He clenched his jaw as she dragged him into the starkly cool air of the corridor. Only a fraction of the light panels were illuminated, with every deck in low-power mode to accommodate the dwindling shields. His eyes scoured the vacant passage, the weight of the abandoned ship looming the farther from the reactor they got.

"Rake, please," he begged, trying not to trip over his own feet as she pulled him forward. "This is my responsibility."

"I get it," she said, tone still flat, autonomous. Her grip on his collar firmed. "You think martyring yourself will prove you're not him."

His lips parted, but he couldn't find the words to rebut it. He still couldn't lie to her.

"But that's not how it works," she continued. "You've already proven it. Knowing the truth changes nothing."

"It changes *everything.*"

"No," she said, affecting that assured tone of hers that made everything a simple fact of the universe. "The Cavalon I know isn't that man, and there's no amount of DNA that can convince me otherwise."

"Why do you get to be a martyr if I don't?" he accused.

"I'm not a martyr. I'm fulfilling my purpose. I took a literal blood oath to this ship, and I swore to Jackin I'd get the Sentinels to safety. And that's what I'm doing." She shook her head, and her determined tone grew wistful. "Everything has been leading to this point, Cav."

"What?" he scoffed. His reluctant, stumbling boot squeaks echoed down the corridor as she kept dragging him forward.

"Letting Kaize go," she replied. "Me being out here in the first place.

Restarting the dark energy generators. Every time it happened, I thought it was just my instincts. But now I know."

"Know . . . what?" he croaked, eyebrows knitting.

"It's the will of the universe. Caelestis. I'm meant to do this. I save the Sentinels. Then, it'll finally be enough."

"*Enough?* Rake, what are you . . ." His lips parted as he stared at the side of her face. At her *determination*—not resignation. An expression that remained steady, unwavering, jaw firm, eyes on the path ahead.

She'd *lied* to him.

That whole spiel she'd given on the *Synthesis* about "*saving those they could*" and "*letting go of those they couldn't.*" That was bullshit. She didn't believe that; that wasn't Rake. He was too tied up in his own shit. He should have noticed.

Losing Jackin had been the last straw. She'd fooled Cavalon into believing she was okay, and now she was trying to escape the suppressed pain in one fell swoop. He recognized it, because he'd tried it himself once.

"This is about losing Jackin," he said, his tone a quiet, flat statement devoid of accusation.

"No, this is about saving you," she corrected. "It's the logical course of action. They're going to need you."

"No, they're going to need *you*," he insisted, voice rising again. "I'm a fucking *mess*, Rake! When faced with your past on the *Presidian*, you held it together. When faced with mine on Elyseia, I totally fell apart."

"You rallied."

"Because of you! Without you, I'm useless."

She reaffirmed her grip on his collar, tone adamant. "You're stronger than you think, Cav. You risked your life to save me from the Divide. You reined me back in after I tried to kill Snyder. You kept it together on the *Presidian*, and guided our escape from the manor. And after you'd found out about Augustus—and lost a hand—you still got what we needed to save our people. Then you came back here, and you made it all work. You just have to accept it. Being competent is a responsibility, yes, but you're more than capable of handling it without me."

"This isn't what Jackin would have wanted," he said. "You know that."

"Ironically, I'm finally being the leader he wanted me to be."

Cavalon ground his teeth, twisting his arms against the unrelenting mag-cuffs. "I respectfully fucking disagree."

"He wanted me to think long-term," she explained, taking a turn down another empty corridor. "To plan ahead, to make the best calls for the whole. That's what I'm doing. I was so certain he was going to try and trade *you* . . . but he didn't. Because he knew we needed you."

"They need *you*, Rake," he growled. "What the hell are they going to do without you?"

She shook her head, voice thin. "There's a whole resistance out there already—Lugen planned all this . . ." Her gaze drifted down for a heartbeat before her expression hardened again. "Soldiers will be a dime a dozen soon. But *you*, Cav . . . that's unique."

He scoffed out a bitter laugh. "That's literally not true. There are at minimum two more of me out there."

"The Sentinels need you," she went on, ignoring him. "The whole galaxy needs you. Not only your brain, but your insight into Augustus, the System Collective, the Allied Monarchies, the Quorum, the whole broken system. How to bring it all down . . . and how to rebuild it after. That all dies today if you do."

He twisted his bound arms, fury welling in his chest. "Fuck whether the Sentinels need you, Rake—*I* need you!"

Her expression tightened, eyes going glassy, though she didn't look back at him. "Don't say that."

"I would have never thought to rig this explosion without you," he said, straining to keep his tone steady. "I wouldn't have even been able to *build* it without you. You force me to realize what I'm capable of. You were right, earlier. I'm not just Augustus's clone. I've become so much more. But only because of you."

She kept marching, but her lower jaw slid out, gaze flitting back to him every few steps. His heart thrummed—it was working. He had to keep pressing.

Grinding his teeth, he called on his Imprints.

"Augustus blames me for my failings," he went on, "but he made me that way—through decades of emotional abuse, through killing my father—and apparently my mother. But then came Rake. Rake, who trusted me from day one. Who believed in me when I was nothing but an arrogant asshole." He flexed his jaw, voice breaking as his composure faltered. "When all I wanted was for someone to kill me, because I was too much of a coward to do it myself."

Rake came to a halting stop, staring forward for a few long heartbeats. Then for the first time since she'd cuffed him, she looked back at him. Her cheeks were flushed, eyes round and glassy, lips slack.

She gave a slow head shake. "Augustus said . . ."

Then her brow knit, jaw firming, and he could practically see resolve weaving back into her presence. Grip firm on his collar, she kept marching, hauling him behind again as she said, tone monotonous, "Your grandmother is on that planet, Cavalon."

His mind went blank as his legs stopped working and he stumbled into her. She caught him, righted him, and kept walking.

His heart pounded as sweat poured down his temples. "She—you—what?"

"She fled the Core for her safety," Rake replied. "Jackin told me. I don't know all the details." She met his eyes again as his heartbeat tried to drown out her words. "I know you miss her. That you loved her. You can see her again, if you want to."

"Yes," he breathed, then squeezed his eyes shut, teeth clenching. "No! Not at the expense of you."

"Jackin asked something of me in that message," she said, returning her placid expression to the corridor ahead. "I have to ask you the same thing. I need you to not need me."

Cavalon growled in frustration, hot tears pooling behind his eyelids. No. Fuck. He had a plan; he had to stay focused. He inhaled a steadying breath, and his shoulders popped as he rolled them forward, biceps pressing tight against his chest.

"How about what we promised each other?" he said, injecting as much accusation into his tone as he could while masking the soft clicks of his Imprints. "You swore to me you'd never let go."

Her relentless pace slowed a fraction, and her chin dropped.

"I don't want to either," he pressed. "I *won't*."

Her lashes fluttered, her grip on his collar loosening so, so slightly.

He let the silence hang, let his tears fall, let it all distract her, because he'd finally worked his Imprints into a sheath on his upper arms, and she hadn't noticed.

She pushed a strand of hair from her forehead. Her gaze remained down, olive cheeks flushed, lips parted.

His Imprints slid a centimeter down his biceps. He closed his eyes, imagined his arms were metal, willed them to polarize, *believed* them to be magnetic . . .

With a slow exhale, his amassed gathering of Imprints slid over his elbows and down his forearms. Bringing the cuffs along with them.

They clattered to the floor at his feet.

He drew back his right fist and caught Rake in the jaw before she'd even turned around. She stumbled while he cursed—he'd aimed for the temple; he had to knock her out.

She recovered with alarming speed and retaliated with alarming ferocity, baring her teeth as she advanced on him so quickly, he barely retreated in time.

Her first swing came so close, her knuckles dragged through his beard. Her follow-up hit him squarely in the gut. He keeled over, stumbling back, nausea twisting his stomach.

Instinctively he ducked, the gust of air from her next swing blowing through his mussed hair. Stance wide, he struck out at her, but she evaded. Her follow-up did not miss.

His jaw cracked and he fell, head snapping against the decking as he slid back. Tears of anger and frustration and regret, but mostly pain, swelled behind his eyelids. Clearly the last time she hit him, she'd been holding back.

He groaned. Blood dripped from the corner of his mouth as he peeled his eyes open.

She stood over him, amber eyes alight, furious. He felt that same sharp kick in the gut he used to get on the *Argus* every time he saw her administering brazen authority as naturally as drawing breath.

Her fists tightened as she loomed over him. "You asked me how many people I was going to let the universe take from me?"

He swallowed blood-laden saliva.

"No more."

She drew back a fist, and Cavalon closed his eyes.

CHAPTER FORTY

✦

Adequin trudged into hangar bay D9, Cavalon's limp body slung over her shoulder. Kaplan stood waiting in the open hatch of the *Callisto.* Adequin ascended the ramp and lowered Cavalon to the deck just inside the main cabin of the small ship.

Kaplan stared at Cavalon, fingers scratching at her jawline. "I'll, uh, go run preflights," she said carefully, then disappeared toward the helm.

Beckar stepped up the ramp, the atlas pyramid under one arm. He paused as his eyes drifted over Cavalon, then up to Adequin. "I . . . have the final jump queued up, sir. Respool will be ready in just a few."

Adequin nodded, then knelt beside Cavalon. Her fingers fumbled over the hook of Jackin's dog tags, then her own. She secured both chains around Cavalon's neck, tucking the atlas medallion and cluster of tags under his shirt.

She wiped the dried blood from the corner of his mouth. Heat scratched her collar as she stared at his flushed cheeks, sweat-matted hair, unfurrowed brow, how at peace he looked when he was unconscious. She gripped his hand, letting the familiar comfort settle her. Though she didn't need it. Since the second Mesa told her, she'd been at peace with it. It'd been the easiest decision she'd ever made.

She cleared her throat. "When he wakes up, ask him to do me a favor?"

"Aye, sir," Beckar said softly.

"When he can, when it's safe . . . bury my and Griffith's tags on Myrdin. Tell him to wait for a thunderstorm."

She stood and met Beckar's haunted gaze. "Sir, you don't have to do this," he insisted, the edge of his voice creaking. "Let me."

"You don't have Imprints to protect you from the heat, you don't know how, and there's no time to explain."

His eyes fell, the muscles in his square jaw flexing for a few long moments before he muttered, "Consider this my formal objection."

She pressed out a bitter smile. "Noted." She held out her hand. "Thank you, Optio."

Beckar frowned, tucking the atlas pyramid against his ribs to extend his other hand. He shook hers in a firm grip. "Thank *you,* sir. For everything." He gave a grim shake of his head. "When I first sent out that mayday six months ago, I didn't think there was a chance in the void we'd survive it. I don't know how you did it—and not only the *Typhos,* but thousands of others . . . Thank you's not really enough."

"It's more than enough. And you're welcome." She looked back down at Cavalon. "But in return, I need you to keep him safe. That's an order."

"I will, sir," Beckar assured.

She gave a grateful nod, then turned and marched to the bay entrance, waiting at the controls as Beckar closed the *Callisto*'s ramp.

She sealed the bay door, blocking the ship from view.

On her nexus, she opened the respool timer, watching as it ticked down, expanding the defense overview to watch as the remaining dregs of the *Lodestar*'s shields soaked up the *Proteus*'s relentless fire. The countdown hit zero, and she triggered the jump.

Her vision swam.

"Jump confirmed," she said into comms. "*Callisto* cleared to launch."

On the bay terminal, she brought up the security feeds. Their ion engines ignited, and they left the hangar. She switched to outboard sensors, then watched as they disappeared, accelerating to warp speed.

She locked the hangar, swiping her clearance to shut down all docking access ship-wide. She checked her nexus. Three minutes and forty seconds until arrival.

She headed back into the abandoned halls toward the reactor bay.

CHAPTER FORTY-ONE

Cavalon woke to anxious boot squeaks.

Sweat slicked his skin, drying in the cool air, prickling his arms with icy goose bumps. His jaw ached and his head throbbed.

"Fucking hell," he groaned under his breath. His eyes cracked open.

Murky forms of gray and bronze aerasteel panels came into focus around him. He lay on a stiff crash bench near the back of a small, dimly lit cabin.

To his right, Optio Beckar paced out a short path, both hands scrubbing nervously over his square jaw.

To his left, a glint of gold caught Cavalon's eye. He craned his neck. The atlas pyramid rested on a flight dash in front of a woman sitting in the pilot's seat, elbows leaned on her knees, staring at the floor through the curtain of long black braids that fell over both shoulders.

Kaplan. An underling of Lugen's. Cavalon had been so busy making a supernova, they hadn't had a chance to meet, though he'd heard Rake talking to her over comms just before—

Fear spiked into his chest. Memories crashed into his mind: Rake dragging him, fighting him, knocking him out.

He struggled to sit up, realizing his arms had been cuffed together in front of his chest again. His fingers tingled—the bindings were far tighter this time around. That would make them more difficult, if not impossible, to escape from. Regardless, he sent his Imprints back into cuff-dismantling position.

"How can you just leave her there?" Cavalon snarled.

Kaplan's gaze shot up, hands dropping into her lap. Her eyes sharpened. "It wasn't my decision to make," she said, accusation thick in her low, raspy voice.

Rage swelled in Cavalon's chest, the veins in his neck tightening as he fought against his cuffs. He turned to Beckar and snapped, "And *your* excuse?"

Beckar's ghosted look remained, but his jaw firmed. "She gave me a direct order."

Cavalon growled, grinding his teeth, his eyes drifting shut. In that perfect engineered clone memory of his, he could see her drifting away from him again, her harness torn, tether floating freely, as clear as the first time. This was what he'd been afraid of for six months, ever since he'd almost lost her at the Divide. She was falling away from him again, and he couldn't do a damn thing to stop it.

He twisted onto his side to try and sit up again, but failed, biceps straining against the cuffs. His dog tags clanked heavy as he turned, sliding cool on his heated chest—far more weight than he was used to. His mouth went dry. Rake had given him her fucking dog tags. Bloody void.

Oh. Wait.

"Uncuff me!" he shouted, half-sliding off the bench as he attempted to stand without first sitting.

Kaplan's brow furrowed as she watched him struggle. Cavalon willed his Imprints to work faster, but they were unable to get under the tightness of the cuffs.

"Please," Cavalon begged, "I can save her!"

Beckar's cheeks blanched, his eyes tapering with a glint of desperate hope. After a few painfully long seconds, he marched toward Cavalon.

"Whoa, wait—" Kaplan protested.

Beckar ignored her. He tapped a code into the cuff's access panel and they slid open, dropping away.

Cavalon almost tripped over his own feet, fumbling at his collar as he sprinted up to the dash.

CHAPTER FORTY-TWO

Adequin stepped into a space suit. Her fingers slid over the seam and the nanite-infused fabric stitched together. She secured her helmet, then climbed the ladder.

At the primary control terminal, she unlocked the hatch, dismissed the vehement warnings, then followed the scaffolding around to the posterior access tunnel. Outside the hatch, she opened her suit nexus, synced it to her wrist nexus, then accessed the *Lodestar*'s primary systems.

Shields at 0.3 percent. Ninety seconds until arrival.

In the lull, her mind searched for something to process, but there was nothing. No reason to question, to wonder if she was doing the right thing. She was done asking other people to give their lives. The best thing she could do for the Sentinels would be to take herself out of the equation before the curse that had followed her since Paxus spread to all of them as well. Her crew aboard the *Argus* had been wiped from existence. Griffith had died on her watch. Jackin was as good as dead. And all the Sentinels she didn't make it to in time . . .

She'd played her role well the last week, but she couldn't continue to act with her head instead of her heart. She just didn't have it in her. As much as she wanted to believe she could, she knew what she was at her core. The Legion had raised her as a cog in the wheel, and she couldn't separate herself from that. She'd been designed as a weapon to be wielded by a surer hand.

Besides, it was what the universe wanted.

She'd thwarted it twice—first aboard the *Argus* and again when they restarted that first dark energy generator—but it still needed its pound of flesh, one way or the other, so she would give it what it wanted, and maybe at last, it would be quiet.

Her nexus beeped. The scanners flashed, confirming the Guardian's ship had jumped in. Their Evorsors deployed, and they began their barrage. She had five minutes.

She summoned her Imprints to coat her neck, chest, stomach—an extra layer to protect her vital organs. The hatch control panel carped out more warnings before finally giving way to her clearance. She stepped inside the airlock, sealed the door behind her, and tapped to access the interior hatch.

The door gave a hissing whine. In her HUD, the exterior oxygen meter dropped to zero, then the hatch's control panel flashed green. She grabbed the inset handles and slid the heavy door open.

Oppressive heat robbed her of breath while her suit attempted to acclimate, her temperature gauge blooming a bright crimson. A brassy, metallic bitterness bloomed on her tongue.

Ten meters down the sloped passage, a narrow, cursory observation window sat in the interior shell. She stepped toward it. Her visor flickered, then shorted out a few times before resetting.

Tapping her suit's nexus, she muted the alarms blaring in her ears and dismissed her HUD's hostile environment warnings. Under her suit, her skin burned. Her boots were too heavy as she dragged one foot in front of the other, slogging down the passage to the window. She had to see it one last time before it consumed her.

She peered inside, into the reactor's core, contorted through the warped glass. The mass churned. Arcs of magenta flame rimmed the edges. The curved panels lining the containment chamber shone with impossibly radiant light, scorching into Adequin's vision. Her eyes watered, and she had to shut them.

She turned away, retreating a few meters up the passage to the local console. She input the admin password Mesa had given her to access the raw code, then carefully made the changes. The holographic display flickered as she backed out to the maintenance menu and unlocked access to panel 18C, home to incoming circuitry for all systems. More passcodes, then more warnings, backed up by verification warnings—all dismissed.

She stepped across the passage to panel 18C, pulled the impact driver from her tool belt, and zipped off the bolts holding the large panel in place. Within, she twisted open two small cogwheels to unlock the vacuum-sealed secondary panel. Inside, heat-shielded wiring ran in tidy paths between an orderly grid of rack-mounted modules.

In her HUD, she brought up the sketch Mesa provided, matching the two modules in question. After tapping the release command into her nexus, one popped free from the rack. She pulled it out, tucked safely inside its sleek, shielded chassis, then inserted it into a free slot beside the second module.

A soft beep sounded in her suit comms. Sixty seconds.

On her nexus, she activated the connection routine Cavalon had designed. Amber status lights on the two modules blinked slowly in unison before finally shifting to solid green.

She drew in a steadying breath and initiated the next routine, the one that would tell the jump drive to activate the ceronite. A high-pitched whine rang out behind her, and she resisted glancing back. She only had twelve seconds to deactivate the compression system, but there was no reason to be delicate at this point.

She reached inside panel 18C, gripped the long edge of the compression system's module in both hands, then ripped it free of the rack—and free of its shielded chassis. It sparked as the metal instantly heated in her hands, and she tossed it away. It skidded across the floor, exposed wires melting before it burst into flames.

Her gaze drifted up. All around, dots of impossibly bright light pricked into existence.

A dozen, then a hundred, then a thousand radiant points crystallized into the air, drifting as her eyes followed the glittering formations up the length of the sloped passage. Her saliva suffused with the taste of metal.

A dense wave of heat assailed her back. She turned around. Within the containment chamber, the mass swelled outward. First by centimeters, then a meter, then two, then five. The magenta flames morphed to a violent red-orange, spiraling into a furious maelstrom around the expanding mass.

The wall of the containment chamber wavered, twisting—a heat mirage, maybe. Or maybe it was liquifying.

A pressure weighed hard against her chest and the air vacated her lungs. Her rib cage withdrew, tightening around her organs, a crushing grip of unchecked gravity. Her suit grew heavy and her shirt stuck to her skin, but not from sweat.

Her leaden Imprints ground against her muscles as they dragged across her superheated skin, aimlessly relocating, spreading thin across her body.

She blinked down at the back of her gloved hand. Where a single, strange speck of black materialized.

The air around her densified, a pressure swelling hot behind her eyes. The hovering pricks of light replicated interminably and every molecule coalesced to white.

CHAPTER FORTY-THREE

✦

Again, she lingers.

She is at once nowhere and everywhere, time is both inert and infinite. The indistinct haze fractures—a shadowed, supernal crack in the ether, an intersection where space and time converge to light.

She yearns for it, this place where form and burden are held in abeyance. She reaches for it, straining, digging her metaphysical fingers into its marrow.

But they slide right through—its substance divine and immaterial, it is nothing, and she can already feel the electric snap of atoms adhering, clinging, saddling her with corporeal strain.

Everything hurt.

Adequin's heart beat long and slow in her chest, each pump brutal agony until it found its rhythm. It pushed blood relentlessly into her aching limbs, her spine stiff against a cold, flat surface. A briny taste coated her dry throat.

A staticky thrum of electronics buzzed, low at first, then escalating to a shrill zenith accented by the sharp scent of burning flesh.

Her eyes flew open. Her visor sparked, spraying searing embers across her cheeks. She clawed at the latches and tossed the helmet off. It caught flame as it skidded across the floor, then fizzled out.

Panting, she pawed at her face, smothering the remaining embers. Her eyes darted around the dimly lit room—a hazy blur of metal panels, glowing green. A meter away at the base of a wide column stood a pair of black boots.

Adequin's clouded gaze drifted up the figure. The rolled sleeves of a muted teal flight suit revealed a weathered, slate-gray carapace, flecked with shades of maroon. They stood with their arms crossed over their chest. Four black eyes stared, unblinking, thin lips pressed flat. "Rake."

Adequin swallowed against her bone-dry throat a few times before she could respond. "Kaize."

The pleated skin lining their forehead bunched, and they glanced at Adequin's charred helmet. "Suit electronics are generally not recommended for transfer through the summoner."

"Noted," she sighed. She winced as she touched her stomach gingerly, where her clothes had fused with skin. It'd started to cool, leaving the impression of crisp, raw burns underneath. "I wasn't aware I'd be . . . transferring," she said.

"I assumed as much."

Adequin's Imprints slid sluggishly as she pushed to sitting. She leaned back, head spinning, slumping against an inset wall console behind her. She inhaled a deep breath while her twisting vision righted.

Behind Kaize, a cluster of floor-to-ceiling columns filled the far side of the room. A bright chartreuse light glowed from within each pillar.

"Where am I?" she asked.

"The *Presidian*," Kaize replied. "Specifically, the summoner control room. I would have brought you aboard somewhere more comfortable, but . . ." They glanced at the sealed doorway across the room. "Some of my crew were not pleased with my decision to come. Keeping you here will allow for quick egress once we arrive."

"Arrive where?"

"We are en route to rendezvous with your aide's ship."

She pinched the bridge of her nose. Her aide? She moistened her dry lips, then remembered: The last time they were aboard the *Presidian*, she'd hastily named Cavalon as her aide to avoid any suspicion about who he was. But how did they know where Cavalon's ship was? How had they even known she'd needed help?

She squeezed her eyes closed, but her addled mind couldn't put the pieces together.

"His Viator is atrocious," Kaize remarked, "but he made a convincing plea for your value."

Adequin raised an eyebrow. "He *called* you?"

"He did."

"And you came . . ." Adequin said, hoping saying it aloud would help it seem more real. It did not. "Even though your people were against it?"

"You did the same for me, once."

Adequin pressed her head against the console, sweat dripping down the nape of her neck. She tugged open the collar of her suit, letting in some marginally cooler air. "How did you even get here so quickly?" she asked, her voice cracking with dryness.

"We were near an Arcullian Gate at the time. Then we took an obscation."

"Obscation?"

Kaize stretched their neck side to side, then said, "A gateless exit."

Right. Because that was a thing now. "I hope it won't delay you too much," Adequin said. "I know you were still working to repair dark energy generators."

Kaize's shoulders shifted. "It took us many hours to arrive, and will take more than thrice that to return, but we will recover."

Adequin pushed a tangle of sweat-soaked hair off her forehead. "Wait. Hours?"

"Yes."

She slid her fingers over her suit's built-in nexus, but the charred fabric didn't respond. She pulled off her glove, hissing as the blackened flesh of her hand stung in the open air. Pushing up her sleeve, she tapped at her wrist band nexus, which stuttered out a few jittering holographic bursts before a wavering orange screen appeared.

Adequin stared, unblinking. It'd been less than ten minutes.

Her eyes returned to Kaize. "When did you get the call?"

Kaize's head tilted. "Roughly four hours ago."

Adequin's mind raced. Cavalon couldn't have called them four hours ago. They were still waiting for the arks to arrive at that point. "That's impossible," she breathed.

Kaize let out a soft hum. "Caelestis, Sentinel. As with the curanulta, sometimes it must weave its way out and back in to achieve its ends."

Her lips parted as she gaped at Kaize. She was starting to think she didn't understand the full meaning of caelestis.

Kaize uncrossed their arms, then picked up the bladed staff resting against the wall beside them, gripping it in both taloned hands to lean against it. "I take this . . . rather aggressive explosion to mean you are at war?"

Adequin exhaled, pressing the air from her lungs for a few moments.

Back to it, then. She'd accepted her fate, but now she had to backpedal, reorient. She had to start thinking about what it meant that she was still alive.

Kaize was right. There was a rebellion waiting for her.

"Yeah," she replied. "It's not war, not yet. But it will be."

Kaize's deep black eyes fluttered with a few short blinks.

"Our reasons are just," Adequin added, the steadfast assurance escaping her lips reflexively. "There's corruption, abuse of power. They're trying to cleanse us, genetically. And we recently learned . . . well, that we may have reason to fear for the survival of our species. They must be stopped—*he* must be stopped. Or we risk everything. I hope you can understand."

"I do," Kaize replied. "You were willing to give your life for this cause. That is a noble sacrifice."

"No," she said, head shaking, Jackin's voice ringing in the back of her mind. "If you love something, it's not a sacrifice."

Kaize's chin lifted. "Well said, Sentinel."

"I can't take credit for that one, I'm afraid."

"Well, then it is invigorating to hear there are other humans who share your capacity for wisdom."

Adequin tried to give an appreciative nod, but a heavy mantle of fatigue settled on her shoulders, and it came out more of a jittering headshake. "I thought you'd be more upset," she said, tone wavering. "That we're fighting more wars."

"I am not pleased," Kaize admitted, "but if what you say is true, then I cannot fault you. Maybe we wouldn't be on the eve of extinction if my ancestors had stood up for their principles and refused war with your kind."

Adequin licked her dry lips, brow furrowing. "You mean the Viator War?"

Kaize inclined their head. "As you call it."

"There were Viators who opposed it?"

"Many. But those who had been named sovereigns were steadfast. They knew what would come, and believed the only safe option was to take this galaxy for themselves. Those who opposed eventually conceded—as you know, one of our core tenants is cohesion. We had to have that in order to escape our home galaxy, to accomplish what we did along the way, to make this place the levalaine. But it is not an infallible system."

Adequin shook her head, unable to translate levalaine. "Your *home* galaxy? Why'd you leave?"

"We had to. It is now beyond."

"Beyond what?"

Kaize's main set of eyes blinked slowly a few times. "Your myth that we came from beyond the Divide is not inaccurate, Sentinel. Simply a case of misconstrued timeline."

Adequin's aching muscles cramped as she blew out a hard breath.

They really had come from "beyond." But it was a beyond that no longer existed. Their galaxy had been destroyed by the collapsing universe.

"And you came here . . ." she said, throat closing around the words.

"Yes," Kaize confirmed. "We fled galaxy to galaxy for millennia, and while we did, we worked, devising the means to keep it at bay. We had only just arrived in this galaxy when the technology was finally ready."

Adequin's head bobbed in an unconscious nod.

"I do not know all the details of that time," Kaize admitted. Their gaze drew distant, tone softening. "Other than the images of our deserted generation ships, burned into the ancestral dreams."

Adequin's brow creased. "Is that the same as your ancestral memory?"

"Similar. Though where the dreams have flourished of late, our memories have waned. In the centuries since your ancestors deployed their retributive mutagen, we've lost clarity regarding our past, as well as that which lies outside this universe."

"*This* universe," Adequin echoed. "Am I translating that correctly?"

Kaize's chin lifted slowly. "I confess, I am unsure what to confide in you, Sentinel. Though I believe you trustworthy, I am not sure how much you can . . ." Their black eyes narrowed. "Handle."

Adequin blew out a heavy sigh. She wasn't sure either, honestly.

A sharp trill cut through the electrostatic quiet of the summoner room. Kaize stood up straighter, glancing at the terminal screen behind them. "Caelestis gives us our answer. We have arrived."

"Wait . . ." Adequin tried to push to standing, but her stomach heaved, and she slid back down.

Kaize stepped to the terminal and began tapping through menus. "The *Presidian* will not be in touch for a time, after this."

"Why?"

"We must travel a great distance. It will take many cycles."

"What? Where are you going?"

"Through the Inward Expanse and beyond the galactic core."

"Void, why?" There weren't even Apollo Gates on that side of the galaxy. Though . . . there could be Arcullian Gates. She'd never thought to check if their atlas extended that far.

"The other sides of our galaxy must be shored," Kaize answered. Their gaze turned from the terminal screen, locking on to Adequin. "The Divide withdraws from more than one direction, Sentinel."

Adequin shook her head, the warmth draining from her face. "But, it must still be so far away—the other side of the universe? Before it reaches our galaxy?"

"There will come a time when those two words will be synonymous."

"Excuse me?" Adequin choked out.

Kaize's look flitted to the sealed doorway before returning to Adequin. "It is why my people have fought so hard for a stake here. As I said, this galaxy is the levalaine."

Adequin tripped over her own thoughts for a few seconds before finding the words. "Levalaine—I don't know that term."

"It is the . . . culmination. The refuge of this universe."

Her lips parted, heart racing. "What the hell does that mean?"

"It means there are darker times to come," Kaize said, then began to speak very quickly. "It means all capable species are fleeing the collapse, and those who survive will eventually be driven here. Some may prove allies, but many may be just as unwilling to peacefully coexist as my ancestors. That is why it is more important than ever your people find equilibrium."

Adequin's ears rang and heat seared her face, her mind unwilling to parse what Kaize claimed.

"I wanted to tell you, before," they admitted. The skin folds on their forehead tightened. "My advisor cautioned against it. They do not always share my same proclivities. At least I have given warning. But we are out of time. For now, you have your own war to fight."

"Wait—" Adequin croaked.

The terminal chimed. Kaize glanced at it, then back at Adequin, the skin folds lining their face stretching thin. "May caelestis favor you, Sentinel."

Adequin opened her mouth to protest, but the sound her throat exhaled disappeared into the ether. Her Imprints scattered, black specks materialized across her arms, and she collapsed into darkness.

CHAPTER FORTY-FOUR

Cavalon stared at the floor of the cabin, where flecks of raw bone sparked into existence. Then sinew. He clamped his eyes shut. He'd already seen it once; he didn't need a refresher.

"What . . . the . . ." Kaplan drawled.

The decking behind Cavalon clanged, and he peeked over his shoulder from behind slitted eyelids. Yep. Beckar had passed out.

"Rake?" Kaplan said, bewildered awe in her tone.

Cavalon opened his eyes.

Rake lay faceup on the floor in a space suit, no helmet, sweaty strands of her disheveled brown hair clinging to the sides of her face.

"What in the bloody void . . ." Kaplan muttered, crouched at Rake's side, hands hovering a few centimeters over her as if she might need to gather her back into existence.

Rake groaned, then twisted away from Kaplan and threw up on the floor.

She rolled back. "Sorry," she croaked. "Doing that twice in rapid succession is *way* too much."

"Shit," Kaplan said. "Are you okay? What just happened? How are you here?"

"Viators have teleportation," Rake mumbled.

Kaplan froze, mouth agape.

Rake clutched her arms against her stomach, eyes squeezing shut with a tight grimace. "Anyone else taste metal?"

Cavalon cleared his throat. "Uh, Kaplan?" he said, and the woman's wide eyes shot up to meet his. "You have a rad kit? Potassium iodide cartridges?"

She started to nod, slowly at first, then with increasing certainty. "Yeah, yeah, in the hold." She stood, skirting a wide berth around Rake. "Be right back." She disappeared through the back door.

Cavalon scratched his beard a few times before dragging his feet forward. He knelt at Rake's side, then sat back on his feet, gaze dropping to his lap.

A confusing mixture of regret and relief soured in his stomach. They'd been punching each other mere minutes ago. But now she was here, alive. It'd worked. Some-fucking-how.

Rake drew in a long breath, a furrow creasing her brow. "The *Lodestar*?" she asked.

He nodded. "The neutrino emissions in that direction are off the charts. It's gone."

She drew in a ragged breath, then pushed to sitting. He moved to stop her, but her arms were already pulling him into a hug. He hugged back, his sweaty cheek pressed against her sweatier temple.

A hard lump stuck in his throat as he mumbled into her hair, "Told you I wouldn't let go."

Her grip tightened.

Hours later, Rake looked marginally less like she might spontaneously turn inside out. Some of the color had returned to her olive cheeks, her wheezing breaths had smoothed out, and her hands had almost entirely stopped trembling.

She sat close to Cavalon on the ship's single crash bench, her left elbow hooked in his right, her right hand clamping his upper arm, her shoulder pressed into his. He wanted to make a joke about not meaning she should *literally* never let go, but from her ongoing silence and far-off gaze, she was dealing with some kind of PTSD, likely from almost being consumed by a swelling mass of stellar fire. Though he couldn't shake the feeling it was something more.

"We're on approach," Kaplan said, glancing back at them, her long black braids drifting over her shoulder.

Rake unwound herself and stood, and Cavalon suddenly felt chilly and asymmetrical in her absence.

He followed to look over Kaplan's shoulders at the wide viewscreen above the dash. Beckar joined them, holding an icepack to the back of his head.

"It's not in the SC registry," Kaplan explained, "so there's no designation. We call it Akhet."

They approached the daylight edge of the planet. From beneath swirls of cloud cover, broad grayish-brown land masses were cut through by swaths of green and meandering paths of cobalt.

Kaplan tapped open comms. "Orbital Defense Command, this is Legator Levi Kaplan aboard the *Callisto*."

"ODC here, transponder accepted, *Callisto*. Welcome back, sir. Please send secondary authentication."

"Sending now."

"Received, *Callisto*. Handshake complete. Proceed to grid Y494 for gate access."

Through the viewscreen, a wide arc of shimmering silver rippled off in every direction. A square opening materialized in the translucent membrane, and Kaplan guided them toward it. Pressure weighed on Cavalon's eardrums, and he stretched his jaw to pop his ears as they passed through.

They had a transmission shield over the whole damn planet. And the fact that they needed a gate meant it wasn't just any old transmission shield, but the ship-ravaging, EMP variety.

"Transit Command, this is the *Callisto*," Kaplan said, "requesting landing clearance. VIPs aboard."

"Understood, *Callisto*. You're cleared to land—kept 6H open for ya, sir."

Minutes later, the *Callisto* cleared through a thin haze of clouds. They dropped into a valley dotted with small copses of short trees, rimmed on either side by broad, dusty plateaus. A shallow river snaked between, looking well on its way to going dry, surrounded by fields of cracked clay.

To the north, a massive metal structure jutted up from the western edge of the river, a wide half circle at least fifteen stories tall—some kind of stronghold, though Cavalon didn't recognize the architecture. In the shadow of the complex, modern buildings perched in neatly aligned rows, their recurring designs of tan and gray making them look like the prefabricated modular constructs from Outer Core colonization adverts.

The surrounding area fell away into cultivated fields. A few swaths of land were hemmed by electric fences, containing tiny dots of white and gray and black and red . . .

Cavalon's stomach growled, and he leaned toward the screen, squinting. "Is that . . . cattle?"

Kaplan slid him an amused look. "Yeah . . ."

Cavalon's mouth watered.

Beckar eyed the prefab structures. "Who are all these people?"

"You name it, we got it," Kaplan said. "Soldiers, scientists, politicians, engineers, exiled former citizens. For over a decade, Praetor Lugen's been hiding people out here, people the SC's wanted killed. The ones he could save, at least."

Rake shifted as she crossed her arms. Her eyes stayed locked on the screen, visage clear and open, but jaw firm, shoulders stiff. Some mix of contemplative, relieved, and pissed off.

Kaplan flew the *Callisto* west toward a ground-level spaceport, a wide expanse of well-demarcated landing pads rimmed with support buildings and repair hangars. Twenty freight ships of varying size filled almost every pad—the arks that'd flown the Sentinels to safety. Soldiers were lined up like ants out the cargo hatches, trailing into makeshift medical tents. Armed guards paced the perimeter and armored vehicles dotted the landing pads, dozens posted to keep a keen eye on the newcomers.

"The MPs are only a security precaution," Kaplan explained, glancing back at Rake. "Medical's on it too; they'll help figure out the rationing situation. Need to make sure we don't shock anyone's system." Then she looked over her other shoulder at Cavalon. "Which means no sudden influx of red meat. For a little while, at least."

Cavalon gave a dutiful nod. "I will not devour the cattle without permission."

Kaplan landed on one of the few open pads near the back, then opened the hold. They stepped out, and Cavalon inhaled the thick humid air. White clouds dotted the deep-blue sky.

Rake looked across the spaceport toward a rim of low hills, which acted as a natural barrier between the inner edge of the stronghold and the rows of prefab multistory buildings. She stared unblinking at the tiny dots of people moving on the gravel street.

Cavalon nudged her with his elbow. "You okay?"

"Yeah." She blinked rapidly a few times, then met his gaze. "Just . . . for once, it feels like the universe is giving."

A smile tugged at his lips.

"Sir," Beckar said, stepping up beside Rake, "with your permission, I'd like to locate Security Chief Warner and Centurion Puck, and ensure we're doing everything we can to facilitate."

Rake nodded, then glanced at Kaplan. Kaplan got on her nexus and connected Beckar with an escort, who appeared in short order, leading him off through the sea of deplaning Sentinels.

Kaplan led them to the nearest medical tent, where a short, lab-coated man gave them each a quick inspection. Rake remained patient and oddly placid as she explained that the biotool's inability to determine her white blood count was likely due to being successfully treated for a Viator infection, only to then receive a concentrated dose of ionizing radiation.

When the medic recovered from that bit of terrifying news, he injected Rake with a slow-release anti-rad medication, treated and wrapped the charred skin on the backs of her hands, then sent them on their way. Outside, Kaplan waited in a small open-air transport.

Cavalon climbed in after Rake, and Kaplan drove them toward the stronghold. The slate-gray stone facade had begun to crack away in places, revealing the metal framework underneath. Colossal stone stanchions— empty bases for long-dismantled artillery turrets—flanked the two visible entrances. A mammoth variety of ivy grew around the structure's base, with bronze-tipped, sea-green leaves, each as large as a small starfighter. The stalks climbed over ten meters, less than a sixth the height of the building.

As they drew closer, Cavalon's gaze stuck on the immense hangar door, framed by towering blades of aerasteel. The metal edges sliced into the stone edifice like the opened vents of a massive grate. The cascade of planar columns came to a peak over the center, where a flat, circular slab of metal sat empty—likely where a plaque or flag used to hang.

"Damn . . ." His gaze drifted up the looming wall. "What *is* this place?"

"A Cathian command post," Kaplan answered.

Cavalon blinked a few times, staring at her. She was being serious.

Though, it made a degree of sense. Cathians were a species eradicated by the Viators well before humans got involved in the all the fun. A Cathian base wasn't likely to be featured on any star chart created in the last three thousand years. It also meant it would be *really* old and *really* run-down, but they were pretty used to that at this point.

"We've added on, clearly," Kaplan explained, jutting her chin toward the prefab structures. "And we're still renovating, but it's working for us. Lots of old, strange shit inside the stronghold, though. Most people prefer to bunk up in the outbuildings."

Kaplan drove toward an open transport access door and into the main hangar. Overhead, a complicated helical pattern of truss crossed the towering ceiling. As Kaplan steered around a cluster of small starships in varying degrees of broken, Cavalon's gaze caught on something strange tucked in the far corner: a massive, worn sculpture of a tall, thin, winged species—a Cathian. It held a long, narrow rifle in its spindly arms, while hawklike feet gripped the edges of the metal plinth. Two compound eyes dominated either side of the oval head. From his overly detailed royal education, Cavalon knew the winged portion was a cultural inclusion—an ornament of war—and not a part of the species' actual biology.

Kaplan parked on the outskirts of a small motor pool near the inner wall of the hangar, lined with a half-dozen lift access doors. "I'll work on getting the big guy on the horn," she said as they climbed out of the transport. "But I'll show you guys to quarters first if you want to get some rest. It could take a few hours."

"CJ . . ."

Cavalon's heart kicked hard against his ribs. The resulting wave of adrenaline instantly nauseated him.

His gaze swung to his right. Where Corinne Mercer stood. Just a few meters away.

Her arms were crossed tight, one hand raised to hold her chin, thin fingers draped over her mouth. More lines etched her ivory skin than his memory could account for.

Cavalon startled as a hand squeezed his left arm. He tore his gaze from Corinne to Rake. She gave an encouraging nod, then followed Kaplan past the conveyance lifts.

Cavalon watched them go until they rounded a corner and fell out of sight. Leaving him alone in the Cathian hangar on a secret planet in the Drift Belt with his . . . grandmother.

He looked back to Corinne. But as she approached, his eyes drifted up to the looming Cathian statue behind her. His sight went unfocused on the mosslike verdigris shrouding the wide plinth.

He didn't look down, but he knew Corinne had stopped nearby from the sweet, mild scent of overmilked coffee, flooding his mind with memories of when things weren't nearly so grim and shitty. Or rather, when he was too young and naive to properly notice how grim and shitty things were.

As she craned her neck to try and catch his gaze, he finally gave in and met her blue eyes.

Her cheeks blanched. Briefly, she looked terrified.

"It's really you," she said, voice paper thin, almost lost in the whining echo of an impact driver. "I can't . . ."

She hugged him. Her thin arms squeezed with surprising strength.

He froze.

He had no idea how to be.

He thought furious might be the right answer, but that didn't seem quite right. So instead, he just stood there and let her hug him and wondered for a fleeting moment if she thought he was his father. Because she'd abandoned them both. She might not even know his father was dead. But she'd called him CJ . . .

Then he realized something that had somehow not occurred to him even once since he'd found out: Corinne *had* to know about the cloning.

Furious started to seem like the right answer.

"I'm sorry, CJ," she whispered into his neck. "I love you."

And with that, every ounce of rising anger evaporated.

He was way too damn tired to be mad at one of the handful of people left alive that gave a shit about him. He didn't want to hold grudges against the people he loved. That list was too few, and life too short.

So he tightened his arms around her, and gave into the warmth of the embrace.

Rake was right. It felt like the universe was finally giving. And at this point, it fucking owed him one.

CHAPTER FORTY-FIVE

Adequin tried to sleep, but it was beyond pointless. Utter exhaustion racked every cell in her body, every neuron in her brain, but every time she shut her eyes, she could see nothing but fire.

And every time she opened them, a heavy, impending dread settled deep into her bones and the room seemed to narrow as the universe crept in from every edge.

A few very long hours later, Kaplan returned to escort her to a secure strategy room.

They entered through a high doorway, where a ramp sloped a half story down into a flattened basin of dark concrete. On the partially re-painted walls hung a few holographic squares of light, one showing a topographical map, another a series of security feeds. A half-dozen indi-vidual control stations sat around the room in varying degrees of instal-lation, though none were active.

Kaplan went straight to the circular command table at the center. She expanded an amber holographic interface and tapped through a few screens before taking a step back. "Call's ready to be patched in. Just hit connect when you're ready."

"Thanks, Legator."

Kaplan inclined her head and left, leaving Adequin alone in the strat-egy room. She faced the glowing amber screen, then tentatively tapped to connect.

The menu disappeared, and a square display projected over the ta-ble. An image flickered into it seconds later. Adequin strove to keep her breath steady.

Lugen. White hair, narrow face, sharp cheekbones, his pallid com-plexion tinged blue in the holographic light. In the years since she'd last seen him, the lines of his face had grown deeper, his brown eyes hooded under a sagging brow.

Adequin's spine straightened, her fist drawing to her chest instinc-tively. She couldn't remember the last time she'd saluted.

Lugen's tired eyes drifted across his feed, then came to a stop. "Dex-tera . . ."

Adequin sucked in a long breath, meeting Lugen's gaze in the video feed. "It's excubitor, sir."

"Right." His dry voice crackled through the speaker. "Old habits."

The static silence rang loud in her ears, and she couldn't formulate a single coherent way to react. So she said, "What the *hell*, sir?"

He sighed. "I know, Rake. There's a lot to discuss."

"You think?" she fumed, a wave of unexpected heat radiating through her. "Let's start with that fucking useless call we had at Kharon Gate six months ago."

"I know," he said, gaze cast down, but voice calm as ever. "That was not ideal; I was caught off guard. I didn't know you were still out there. I saw the memo announcing the withdrawal, but I didn't know they'd never actually passed down the orders." His gaze lifted again, lips pressed thin as he shook his head. "I want to explain everything, Rake, but we don't have enough time. This connection's routing integrity will be compromised in just a few minutes."

Her jaw firmed. She didn't care. She saw no better way to use the time. "What about the Divide? Did you know it would collapse?"

"No," he said, resolute. "I had no idea. That was a coincidence. A terrible one. I never would have sent you out there if I'd have thought that could ever happen."

She glanced down, rubbing at the edge of the gauze wrapping her burned hands.

Lugen pinched his eyes closed for a few long moments. Then his voice crackled through, quiet and soft. "I know stationing you out there felt like a punishment, but I did it to protect you. In case Akhet was discovered before we were ready . . . so you'd still be safe." He leaned forward, his brown eyes glistening as they caught the light. "I've lost so many good soldiers fighting this cold war, Rake. For over fifteen years. I didn't want you to become another person I couldn't protect."

She assessed his weary expression, his fervent tone of voice. She believed him.

But she also knew how his mind worked. There was no way that was the only reason. It was too convenient to be mere coincidence.

"So the Sentinels were always part of your plan?" she said, not sure why she bothered to form it as a question.

He gave a thin smile. "Perceptive as always." He sat back again, nodding. "It *was* primarily to protect you. But yes. I assigned you to the Divide and gave you that rank because I knew we had a veritable army wasting away out there. And I knew if anyone could unite them and bring them to me in one piece, it'd be you. I thought we'd have a few more years. That we would be able to plan that together and execute it on our own terms. But I'm not surprised you still managed to muster an army without me even telling you you needed to. We were always in sync."

A twitch of relief tugged at her ribs and she gave a stilted nod.

She could—*should*—be pissed at him. For lying all these years, misleading her, positioning her like any other pawn in his galactic cold war. But it meant one very important thing: It'd had meaning. She hadn't lingered at the Divide for over five years for nothing, for no reason. She still didn't know if the ends would ever justify the means, if anything could ever make up for the losses she'd endured. It was a small, bitter solace. But it *was* a solace.

"I'm proud of you for taking the initiative like this," Lugen went on. "We're going to need you and your best officers to take the mantle out there. We have a lot of civilians right now; I'm hoping this influx of trained soldiers will help fill some leadership gaps. Is Bach with you?"

Her fingers drifted to her neck, but the chain was gone, along with Jackin's. Cavalon still had them. "No, sir," she said, voice creaking. She cleared her throat. "Bach's gone. Dead."

"Void." Lugen sat back, scrubbing a hand over his mouth. "I'm sorry, Rake. I know you two were close." He seemed truly distressed, grief tightening his visage as he pushed a hand through his thinning hair. "I understand you lost North infiltrating Mercer Manor?"

Her cheeks heated. "Yes. He traded his life for mine."

She drew in a breath and steeled herself, preparing for the reprimand. She'd left someone behind—someone who knew the location of this place. She'd made Akhet far more vulnerable than it'd ever been.

Instead, he said, "I'm sorry."

She blinked rapidly a few times.

"Were you close?" he asked.

"Yes," she admitted. "I'm sorry, sir. I know that's dangerous."

"Don't apologize. I'm not mad. Your heart has always been your greatest asset, Adequin."

Her expression slackened, warmth filling her chest. This conversation kept taking turns she didn't expect.

"We are going to need that moving forward," he went on. "Our soldiers need to see it in Command. And after this whole debacle, especially. I'm going to have to go radio silent for a long while. Can I count on you to take the helm?"

She gave a soft head shake, brows knitting together. "Won't you be at the helm, sir?"

He wet his lips, head shaking slowly. "There's very little chance of me surviving this. My cover will eventually dissolve. Maybe sooner than we'd planned."

"Then leave," she pleaded. "Now."

"I can't. The job's not done yet, and we can't play our hand before we're ready. I've been walking this line, Rake . . ." He blew out a shallow breath. "This terrible line. For so long. We have to make it worth it, in the end."

Adequin blinked heavily, eyes scanning his hewn, glassy-eyed visage. She'd seen that look before, just once. He was afraid.

She cleared her throat. "Is this 'line' why Augustus Mercer talks about you like you're friends?"

After a few long moments of silence, he said, "Yes."

She nodded slowly. It was starting to feel like Lugen was as much of a manipulator of the galaxy as Augustus. Two sides, same coin.

But she had a hard time caring. They would need their own puppetmaster if they were going to win this. And at least this puppetmaster she trusted with her life.

"If I leave now," he said, "we undo decades of work. Thanks to the data you secured from the manor, we'll have more details and a clearer timeline on the bioweapon than ever before."

Her brow creased. "You already knew about that?"

"Yes," he admitted with a sober incline of his head. "It was a large part of why Corinne had to leave all those years ago, once she realized the project's true purpose and what Mercer intended to demand of her. But we knew nothing substantive, until now. And I have so much to do to prepare." He rubbed his knuckles across his chin, then stared earnestly at the feed again. "I need you to act on that preparation."

Her lips parted speechlessly.

"It's not a demand," he went on, voice thin, weary. "Please know that. I'm done giving you orders."

She swallowed, her ability to respond barricaded in a stirring mass behind her sternum. She stared at him, at years of struggle and decades of scheming, all weighing heavy on his stooped shoulders and gaunt cheeks.

"Will you do this, Adequin?" he asked.

A chill flooded her limbs with an icy, invigorating energy. The concept should terrify her—far more than commanding the *Lodestar* ever had. But everything had grown so much smaller in the last twelve hours.

She met Lugen's gaze, or as much as she could through a holographic screen and thousands of light-years. "I will, sir."

CHAPTER FORTY-SIX

That evening, Cavalon roamed the ground floor of the massive stronghold, ogling the ancient architecture while he gnawed on his approved caloric ration. On his way through the hangar, he passed a group of Akhet and Sentinel soldiers hoisting the Sentinel banner onto one of the side walls. Evidently, they should be painting the Corsairs' diving hawk symbol up there too.

He wandered outside, where he finally found Rake.

She sat atop one of the low hills along the eastern side of the stronghold overlooking the collection of prefab structures. Beyond the fields and shallow river, the massive plateau stretched as far as the eye could see in either direction. Dark, marbled clouds covered the eastern horizon, cut through by tiny sparks of lightning. Thunder rumbled in the distance.

Cavalon trudged up the slope through clumps of dry, wheat-colored grass. Rake sat on the ground in front of a large, flat slab of tawny stone. A few meters to her left sat something that looked a bit like an art installation. Dozens of multicolored squares of holographic text shone within a large piece of glass, framed by a thin border of stone. A collection of loose debris and alien flora littered the ground in front of it.

"So," he sighed as he approached Rake. "Puck says you own the Corsairs and all their assets?"

"Yeah . . ." Her gaze remained locked on the horizon. "Parting gift from Jackin."

Cavalon scrubbed his right hand through his beard. "Meaning they were Jackin's to give?"

She merely nodded.

Cavalon plopped down beside her. "An enigma, that guy." He glanced past her at the holographic installation. "What is that?"

"A memorial. People they've lost in this . . ." Her hand fanned open in a vague, all-encompassing gesture.

"Oh . . ." He looked back at the installation and saw the pieces of debris for what they really were: offerings.

He took in Rake's distant, hardened stare. That same haunted look she'd carried since the supernova.

His hand drifted to the back of his neck, to the three chains chafing his sweat-sticky skin. He singled one out, twisting his fingers around the clasp until it fell free with a soft clatter.

Rake looked over at him. He picked up the fallen chain—the one with her tags, Griffith's tags, and the atlas medallion. He passed them to her.

Her eyebrows drew down. She inhaled a long breath, then stood and walked to the memorial, kneeling before it. She slipped two of the etched glass and metal pendants off the chain, then set them on a ridge of the carved stone base.

Cavalon waited, rubbing the inside of his left elbow. Over the plateau, lightning forked across the black stormfront as the clouds rolled closer.

After a few minutes, Rake broke the silence. "Do you know any of the traditional Cautian elegies?" she asked. "There's one where it's talking about sharing a final drink before saying good night."

"Uh, yeah," he replied. "I know the one you mean." More of his princely education he never thought he'd need.

When she didn't respond after a few seconds, he realized it'd been a request.

Tucking his left arm against his side, he pushed up and joined her, kneeling in front of the memorial. She kept staring at the ground.

He drew in a steadying breath. Striving to keep his voice quiet and even, he recited the elegy, glad he didn't have to hate his relentless perfect memory, for once.

"Thanks," she said when he was done. She didn't look up.

Cavalon returned to sit in front of the flat rock and waited. A minute later, she sat back down beside him.

"You know . . ." His chin lifted to look at the darkening sky overhead. "Today we kind of accidentally designed a weapon."

She rubbed the nape of her neck. "Yeah . . ."

"You could fly one basically anywhere, and . . ." He pinched his fingers then flowered them open, blowing out a fluttering breath in a small explosion noise.

"Yeah," she repeated with a heavy sigh. "We shouldn't tell anyone."

"That's what I was thinking," he agreed, then edged his shoulder into hers. "Puck told me the rumors are already spreading through the ranks."

She raised a brow. "Rumors about what?"

"That our excubitor survived a supernova. He says they'll follow you anywhere now."

"Good," she said, oddly with no hint of sarcasm in her tone. "We're going to need them."

He scoffed a laugh. "Dang. Who's got those rose-colored glasses now?"

A fraction of that same haunted look slipped back into her expression, and her lips pressed into a consoling smile. "Yeah. Something like that."

The storm rumbled softly on the horizon. They stared out over the edge of the hill again.

"Quite a safe haven your mentor has built," he said. "Are you pissed he didn't tell you?"

"No," she said softly. "I understand why. Just wish the Divide hadn't started killing us before he found a way to get us here."

"So, he really was planning for you to join him here the whole time, huh?"

She shook her head. "Not just join."

He lifted a brow.

"Lead."

"What? Won't . . . *he*?"

She shook her head. "The SC has him on a tight leash."

He gave a dry swallow, thinking about how easily that leash could turn into a noose.

"With all this, he's had to go dark," she explained. "I agreed to take the helm."

His eyebrows climbed. "Well. Void. No pressure."

"We can handle it," she said, tone assured. "But first . . . I'm going to try and take a minute." Then under her breath, she added, "Maybe two."

His lips twitched in a weak smile. "That sounds like a good idea."

A rumble of thunder sounded and a cool, bracing wind picked up. The weather was turning.

"How about you?" she asked. "Are you doing okay, all things considered?"

He drew in a deep breath. "Fine, yeah," he forced out, though it sounded weak and thin, and clearly a lie. He didn't know if he'd ever be "*okay, all things considered*," when the list of considerations grew so increasingly grim. But she didn't need the weight of that on her too. "There's a lot to process," he conceded, then by way of evasion, added, "But I'll manage. Especially with *the* Adequin Rake by my side. Evader of Supernovas. Exploder of Stars."

She gave a lazy eye roll and a ghost of a smile creased her lips, gone within seconds. Her brows knit, and after a few silent moments, she said, "Actually, it's Idra."

Cavalon froze.

"Idra Le Calvez." She leaned her elbows on the stone ledge behind them. "It's strange how foreign it feels now, when it was so hard to get used to at first. For a long time after I changed it, I felt like I was playing a part, walking around in someone else's skin. That I wasn't me anymore. I know it's not the same thing, but . . . I do know what it's like to feel like you're not who you thought you were."

Cavalon chewed the inside of his lip, gaze drifting down. He should have known she'd see right through his pathetic attempt to write it off, to make light of it and shove it back down into the dark place he'd been sequestering it for the last two weeks.

"It took a long time," she went on, "but once I accepted it, I stopped feeling so . . . *trapped* by it. Instead, I was someone new, reborn, could be whatever I wanted to be. Who I was before didn't define me. Nothing and no one was holding me back but myself. If you accept who you really are, you can use it to start fresh. Let it fuel your purpose, not drag you down. Otherwise, Augustus wins."

Cavalon bobbed his chin in a wavering nod. As usual, she was right. He just needed to find a way to get there.

And since they were on the topic of each other's deepest traumas, he asked, "How are you doing about Jackin?"

Her jaw firmed, and she looked out across the base again. "He's strong," she said, tone flinty, but quiet. "This place is too important; he won't give it up. And that'll keep him alive. We'll have time to get him back."

Cavalon let out a sigh. "Yeah, over Augustus's dead body."

"That's the idea."

He blinked, his response catching in his throat for a few startled seconds. "Well. That's the best present a guy could ask for."

She gave him a forced smile. "That's what friends are for."

Then an intention slipped right past his conscious thought filter and out his mouth. "I want to be the one to do it."

She looked at him steadily, expression curiously vacant.

"I'm serious," he said, tone hardening. "I should have done it years ago. I was too much of a coward."

"Are you sure?" she asked. "Killing family, that's a whole . . . thing."

"He ceased being family a long time ago. There's nothing left but the corrupt, lying, murdering, psychopathic parts. Even if we forget about the captive clone boy and the list a kilometer long of crimes against humanity—he killed my mother, and my father, and drove away my grandmother. He took away my family. He made it personal."

The cool breeze kicked up, chilling his heated face. A long peal of thunder jittered in his teeth as the dark clouds moved closer.

Rake gave a slow nod. "I understand. But you do have family."

Warmth swelled in his chest, and he gripped her hand in his.

She took another long look out across Akhet. "You know, when you saved me at the Divide . . . I was worried that together, our force might break the tether." She locked eyes with him. "Now, I'm counting on it."

ACKNOWLEDGMENTS

Thank you to . . .

- ★ **Dave Dewes**, for feeding and watering me at regular intervals.
- ★ **Mom, Dad, Jessie, DJ, Skyler, Dawson, Lincoln**, for their endless enthusiasm and support.
- ★ **Ember, Arya**, and **Sylvanas**, for evaporating my anxiety.
- ★ **Matt Olson**, the Glinda to my Elphaba.
- ★ **Dave Hollis**, my preferred model of Hollis-bot; if I were to buy you all the Guinness I owe you, you would die.
- ★ All my amazing critique partners for their insight and encouragement: **Rebecca Schaeffer, Tina Chan, Tullio Pontecorvo, Marco Frassetto, Francesca Tacchi**.
- ★ My agent, **Tricia Skinner**, for her incredible enthusiasm and guidance.
- ★ My editor, **Jen Gunnels**, for believing in this series, and for her patience and council through a very trying year.
- ★ **Caro Perny, Renata Sweeney**, and the entire team at **Tor** and **Macmillan Audio** for their tremendous support. I couldn't have asked for a better home for my Sentinels.

No thank you to . . .

- ★ COVID-19
- ★ Fascism
- ★ 2020

ABOUT THE AUTHOR

J. S. DEWES has a bachelor of arts in film from Columbia College Chicago and has written scripts for award-winning films, which have screened at San Diego Comic-Con and dozens of film festivals across the nation.